MISS MABEL'S
SCHOOL FOR GIRLS

THE NETWORK SERIES
by Katie Cross

Mildred's Resistance

Miss Mabel's School for Girls

The Isadora Interviews

Antebellum Awakening

MISS MABEL'S
SCHOOL FOR GIRLS

Katie Cross

Antebellum
Publishing

Miss Mabel's School for Girls

Young Adult Fantasy

Text copyright ©2014 by Katie Cross

Cover designed by Cory Clubb at www.goboldddesigns.com
Typesetting by Atthis Arts LLC www.atthisarts.com

Published by Antebellum Publishing
www.antebellumpublishing.com

ISBN (trade paperback)   978-0-9915319-0-5
(ebook)   978-0-9915319-1-2

Visit the author at www.kcrosswriting.com

Visit The Network Series at www.missmabels.com or on
Facebook at www.facebook.com/missmabels

For Mim.

Because you believed in me.

Acknowledgments

Miss Mabel's School for Girls started in the fall of 2012 while my husband and I hiked through a forest that later inspired Letum Wood.

Every time we ran the trails, an eerie feeling followed me. Surely, I thought, a witch lives here. She had an alluring presence, and seemed to always be watching. I never met her.

I didn't understand it at the time, but I had a feeling that something great had started. Months later this witch found her way onto the page on a writing whim, and my journey with Bianca and Miss Mabel began.

Since then, Miss Mabel's School for Girls has come a long way. To my editors, Robin and Catherine, your insight and guidance was truly a book-saver. Thank you for polishing and shining and buffing. You taught me about the art of writing, and helped me believe in myself.

Cory Clubb, you are the best cover designer in the world and possibly the most patient man alive. Musers, you'll always have my heart. Thanks for your guidance and listening ear. Dizzle, the best web-hoster-blog-fixer-ever thanks for showing me the path on the interwebs.

Jason Anderson, Stephen Cross, LaDonna Cole, Kelsey Keating, Stephanie Karfelt, Dennis Clough, and all the readers on Fanstory who made the journey of the first draft with me, thank you for beta-reading and believing in Bianca, and me, from the beginning.

To the loyal followers at KCrossWriting, thanks for your insight and feedback, and straightening me out when I got myself crooked, which we all know was far too often. To my family, thanks for your unrelenting support – Mim (best friend and financial guru), Mikey, Courtney, Grandma, Grandpa (you're always in my heart), DJ, JaiHo, Cindy-Mom, Father Stephen, and Dahrling.

Husband, love your face. Thanks for taking care of the pandas on the days I had to frantically write and edit myself into a tizzy, and then tolerating me when I spazzed out over plot lines and lacking characterization.

You rock.

Isadora's Interview

I stared at the lavender flowers on the white china and willed my heart to stop pounding. Papa's advice whispered through my head like the balm of a cool poultice, settling my nerves.

Don't be afraid, Bianca. The old woman will perceive your personality no matter what you do or say. You can't hide information from a Watcher. Let her remain in control of the conversation and things will be easier.

"You said that your family is from Bickers Mill?" The old woman, Isadora, startled me from my thoughts with her question. "That's not very far from here."

"Yes," I said, turning around to face her. "I grew up in a cottage outside the village."

Don't think about how important this is.

That wouldn't be too difficult. She only determined the rest of my life.

Isadora smiled in a distant way, as if she were lost in thought and only keeping up with the conversation to be kind. She was a stringy old woman, with a curved back and foggy, pistachio-colored eyes, although one of them looked more blue than green.

"Your grandmother is sick, isn't she?"

My throat tightened.

"Yes," I said, swallowing past it. She studied me while I continued. "The apothecary said she may not have much longer to live."

"Well, I'm glad you were able to come here today so that I did not have to come to you. Living near the school helps me keep this part of Letum Wood safe for the students. Now that school has started, I don't like to leave."

"I'm sure they appreciate your work as a Watcher," I said, circling back around to face the tea set. *Confidence,* I told myself. *Even if she can see into your soul and it isn't very organized.*

My hands trembled when I set the fragile cups and saucers on the antique silver tray. Was that right? No, the teacups went on the plates. Or did they? Was I supposed to set out a fork for the little cakes? Or tongs? Or nothing at all? An interview I'd prepared for my entire life, and a tea set flummoxed me. This was a promising beginning. Deciding to leave the cups off the plate, I set them off to the side, lifted the tray and turned to serve the tea.

Isadora moved away from the window with a hobbled step while I approached the little table. Her quaint cottage at the edge of the trees aged with a quiet grace, decorated in an opulence that made me nervous, afraid I'd take one step too far in any direction and break something, like the witches' bottles hanging from one wall by strings of twine. A simple nudge and they'd fall, shattering, the whispers of their bottled incantations rising into the air like a mist.

Despite her reputation as one of the most powerful witches in our world, Isadora lived a discreet life in the midst of her porcelain tea sets, of which she had many, and her white curtains. A buttery loaf of bread gleamed nearby, smelling of warm yeast and flour.

"Is this part of Letum Wood dangerous?" I asked, taking measured steps so I didn't rattle the china. Letum Wood, the weather, my chances of survival at the school, I would have picked any of these topics for conversation. Anything to avoid the silence that meant she searched my soul, hoping to understand the secrets of my mind.

"It can be a frightening place," Isadora said, lowering into a wooden chair. "But not when I'm watching."

For all my precautions in getting there, the tray landed on the table with an ungracious clunk, and I murmured a nervous apology.

She smiled, surveying the layout of the china with puckered lips that looked suspiciously close to a smile. I'd gotten the tray wrong, of course.

"I was an awkward teenager too, you know," Isadora said. "Big teeth and whatnot. That all changed when I turned sixteen."

"Oh?" I stammered, forcing myself to sit down. "Sixteen?"

"Yes, your age."

She's going to know many things about you. Don't be surprised if she mentions details you haven't told her. She sees.

"It's a wonderful age," she crooned before I could reply, lightly sliding her cup onto her tea plate. "I started learning how to control magic at a Network school, though not Miss Mabel's School for Girls. It changed the course of my life." She paused for a second, then continued as if she'd never stopped. "Miss Mabel's is a grand place. There's so much history in that big old estate, you know, and so much to learn."

"Mmm-hmm," I hummed as I reached for the pot. The tea tumbled in a coral waterfall into the fragile porcelain cups. Steam rolled off the boiling liquid, filling the air. A drop or two slipped out, falling to the white tablecloth when I tipped the spout back. An instant stain spread.

"Miss Mabel's been teaching there many years," I said, quickly setting the teapot on top of the diffused pink circles, hoping she didn't see. My heart pounded. This wasn't the time for mistakes. Perhaps I'd spent too long perfecting the big things and too little on the mundane.

Our eyes met for the first time. Isadora didn't smile, just stared into me with a troubled expression. I waited under the scrutiny of her gaze, my heart pulsing in my throat, making me sick to my stomach. Her worried expression had nothing to do with my inability to properly set out and pour tea.

Isadora doesn't care about trivialities.

"Yes, Mabel has been teaching for a long time." She finally took the offered cup to sip, breaking her intense study. "She's one of the best teachers in the Network."

Her face scrunched a little, and I fought back a frustrated sigh. I had steeped it too long again. Herbal teas always stumped me.

"So I've heard," I said.

"Mabel gears her teaching toward action, not books. Education these days involves too much reading. Learning magic should be about practice, not recitation."

I heartily agreed but remained silent. Bookwork was never my cup of tea, so to speak. Her cup set itself down as I reached for the sugar. I didn't know how to respond, so I remained quiet and stirred the sugar into my tea. *Above all, show confidence,* I reminded myself. *Sometimes silence does it best.*

"Tell me, Bianca, why you are here today."

I looked up in surprise. Part of me hoped that our entire interview consisted of this strangled, awkward small talk. Then she could probe into my mind and personality in silence, discerning what I already knew. *You're determined to attend this school. You've spent years learning magic to prepare. You hope to control fate, but you can't because she's a fickle mistress.* Then she'd tell me I passed and I'd never have to really answer anything.

She lifted her eyebrows, waiting for my response, shattering any hope of an easy escape.

Never lie to a Watcher, Papa's voice returned. *Most of the time they already know how you are going to respond. The test is in your emotions, and you can really only control how you use them.*

Elaborating on all the possible life benefits of attending Miss Mabel's tempted me, but she'd know I didn't really care. Trivialities, I reminded myself. Isadora may already know the answer to her question, but she might not.

A bargain I couldn't ignore.

I finally settled on the one answer I knew would be true.

"I want to work with Miss Mabel."

We sat in silence for several minutes. The snap of the fire filled the background. I stirred my cup. Most girls probably had a ready answer for that one. Perhaps I'd been learning how not to set out tea.

"Yes," Isadora said, taking a sip of her tea with a quiet chuckle that didn't sound humorous. "You certainly don't lack motivation, do you?"

She looked out the window again. I pulled the tiny silver spoon from my tea and set it next to the cup. My hands still shook, so I folded them in my lap instead of taking a drink, braiding them into a ball of icy fingers. I wondered if she'd notice if I didn't take a sip. After her reaction, the taste probably wasn't worth it.

Isadora opened her mouth to say something, then closed it again. I began to wonder if I could stand a silence so loud.

"My job is to interview prospective students to see if they would be a good fit for Miss Mabel's School for Girls," she said, turning away from me. "It's a difficult education to complete, with a demanding schedule, and isn't meant for everyone. That's why the High Priestess of the Network requires you to qualify."

My knuckles tightened until my hands blanched to a shade of white. This was it. She would turn me down, say I wasn't the right kind of girl. My whole life and future hung in the balance. It would be quick as a guillotine but infinitely more painful.

High stakes are what you get, I reminded myself, *when you have a lot to lose.*

I wished I'd worn my hair in a bun instead of loose on my shoulders. But I couldn't act myself by pretending to be something I wasn't, so my hair remained down where I liked it.

"I've met a lot of students, but never in my life . . ." she faltered. Her fidgeting and blank stares began to unnerve me. Wasn't this a witch of great magical knowledge and power?

She set the china cup down with a resolute clank.

"I'm going to let you in, Bianca, but I do so with one warning."

Her creaky, anxious voice took away any chance to feel relief. I waited, holding my breath, while she stared into my eyes.

"Don't underestimate her."

I didn't need to ask whom she meant. The name hung in the air between us like an anvil on a fraying string.

Miss Mabel.

We stared at each other. I wondered just what she saw about me, what facets of my personality, and what motives she understood that I didn't. Before I drew up the courage to ask, Isadora turned away again, as if she couldn't stand to look at me, and took another sip of her tea.

My right wrist burned. I grabbed it, which gave only a moment of relief.

When I pulled my hand away, a black circle of ancient, minuscule words lay on the inside of my wrist. The circlus. Without it, the magic surrounding the boundaries of Letum Wood that housed Miss Mabel's School for Girls wouldn't allow me in.

My stomach flipped.

I did it.

My chest sank, heavy with fear and weak with relief. I suppressed the rush of panic, banishing it to the corners of my mind. No panic here, just confidence.

I spent years preparing for this. It won't frighten me now.

I was a terrible liar. Attending Miss Mabel's School for Girls did frighten me, but so did staying home, forfeiting my only chance at freedom.

Isadora seemed to recover her wits with surprising speed. She sat up, set her napkin on the table, and straightened her wobbly legs.

"Have you said goodbye to your mother?"

"Yes," I said, wincing inside. The fear in her eyes haunted me. Mama didn't want me to go, not like this. *There has to be another way,* she whispered to me last night, tears in her eyes that she never shed. *I don't like this, Bianca. What if something happens to you?* I hated leaving her.

But I still did it. Because I had to.

Nothing bad will happen, I had promised her. *I can do this. I know I can.*

Isadora nodded once. "Very well, come. Let's continue your education. I can see that Mabel will be quite . . . pleased to have you."

Grateful to get out of the close little parlor, I walked past the window to see a figure moving out from behind a tree. Mama stood amongst the dark woods with her queer gray eyes, her ebony hair restless in the wind.

"Merry part, Mama," I whispered. The memory of Papa's voice ran through my head as I stared at her, my homesick heart already raw and throbbing.

Mabel is the one of the cleverest witches in the Central Network. She's the only one that can remove your curse. You must remember: Mabel does no favors. Be careful, B.

Your life depends on it.

6

Isadora led me through her house to a rickety back porch where a torch illuminated the ground. A single trail ran from a set of wooden stairs, disappearing into trees and deadfall beyond. The gray and muted brown leaves matched my simple brown dress. Winter robbed Letum Wood of color, leaving it stark and ugly.

"Well, keep to the trail." Isadora cast a look at the sky. "It looks like rain, so you better hurry. It's at least an hour's walk to the school from here."

"Thank you."

I pulled the hood of my cloak over my long black hair and took a few steps forward. Every minute of my life led to this moment. *Fate may be a fickle mistress*, I thought, glancing at the sky, *but she isn't entirely unforgiving.*

Isadora called to me, stopping me in my tracks.

"Did you know they are taking volunteers for the Competition tonight?"

I kept my hood up and my eyes on the ground so she couldn't read my expression.

"Yes," I said. "I heard that rumor."

I left before she could ask more, evaporating in the mist of Letum Wood.

Merry Meets

The tree branches rattled together in hollow knocks from the wind, and a few brittle leaves fluttered past my legs as I started. A chill bit through my black cloak, wrapping me in a crisp blanket of cool air. Once I'd put some space between us, I looked back. Only an empty porch and extinguished torch remained.

Glad to leave the interview behind, I whispered a special incantation, one Papa found just for me. The folds of my skirt lifted up, like an invisible hand was drawing a pair of drapes, until they stopped around my waist. My frilly white knickers, lovingly sewn by Grandmother's arthritic hands, revealed themselves to all of Letum Wood. No one would be here on the trail, but I cast my eyes around just in case.

Clear.

I took off at a steady jog, holding my cape so it wouldn't tangle in my legs. My muscles warmed to the movement with little preamble, and I gave them room to fly. The forest soared past, a whiz and whir of spindly branches and old moss. The familiar staccato rhythm of my heart soothed me; all of my anxiety melted into the cool earth. I pounded down the path.

A storm threatened to break with every gust of wind that hurried me along. My thoughts spun, recalling the smell of lavender tea in Mama's cup, the down pillow I left behind, and the garden of spices in front of our little cottage that Grandmother loved so much. The melancholy caw of a crow reminded me that I was alone.

A change in the trees slowed me to a walk. I shoved my skirts down and dropped the cloak, suddenly nervous I'd be seen. What a great first impression that would make, trotting up to school with my knickers blaring for all to see.

I'm Bianca Monroe, and I run in the woods with my skirts up. I also don't know how to steep or pour tea.

Catching my fast breath, I peered through the thick foliage to see an unnatural color between the branches. The school.

My cloak drifted ahead of me in the breeze when I walked out of the deadfall and stopped at a black, wrought iron fence. A loose gate moved with a shrill cry in the wind.

The old manor was a gothic structure, made of shadows and aged stone that faded to light cream color. Ivy crawled across the front in brittle strands, shuddering in the wind. A steady stream of smoke drifted from two chimneys on the far right side. The late evening gloom overshadowed the sprawling beauty, leaving the manor both depressing and intriguing.

Twelve darkened windows marched across the second, third, and fourth floors. They must be student bedrooms. Five sat on either side of the front door on the ground level. Candles illuminated several glass panes with warm, buttery light. A wooden board introduced me to the school. It looked ancient and worn, like a standing citadel stained with shadow. A shudder spun down my spine.

Miss Mabel's School for Girls.

After taking a deep breath, I pushed through the cool gate and strode forward. "Here we are," I whispered, pulling in a bolstering breath. "Here we go."

Confidence.

When I knocked on the thick wooden door it seemed to reverberate inside. A quick fall of steps came soon after, and when the door opened, an older woman with green eyes stood to welcome me. Flour dusted her apron, and her hair sat like a gray pillow on top of her head.

Her shrewd eyes narrowed.

"Bianca Monroe?"

"Yes."

"Come in." She opened the door wider. "Isadora just finished meeting with Miss Mabel. We weren't expecting you so soon."

A few leaves scuttled into the warm entry ahead of me. The woman had to push against the wind to close the door.

"Your bags are up in your room already. My name is Miss Celia. I'm a teacher here."

I stepped into a vestibule. The ceiling rose several floors, following the twirl of a wide staircase. A silver chandelier with dripping candles hung from the very top floor several stories above, illuminating the ground and walls of cream-colored stone. A crimson rug climbed along each stair, accenting the carved ivy leaves twisting through the railing. Skinny candles flickered from iron wall sconces and cast dancing shadows on the grainy wooden floor.

It was warm, at least. If not a bit old.

"Wait here."

She disappeared down a hallway at the end of the entry, leaving me to feel small in the dominating presence of the room. When I turned my focus to listening, the distant clang and clatter of pots came to my ears first. A buttery smell filled the air, making my stomach growl.

"This is Camille. She's a first-year like you. Camille, show Bianca up to her room, please."

Miss Celia reappeared with a girl my age in tow. She had curly blonde hair held away from her face by a white headband. I assumed that the navy blue dress over a long white shirt fitting down to her wrists was the school uniform, as a few other girls walked by in similar blue dresses. A kind smile lit her face.

"Merry meet, Bianca!"

Miss Celia ushered us up the staircase with a frantic wave of her hands.

"Go on, go on!" she exclaimed. "It's just about time to eat. Heaven knows I don't have time for interruptions."

Camille beckoned me to follow her as she started up the stairs, leaving me to trail behind. Miss Celia's tirade faded into the background.

"Don't mind Miss Celia," Camille said with a roll of her hazel eyes. "She gets really stressed at mealtimes. She runs the kitchen and has for years. Her cinnamon buns are legendary, and so is her bread. Trust me."

"Oh, that's good to know."

"Did you just get here?" she asked, as if my clothes and lack of know-how weren't any indication.

"Yes."

"You must be cold then! We'll get you by the fire in the dining room soon. Miss Celia's prepped a feast tonight that will warm you up faster than anything. It's the Feast of the Competition!"

We approached the second floor. The stairway continued up, but the landing opened to a dark corridor filled with doors and a tarnished wood floor. A warm fire blazed at the end of the hall, where girls in similar blue dresses moved around.

"This is the third-year corridor. Don't go in there!" Camille said, pulling me back when I stepped across the doorway. "They get really picky about first-years in their area. Especially Priscilla." She lowered her tone and spoke behind her hand. "She gets really upset. Her dad is rich so she gets away with it."

Camille grabbed my arm and spun me back toward the stairs. Our shoes clacked on the floor as we climbed. "The second-years are okay, but most of them spend time trying to get the attention of the third-years. They usually ignore us."

We passed the second-year floor. Their common room sat right off the stairwell, filled with long tables, plush cushions on the high back chairs, and a wall of landscape portraits clearly done by students still struggling to find their talent. A burly second-year sent us a warning glare when we peered in.

"Second-years," Camille said, then stuck her tongue out at the girl near the door and quickly ushered me toward the stairs again.

"Where are the classrooms?" I asked, studying a carved floral design on the stair bannister. It looked like the ropes of Letum ivy that hung in the forest in the summertime.

"On the first floor. So are the dining room and the library. The teachers live in cottages just outside the yard. Here it is!" Camille announced, spreading her arms out. "The first-year floor."

My first impression told me it wasn't anything to get excited about. We had to walk down a chilly corridor to reach the empty first-year common area. Although a fire burned in the grate, I saw no one enjoying the sweet warmth. I moved closer to it, grateful to feel my fingers thaw. Camille kicked aside a few wrinkled scrolls and plopped onto a straight-backed, firm sofa. It looked as comfortable as a pair of shoes that pinched.

"I think you'll like it." Her face turned down as she leaned forward, propping her head on her palm. "Well, it's less dreary when the students are actually out here. Everyone is getting ready for the feast downstairs."

"It seems really nice," I said, lying through my teeth. The stone walls were cracked and stained with dust. Floorboards stuck up at random intervals; black—perhaps from years of soot—edged the walls. Homework tables occupied most of the free space, lined by benches instead of chairs. Books cluttered the shelves in obvious disarray. Camille snorted.

"Nice, sure. Not compared to the second-years. The third-years have the best of everything. Follow me." She bid me to follow her down another hallway with a wave of her arm. I obeyed, pausing to gaze at a portrait of a woman with black hair and solemn eyes. A previous High Witch, no doubt.

"Your room will be right next to mine," she said. "Leda and I came a little late too. We just got here a week ago, so I know how it feels to be in your shoes. Don't worry. It's not so bad here."

Her hair bounced to a stop. She opened a door to reveal a tiny square of a room with bare, wooden walls and a handful of built-in shelves. A scarlet blanket covered the narrow bed and a desk sat below the window. Age cracks snaked through the window panes, allowing a whistle when a gust of wind hit the house. The slow plod of a new rainstorm hit the glass with a soothing, gentle hiss.

"Looks like your stuff came already." Camille nudged my trunk with her toe. "That's lucky. One of the second-years is still waiting for her stuff to come. I think her parents sent it with a bad spell. I don't think they'll ever find it."

A candle flame came to life as I stepped in. The shadows loomed like creatures dancing on the wall, making the room feel even more dismal and grim. I longed for the comfort of home, of familiarity.

Confidence in all things.

"When did school start?" I asked, hoping to distract my rising unease. Surely I'd lost my mind, coming to Miss Mabel's School for Girls.

"Two weeks ago." Camille sat on the end of my bed and let her legs swing. "But you haven't missed much. Leda can help you catch up. She's the smartest first-year because she likes to study, but she doesn't really like people. You'll meet her at dinner."

She sounds delightful, I wanted to mutter, but bit my tongue. Despite what she said, the warmth in Camille's tone told me Leda was a friend of hers.

A tinkling chime came from downstairs, so faint I thought I'd imagined it. Camille jumped to her feet.

"That's dinner. We better get going. Miss Scarlett takes roll and she doesn't like it when anyone is late."

"Just follow me," Camille whispered. We stood outside the dining room, peering in.

Six long wooden tables with benches filled the open area. A fireplace big enough to stand in warmed the room with crackling flames. Every spot at the tables was full, except for one in the back next to a girl with white-blonde hair, who appeared to be buried in a book.

"Are we going to get in trouble?" I asked.

"No, but I hate it when Miss Scarlett singles me out. She's terrifying."

Camille started into the room along the back wall at a cautious creep, and I followed close behind. The moment I stepped into the room every eye fell on me like metal to a magnet.

Fantastic. An entrance.

"Care to explain why you're late, Miss Duncan?" A booming voice came from the front of the room. Camille halted with a wince.

"Y-yes, Miss Scarlett. Miss Celia asked me to show Bianca to her room before dinner."

Camille stood at my side instead of retreating to her seat. I felt a moment of gratitude that she didn't leave me standing in front of the school alone.

"You must be Bianca Monroe," Miss Scarlett said, turning toward me. "I just heard of your coming. You're a bit earlier than expected."

"Yes, Miss Scarlett," I straightened and looked right at her in the hopes of feeling more sanguine than I felt.

I arrived early because I lifted my skirts and ran here. Hope that qualifies me to fit in. If not, let me impress you with my secret talent at brewing the perfect tea.

Miss Scarlett stood in front of the fire at the top of the room. Her tall, broad shoulders, backlit by the flames, made her seem like a tree rising from the ground. Her reddish brown hair shone, pulled away from her face in a tight bun. Red bracelets dangled from her right wrist and sang when they touched. I couldn't decipher whether she was friend or foe. She studied me with narrowed eyes.

"Welcome to Miss Mabel's School for Girls." When the silence stretched a beat too long she broke it, gesturing to the other side of the room with a hand. "Miss Bernadette will be your advisor."

A slender woman in the corner stepped forward with a warm smile. Her short-cropped hair framed a lovely, heart-shaped face.

"Merry meet, Bianca," she called in a voice that sounded like wind chimes. "It's always good to have a new student."

A rush of relief flooded me. She seemed very kind. I smiled and nodded in return.

"Merry meet, Miss Bernadette."

"Sit with Camille," Miss Scarlett ordered, turning back to a scroll of parchment floating in the air next to her. "Miss Bernadette will find you later to go over the rules and expectations. Dinner starts promptly at six every evening. This is your warning. Do not be late again. Jackie Simmons?"

A voice called out from across the room, "Here!" Camille and I quickly made our escape.

"Miss Scarlett is a real stickler for rules," Camille whispered. "Don't let her see you break them."

"Thanks for not leaving me on my own."

She smiled. "You're welcome."

Camille motioned the girls on the back bench to scoot down, and they made room for me at the end. The girl with white hair looked up in surprise, her book now hidden in her lap from Miss Scarlett's roving gaze. She had two different-colored eyes, light brown and olive green, set against pale skin.

Miss Scarlett cleared her throat to get our attention.

"Now that roll is complete, we will proceed with the feast. After that I will take the names of the third-years who want to join the annual Competition. Miss Celia, we are ready."

A swinging door banged open, streaming platters and bowls piled high with a succulent array of food. Miss Celia stood at the back, orchestrating the placement of the trays that didn't obey her magical commands to exactness. Once every dish found the right spot, they descended on the tables with a light clink.

"Oh," Camille groaned with a hand on her stomach. "Look at all this food. I'm starving! I'm going to eat until I die, and then it'll be a happy passing."

The quiet anticipation in the room exploded. Camille grabbed a fork and stabbed into a nearby pile of roasted potatoes. "Get it while it's still here, Bianca. Food goes fast. Trust me, you don't want to miss a single bite of Miss Celia's cooking."

Leda didn't move. In fact, she still didn't surface from her book, even after the scrumptious fare arrived. Following Camille's example, I surveyed the options. Fruit salad with a shiny glaze. Slivered green beans with flecks of almond and butter. A pork chop with apple gravy landed on my plate last. No wonder Miss Celia had been stressed. The food on all six tables would be enough to feed a small contingent of Guardians. I had no doubt, after glancing around, that this small horde of girls would take care of it.

"So, Bianca," Camille said through a bite of strawberry tart. "Where do you come from?"

A gleaming wheat roll tumbled off her loaded plate, hitting a glass of light green winterberry lemonade. The sugared, minty smell drifted toward me.

"Bickers Mill."

Her forehead wrinkled as she swallowed. "Where's that?"

"Not far from here. Just outside the border of Letum Wood on the west. What about you?"

"Leda and I come from Hansham. It's on the border near the Eastern Network. It's a part of Letum Wood as well. I think it's the most beautiful place in all of Antebellum, but I haven't even been outside of the Central Network." A sheepish blush covered her face, and she licked a little strawberry glaze off the end of one finger with a murmur of enjoyment. "Mmm. Delicious. Anyway, this is the farthest I've been from my aunts' home."

I noticed the way she said *aunts' home* and wondered about her parents.

Letum Wood encompassed nearly all of the Central Network. Because of Letum Wood, most of our Network consisted of trees and gentle hills, a continuous emerald wave of farmland and woods. We were the largest of the five Networks, nestled in the middle, away from the harsh deserts of the West and the breezy coastline of the East. Below us, the Southern Network hibernated most of the year in snow. A rugged, domineering mountain chain separated the Northern Network from the rest of us. It had been years since the other Networks last contact with them.

Camille helped herself to a bite of pork chop slathered with baked apple wedges and motioned to the girl across the table.

"This is Leda, by the way. I mentioned her earlier."

I didn't tell her that I'd surmised it myself. Leda acted as if she hadn't heard and kept her face in the book in front of her. Camille dished food onto Leda's plate, most of which consisted of vegetables and fruit. No meat. The scrumptious fare went unnoticed.

"Nice to meet you too, I'm sure," I muttered and bit into a crusty piece of brown bread smeared with tart raspberry preserves, my jumpy nerves almost forgotten under the tantalizing fragrance of the feast. The yeasty, warm smell of Miss Celia's fresh bread proved her talent at once. Camille hadn't been exaggerating.

"We've been waiting for you to come for a while now," Camille said.

I almost choked.

"What?"

She smiled her apology. "I just meant that we didn't have a full first-year class, so we knew that one more girl would arrive soon. Miss Bernadette said Isadora has been looking."

Camille turned to fight another girl for the butter plate before I could respond. Leda shifted, snatched a strawberry off her plate without moving her eyes from the text and popped it into her mouth. I studied the spine of her book. *High Priests of the Southern Network.* As if she felt my gaze, Leda slowly pulled the book down and peered over it, one eyebrow quirked high.

"How is it?" I asked, pointing to the book as if I hadn't just been caught and didn't feel stupid. Perhaps we had a mutual love of history.

"Bianca, do–" Camille whirled around, her hair whipping my cheek. "Oh, you're talking to Leda, sorry. I didn't mean to hit your face. My hair has a mind of its own. Do you want a fruit tart? They are simply my favorite. I love the sugary crust."

Leda disappeared behind her book yet again.

"No, thank you," I said, giving my brimming plate a quick glance. "I don't have any room."

Camille leaned toward a first-year with large eyes and even larger glasses, asking her the same question.

Using it as a chance to gain my bearings, I took inventory of the dining room. It was large, with scalloped edging running along the ceiling and a sprawling mantle with the same Letum ivy carved into the wood. Thirty-six girls, four teachers, and a calico cat perched near the fire. A typical size for a Network-run school. There were two doorways: the swinging door into the kitchen and the double doors that led to the main entryway.

Where is that old dragon Miss Mabel?

Camille spun around, a berry-stuffed croissant slathered with a fluffy cream in her hand.

"Oh, Leda, guess what I found for you! It's your favor–"

She stopped with a little sigh. Leda had given up on the book and stared at the table instead, a glazed look in her eyes. Camille turned to me and held the pastry up.

"Do you like chocolate and strawberry? I don't think Miss Celia should have put blueberries in the sauce, but it still tastes okay."

"No, thank you. Is something wrong with Leda?" I asked. Camille followed my gaze to her odd friend and then waved her hand with a high pitched laugh.

"Oh, she's fine. Just—"

Leda snapped to attention, blinking several times. She shook her head.

"Thinking," Camille finished with a fixed smile. "She likes to think. A lot. Don't mind her. Are you sure you don't want the croissant?"

I refused it again with a shake of my head.

"No, thank you. Can you tell me—"

"Miss Mabel doesn't come to meals," Leda said, brushing her white blonde hair away from her face with a careless flap of her hand. "In fact, she doesn't show up very much at all. At least not so far this year. School started two weeks ago, and we have yet to meet her."

My fork fell to the table with a loud clatter. How did she know what I was about to ask? I quickly retrieved it. "Butter on my fingers," I said with a sheepish look. "Sorry."

Camille shot Leda a sharp look, which faded into her sweet smile as soon as she saw I was watching.

"Miss Mabel is very busy, I'm sure, as High Witch over the school and Coven leader for this part of Letum Wood," Camille said with a stiff voice. "A feast with teenagers is far from priority."

My eyes drifted past Leda, falling on a banner stretching across the broad hearth that said, *'Feast of the Competition.'* Garland crept around its edges, ornamented with cranberries and strung with twine and deep red ribbon.

A girl with strawberry blonde hair called from a few places down the bench.

"We're taking bets on how many volunteers there will be and who the final winner is. What are your guesses, Camille?" she asked.

Camille straightened with a proud swell of her chest, obviously gratified to be included.

"Priscilla," she said with confidence. "And I think four will be the final number of Competitors."

The rest of the table broke out in a chorus of agreements. The girl with strawberry blonde hair wrote her answers on a scroll, then turned away, pointedly ignoring Leda.

"The third-year you told me about?" I asked Camille.

"Yes," she said, spearing a caramelized carrot with a stab. "Everyone knows that Priscilla is going to win. She's so smart. You've heard of the Competition before, haven't you?"

My stomach fluttered at the question. Heard of it? *Every year of my life.*

"Yes, I have. My village likes to hear about the Competition after it's done. What is Miss Bernadette like?" I asked, hoping to deter Camille onto something more mundane. Thinking about the Competition killed my appetite, and I still had piles of food to try.

Leda's eyes flickered briefly to me, her teeth sinking into her bottom lip and her eyebrow lifting in suspicious question.

Leda's going to be a hard one to fool.

Camille, to my luck, proved easy to distract.

"I love Miss Bernadette," she said with a dreamy breath. "She's just lovely, isn't she? She's so kind and patient. She's even been helping me with geometry after class. I'm terrible at math."

Camille took over the conversation for the rest of the meal, chattering about people I should meet, and who to avoid. A third-year with a tilted nose and porcelain skin, the famous Priscilla, shot a few curious looks my way. I ignored her. She had the sour pinch of someone sucking on a pickle.

Once conversations began to slow and the pastries disappear, Miss Scarlett stood up. She didn't have to say a word to get total silence.

"I trust all of you will let Miss Celia know how much you appreciate her hard work in the kitchen, as well as the third-year Culinary Mark students who helped. Michelle and Rebecca, you have done an exemplary job in such a short time. It's no wonder the students from Miss Mabel's are first pick to work for the High Priestess at Chatham Castle."

A polite smattering of hands came from the crowd, and two students standing near Miss Celia in the back flushed and waved. It died down shortly, and Miss Scarlett continued.

"The Competition is a centuries-old tradition that dates back to the time when the five Networks formed, when mortals and witches coexisted in peace throughout all of Antebellum."

Smoke from the fire twirled in the air near her, forming two groups of people at war. Her voice lowered, resonating through the room. I'd heard the legend hundreds of times, but it never felt more real than now, watching it unfold.

"Then the great division took place when greedy mortals began killing witches for their land. The witches cursed the mortals in retribution, and so the Reformation began. Witches grouped together for protection and birthed the five Networks."

The smoke people fled, running to each other and forming five separate groups.

"Banded together, the Networks drove the mortals out of Antebellum and sent them across the ocean to find a new land. The race of witches won. Esmelda, the first High Priestess of the Central Network, formed special schools to educate natural born leaders from a young age."

The vapor twisted into a haunted building like the school.

"Only the worthy enter these schools as students. You are the chosen few, evidenced by the circli on your wrists."

As one, almost all the students looked down at their wrists. I kept my eyes on Miss Scarlett, preferring not to look at the ring of ancient words. Legend had it that the words were different for every witch, encompassing their strengths and weaknesses, written in a language that none remembered.

"You will attend this school for three years. The first two years of your education will encompass knowledge of our witching world. Potions. Alchemy. Geography. Algebra. Herbology. Divination. History. Symbology, and the like. But the third year, the final year, you'll work for the three marks that will determine your place in the Network."

The smoke building drifted apart, forming a wide circle in the air, shimmering from the embers of the fire. Symbols appeared. Triangles. Circles. Interlocked lines. There were too many to see them all.

"The three marks you earn will appear in your circlus. It's a sign of education, of pride, that will never leave." Miss Scarlett elevated her chin. "One you should remain worthy of at all times."

The vapor twisted again, churning into several willowy, girlish figures. Shadows climbed the wall behind Miss Scarlett, giving her a ghostly, ethereal look. Most of the students watched, transfixed, leaning forward in their seats until the edge of the table stopped them. Even I couldn't fight the draw of her storytelling.

"But this is not all Esmelda began." Miss Scarlett shook her head, her voice dipping low. "She instituted the Competition. The prize was a one-on-one education with the High Witch of the school to the girl who is clever above all others."

The smoke figures dissolved, leaving one behind that wavered in the warm air.

"Tonight, the third-years may volunteer for the Competition. Whoever wins will become Miss Mabel's pupil and her Assistant. I don't need to remind you what an honor that would be."

The smoke figures disappeared with a pop, breaking the gloomy atmosphere. Students startled back into reality, blinking as if they'd stepped into a very bright light.

"Are there any questions?"

The only sounds were the crackle of the fireplace and the purr of the cat. Miss Scarlett rubbed her lips together and pulled in a deep breath.

"Very well. We will now take volunteers for the Competition."

Miss Bernadette stepped forward with another teacher in a full yellow dress and wide blue eyes. She had a rigid wooden smile and diamond earrings so long they touched her shoulders.

"If you would like to become a Competitor, raise your hand now," Miss Scarlett directed.

Priscilla's hand shot into the air first. She waved a lock of her long red hair over her shoulder, smiling at the third-years around her who made a sighing sound of support. Leda rolled her eyes and returned to her book.

Two more third-years volunteered. "That's Jade," Camille leaned over to whisper in my ear, motioning to a girl on Priscilla's left. "The other one is Stephany. The three of them are best friends, and they're all very competitive, not to mention popular. Each one of them is determined to win. It's all they ever talk about. Should be interesting."

Ah, the three most well-known girls decided to compete against each other. This would be a bloodbath by the end, if their tight smiles and fake exclamations of delight meant anything. The burly, thick-shouldered girl named Michelle that helped in the kitchen volunteered next, unnoticed by most of the school still gossiping over the previous three. Another silence settled on the room as every girl looked, waiting. My stomach gave an uneasy turn.

A gasp of shock came from my left, and I turned to see a student raising her hand on the other side of the room. The girl next to her tried to grab her arm and pull it down, but she fought her off, resolute.

I couldn't help but notice how her hand trembled.

"What is Elana doing?" Camille asked. "She's lost her mind! Second-years can't volunteer."

The room exploded in similar exclamations of surprise. Leda came out of her book to watch, and even Miss Scarlett's mouth dropped open.

"Elana," Miss Scarlett finally snapped, recovering. "What are you doing?"

"I-I'm volunteering, Miss Scarlett." Elana stood up, her small shoulders squared. Priscilla, Jade, and Stephany clumped into conversation together. I could hear their mocking laughter.

"No, you're not," Miss Scarlett said. "You're too young."

"With all due respect—"

"I said no."

"But Miss Scarlett—"

"You're a second-year, Elana. Third-years are the only ones who may enter. I won't accept you. It's against the rules."

Elana's voice shook.

"Excuse me, but second-years are not excluded from entering. I checked the book."

She nudged an old tome splayed open on the table with her hand. At Miss Scarlett's silent nod of command, Miss Celia bustled to Elana's side and read over her shoulder, turned a few pages, then looked up.

"She's right," Miss Celia said. "There's no specific rule that it only be a third-year."

Miss Scarlett's eyes constricted, reminding me of a hawk.

"Do you know what you're getting into?"

"Y-yes, Miss Scarlett. I attended school here last year. I spoke to the Competitors then. I've prepared myself all summer."

An unreleased denial lingered in Miss Scarlett's voice. "You really want to do this?"

Elana didn't falter. "Yes."

The room seemed to hold its collective breath, waiting for Miss Scarlett to grant or deny permission. My heart pounded beneath my ribcage on Elana's behalf.

"Very well," Miss Scarlett said with a tone that clearly said she washed her hands of the consequences. "Enter at your own risk, but know that I don't like it. Miss Mabel will not change the challenges to make them safe for a second-year."

Miss Bernadette hesitated, her hand lingering over the parchment. Miss Scarlett nodded to her, and Miss Bernadette slowly started to write, casting a worried glance back to Elana.

Elana lowered herself to her seat and placed her hand on her stomach, her face ashen.

"Anyone else?" Miss Scarlett looked over the third-years.

My father's voice returned with a less-than-reassuring reminder as to why I was really here.

Mabel does no favors. Be careful, B.

With a deep breath, I raised my hand.

A Bit Mad

A ripple of astonishment moved through the room. Miss Scarlett appeared at my side in what seemed like an instant.

"Follow me." She yanked me to my feet. "Now."

We went to the library next door, a warm room filled with shelves and yellowing maps on the wall. Volumes of old books occupied every available slot, tumbling over each other in piles on the floor near a few study tables. Sheets and rolls of parchment were scattered across a few tabletops, along with jars of ink and skinny feathers.

Miss Scarlett pushed me into a dusty chair. It faced a wall with two windows and a low fire that burned in the grate.

Miss Bernadette entered not far behind, closing the door after her. Miss Scarlett circled me like a slow vulture, her back ramrod straight.

"Are you a fool, Bianca Monroe?" Her voice came out in an annoyed burst, each word punctuated with emphasis. "You can't volunteer for the Competition within your first hour of arriving. It isn't done."

Well, it is now.

I remained quiet, certain that anything I had to say would only make her angrier. She continued. *Stay calm,* I told myself. *Miss Mabel is always watching for weakness.*

"It's not safe. It takes years to prepare for something like this. Years! You're insulting Miss Mabel and the third-years. I hope you know that."

Her raised eyebrows indicated that she wanted a response. Despite my determination to see this through, I couldn't help the slight tremor in my voice.

"I-I mean no insult, Miss Scarlett."

"You couldn't even know what you're up against. This Competition is too much for some of our third-years. And now you expect to join. A first-year!"

Miss Bernadette stepped forward.

"Bianca," she said. "Miss Scarlett is right. You have some explaining to do."

Yes, but I wouldn't explain anything, not really. I'd practiced this conversation over and over in my head for months now and knew exactly what I wanted to say.

"What would you like me to explain, Miss Bernadette?"

My hands hurt from clenching and I forced them to relax, grateful to speak with Miss Bernadette instead. Her calm voice had a soothing effect, sweeping over me with a warm breeze that brushed against my cheek.

"Why do you want to compete?"

Keep to the facts. They rarely lie.

"I want to learn from Miss Mabel."

They both stared at me. A long silence swelled, expanding until it felt like the quiet had pushed out all the air. The creak of the door opening broke it, and I felt as if I could breathe for the first time in minutes.

"Excuse me." Miss Celia peeked in, looking at the teachers. "Mabel would like to talk to both of you."

They glanced at each other with unreadable expressions.

"We'll be right there, Celia," Miss Scarlett said. Miss Bernadette let out a heavy breath and folded her hands in front of her, addressing me as she would a younger child.

"This is no game, Bianca."

"I know."

"Are you sure you want to do this? Mabel will not guarantee your safety."

"I want to do this, Miss Bernadette."

It's more than that. I had to do it, but I didn't mention that to her. The less they know, the better.

"There's magic at work you couldn't possibly know yet, and Mabel loves to challenge witches in the Competition."

Miss Scarlett spoke from the doorway.

"Let's go, Bernadette. We don't want to keep her waiting."

Miss Bernadette kept her eyes on me for a few moments more, then nodded.

"Okay."

I stood up as she walked away.

"I can do this, Miss Bernadette," I called after her, holding onto the back of my chair, feeling suddenly desperate. Why did all my plans hinge on the decisions of other people? "Will you tell her?"

Miss Bernadette stopped in the doorway.

"I'll let her know you said that."

The calico cat leapt onto a nearby table as the heavy door closed behind them. I stared at its strange yellow eyes and wondered how long it had been there.

The candle in my room sputtered whenever the wind blew past. It fluttered, threatened to die, and then straightened back up. I felt an odd kinship with it.

Although I ate plenty at dinner, the gnaw in my stomach afterwards had nothing to do with food. I sat on the floor, with my back against the wall and my knees drawn into my chest. It felt safer that way, like I could keep myself inside, protected from the wolves of my new environment. The sound of the girls shuffling to their separate rooms drifted in from the hallway. Their low voices disguised nothing.

"Do you think the new girl is serious?"

"Are they going to let her do it?"

"I don't know."

"I've never even heard of a first-year volunteering."

"It's not possible for her to actually win, is it?"

My fingertips skimmed the circlus. The red, swollen skin smarted with offense. I stopped touching it, instead covering it with my sleeve. It felt like a brand, properly categorizing me. Girl, witch, student. Nothing more, nothing less.

I am more than what they train me to be.

Something slid underneath my door, and departing footsteps left me in silence. A thick brown envelope, tied by a length of twine with the stem of a purple flower held in the middle of a knot. I held it in my hand, barely willing to breathe on it, as if it were a sheet of glass about to break.

When a knock came to my door, I jumped.

"Come in."

Camille's blond hair spilled in first. She gazed around, only half of her face visible.

"Are you busy? No? Great."

Leda followed, then quickly shut the door and pressed a finger to her lips. We waited in a stressed silence until her shoulders relaxed a little. I wasn't sure what we paused for until Leda said, "You've only got a few minutes before Miss Celia comes to do final checks."

Camille hopped onto my bed and stared at me with wide, distressed eyes.

"Are you okay?"

I tucked the envelope in my sleeve and stood.

"Yes, I'm fine."

Back to calm and confident, I thought, pushing my worries away to deal with later. *No fear.*

"Then are you crazy?" Camille said in a high screech. "Why did you volunteer? No first-year has ever volunteered!"

"That's not true," Leda said, still standing by the door. "There's been one other, but it was decades ago. They were injured in the first match and had to drop out."

"Whatever." Camille rolled her eyes. "My point is the same. You just volunteered for the Competition. On purpose. I can't let the new girl do something so stupid without saying something."

I had the feeling that there was a lot Camille couldn't stop herself from talking about.

"I want a chance to learn from Miss Mabel," I said.

Camille looked dubious. "Sure, but is your life worth it?"

"It can't be that bad," I countered, looking up to Leda for help, but finding none. The same distant expression covered her face, her forehead lost in deep furrows and lines.

"Brianna, she's the second-year with really curly brown hair, told me that last year there were only two participants," Camille said. "They left one morning after opening their envelopes and came back three weeks later. The loser had broken a leg."

Camille leaned in toward me to emphasize her point.

"Broken. Leg."

"I'm sure that's a rare exception," I said with false bravado, my voice breezy. "I won't break my leg."

Camille huffed.

"Or not an exception at all. What do you think Leda? Does she have a chance?"

A change in Camille's tone caught my attention, but I didn't have time to analyze it before Leda spoke up, restored to her normal, moody self.

"I think it could go either way."

"What do you mean?" I asked. Leda didn't seem like the sort to give an idle opinion and I needed all the information I could get.

"We have to go, Camille," she said instead, opening the door a crack and peering into the hallway. "Miss Celia is on her way up. If she catches us, we'll get kitchen duty again. I just found a new book on the formation of the Council during the early days of the Networks. I don't feel like washing dishes."

With that delightful book waiting, who would want to wash dishes? I almost quipped, but had a hunch that Leda would take me at my word.

Camille stood and straightened out her skirt.

"Look, Bianca, I think you're a bit mad," she said, with more warmth in her tone than I would have expected. "But you're also new. I know how that feels. We'll come by for you in the morning and show you to class."

"Thanks." I managed my first smile, a little humbled by her quick friendship. I didn't blame her opinion. I felt a bit mad myself most days. "I'd appreciate that."

After they left, I stared at the envelope in my hand and saw it tremble.

Dearest Bianca,

The Competition you entered is no ordinary game. As a Competitor, you cannot afford to be anything as boring as ordinary.

This year, there are six Competitors, meaning there are three matches in the first round. The three winners will advance to the second round from which only two may go on. These two winners will compete in the final match. The result decides my next pupil and Assistant.

The first round will begin in three days, as the moon rises. Because of the delightfully diverse selection of participants this year, I have decided that the whole school will be able to attend to watch you compete. Won't it be wonderful?

Bring a cloak, nothing else. Oh, and keep this in mind: a winner is by no means a winner, who does not win it all.

Good luck, my darling.
Miss Mabel

A Reliable Weakness

The next morning dawned bright but cold.

Frost coated the windowpanes with spirals of ice. Outside, the grass had become a field of thousands of little white spears. I sat on top of my desk and stared out, my forehead pressed against the cold window frame. My eyes burned from lack of sleep. The candle had sunk to the holder in a pool of wax before the sun rose. Beneath it rested the letter from Miss Mabel.

I stared past the frozen world, as if by looking I would see through the miles that separated me from my mother and grandmother. A low ache radiated from my chest, making my throat thick. I wanted to tell them about my first day, about Camille and Leda, and the frightening experience of volunteering for the Competition.

Later, I resolved, straightening my shoulders and banishing the morose thoughts. *Don't think about it. No time for pity.*

The sound of a couple pairs of feet approaching my door brought me out of the reverie, and I slid off the desk just as Camille tapped on my door and called through it.

"Bianca, are you awake?"

"Yes," I said. "Come in."

Both Leda and Camille stepped inside. An old ratted bag with fraying seams sat on Leda's shoulder, strained by the books bulging inside. She took one look at me and lifted her eyebrow.

"Did you even go to sleep?"

It was her first display of any emotion outside the range of annoyance and obligation. I was so surprised I didn't know how to respond.

"Rough night?" Camille asked, looking me over. A few girls walked down the hall behind her, their dark dresses and long white shirts flashing as they went. I'd been dressed for hours, too nervous to sleep. I hated waiting for the day to start and spent the time reading a few books on defensive magic. Wrinkles creased my dress.

"It's a lumpy mattress," I said with a weak wave of my hand. I didn't want to tell them that in my nightmare I failed the first challenge and had to kneel before Miss Mabel with blood on my hands. "I'll get used to it."

"No," Leda shook her head with a grim purse of her lips. "You won't. But eventually you'll get tired enough you won't care."

Something in her serious tone sparked my fatigued brain, and I laughed. Camille smiled, but it looked tight, as if she'd missed the joke and couldn't figure it out. The corners of Leda's lips raised.

So she isn't made of stone.

Camille fidgeted for a second.

"Are you going to wear your hair that way?" she asked.

I instantly took in their hair, pulled back into a tight bun at the nape of their necks. Mine fell down my back in a thick ponytail.

"No," I said. "I was just about to put it up."

Leda's eyes slipped down to the hem of my dress, where a pair of leather shoes from Papa covered my feet. The soft suede made it more like a slipper than a shoe. I curled my toes to draw them further under the skirt and wondered how long I could get away with it. The rigid black shoes I saw most of the girls wear, a pair of which sat now under my bed, meant a world of blisters and pain. If she saw them she made no indication.

"Let's go," Leda said, motioning to the hall with her head while I grabbed a matching dark blue ribbon from my desk. "Miss Celia's porridge tastes like chewy leather when it's cold."

The dining room was only half full when we arrived, so I didn't have to fight for a full seat on the bench. Camille prattled on about a lesson in Herbology while I put the finishing touches on my hair. The skin on the back of my neck prickled. Instantly alert, I looked around without moving my head and tuned into the sounds about me, focusing my attention on what I could hear through the everyday clatter.

Close footfalls. One set, and then another. Three pairs of shoes walking through the dining room. The light talk of the girls at our table died down.

"Uh oh," Leda muttered, her pale face darkening. "Here they come."

Someone approached from behind me. I shot to my feet and spun. My quick movement jarred the bench, and a couple girls squawked, almost tumbling backwards.

"Oh, dear. Did I scare you, Bianca?"

An enchanting face with the lightest kiss of freckles met me. Priscilla and I stood eye-to-eye in height, and, I suspected, determination. Up this close, her eyes were a light green color flecked with gold.

Hoping to distract attention from the over-active jump to my feet, I gave her a smile.

"Not at all," I told her. "Thought I saw a spider."

She glanced down and danced back a step, her nose twitching with a cringe.

"Yes, well, that's not entirely unexpected in a school this old, is it? Nasty things. My name is Priscilla." She spoke with the drawl of someone from Ashleigh, the richest village in the Central Network. The affluence of her family was unquestioned if the pearls in her ears gave any indication. School uniforms supposedly kept everyone on an even standard, but poverty and wealth had their own way of bleeding through uniformity. "It's nice to meet the bravest first-year in the school."

Priscilla smiled beatifically, as if she thought she'd done me a favor by introducing herself. The two girls that came with her sniggered behind their hands, privy to an inside joke. One of them had the nose of a pug, turned up and pressed in. Her blonde hair flaunted her jaw in an unflattering line. I recognized her as Jade from last night, the first to volunteer after Priscilla. The other one had to be Stephany. Tall and skinny, a little like a twig with arms. Even her nose was thin and pointy.

Priscilla's sweet smile never faltered.

"Merry meet," I said with cool indifference. "I'm Bianca Monroe."

"Yes," she said, brushing her hair off her shoulder. "I know. We came to talk to you about the Competition."

Something in the rise and fall of her tone belied her words. Her speech too measured, her blink too practiced. Priscilla held all the cards and wouldn't have it any other way. Apparently I'd upset a more delicate balance by volunteering for the Competition than I'd thought, one that these girls wouldn't stand by and watch.

A controller. Perfect. They were easy enough to deal with.

"Of course," I said with gracious invitation. "Love to."

She paused, her eyes flickering. If she expected me to get nervous just because she dropped from the heavens to speak to me, a first-year, she'd be very disappointed.

"We're worried about you, Bianca. This Competition is very difficult."

"Yes," I said, my composure firmly in place. "So I've heard."

Her nostrils flared. She smiled with just the corners of her lips.

"Yes, well, are you sure you know what you're getting into? There's no shame in dropping out, you know. You are only a first-year. How much could you do?"

She let out a petite little laugh, and Stephany and Jade joined in a few seconds too late. It didn't take long for the false amusement to subside.

"I think you'd be surprised," I said, matching her cool hauteur. Her pupils constricted. She pressed her lips into a line and lifted an eyebrow.

"You certainly are a confident little monster, aren't you?" she muttered.

"Better than manipulating a sixteen-year-old into quitting because I'm scared to lose, I think."

Camille gasped and slapped a hand over her mouth. Leda sniggered. Priscilla and her friends sucked in a deep breath together, operating from one mind.

Ah, vanity. A most reliable weakness. Papa's advice stirred from the deep recesses of my mind.

Your first job in every confrontation is to establish your opponent's weakness. Strategy starts with weak spots.

"Oh really?" Priscilla said, her tone quivering. "I'll tell you exactly what I—"

"It's been great to meet you," I said with exaggerated politeness. The shift of power from her to me was palpable. Taking away her control over the conversation would be the only way to stop her. "I can't wait to see you around. If you have any questions about the Competition, let me know."

Her eyes narrowed into spikes. "Don't get too sure of yourself, first-year," she whispered. "You don't know anything yet. The Competition is no game for babies."

"Then I'm sure you can quit at any time. There's no shame in backing out, Priscilla," I parroted her cloying tone.

We stared at each other for a long time. The dining room held its breath. And then she broke into a wreath of smiles. Her voice carried through the dining room with an airy roll.

"Just let me know if I can be of help. Wouldn't want you getting hurt or embarrassing yourself."

I wondered how long she'd be able to keep that fixed smile in place. I smiled and turned around, effectively dismissing her before she could leave.

Priscilla moved away with a low grumble of what sounded like murderous intent. Stephany and Jade followed suit. I sat back down, trying my hardest to act as if nothing had happened.

Camille turned to me in awe.

"You were amazing!" she whispered in an exultant cry. "You really gave it to that witch!"

Leda took a more practical approach.

"Better be careful," she said. "You don't want to mess with people like Priscilla."

"She seems like a delightful friend."

"That delightful friend has talent to brag about."

Well so do I. Except using it would earn me a fast ticket out of here.

"Like what?" I asked, unfolding the cloth napkin and spreading it on my lap.

"She's at the top of the third-year class for one, and the Network Protector program has their eyes on her."

I laughed so loud it drew the attention of a few first-years nearby, who shot me a dirty look before resuming their conversation.

"They would not take her as a Protector," I said.

"Why not?"

I could tell her curiosity was triggered by the certainty in my tone and realized I may have gone too far. The Protectors were the High Priestess's spy system. They did anything, and everything. From protecting the High Priestess to infiltrating dangerous places like the Northern Network, to fighting pockets of black magic. By necessity they were secretive; as a sixteen-year old schoolgirl, I shouldn't know much about them.

"Because she's too pretty," I said, and left it at that.

"Well, if that doesn't work out than she's still got options. She's going to graduate with the Curses and Hexes mark, Advanced Transformation, and Astronomy. Not to mention her family is so rich they burn money for fuel."

I met Leda's eyes.

"She's not worth being afraid of," I said. She blinked several times and then looked away. For all her disdain and indifference, I sensed Leda hid what she really felt. There were things in my life to fear. A bully with flawless features wasn't one of them.

To my relief, a soft tinkling sound filled the air, cutting off our conversation. Miss Scarlett stood, seeming to appear from nowhere, for roll call. I realized the dining room had filled during my moment with Priscilla. Six cauldrons flew out of the kitchen when Miss Scarlett finished and landed with heavy thuds on each table. Bowls and spoons distributed themselves amongst us.

Camille let out a sigh.

"Leda's right, Bianca. Priscilla is the best witch of all the students. You should see her do transformations. She changed a bat into a dove. She even made Michelle look pretty! She's going to crush you during the Competition."

"Thanks," I said in a dry tone as Camille scooped a pasty blob of oatmeal into my bowl with a resounding plop. "I appreciate your support."

Camille muttered under her breath, violently shaking out her napkin and almost whipping the girl to her left. But I saw the corner of her lips turn up for just a moment.

We started into breakfast without another word.

Are You Afraid?

Miss Bernadette's classroom smelled like fresh pine needles. Two windows with ledges full of cream-colored candles looked out onto the gloomy wood, and a blackboard covered the whole wall behind her. A few obscure paintings of previous teachers filled the space between the windows, and bookshelves ran along the back wall.

The desks in the front buzzed with prattling students. Only Leda sat by herself in the very back, as far from everyone else as she could get, her desk pushed against the wall like a little island in the sea of chairs.

When I walked in, the curious stares of the first-years unnerved me more than meeting the whole school the night before. The calico cat jumped onto a chair in the back, near the fire, and sat like a stoic statue.

"Welcome to the first-year classroom, Bianca," Miss Bernadette said with her lilting voice. Her smile infused her whole face, like an angelic pixie in a beige dress. "Leda will help you get your textbooks in the library after class."

Miss Bernadette looked back to Leda, who agreed with a nod.

"Thank you, Leda."

All traces of Miss Bernadette's worry from the night before had vanished, filling me with relief. Miss Bernadette was someone I wanted on my side.

"Yes, Miss Bernadette."

"Go ahead and pick any seat you like. Class will begin in four minutes."

Camille stayed at my side like a shadow, motioning to the vacant desk behind her.

"What about Leda?" I asked.

"Leda doesn't like people," she said. "She sits there for a reason."

The girl sitting behind the open desk leaned forward and caught my eye.

"Are you really going to go through with this?" she asked.

She had smooth skin, the color of coffee mixed with cream. Her hair spiraled out around her head in a halo of black wires. She was lean and wiry, moving with long, graceful movements.

"Yes," I said. *No*, I wanted to say. *I just thought I'd do this as a fun joke. Are you laughing yet?*

A few other girls clued into our conversation and leaned toward us.

"This is Jackie," Camille said by way of introduction. "Jackie, this is Bianca."

"Oh, we all know her," Jackie said, leaning back in her chair with a surprisingly white smile. "I think the whole school knows this girl. Do you think you can win?" she asked.

"I wouldn't have volunteered if I didn't think I had a chance." My response had a bit more energy than I expected. "Uh, yes, I do think I can win," I said in a slower, more controlled tone.

"I think you're a raving lunatic to even try," Jackie said with her full-lipped smile. "But I kind of admire you for it too. You must have courage."

I hated the surge of pride I felt at her words. Maybe she didn't know that there was a fine line between courage and lunacy. I felt like I flirted with it often, dancing with one foot on either side like a child. Except now I felt like I'd stepped fully to the side of lunacy, coming to school here and attempting the Competition.

Another first-year piped up from behind me. She had a chubby face and spoke with a lisp.

"Aren't you afraid of Prithilla, Jade, and Thephany?"

A sea of faces stared back at me. Here was my chance to establish a bit of solid ground against the opposition.

"No, of course not," I laughed with breathy amusement. "Why would I be afraid of them?"

The girl's eyes widened.

"Why wouldn't you be?" she asked, dubious. "They know what they are doing. They're third-years. I think Prithilla will win."

"I've seen the transformations she can do," Jackie said with a low hum of agreement. "Jade isn't too bad with healing incantations either, if she were to get hurt. She'd have a good advantage there."

Several girls agreed, launching them into a discourse on the faults and strengths of the three third-years. I noticed that no one mentioned Michelle, or even seemed to consider her much of a contender. Stephany didn't seem to have one area of magical strength, just a general ability to perform most incantations. Priscilla, it was unanimous, would win. I listened, trying to absorb any information that could later give me an advantage.

"What about Michelle?" I asked, interrupting a heated discussion on whether Jade could outmatch Stephany in transfiguration magic. They all looked at me in surprise.

"What about her?" Jackie replied.

"She volunteered as well."

They all stared at each other.

"Mithelle?" the lisp-girl repeated with shrug. "Well, thee will do all right."

"And Elana?" I pressed.

They seemed to have forgotten about the other competitors. Jackie responded first. "Elana might give you a run for your money in the first match, but I don't think she'll make it to the third."

The rest of the first-years murmured their agreement. *Sheep, all of you,* I wanted to say, but held my tongue.

The tiny silver bell on Miss Bernadette's desk rose into the air and signaled the start of our class with a musical clatter. Through the shuffling of girls turning around and pulling out books, I heard Leda's quiet laughter from the back of the room. I glanced over my shoulder, unable to imagine what she found so funny, but couldn't catch her eye.

"Bianca, take a seat. Everyone, pull out your blue books. The one titled, *Essays on Incantations and Their Importance in the Network.*"

I moved to the desk behind Camille and slipped into the seat. The cat purred itself to sleep on the hearth behind us, and my first day at Miss Mabel's School for Girls began.

Predictions and Possibilities

"These are the textbooks we use the most. I'm afraid there's only a few old tattered ones left over, but you can deal with it."

Leda's less-than-sympathetic words as she scoured the library shelves came from inside a rather large bookshelf, where her head had disappeared in search of a missing page.

A stack of worn-down, ancient books grew in size as she pulled the volumes down from her perch on an old rolling ladder. I noticed someone's old grimoire amongst them, and shuffled through the pages of handwritten spells and notes on potions. Grimoires were my favorite. I loved learning what magic the original owner knew, what secrets and spells they passed on, like a magical diary.

The library was made up of two floors of books with a short walkway ringing the second floor accessible only by a twirling, rickety staircase. Hazy murals covered the ceiling, coated in a film of dust. It smelled musty, like old paper and ink. A few second-years sat around the fire, bent over rolls of parchment. They gazed at me every now and then, but looked away before I could make eye contact. It was a droll celebrity status I had attained my first night here. They looked but never spoke. While I found it easy to ignore for the most part, their constant stares and whispers were quietly unnerving.

"Thanks for your help," I said.

"Don't thank me yet," Leda replied, reappearing with a poof of dust and the lost paper in hand. "We haven't even started catching you up."

I eyed the books. *Mr Gulliver's Guide to Potions* sat on top of *Topography of the Central Network*.

"I'm sure it won't be too bad," I said with little conviction, hoping it was true. Sitting down to study felt like a special form of torture. Growing up, most of my education occurred outside, in the dirt and fresh air. The idea of restricting myself to books and worksheets seemed less than enticing. Leda gave me a funny look, spaced out for a second, then quickly shook her head to clear it.

"Well, let's get started."

We both took an armful of the old tomes, but just as we headed to a lonely corner of the library, a group of obnoxious third-years moved in. I recognized Stephany in the midst of them, a good six inches taller than everyone else. Her smug expression grew when she saw us.

"Watch out girls," Stephany called, her skinny arm reaching out like a giant branch to point to us. "Leda's out. Cover your eyes, or her skin and hair will blind you!"

The third-year students let out a burst of tittering laughter. Leda rolled her eyes.

"Let's just go to my room," she said under her breath, avoiding eye contact with the older girls.

"Don't look right at her," another called amidst the laughter. "It's like looking into the sun!"

I sighed, watching Leda's neck flare to a bright red color.

"Aren't you going to say something?" I asked.

"What would I say?" she retorted. "I am really pale."

I shot her a dismayed look. "You're just going to let them win?" I asked. She stared at me in response. "If you aren't going to say something, I will."

Leda shrugged, staggering under the weight of the books.

"Go right ahead. I'd love to see you try to put them in their place."

I had a feeling her willingness came more from a desire to see me fail than to see Stephany cut down to size. The way she emphasized the word *try* left little doubt. The gauntlet thrown, I couldn't back down. If Leda wouldn't stand up to the third-year bullies, there was no reason for me to leave without taking a swing.

Following Leda's example, I turned to depart from the library, smiling at Stephany as I approached. Her amusement wavered, dwindling into a confused question mark on her face. Apparently she wanted the first-years to scuttle away, intimidated, and certainly not making eye contact with her.

Well, not this first-year.

"Have a great day, Stephany," I sang. "Always lovely to see you."

Then the rug underneath her feet slipped and she fell on her bottom with a yelp.

"Look out," I said over my shoulder as I sailed out the doorway. "A tree just fell in the library."

The double doors slammed closed behind us. Leda's eyes grew wide.

"What have you done?" she cried, breathless.

"Evened the playing field a bit," I said in a dry tone. "Girls like that feel like they can get away with anything."

Despite my boldness—or perhaps because of it—we sped up the stairs as fast as we could, neither of us relishing the idea of them coming after us. Leda slammed her bedroom door and propped the wooden chair from her desk underneath the old handle.

"There," she said. "That might hold them for now."

I had my doubts but didn't voice them. A chair wouldn't stop third-years on the rampage.

Her room wasn't bare like mine but remained just as simplistic in design. A worn homemade quilt covered her bed, a few history books littered the windowsill, and the recent edition of the newsscroll *Chatham Chatterer* lay open on the floor. Leda kicked it to the side with her toe and unloaded all her books on the bed. All her possessions had a faded look, as if they'd gone through one person too many before settling on her.

"Grief!" she cried, shaking out her skinny arms. "Those stairs are awful with a load of books. I can't wait until we learn levitation, and I can float them up. I'm too skinny for stuff like that."

I carefully set my own armful beside hers, shaking out my arms as if they ached too, hoping she didn't notice my poor show. The long sleeved uniform didn't show it, but all my training and running with Papa had left me unusually strong for a girl.

"Finding the books took longer than I thought," she said, casting an eye on the clock. "We don't have very long. I can at least show you where we are in each subject."

She sat on the edge of her bed as I gathered the books, pulling a new one out of the middle of one pile. *The Natural Laws of Antebellum and Their Magical Application: A study of the physical world and how magic works.*

"This one looks interesting," I said, sifting through the pages written in a loopy, cursive script. When I turned to Leda, she was back in her trance-like state. She came out of it with a start and stared at me.

"You already know how to do this, don't you?"

"Do what?"

Leda grabbed the nearest book and pushed it onto my lap. *Basic Incantations and Their Everyday Use.* I met her gaze.

"I-I don't know what you're talking about."

"Do a levitating spell."

"No!"

Leda grabbed a feather quill and held it out. "I know you can. Levitate the feather."

"How do you know I can?" An uncomfortable prickling feeling climbed up my spine. "We just barely met."

She didn't say anything else, just lifted her infernal eyebrow. It got so much exercise I wondered why it didn't bulge with muscle. All the same, I knew I wouldn't win. I could see it in her eyes.

"Fine," I whispered on a sigh. The feather zipped out of her hand and hovered in the air between us. A triumphant look crossed her face.

"Ha!"

"How would you know that?" I hissed.

"I know a lot of things," she said vaguely, trying to wave it off. "This will be a lot easier than I thought. All right, well, in this book–"

"Wait." My hand shot forward to stop her. She quickly jerked out of my grasp. "What else do you know?"

She released a burdened sigh.

"Look, I just said it as a guess. The way you looked at the books seemed like you had seen them before. Don't read too much into it."

Her eyes shifted away from mine. Her free hand made a white-knuckle fist, and there was a hesitant, rushed tone in her voice.

"You're lying," I whispered. She looked up at me with a flash of anger, and for a second, I almost lost her to another mini-daze. But she pulled herself out of it with a growl.

"No, I'm not."

"Tell me what you're lying about."

"I'm not lying!"

"Then why can I see your heart pounding in your throat?"

Her eyes jerked to mine for the first time since my accusation.

Watch their throat, Papa's voice whispered through my mind. *If they really are lying, and they aren't used to it, you'll be able to see their heart beat in their throat. They might look breathless or flushed.*

"Fine," Leda said, slapping her book shut. "You want to know more? I'll tell you what I know. I know that you're scared. I know your grandmother is very sick and could die at any moment. I know that you look like your mother and dream about your father at night. I know that your family has a curse that ties you to Miss Mabel and—"

She stopped with a nervous breath, her steam dying like a kettle taken out of the fire.

My heart beat so loud in my chest that I almost didn't hear her finish. I pushed off the bed and turned my back to her, trying to hide my fear.

"Sorry," she whispered. I heard the wince in her voice. "I should have handled that better. I don't . . . I don't really have friends except for Camille."

"So I've heard," I muttered, pressing a hand to my chest. I hadn't felt this kind of heart-fluttering panic in a long time, and it was hard to get under control.

"Look, I'm not going to sell your life story for money, all right? No one would want it. You're not that exciting. Except for the Miss Mabel part. You'd probably get a few headlines in the *Chatham Chatterer* if they knew that your teacher held a curse over you. Pretty horrific, by the way. Poor stroke of luck for you."

Her droll tone and bad attempt at rectifying the situation were half-hearted and pathetic. I turned around to find her face screwed up in a grimace.

"I know you have a lot of questions," she said in a rush when I opened my mouth. "I'll explain myself, okay?"

I sat back on the end of the bed, but further away this time.

"Go ahead," I said.

She let out a frustrated breath.

"I'm not sure where to start," she murmured.

"Start with how you know that much about me."

"Because I'm alive."

My forehead ruffled in confusion and she readjusted, shoving the books away from her with a sharp movement. "I perceive things before they happen that normal witches can't. It's an involuntary function of my mind. It just happens. Strong emotions give it power, just like any magic in our world. So when I get frustrated, or happy, or sad, it brings a rush of images into my head. Possibilities."

"Is that why you space out?"

Her face flushed and she looked at her shoes. "I don't have a lot of control over it right now. All the emotions of starting school and moving from home make it unpredictable. I have a hard time keeping my thoughts in control."

"Camille knows about it, doesn't she?"

"Yes. We've been friends for years. She's the only one who does." She gave me a pointed look, a warning to keep her secret.

"I won't tell either," I promised, to put her at ease, knowing I wouldn't get answers if I didn't.

"Thanks," she said, looking down again, clearly uncomfortable. She really didn't know how to have friends.

"Not even Miss Bernadette?" I asked.

"No," she said forcefully, reddening again. "I don't want her to know either."

Leda wasn't that different from me. I drew in a deep breath, feeling a little calmer.

"Did you see that I had levitated before?" I asked, eyeing the feather that sat on the edge of the desk, precariously close to falling.

Leda pressed her lips into a line. "No, because I don't see the past. I saw you completing the magic in the future and took a guess."

"Then how do you know I dream about my father?"

Just mentioning him sent a nervous thrill through me, and I had to suppress the need to change the subject. I never talked about Papa. We had to keep him safe, so we never mentioned him.

"I saw the possibilities. You may have a dream about your father tonight or the next night. Based on your possible reaction, you have it often. That's how I knew."

"Does this happen with everyone?" I asked, thinking about how exhausting it would be. How did she learn anything in class? Her lone desk and penchant for avoiding people suddenly made sense.

"Yes, for the most part. Sometimes choices they make cloud it, but I see it all the same. Crowds give me a headache because everything changes so much."

I laughed in spite of myself. "Is that why you're always reading books at mealtimes?"

A shy smile showed up only briefly. "It helps me focus on one thing when I read."

"You'll probably have the whole library read by the time you graduate."

"I plan on it," she said in a serious tone, taking me by surprise. Apparently Leda had more aspirations than I had given her credit for.

I couldn't help wondering what her foresight could mean for me in the Competition. "Is what you see guaranteed?" I hoped she didn't hear the edge in my tone.

"When it's in the very near future," Leda shrugged, leaning back against the wall, stretching out legs covered with the thick white stockings that enslaved us all. "I mean within minutes, then what I see is pretty certain. Miss Bernadette is going to come back to the school from her cottage in a few minutes, for example. As time passes, the options narrow. Everything else I see is just . . . something that could happen."

It was difficult to know what to say. My initial horror had faded because she didn't seem malicious. We sat there for several minutes in silence.

"Were you born with it?" I finally broke the quiet.

"No. Someone cursed me."

Stunned for the second time, I just stared at her. I'd never met another witch my age with a curse. Having a curse was like having a disease, ostracizing and terrifying. Everyone assumed you had it because you did something wrong.

"What? You're cursed?"

"No, it wasn't Miss Mabel," she said, anticipating a question that hovered on the tip of my tongue. "It happened when I was a baby. My father made a stupid decision and hurt a friend. His friend cast a curse on me in his anger. I believe his friend really thought he was doing my father a favor, giving him a daughter that could see possibilities in the future to stop him from making any bad mistakes again. But it's far from that. It's a nightmare."

"Oh."

"Don't worry," she said quickly. "My father is a great guy now. That's all it took to shape him up."

I managed a smile, and she looked away with another sheepish blush.

"His friend won't take the curse away?" I asked.

"The man died. He had no family or relatives, either, that would be able to remove it after he passed."

She spoke about it with an ease that I envied. Sometimes I wished my curse could just be something in the background, and not an existing presence, looming just above me with its hands around my neck.

"I don't want anyone to know about my curse, so why are you telling me about yours?" I asked.

Her reply was simple and wry, as if she wasn't sure whether she'd come to terms with it or not.

"Because we could be great friends."

Something about her strange eyes and white hair made me like her. Leda was all edges, like a broken piece of glass, but it worked for her.

"Aren't you going to ask the most important question of all?" she asked.

I understood by her tone exactly what she meant.

"No," I stated with a firmness that took us both by surprise.

"You don't even want to know what could happen at the first match of the Competition?"

I came to my feet, uncomfortable with the temptation. Of course I wanted to know. But what if it showed me losing? Knowing what could happen would play with my mind, and I'd become obsessed, or paralyzed, by what she saw.

"No. Don't tell me. I won't tempt fate. If I win, it has to be because I did it. On my own."

"Good for you," Leda said in a quiet voice. A new glimmer came into her eyes. And I hoped, for the first time, that we really would become great friends.

A knock came at the door, surprising both of us.

"Miss Bernadette," Leda murmured. She went to the door and pulled the chair away. "Come in!"

The door creaked open, revealing Miss Bernadette's warm brown eyes and heart-shaped face.

"Hello Leda, Bianca."

I stood, our voices echoing the same words in sync.

"Miss Bernadette."

"I'm glad I found you, Bianca." she said, breathless and flushed. "I've been looking for you everywhere."

"Is something wrong?"

"Miss Mabel moved the time of the match."

My stomach dropped, already guessing what she was about to say.

"It's tonight. The first match is tonight, after the sun sets."

Play It Smart

I felt an odd sense of calm when Miss Scarlett called us forward.

"All right, Competitors, I have your envelopes."

The fading blue tones of twilight, normally so calming, put me and everyone else on edge. Six torches flickered in a line along the wrought iron fence in front of the school. Beyond their circle of light, the forest faded into black. Our breath misted out in front of us as we waited. The entire school stared at our backs, only a few steps away. I got the sense that they weren't the only ones watching.

To my right stood the only second-year volunteer, Elana. Her clenched fists and compressed lips made her seem a formidable opponent, despite her petite body and pale face. She met my eyes for a second and then looked away. Michelle lurked to my left with her stocky, broad shoulders. Her lips and nose were too big for her face, making her eyes look small and beady. She hunched her shoulders forward, as if she was trying to make herself small, out of place in a world so far from her usual work in the kitchen.

Priscilla, Stephany, and Jade stood together several paces away from the rest of us. Priscilla caught my eye and sent me a little wave and smile. A heavy cloak lined with white fur framed her porcelain face, and her red hair fell in perfect curls onto her shoulders. If the mocking laugh that followed her gesture hadn't come soon after, it would have almost looked kind. I acted as if I hadn't seen her.

Focus, Bianca, I thought, sucking in a calming breath. *If you don't think about failure as an option, it won't be.*

The students chattered like nervous chipmunks in a huddle by the back door. Miss Celia attempted to calm them by handing out steaming mugs of cider and cinnamon sticks to stir with. I wished I had one to wrap my cold hands around to quell the nervous ache in my belly.

The blonde second-year advisor, Miss Amelia, stood with Miss Bernadette in quiet conversation off to the side. Once we left, Miss Scarlett would tell the students our challenge. For now, they were as blissfully ignorant as the Competitors.

All sound dropped from the air when Miss Scarlett stepped into the rings of torchlight. I straightened up. Six familiar envelopes filled her hands.

"The match begins as soon as the envelopes are open, not a moment before," she said, swiveling to make eye contact with each one of us. "Good luck."

She threw them straight out, and they headed toward us with all the velocity of a dart. I caught mine with a flinch. Miss Mabel's familiar wax seal sat on the flap. I tore through it, almost dropping the envelope when something gossamer drifted out.

It was a butterfly made out of a sheer substance, like a wisp of smoke. The wings shimmered green and blue, like a rolling ocean wave. It stayed in front of me, hovering a few inches from my face. I studied it for several moments before remembering the letter.

Dearest Bianca,

I always look forward to these matches, but never more than when a first-year volunteers. Since this is your first match, I would like to give you some advice.

Play it smart.

Each Competitor is paired with one another. Whichever witch out of the pair finds her individual butterfly first will win. The butterfly you see is specific to you. Your objective is to find and catch it before Michelle discovers hers. If you find your butterfly and return to the school first, you will advance to the second round and Michelle will not.

Sounds simple, doesn't it? Another piece of advice: Nothing is ever what it seems.

Your doting teacher,
Miss Mabel

I glanced up at Letum Wood with an uncertain eye. Nothing in that forest would make this as simple as it sounded. The eerie darkness crept about like a lazy fog, filled with unknown shadows and creatures you couldn't always anticipate.

The rest of the Competitors finished their letters, and Priscilla showed off her transformation skills by folding her letter up and turning it into a little bird. It fluttered over to a few students on gentle wings before settling on the shoulder of a girl with bright green eyes and letting out a quiet cheep.

Michelle gave me a quick sideways glance. Her silver butterfly sparkled with every move. Mine fluttered in a circle around my head and finally faded from view.

I closed my eyes to block the students out. When my thoughts gathered together, I could hear the whisper of my father's voice in my mind.

Magic is nothing but the reorganization of elements. Because you change the way things are, it leaves an impression behind.

My butterfly was magical, which meant that as it flew, it would leave an impression behind. All I had to do was search for the impression of my butterfly with a revealing spell. A dozen other methods came to mind, but following the impression would be a more obscure magic, something the other students wouldn't attempt. Having a plan eased my tension somewhat.

But my mind soon wandered over the possibilities, making me uneasy. A sense of foreboding overcame me when I opened my eyes and took Letum Wood in one more time.

Nothing is ever what it seems.

The movement of girls filtering through the brush broke my worried thoughts. The row of Competitors disappeared, leaving only Elana and me behind. Michelle headed to the left in her awkward, heavy gait, toward the pitch forest that swallowed the girls one by one.

Elana nodded once, set her shoulders, and moved away. The cat rubbed against my leg with a stuttering purr.

"Go, Bianca!" Camille called. "You'll do fine!"

A few twigs cracked beneath my feet when I started forward. The chilly air hurt my throat. When the darkness of the tree line hid me, I turned around. The sense that someone watched from the shadows increased. The hair on the back of my neck stood up.

The drapes in the largest of the four attic windows stirred and fell back into place.

Light from the torches faded fast. Stumbling over tree roots and stones in the darkness kept my pace slow. Even the stars couldn't poke through the bare canopy. Without the moon as a guide, it was impossible to keep my bearings.

When the lights of the school lay far behind, I stopped and listened. No noise. Not even the rustle of a bird's wing. It was unnatural, this quiet gloom.

Willing myself to not think about the ghoulish possibilities, I grabbed a handful of dirt and whispered the revealing incantation Papa taught me at eight years old. My fingers opened one at a time, revealing a mound of white sand. The perfect tracker.

When I blew on the pile, it billowed out like a muted powder. The cloud spread, thinned out and drifted higher. Then it disappeared into the treetops without a trace, detecting no impression. If my magic had left a trace, the sand would have turned a bright blue color and lingered. Any other color would indicate a different witch.

A magical impression was easy to miss. I could saunter right past it, send out the detection powder a few steps away, and miss it completely. It may not spread far enough, or the impression could be old enough by the time I found it that a powder wouldn't change.

This isn't a good plan, I thought.

Good plan or not, I didn't have a choice. I had to press on while thinking of something better. Branches raked my skin when I passed through their gnarled, spiny fingers, seeking the next spot to send out the revealing spell.

I repeated the same ritual an innumerable number of times and never stopped moving. The night air crept in with cramping chill, making my movements sluggish, like a toddler scratching at the dirt with chubby fingers. Once bent, my stiff fingers had a difficult time unfolding. I blew on them to no avail.

"Cursed night," I muttered.

And then a noise came from the right.

I stopped, crouched on the balls of my feet. A panicked rush of blood hurried past my ears, making it difficult to hear. My mind raced. The noise could be anything, or nothing.

No, not nothing. Whatever it was, it moved fast.

Don't panic, Papa's voice whispered in my ears. *When you feel fear, never panic. Fear is an ally. It tells you something is wrong, like pain. Think through it and be calm. What is it? Where is it coming from? What assets do you have?*

My breath evened. *Think through it.* Although I couldn't see well, the night did nothing to muddle my hearing. I forced a long breath out, diminishing the heartbeats clogging my ears. The sound came again and I turned toward it. A snapped twig. Shuffling, heavy steps. Grunting breath. I straightened, searching again for visual cues in the dark.

Thirty yards away and closing in.

Based on how often I heard the footfalls, it had four legs. It would be at least three times my weight. Letum Wood held creatures that most witches had never even heard of. Four legs to my two, and not to mention my almost perpetual blindness.

Beautiful odds for survival, Bianca, I told myself. *What have you gotten yourself into now? No matter. The secrets of the forest are nothing to wait around for.*

I abandoned the dirt and jumped to my feet. The darkness made it impossible to work through the trees with any kind of grace or ease, so I stumbled through the twigs and vines, heading right into a thick underbrush that snagged my cloak and hair. My heart thudded dully in my chest.

Relax, my father's voice said. I was a young girl again, standing in front of a hulking brown bear that I'd stumbled across, in a different part of Letum Wood. Papa stood at my back, facing the monster with me. I could feel the rise and fall of his chest against my spine, the rhythmic thump of his heart. He put a hand on my shoulder. His steady voice reassured me. Papa had no fear, but my hands shook with every raspy breath the bear took.

Breathe deep, Papa said. *Think. Don't panic. Just relax. Keep your shield out in front of you. Yes, good, just like that. You know how to fight if you have to. Use the skills you have, but only if there is no other choice.*

This time I didn't have a shield, and Papa didn't have my back.

Use the skills you have.

I skidded to a stop on a carpet of leaves, turning my ear to the direction I'd just come from. This time I felt the creature before I heard it. The ground pulsed beneath my feet in a fast, staccato rhythm. Running.

Batting aside a spiny twig, I ducked around a large oak and pressed my back to it. Running would only guarantee an injury, not an escape. I slid down the tree and groped around until my hand closed on a thick, fallen branch. I hefted it, feeling only a bit better with a weapon in hand.

Twenty yards.

Another noise came from my right.

I froze, hearing an uneven, gasping sound, and waited several seconds to see if it would come again. When it repeated, I paused, wondering if I should call out.

Fifteen yards.

My hesitation won when I realized it could be a Competitor.

"Hello?" I called, crouching down.

Silence.

"Hello?"

A shaking voice replied.

"Bianca?"

A dead bush slapped my face when I headed toward the girl's voice. It wasn't until I almost tripped over her that I made out Elana's

figure on the ground. In the inky air, I couldn't tell what she was doing down there.

I fell into a crouch next to her.

"Are you all right?"

"I sprained my ankle running away," she whispered. "That thing
sounds like it's going to eat us."

"It won't." I put a hand on her shoulder. "Just stay here."

"What are you doing?"

I silenced her with a tight squeeze of my hand and turned toward
the crunching branches. Ten yards. The thicker undergrowth of this
area, probably a dried stream bank, had slowed it down. It was close,
probably circling around, scenting us out.

Silence.

I busied myself with gathering a bunch of pine needles, commanding them with a silent incantation while keeping my eyes up,
glancing around despite the blackness that met me on every side.

Elana grabbed my arm and pulled me close.

"Are you crazy?" she whispered, so lightly I could barely hear it.
"Get out of here while you can!"

I ignored her.

The pine needles congealed into a cool poultice in my palm. I
wrapped it around her swollen ankle, the putty clinging to her skin
like a slug. Within moments her breathing evened. It would only take
a few minutes to numb the pain. I grabbed my wooden club and
straightened up again. A twig snapped to my right. I whirled around,
rotting branch at the ready.

Darkness.

Come on, mangy animal. I want to live far more than you.

Another twig snapped, and another. The huffing started again.
The footfalls so close that I could smell a rotten, musky odor. I lifted
the branch so it hovered a few feet off the air when a low growl sounded just a few steps away. The darkness hid her quarry.

Then a stomp, a rustle, movement. The sounds faded, disappearing into the night. The creature was running away. Five minutes later
and I could no longer hear it, even when I strained. I let out a heavy
sigh and finally dropped the branch. My arms trembled.

"It's gone," I announced in a quiet voice. Elana peered at me through the darkness.

"What was it?"

"I don't know."

I helped pull her to her feet. The dirt shifted beneath her when she put weight on the offended ankle.

"Thanks," she said. "It feels great now. I think I'll be able to walk."

"Good."

"What did you put on it?"

"A little family secret my grandmother taught me. Are you going to be okay?"

"Yes," she said, a little too quickly. She cleared her throat. "I'll be fine. I still have to find my butterfly. You should go. I've kept you here long enough."

I held out the thick wooden stick. "Here, take this with you. It'll give you some protection if you need it."

Elana reached out and grabbed it. "Why are you doing this, Bianca?"

"You're hurt."

"No, I mean the Competition."

I didn't answer for a long time.

"Why are you?" I asked in return. The question felt personal, but then, so were the secrets that drove me.

"Because my parents expect me to win."

"You're only a second-year."

"That doesn't matter to them."

Even though she couldn't see my eyes, I looked away, embarrassed at such a revealing response. She swallowed and let out a sigh.

"It's all right, you don't have to tell me. I probably shouldn't have asked you anyway. For what it's worth, I think you're crazy to help someone that will just be working against you later."

Maybe.

"No Competition is worth losing my humanity over," I finally said.

She didn't answer. I felt around and grabbed another fallen branch for myself.

"Good luck, Elana."

Her eyes were on my back as I left, even in a dark so thick.

The cold began to wear into my bones.

Every step felt like a grinder turning on my hips. The constant fear of unknown creatures made the rustle of a leaf sound like the rush of an attack. The jittery stress felt like it would age me ten years in a single night.

Each attempt to find the impression of the magic turned out fruitless and frustrating. The sting of a gash on my cheek reminded me to keep my arms in front of my face as I walked if I didn't want to risk running into the sharp ends of the trees. When a pinecone fell on my head, I whacked it away with a growl and a curse. It flared into a fireball on the ground, reduced to cinders in seconds.

Miss Mabel had planned this on such a horrid night, of that I had no doubt.

A cracking sound in the trees caught my attention. This time the noise wasn't loud, just a quiet breath of wind that didn't belong in the stillness. I groped forward to investigate, blind. A bulky silhouette leaked through the night. At first I thought of a misshapen tree.

No, it was Michelle.

Her legs trembled, tense and unmoving. A flicker of light came from the darkness. It started as a meandering dot and slowly grew. Then I noticed something glowing in her shaking, outstretched palm.

My breath faltered. A glowworm. Michelle found or produced a glowworm to draw her butterfly in.

"Brilliant," I whispered to myself. "She's got everyone fooled."

I didn't wait around, struggling backward. Despite not being able to see, I started to run. My ankle twisted once, and I almost ran headfirst into a tree.

Pausing only long enough to scoop fistfuls of dirt in each hand, I blundered on, repeating the incantation under my breath and letting the powder drift behind me. I tripped over a root and slammed into the ground with a thud that paralyzed my chest. The impact ricocheted through my ribs and down my spine, numbing my leg for a moment. I rolled onto my back with a gasp and struggled to breathe.

A thin trail of dazzling blue powder caught my eye.

Instead of fading into the sky, it stretched out, heading the opposite direction. I forced myself to my feet with a moan. Of course the revealing spell worked now that I'd almost crippled myself.

The glittery mist ended at a wall of rock that gave way to a cave with clammy air. A muted glow came from the back and illuminated a corner. Hope filled my heart. What else would light up a cave in this dead forest?

The corner turned into a room of glowing sea-green butterflies. Their wings fluttered.

All of them were my butterfly.

Nothing is ever what it seems.

My jaw dropped. How would I find mine amongst hundreds? Michelle could be on her way back by now, butterfly in hand, trophy in her triumphant bag.

A summoning spell. Of course.

I cast it without thinking. Seconds later the ocean wall turned into a fluttering mess of sapphire and emerald.

"Wait," I said, stepping back too late. "Wait, no!"

Boiling out of the wall with their filmy wings, they bolted toward me as one, sweeping around me in a tunnel of color. Light and wind tossed me, forming a tight cocoon. My hair danced around my face and eyes.

"Stop!"

They flew back to the wall, lining it with their shimmering wings as if they'd never left.

One butterfly remained behind, settling on my shoulder. She waved her wings, an exact replica of another one on my knuckles. The sight of the hundreds of butterflies almost brought me to my knees. Too many.

A winner is by no means a winner, who does not win it all.

A third butterfly came within a few inches of my face. Her gauzy wings whispered while she hovered there, bobbing up and down, sprouting an idea in my mind.

Who does not win it all.

Overpowering

O ne of the first lessons Papa ever taught me rose from the depths of my mind.

Overpowering another spell is one way to stop the magic, or channel it into a different direction. It takes concentration, and, depending on the magic used, power. Keep in mind that not every spell can be overpowered.

"Follow me," I told them after casting a following incantation. They would obey as a group. The real test of my power came when I tried to find the one butterfly I had to return with. "We'll all go back."

The butterflies peeled away from the cave wall, flying out in torrents that slowed to a graceful flutter, thousands of winking wings illuminating my path back to the school.

"We have to hurry," I said to the mass, like talking to an old friend. My shoes pinched when I jerked at the laces, pulling the knots apart while balancing on one leg. "Michelle probably has hers by now. We're going to run. You better keep up. I'll need your light."

Within a breath I had both shoes off, and my socks with another. Papa's spell gathered my dress into my waist. I hoped that I wouldn't pass Priscilla in the woods; she'd never stop teasing me about running in my knickers. Holding one shoe in each hand, I gripped my toes into the cold earth and took off.

A rapid heartbeat filled my ears again, and the wind pressed my hair out of my face. Trees whizzed past, lumpy shadows in the night. The cloud of butterflies surged ahead by just a few strides, lighting my path, pressing hard like galloping horses. For a moment I heard Papa laugh, coming from just behind, as he always did. But no sooner had it come than it vanished, another ghost in the night.

When the torch lights of the school yard were specks in the distance, I skidded to a stop and whirled around to face the butterflies.

"Stay here," I said through a heavy breath. Enough ambient light filtered through the trees to help me find the way, keeping my tread light and my body in a low crouch.

When the giggle of voices met my ears, I slipped behind a tree and scanned the schoolyard. Less than ten people remained outside, clustered in closely packed huddles.

I turned around and whistled two soft notes, casting a silent spell to call the one butterfly back to me while the others continued on. It would separate from the others and stay behind with me.

If I could continue to overpower the original magic.

The forest gave up nothing at first. Talking amongst those outside continued. Then a sound from the trees began to grow. A few flickers of light twinkled behind me. The flickers turned into dots. The dots spread through the trees like tiny lanterns, becoming lines.

Camille noticed it first and let out a shriek.

"Look! That's Bianca's color, isn't it?"

Miss Bernadette followed her gaze.

"I believe so."

"Hey!" Camille yelled, "Bianca's coming back! Hurry up!"

Several girls stumbled out from the main entryway, where everyone else had gathered to stay warm. Camille took a few steps toward the forest.

"It's getting bigger."

More students streamed out, filling the yard. The sound of beating wings, moving in unison, created a symphony. The rolling turquoise cloud grew. I could distinguish individual butterflies as they approached and then passed me.

"Oh." Camille's eyes widened. She stumbled back. "Uh, Miss Bernadette? I think–"

The army of butterflies swooped into the yard, flying toward the girls in a stream. Several students shrieked, forming a circle when the butterflies parted and flew around them.

A few first-years giggled and tried to catch one, but the saccharine wings slipped through their fingertips. Five or six of the ethereal creatures spun around Camille, turning her in a circle. They zipped around the students, spiraled up into the sky in a great plume, and erupted, dissolving into glittering cobalt and jade snowflakes.

The students laughed, spinning through the shimmering flakes with their hands in the air.

Miss Bernadette peered into the trees, searching. Her arms hung at her side, sparkling as the fragments continued to fall and fade.

"Come on," I whispered, my skirt falling back to cover my dirt-dotted ankles. My butterfly landed on my shoulder with a little flutter, having been the last in the group. We left the seclusion of the wood behind us. It felt so good to do magic again that I felt like flying.

The girls quieted into whispers as I came out of the darkness. They stopped dancing to stare.

"Look!" A second-year pointed. "There's another butterfly."

"It's not just a butterfly. That's Bianca."

"She's back!"

My hair drifted around my shoulders and back, my shoes still in my hands. Leda stood behind Camille on the edge of the crowd. Camille bounced on the balls of her feet in excitement, her hair looking like webs of blue and green, reflecting the butterflies.

"Great job, Bianca!" she cried, clapping.

"Did she take her shoes off?" Isabelle whispered.

"Raving lunatic," Jackie said with a bright smile as I passed her. "That girl isn't afraid of anything."

The speculative whispers ceased as I approached Miss Bernadette and Miss Amelia, who fought an amused look of her own. The school held their breath. With a gentle quiver, the butterfly came off my shoulder and flew to Miss Bernadette.

She gave me a smile, but her lips twitched and her eyes remained distant. Despite the relief and joy in my own chest, Miss Bernadette did not share my feelings.

"Congratulations Bianca," she said loud enough for all to hear. "You won your first match."

Some Dangers

The rustle of paper distracted me from studying early the next morning.

A thick white envelope slid into my room from the crack at the bottom of the door, followed by the retreat of footsteps. I looked away, pretending it wasn't there. I didn't want to read it. Thinking about the next match all night kept me from feeling any relief that I passed the first.

The second match would not be as easy. Despite the frustration—and even danger—of tripping around in the dark and confronting unknown animals, we'd gotten off easy. I lifted my hand and touched the scabs on my cheek from the sharp whip of the tree branches.

At least it was over.

Diffused winter light filled my bedroom with gray. Outside, the dreary day blew in with low hanging clouds from the south. A few stray leaves rattled along the black iron fence in the gusty wind.

Apprehension filled me when, at last, I pushed away from the window and moved over to the letter. I couldn't ignore it forever. Like the last one, twine anchored two purple flowers to the envelope with a knot, tied over the looping scrawl of my name.

Repulsed again, I left it on the desk and snuck out of the room with the quiet snick of the handle closing behind me.

Later.

An array of students bustled around the dining room, talking over each other in shrill laughs. A blazing fire in the hearth warded off the blue chill of the morning. The smell of fresh bread filled the room.

The nearest table of second-years exploded into whispers when I passed by.

"Can you believe she took her shoes off?"

"All those butterflies!"

"How did she do it?"

I let them talk, acting as if I didn't hear.

Camille and Leda saved me a place at the same long table on the right side of the room. Several parchments littered the table around Camille, and Leda had a few books opened in front of her.

"No, Camille, that's not the right answer. You shouldn't use comfrey tea. It'll kill you if you drink too much. Look at the other options."

The both looked up when I sat down, and a look of relief spread across Camille's face.

"There you are Bianca! How are you this morning?"

"Good."

"You look terrible," Leda said.

"Thanks," I muttered, "I think."

Camille patted my arm and shot Leda a perturbed glare.

"You look lovely this morning. Maybe a little pale but lovely. Have you finished the homework?" Camille asked, her eyes widening. "It's quite difficult, isn't it?"

"It was tricky," I said to ease the stress lines in her face. Camille turned back to it with a heavy sigh, leaving me grateful she hadn't asked more. The worksheet sat in my textbook on my desk, incomplete. I'd have to end breakfast early to finish it.

"Yes," she agreed with a bitter sigh. "Tricky."

Stray whispers from the first-years next to me filled the silence.

"Like a savage! Who runs through the forest in their bare feet?"

"Well, she did win, didn't she?" Jackie's voice pointed out. "Who cares if she was wearing shoes or not?"

"She's certainly no lady."

"They're afraid of you," Leda said, motioning with a jerk of her head to the other end of the table. "Not just because you were barefoot in that bitter cold."

"I didn't walk barefoot," I said. "I ran barefoot. There's a difference. Walking is colder."

Leda shrugged. "All the same. They think you're a little, you know—" She made a twirly motion in the air with her finger.

"Oh?" I lifted an eyebrow. "They are easy sheep to control, aren't they?"

"Yes," Leda said, taking my comment too seriously, as she often did. "Well, they may have forgiven running barefoot due to the stress of the match. But now they don't believe that you're actually a first-year because of your big display last night."

"Right," I said. "A beautiful display of magic. That's something to distrust at a Network school."

Leda agreed with a nod. "It is when you're an inexperienced first-year. But don't worry. They won't say anything to your face. Camille called them off before you came down."

"Saying it to my face would just be horrible," I muttered. "It's so much easier to bear behind my back."

Camille joined the conversation, grateful for any reason to not do her homework. "Leda's right. You freaked them out, even if most of the girls liked the whirling butterfly thing."

"Thanks. I'm feeling so much better about my new life here now that I know the entire school is afraid of me."

"Oh no!" Camille cried, grabbing one of my hands. "Leda and I still like you."

A bleak outlook, to be sure. I couldn't help noticing that Leda didn't chime in with agreement. Making friends was hardly my purpose for attending Miss Mabel's, so I smiled to thank her and changed the subject.

"What's for breakfast?" I asked.

"Great choice, by the way," Leda said, closing the book *Justice in the Five Networks* and stuffing it into a bag at her feet, not ready to let the subject drop. "Taking all the butterflies in order to find the one, I mean."

"I liked the glitter at the end!" Camille cried. She fluffed her hair with a hand and watched a few remaining sparkles fall out. "I think I still have some in here. It'll probably be in there for decades."

"Porridge again?" I asked, looking over the sea of heads, desperate to stop talking about the Competition. "We had it yesterday though, didn't we? I hope there's eggs today. I'm starving."

"Elana did a stunning spell and beat out Jade," Leda said. "Priscilla won over Stephany because she transformed a few dead leaves into a companion butterfly, then snatched hers when it came to investigate. At any rate, the three of you are advancing to the next round. Should be interesting."

"Yes," I echoed in a hollow tone, giving up. "Interesting indeed."

Brutish. Barbaric. All kinds of words came to my mind in place of *interesting*. Elana's determination to keep going despite her sprained ankle came back to me, a stark reminder that I wasn't the only one with something to lose. I didn't relish the thought of facing Priscilla, and had been entertaining the hope that she'd tripped on a branch and knocked herself out for a week.

"How's Michelle?" I asked.

Camille's face scrunched.

"She didn't come down to help with breakfast this morning. At least I didn't see her with Rebecca and Miss Celia."

"Probably embarrassed to lose to a first-year," Leda said. "And a second-year, for that matter. She came in right after you. I'd be embarrassed."

Yes, except you don't really have emotions, do you?

"Will she be okay?" I asked instead, giving her a pointed gaze. Leda concentrated on a spot on the table. Her eyes glazed over. She was seeing. She resurfaced after just a moment.

"She'll be okay. From what I can see of her future, it wouldn't have been a good thing for her if she had won the Competition. There's a chance the two of you could be friends."

Camille turned back to her homework with the pained sigh of a martyr. At this rate, she'd never finish.

At least she's started, my conscience nagged, reminding me how much I hated homework.

"As far as game play goes, it wasn't very smart of you to go that big early on," Leda's voice lowered. "Now your opponents know what they're up against. More than that, Miss Mabel will keep a special eye on you."

"I know," I said. "But entering the Competition as a first-year guaranteed that I'd have Miss Mabel's attention from the beginning."

"Then again," Leda concluded, "maybe that was what you wanted."

"Maybe," I whispered, my eyes narrowing. I hated it when she anticipated my motives.

"You've been planning on doing this for a long time, haven't you?" Just my whole life.

"Something like that," I said with a dismissive wave, pondering over the homework I was putting off. Miss Bernadette would not be pleased if I didn't turn it in with the rest, and I didn't want the other students thinking I thought I deserved preferential treatment because of the Competition. The ice I skated on grew thin enough.

Leda glanced to my left. Camille had scooted down a few inches to talk to Grace, another first-year, and wasn't listening, her homework shoved off and abandoned.

"It all ties back to your curse, doesn't it?" Leda asked.

I again swallowed back the discomfort of Leda knowing so much about me.

"Yes. Why do you ask?"

"I'm trying to figure out why you're doing this."

"Does it matter?" I snapped.

Leda's eyes, so bright against her creamy skin, showed signs of trouble. She hesitated.

"It might. You're doing this for your grandmother, aren't you?"

My gaze snapped up to hers in fear. She had my total attention. I leaned forward, clutching the table.

"What have you seen? Is she okay?"

"Nothing I can make sense of. It all comes in snippets and images. I've tried to keep away from your future, but for some reason I can't. You have an annoyingly strong presence," she muttered.

The slow recovery of my heart made me feel weak and tired. Leda sagged back.

"All I can really do is tell you to be careful. Some dangers aren't worth flirting with." She paused to stare at me. "Not even to save your grandmother from dying."

The slamming kitchen doors announced the incoming breakfast. I looked away, no longer hungry.

"I forgot some homework," I said, jumping to my feet, ready to be done with her, and this conversation. "I'll be back."

I hurried up the wide staircase, leaving the busy dining room, and all its occupants, at my back.

The Second Letter

The letter stared at me late that night, long after the school had bedded down for the evening and tucked itself into silence.

The two flowers had wilted in the twine knot, now nothing more than a droopy pair of petals that once looked beautiful.

That's just like life, isn't it? Glorious one moment, ugly the next.

Candles cluttered my desk and provided the only light in the room, casting agitated shadows. Outside, the wind rattled the windowpanes and sent occasional bursts of cold air through the cracks in the glass. I shivered and pulled my shawl closer around my shoulders.

A heavy book on the proper cultivation of herbs and spices lay open in front of me, but every time I looked at the pages, the flash of butterflies in my mind distracted me. My thoughts meandered from the darkness of the first match to the unknown of the second to Leda's conversation with me before breakfast and then to my grandmother. Did I have time to save her life?

When I snapped out of my troubling thoughts, a long tear ran down my cheek. I brushed it away and shut the book with an emphatic slam. The sound reverberated off the stone walls with a dull echo. Self-pity wouldn't help.

I glanced back outside. What I wouldn't give to be able to sneak outside and run through Letum Wood one more time, abandoning all my fear for just a few minutes. I mourned the loss of my time outside with Papa, training and running, deep in my heart. These four walls made me restless. It felt unnatural, being trapped inside, learning by ink and paper.

The flowers tied into the letter dropped even further when I pulled on the twine. A square of paper fell into my hands.

Darling Bianca,

Congratulations! You passed your first match and will advance to the second round with two other Competitors. This match decides the final two. I look forward to seeing you in six days. Meet that evening in the library after dinner.

Your loving leader,
Miss Mabel

The sight of her name made me sick. I shoved the paper back into the envelope and held it over the candle. It caught fire at the corner; the rolling yellow flame left a black trail of ash behind. I forced the window open and threw the remains into the windy night.

An unbearable six days.

I dropped my head to the desk and closed my eyes until the wind faded and sleep overcame me.

"Now remember, students. When you address a Member of the Council, you do not use their first names unless given permission to do so. It's a breach of conduct that I will not tolerate. If I hear you have done so, I will bring you back to Miss Mabel's and teach you this etiquette lesson again."

Miss Scarlett's voice rang over the dining room with all the force of a rolling storm, filling in the warm cracks and crevices while simultaneously preventing any of us from having a nap at her expense. An etiquette class during our usual free hours after dinner was a fresh form of hell. I stared at the tops of my shoes and wished I could pull my hair out of the tight bun at my neck. It pulled on my temples, giving me a pounding headache. Despite the falling rain and the bone-numbing chill, I'd still rather be outside. It had only been two days since the first match finished, and already my gut churned with nervous fear of the next one.

At least I'm not sitting alone in my room, thinking about how nervous I am, I thought, in my last attempt at being optimistic. Then I laughed under my breath. A dry etiquette lesson only made me think of the second match more, as that would be less painful, surely.

"Can you imagine?" Camille asked, leaning her back against the table and folding her hands on her lap. "I'd love to have tea with a Council Member."

A distant look came to her face. It was the first thing she'd said all day. An unusually melancholy air hung around her, and I wondered what could be horrible enough to drag Camille into a slump.

"So would I," Leda muttered. "Then I can tell them what I really think of what they do for a living."

"Yes," I said in grouchy response, agitated from being inside all day. "But then you'd be kicked out for calling them imbeciles and telling them how to do their job."

"Someone needs to tell them how to run the Network," she replied without taking her eyes off of Miss Scarlett, unruffled by the snap in my voice. "Because some of them don't seem to get it. Did you see the article in the newsscroll today about the Council Member that wants to put a tax on messenger paper? He plans to charge a sacran for every ten sheets of paper. It's outrageous."

I hadn't seen the article, and, at the moment, didn't care. A golden sacran wasn't that much money to spend. I wondered about Leda's agitation over it. Instead of giving my thoughts too much energy, I stared dully at Miss Scarlett, wishing myself far away.

"Now, if you are lucky and earn a chance to meet the High Priestess," Miss Scarlett said, annoying me with her strict aplomb, "which I hope all of you do, you will have one opportunity to introduce yourself to her. Use it well. Never address her by anything but her title, and be sure to start by saying *merry meet.* Everyone practice together."

A chorus of diffuse voices mumbled it back, but none with as much growl as Leda. I joined, but only faintly. If I ever met the High Priestess, I'd like to find something original to say. She must tire of the same old drivel. I would. *Beautiful day to be one of the most powerful women in Antebellum, isn't it, Your Highness?* I imagined myself saying, the required curtsy exchanged with an arm grasp, as a Protector or Guardian would.

"Don't you agree, Miss Monroe?"

I startled back to the class with a jerk.

"What?"

Miss Scarlett's bird-like eyes locked onto me.

"We were discussing the importance of punctuality when meeting with a Council Member, or anyone else for that matter. I hardly dare think I need to go into the merits of paying attention?"

A few girls snickered nearby, Priscilla, Jade, and Stephany in particular. I suppressed an embarrassed blush.

"No, Miss Scarlett."

She eyed me. "Very well. We'll continue, now that I have your attention again. And won't lose it."

Her emphasized words were a command, not a request. I nodded. The class resumed again, with Miss Scarlett rambling off on which blessings and invocations were appropriate in a Network setting. Boredom returned on swift wings despite her reprimand. It wasn't long before other students became noticeably fidgety and restless.

"You should try to be Council Member one day, Leda," I said in a low voice, half-joking, hoping to provoke her into a conversation to remove the misery of sitting there without moving. "I think you'd be wonderful because you'd tell people exactly what you thought."

"Why else would I be here, Bianca?"

Leda's cool tone told me she didn't mean the etiquette lesson. I felt a mixture of amusement and anxiety. If Leda did gain power, I feared for her secretary.

"The Central Network could benefit from your, *ahem*, gift," I said, marveling over how Miss Scarlett's back didn't seemed to bend or fold at all as she executed the perfect curtsy. Despite her wide shoulders and thick frame, it looked quite graceful. *Well,* I thought, *I'm sure I'll manage to make it look atrocious.*

"No," Leda said. "The Central Network isn't ready for me yet."

I looked out of the corner of my eyes, expecting to see a smirk. Leda surprised me with a serious expression. Did she ever joke?

"Yes," I agreed after mulling it over. "I think you're right."

"Now," Miss Scarlett called the attention of the class. "Everybody stand and practice together. Any witch who cannot fulfill my expectation will stay after for more practice. Remember: this is the High Priestess. Represent yourself, and Miss Mabel's, with pride."

Leda rolled her eyes. Camille and Jackie were already dipping and bowing to each other while critically assessing the other's performance. Jackie folded with a lithe grace I envied. I turned away, watching Miss Scarlett instruct a second-year as I gained my feet.

"Do adults really curtsy to the High Priestess?" I asked. It seemed like an outdated tradition, but then, I felt that way about skirts sometimes too.

"I doubt it," Leda scoffed. "But we aren't significant yet, remember? Let's just get this over with."

The beauty of Network education. Some traditions never went away, even if the High Priestess didn't enforce them. While I didn't know the High Priestess personally, from what I knew of all the positive changes she had brought to the Central Network, she certainly didn't seem like someone stuck in the past.

"Right," I muttered. "This wouldn't be half so boring if we didn't have to wear shoes."

"If you wore real shoes then I might feel pity," Leda said, glancing at the leather sandals Papa had fashioned for me. They had a low rise, making them perfect to wear inside. So far, no one had asked me about them. It made me feel deliciously wicked some days, like I'd circumvented tradition with a careless *ha!*

"You first," I motioned to Leda. She bobbed an awkward rendition of a curtsy.

"Close," I said. "Not so deep next time. You aren't cleaning the floor with your nose."

She repeated it. I copied her with dramatic flair.

"Council Member Leda, it's a pleasure to meet you. I'd like to discuss the current horrors of the first-year common room at Miss

Mabel's. My toes have massive splinters I can't seem to pluck out because of the deplorable floors."

Camille sat back down on the bench and stared past us with a distant, sad expression. I recovered from my exaggerated curtsy and motioned to her with a jerk of my head, looking at Leda in question. Leda's face fell. She opened her mouth to explain but stopped and shook her head. A glimmer of silver around Camille's neck caught my eye. A chain fell down onto her chest, holding a round silver ball the size of a fingernail. I'd never seen it before. Camille's curtsy must have knocked it out of its hiding place beneath her dress. My breath stalled.

A memento.

Mementos kept a piece of someone who had passed on, normally a lock of hair, close to the heart. They were meant to be worn on the anniversary of the loved one's death. I sat down next to her.

"Camille," I said quietly, startling her from her reverie. "Tell me about your memento."

Her hand wandered up and wrapped the little ball into a fist. She didn't fully recover from her daze, her voice sounding wooden and distant.

"It's my parents," she said. I looked to Leda, who turned away to watch Miss Scarlett correct the awkward attempts of several first-years. "They died when I was eleven," Camille explained.

"Five years ago?"

She nodded. "Yes."

"Is that why you live with your aunts?" I asked, recalling the first day I met her.

"Yes. They died in the kimeral plague. It was so sudden. Within two days. And then Bettina came and arranged the funeral. I moved in with her and Angie, my mother's sisters."

I swallowed back the rising hysteria this conversation evoked in my chest. *Death. Loss. Failure to save them. Pain.*

"What's in your memento?" I cleared my throat, desperate to get away from my own thoughts.

"A lock of my mother's hair." A flicker of a smile came to Camille's lips and she looked at me for the first time. "She had thick curls just like mine. Papa loved cigars, so I kept some of his favorite tobacco."

Her hand tightened around the memento until the knuckles turned white. A watery flash appeared in her eyes, but she smiled through it, acting as if the tears weren't there. I let it go, hoping Camille would cry it out in the loneliness of her room tonight. Part of me told me not to let it happen, to reach out and be her friend, help her through the bitter loss so she didn't feel alone. But I couldn't, because grief was too personal.

Too real. Too close to my own future. I wasn't brave enough to help Camille through hers when I could barely face the possibility of feeling it myself.

Instead, I squeezed her hand, like a coward.

"Will you show us how to do a curtsy? Leda and I did a horrid job, as you probably saw. Leda is going to go into politics, and she can't jeopardize her career because of a bad curtsy. Miss Scarlett is positive that one breach of etiquette will end it before it begins."

"Of course," Camille brightened. "Bettina taught me how."

We laughed and made a show of our exaggerated curtsies until Miss Scarlett called us back to order. The laughter and merry change in pace jarred the awful gloom in my heart as we sat back down, breathless and giggling. Then Miss Scarlett dismissed us with a wave of her hands, grateful to be done with us, and we all escaped to our freedom.

A couple of days later, Camille fumed at the off-white square of paper in her hands with a cherry-red set of cheeks that made me laugh.

"Agh!" she muttered. "It never works!"

Miss Bernadette sat at her large desk in front of the class, grading papers and remaining purposefully oblivious to the struggling first-years. A list of instructions on the board explained how to fold messenger paper into an envelope that would deliver itself. It was flighty stationary. Most girls that came from bigger villages already knew how to fold it because so much communication in the cities relied on messenger paper. Grandmother ran the *Tea and Spice Pantry* in the small town of Bickers Mill, which meant I'd been working with it since I could fold a straight line. The rest of the students who came from the smallest villages, like Leda and Camille, had never used it before.

Camille frowned at her fourth misshapen page.

"You'll get it," I said in an encouraging tone. "Try starting over again. I'm not sure that one will even fly."

"Oh, my aunts can hang it. They never write me back anyway."

"Do you have anyone else you can send a letter to?"

"No," she muttered, looking more flustered than ever. "Well, maybe Leda's mother. She likes me."

Leda bent over her own letter, oblivious to the rest of the world and intent on her task. My envelope, addressed to my mother, tried to escape from the books I set on top of it. The desk jerked and spasmed, forcing me to hold onto the sides to keep from getting bucked out.

Camille rolled her eyes, scrunched the paper into a ball and flicked it off her desk. It flew to the other side of the room and circled around a few desks before landing in the fire. Camille perked up.

"That's a good thing," I said, looking down to her other papers flopping on the floor. "At least that one flew somewhere."

She perked up a little and started to the front of the room to get another one. Isabelle, a first-year with wide glasses that made her eyes as large as the circular lenses, distracted her with a question, and soon Camille was deep in conversation, her task forgotten. I eyed one of her discarded pieces on the floor. Although tattered and wrinkled, it may still fly. I picked it up and smoothed it out with the heel of my palm. After a quick check to make sure no one was paying attention, I started a second letter.

P

I miss you. I don't have a lot of time, but I'm okay. Things are going as they should. Lots of big tests to pass, another one tonight. I'm keeping track of the news, so be careful out there, please?

Love,
B

Camille returned to her desk when I started to fold the paper. By the time I finished, she'd plopped back into her chair and caught a glimpse of my letter.

"Oh!" she cried, perplexed. "You folded another one. How did you do it so fast?"

I shoved it under the textbooks with the other and attempted an innocent smile.

"Lucky, I guess."

She didn't appear convinced.

"Luck, sure. Who was your letter to? You've never mentioned any friends at home."

Leda looked up now, almost complete with her third attempt. It was just about ready to fly, which made it squirmy. I stumbled for a viable response to satisfy their curious gazes.

"I-it's for a friend."

"At home?"

"Yes!"

Surprised by my vehemence, Camille recoiled, suspicious.

"You must really miss them," she said slowly.

"Yes," I nodded, hoping it didn't come out strangled. "I miss them a lot."

Camille opened her mouth to say something else, but Miss Bernadette took her chance by calling out a warning for time. Frantic, Camille turned back to her letter, her hands flying with surprising speed. I held back my relieved breath and buried myself in a textbook before they could ask more questions.

Ten minutes later, Miss Bernadette gave us permission to release the letters. A cloud of square papers of various sizes cluttered the air, flying in circles around our heads. A few of them straggled near the desks, flopping like dead fish in an attempt to fly, Camille's latest attempt included.

When Miss Bernadette opened the window the letters spilled out, fading into the blue sky. My letter to Papa disappeared in the anonymity of the crowd, with no one any wiser.

We left class shortly after, congregating in the hall at the same time as the third-years. Priscilla sent me another false, cheery smile, to which I responded with a twiddle of my fingers, as if we were the best of friends.

"I can't wait until you crush her in the next match," Leda said under her breath when Priscilla disappeared with a smirking Jade in tow. "That's all anyone talks about in the library anymore."

"Me as well," I said.

I trailed just behind Leda up the stairs, only half-listening to her talk about a flaw in the Council system that she wanted to correct when she came to power. The rest of the afternoon stretched in front of us, and it felt glorious, like flexing a well-worn muscle. I wanted to take the day for a run. If I had been at home, I'd try to track down Papa, see if he was free to give me another lesson on sword work.

"Are you listening?"

"What?" I asked, jerking to attention. Leda shot me a glare.

"Why isn't anybody interested in politics?" she said with a hot breath and her usual annoyed eyebrow lift. "Everyone spaces out when I talk about them."

"I'm listening now. Promise."

"Too late," she said, throwing her bedroom door open. "I'm done."

Her door closed in my face with a final bang. I sighed, then turned to go to my own room, but a cry from some other first-years stopped me in my tracks.

"Bianca, come join us!"

Camille beckoned me from one of the tables in the common room. I walked up to find Isabelle setting out a couple of pieces of canvas and paper.

"I'm teaching Camille watercolor if you'd like to join," Isabelle said. "Miss Amelia ran a class on the weekend. She said I have a lot of talent, and wants me to take the Watercolor mark with her in a couple of years."

Camille glowed with excitement, already rattling off on all her plans for the paper. Jackie sat at the window seat, shifting through a Divination book and lounging back against the wall in lazy, feline grace.

"You can draw me a deck of Diviners' cards, right Izzy?" Jackie asked, her lips pursed. "I'd like to have my own. With pictures no one else will ever have. A one-of-a-kind original. Something that would shock my grandmother."

"Of course," Isabelle shrugged, as if it wasn't a big deal. I plopped into a chair.

"Are you an artist, Isabelle?" I asked, perusing a few sheets of paper she'd set out. The drawings were extraordinary, still-life pictures brought to life through charcoal and paper. A few crinkled paintings rested next to them. The bright, explosive colors startled me, a sharp contrast to the even tones of the drawings. I had to turn away, the pictures were so vivid. If Jackie wanted a deck of Diviners' cards to surprise her grandmother, then Isabelle was the painter for her.

"Yes. I'm going to go for the Landscape and Watercolor Mark when I'm a third-year." Isabelle's chest puffed out a little bit. "My mother and I sold some of my paintings at the Spring Festival in Chatham. The High Priestess walked by and lifted her eyebrow when she saw one of my works. I think you could say that's a good sign."

I imagined that the High Priestess probably meant, *Blessed be, what is this exquisitely horrifying mess of colors? Did a rainbow vomit on the page?*

"They certainly do catch your eye," I said, striving for diplomacy. Isabelle grinned, oblivious to my need to squint.

"Thank you."

Jackie looked at me askance.

"She'd make an interesting Diviners' deck, don't you think?"

I sent her the same inflexible smile.

"One-of-a-kind," I agreed, and Jackie winked at me.

Camille and Isabelle threw themselves into the drawings with gusto. I sat down near an empty sheet of paper and stared at it. An awkward lump of charcoal sat discarded nearby, and I picked it up.

"Try it with your eyes closed," Isabelle said, startling me. I looked up to see her watching me, her great glasses drooping on her nose. "Don't think too much about it. Just put whatever picture first comes to your mind on the paper."

"With my eyes closed?"

"Yes," Isabelle said. "It's amazing what the mind's eye can express if we just let it."

I hesitated, looking from Jackie to Camille and back to Jackie. Isabelle had already turned away, paintbrush in hand, pointing out a few different tubes of color to her mesmerized student. No one else paid attention to me. With one final pause, I closed my eyes and lifted my hand to the page. At first I envisioned a trail, with Letum ivy hanging from the soaring branches, and Papa behind me, walking hand in hand with Mama. I started to draw the lines of the trees, their great arms reaching out. Then I saw the emerald colors of spring and summer. The blur of the colors when I ran. It all built on itself, and my arm moved faster and faster until I opened my eyes. Expecting to see the outline of the green tunnel that lived in my memory and dreams, my hand fell to my lap in disappointment.

"Oh," I whispered. "That's not it at all."

An odd conglomeration of lines and twists met me. None of my leaves came together. Not a single point or shape seemed purposeful. A massive blob of smudged black lines stared back at me. Isabelle moved behind me and looked at it with her head cocked to the side.

"Don't be discouraged. Drawing with your eyes closed isn't done to produce a masterpiece. It's done to help you see."

I stared at the mess in skeptical regard. Even if I turned the picture upside down, it remained a mess. A disaster, even in art's name. A sudden melancholy took over me, and I didn't know why.

"See what?" I asked.

The mess that is my soul?

"I don't know," Isabelle shrugged. Her cryptic voice annoyed me. "That's for you to decide. Don't give up on it yet."

Jackie slinked over and stood behind my shoulder.

"That looks like a raven," she said, motioning to a group of lines meant to be, I imagined, the thick overhead canopy. "Ravens are the harbinger of death, you know. At least, in divination, when they stand alone like that."

The words struck a nervous chord inside me. *Harbinger of death.* Jackie pushed against my shoulder with one hand. "You should let me do a reading with you one day," she said. "I think it would be very interesting."

More like terrifying.

"Sure," I said, with more conviction than I felt, motioning toward Isabelle with a nod of my head. "As soon as you get those Diviners' cards."

"Put it somewhere you can see it," Isabelle instructed, shoving her glasses higher on her nose. "Sometimes the answer will come to you when you least expect it."

Resisting the urge to crumple it and use it for fuel in the fire, I stood up from the chair. "Yes, Isabelle. I'll do that. Thank you."

Pleased again, and oblivious to the underlying tone of frustration in my voice, she returned to Camille's side. I took my appalling piece of art to my bedroom, and just to be contrary, tacked it on my wall, where I'd see it every day.

A Terrible Thing

"**B**ianca?"

Camille's voice from behind my door interrupted my agitated pacing on the night of the second match. I yanked the door open so hard it slammed against the wall with a crack. Camille let out a little yelp of surprise. Leda just rolled her eyes, undisturbed as usual.

"Hi," I said, grimacing as I recovered the door. "Sorry to scare you. I guess I'm more nervous than I thought."

"We came to wish you good luck," Camille explained, wringing her hands until the knuckles blanched white.

"Thanks."

"You'll do g-great," Camille said and bit her bottom lip. "I-I-I'm sure the second task won't be too difficult."

"Great job making her feel better," Leda muttered.

"I'm sorry!" Camille cried. "I-I'm just so nervous for you!"

Leda grabbed Camille's elbow and directed her to the stairs. "You'll be fine, Bianca," she said, turning to me. "Just do what you always do."

"Is she going to be okay?" I asked, motioning to Camille, grateful to take my mind off the task for even a few seconds. The urge to pull them back into my bedroom, to force them to stay with me until the last minute, took over me. I forced it back.

Confidence.

"I'll handle her. We'll see you in the library."

Camille shot me one last agitated glance, mouthed the words

good luck and disappeared around the corner with Leda pushing from behind. I thought of calling after them, but I didn't. Instead I stood back on my heels, feeling lonelier than ever before.

I returned back to the confines of my room with a shaky breath.

It was pointless to prepare for a task that could be anything, so I ran through a few sword routines I'd practiced since I started learning sword work at ten. The familiar movements comforted me, even if I felt a little foolish with my empty hands.

"Bianca?"

Miss Bernadette knocked on my door. I jerked and hit the candlestick. It fell onto a roll of parchment, immediately spreading the flame.

"No!" I cried.

"What?"

"Just a second!" I called, then extinguished the fire by slapping it with my hand. The doorknob turned, and Miss Bernadette peered in.

"Everything okay?"

The parchment burned beneath my palm.

"Yes," I said through gritted teeth. "Just finishing up some homework."

"Are you ready?"

"Yes, Miss Bernadette."

"I'll walk down with you."

We descended the stairs with no sound except for the rustle of her royal blue skirt. She wore a white jacket with it. The colors were the same that the students wore, but the style infinitely kinder. She looked like someone I would want as my older sister, and for a moment, that calmed my frayed nerves.

"Thank you for coming to get me, Miss Bernadette."

She smiled and put a hand across my shoulders.

"It's my pleasure. I'm very proud of you for getting this far."

The look in her eyes when I finished the first task didn't support this assertion. My response stalled on my tongue as I struggled over what to say.

"I-I wanted to ask you about the end of the first match," I said. It came out so breathy and rushed I wasn't sure she understood it until her forehead wrinkled. She stared straight ahead, her lips pressed together.

"What about it?"

"It's just that I . . . I-I wasn't sure . . . You seemed so concerned when I finished. I thought that maybe—"

Miss Bernadette turned a corner and started down the wide stairway; I followed close behind.

"I had been concerned for you out in the woods is all," she said. Her tone seemed off, like she was trying too hard to make it light. "You must have mistaken my relief for worry."

"Yes," I said, eyeing her from behind as she continued on a few steps ahead of me so that I couldn't look into her eyes. "A mistake." Soon we turned past the dining room, so eerily empty and quiet, and headed down the hall.

"Good luck," she whispered. Miss Scarlett stood outside the library, waiting like a dark specter.

"Late," she quipped in a low voice only I could hear. "Unseemly."

The students split into the three year groups. The grave faces and nervous whispers made me wonder if I'd walked into a funeral. Even the musty smell of books seemed close and overwhelming. Camille, Leda, and Jackie stood in front of the first-years. I had three champions, at least. Camille still wrung her hands, so I gave her a smile that seemed to reassure her.

Priscilla and Elana stood at an old table near the fire facing the room. Three thumb sized glasses stood along the middle of the desk, half full with water. A single envelope rested against the glasses. A tattered collection of old books lined the edges. Next to the table was a circular stand packed with glass jars of herbs and potions. I recognized hemp, kawakawa leaves, and dried lemon zest.

Elana met my eyes briefly and returned her gaze to the far wall. That steely expression owned her face. Priscilla and I made a mutual point of ignoring each other. Miss Scarlett closed the library door as the cat ran by in a flash of black and brown.

"You may open the envelope and begin," she announced.

So that was it. One of us would lose a dream, or our life, and it all started with a simple *have a go.* The lack of preamble felt anticlimactic, but delaying the inevitable would have been worse.

Priscilla snatched the letter with a toss of her gleaming red hair.

I envied her for getting to it first and tried not to look as nervous as I felt.

Confidence, I reminded myself.

"I'll read it," she said, sending me a smug look.

Satisfied she had everyone's attention, she cleared her throat and began to read.

Beloved Competitors,

Welcome to the second match!

In front of you is a glass of what appears to be water, but looks can be deceiving. It is not water. To begin, the three of you will drink the contents. You will then create an antidote to the symptoms. The last person to figure out the cure will lose. Feel free to use the books on the table for reference, as well as the herbs and spices to the right.

As you already know, nothing is ever what it seems.

Always yours,
Miss Mabel

Priscilla folded the letter and set it on the table, compressing her lips in a poor attempt to hide a smile. I could see her certainty in the smooth way she shot the third-year group a wink. The three of us sat there for several seconds, waiting.

All arrogance aside, no one wanted to be the first to drink.

With a sinking feeling in my stomach that told me this wasn't going to be good so I might as well get it over with, I reached for the glass and drank it in one swallow. Another wave of shock went through the school. I heard a few whispers.

"She took it first!"

"Demented."

Priscilla slipped me a private scowl and took her own.

The effects were immediate, and intense.

Fire coated my stomach like a hot glove. I doubled over with a cry of surprise. My stomach rolled and twisted in molten heat.

The cramps eased as fast as they came, giving me time to grapple for a book before Elana or Priscilla moved. Once the feeling abated, it grew again. I fell to my knees, knocking the empty glass to the floor. It landed with a dull thud and spun in a circle on its side.

This challenge had to be about more than creating an antidote. Miss Mabel could have tested our skills for potions in an infinite number of ways. Agony like this didn't come without reason. The tightening started in my bowels again. I held my breath and waited it out, only able to think in bits and pieces.

Priscilla whimpered nearby. I thought I saw Elana doubled over, but couldn't be sure of anything.

The pain receded enough for me to grapple for *A Complete List of Medicinal Herbs and Their Purposes* again. Using the table as a crutch, I pulled myself up, then leaned against the edge and flipped to the table of contents. The knotting misery swelled too soon.

Gripping the edge of the table and clenching my teeth helped me pass the next wave. It lasted for ten eternal seconds before loosening. I turned what little brain power I had to the book and had to blink several times to understand the reference for *stomach ailments*. It took me two waves before I got to the right page in the book.

I skimmed with desperation.

Nothing.

Nothing described this kind of pain. It wasn't a stomach ailment. This was a form of torture. How could I create a potion if I couldn't even hold myself up?

Elana followed my lead and used the table as a support. The occasional exclamation of horror and fascination from the students behind me filtered through my mind.

"What's happening to them?"

"I can't watch."

"Is this allowed?"

Startling me with a half-choked, half-exultant cry, Elana ripped a page of her book out. She collapsed to the floor and started to crawl toward the table of herbs. Miss Celia waved the students away when they tried to help, forcing them to back up into each other. Priscilla stumbled after Elana, her face pale beneath a small smattering of freckles.

I looked up to see Camille watching with her hands slapped over her face, her eyes round. Leda dazed out, her jaw tight and lips compressed. I wasn't sure I could beat this. By the looks on their faces, they weren't either.

The cramps overwhelmed me, and I fell to my knees again with a cry.

There was one thing it could be. One thing Grandmother warned me about years ago when a man came into the shop looking for a specific solution.

The Vibrio is a terrible thing, she had told me in her shaky voice.

It hides in many places. Never drink a clear potion if you don't know exactly what it is. It could be the Vibrio. It has no taste, no color, and no smell. Nearly undetectable, if it didn't make you so sick.

It's a terrible experience to survive.

Surely the pain made me batty. The Central Network didn't allow Vibrio. The High Priestess banned it when she took power forty years ago. The previous High Priestess, Evelyn, had used it on innocent witches to force false confessions from them.

Scrambling through the book, I skimmed its pages until I came to a collection of potions at the back. At the herb table, Elana stuffed a few dark green leaves into her mouth, mewling as she chewed. Priscilla sorted through the jars, then fell to her knees with a shriek, her eyes screwed shut.

I found the entry.

The Vibrio potion was originally intended to cure stomach ailments, but over time evolved into many different forms. Mild concoctions are used to treat stomach cramps, while stronger forms may induce extreme spasms and pain immediately upon consumption.

Vibrio has no treatment. Using herbs or potions to alleviate the symptoms may prolong the effects.

It took me three attempts to comprehend, and by then, I wasn't sure I read it right.

This was a bloody nightmare. One I wouldn't survive. I doubled over from a new wave of pain, my stomach churning and grinding.

Dying from this curse would be a welcome reprieve. I embraced the thought.

"You can do it, Bianca!"

Camille's voice broke through my glazed mind. She dropped to her knees so I could see her, calling so frantically over all the other voices that she sounded like a bleating sheep.

"You can do it! You'll survive this. You'll survive!"

I started to shake my head. No. They couldn't understand this pain, this cramping horror. No education was equal to this misery. But then Leda fell to her knees next to Camille. She just stared at me.

"It's worth it," Leda said. "It's worth it."

"You can do it," Camille said again. Underneath the pain bloomed a new determination, the only thing I understood. They believed it was worth it. It must be. Grimacing through the agony, I straightened, trusting their judgment when my own felt so skewed and twisted. Camille smiled.

"Yes!" she cried. "Yes, you can do it!"

A strangled sound came from the herb table, drawing my weak attention.

"Stop," I called to Elana, my voice coming out in a weak gasp. The waves turned into a constant, uncontrollable burn, like pouring a bowl of cinders into my abdomen. "Elana, Priscilla, don't–"

They continued to sort through jars in desperation.

"Elana!" I yelled. It came out strangled at best. Using my elbows, I crawled over to the table.

"Stop! Stop! It's Vibrio!"

Someone behind must have understood my garbled cry because students began repeating me in whispers.

"Vibrio?"

"She said it's Vibrio!"

"No!"

The crash of glass broke through my thoughts. Priscilla fell over again, taking several jars with her. Miss Celia called all the glass shards to her hand before Priscilla fell into them.

Elana grabbed another jar with a wild look in her eye, stuffing whatever she could find into her mouth.

"Stop!" I yelled, with all my strength. "Elana!"

It didn't matter. A wave of sweet blackness came as the pain ballooned, crushing me.

I fell into it and knew no more.

Are You Scared?

The silence woke me.

For a moment, I thought I was home, with my mother bustling in the background as she boiled water for raspberry leaf tea. Grandmother sat at the table, tying the new crop of basil in little white packets while humming under her breath. Expecting to see the sun streaming through the windows, I opened my eyes. The darkness dissipated enough to reveal Miss Bernadette at my side.

No tea, no basil leaves, and no sunlight. Just the shadows cast by my new life and remnants of my old one.

"Bianca," Miss Bernadette said, her melodic voice wavering like the ripples on water. The blackness ebbed away, escorting me into reality by the sore throb of my stomach.

"Are you okay?"

She hovered over me with the concerned touch of a mother, brushing my hair out of my face. I wanted to fall into her warm hand and disappear.

"I think so," I whispered, sounding petulant.

"Tough match," she said.

I wanted to laugh, but the muscles in my stomach refused.

"Do you remember anything?" she asked.

"The Vibrio potion." My eyes adjusted enough to the candlelight that I could see her features. "I think—"

"You passed out during the second match."

I placed my hand on my stomach to quell the memory of the

pain. The sound of shattering glass and the feel of the fire ripping through my body came to me again.

"Did I make it?"

Miss Bernadette leaned back in her chair. As she moved, her flowery perfume washed over me, and my stomach revolted.

"You didn't lose," she said with a sharp intake of breath. "There are no winners in a match like that."

Her jaw tightened, and I saw her hand ball into a fist. But she soon relaxed when she saw me observing her.

"You and Priscilla are advancing to the final match. Elana lost. She kept taking herbs to try and fix it. Unfortunately, according to Miss Amelia, she's still in a great deal of pain."

My queasy stomach didn't burn anymore. The miserable cramping and twisting was finished. I couldn't imagine how Elana dealt with it still. With an exhale, I closed my eyes and leaned my head back against the pillow. The completion of the second match meant I only had one left.

Relief came slow and didn't taste as sweet as I imagined it would.

"So it was the Vibrio," I said.

"Indeed."

"What time is it?"

"It's going on midnight. You slept for several hours."

My muscles felt weak and wrung out. I wanted to go back to sleep. When I opened my eyes again, Miss Bernadette stared out my window, her hands folded in her lap. She had a lovely jaw line, accented by her elegant neck.

"Are you sure you still want to do this?" she asked when she turned her attention back to me.

"The Competition, you mean?"

"Yes. You still have one match left, and it's the hardest."

I put my hands below me and pushed myself into a sitting position, my nostrils flaring in a poor attempt to conceal the pain.

"I'm not going to quit now."

I recalled the moment in the match when I would have given up if I could have. The moment when Leda and Camille came to my rescue. A sense of shame rushed through me. Had I really been willing to give up? I'd dedicated most of my life to seeing this through, and one potion could have stopped it. *Too soon,* I reassured myself. *It's too soon to analyze how you acted under extreme circumstances.*

I forced the thoughts away to consider later. Or never.

Miss Bernadette picked up my feather quill from the desk and ran her fingers along the silky strands.

"Are you afraid of the last match?"

"A little," I admitted.

"Good. You probably should be. I've been here for several years, and these are the hardest challenges I've seen so far."

"The first one wasn't so bad," I said, hoping to dispel some of the tension in the air, but I only made it worse.

"Maybe not," she said, setting the feather aside and meeting my eyes. "But it was very dangerous. You were lucky to come away with little more than a scratch on your cheek, and Elana was lucky you came by and helped her with her injured ankle."

"She told you?" I asked.

"No, she told Miss Amelia, and Miss Amelia told me. That was a very kind thing of you to do."

I brushed off her praise. "Would the animal, or creature, or what-ever, have hurt us?"

"No," she said, but couldn't hide the momentary hesitation. "Isadora wouldn't allow any student to be hurt on school grounds. She is probably the reason the animal eventually turned away."

Isadora. How had I forgotten? No matter how much she tried, Miss Bernadette couldn't hide her reticence, or her worry, when the Competition came up. I thought about her for a second, wondering how such a lovely person found herself at Miss Mabel's.

"Did you compete?" I asked.

"Heavens no," she laughed under her breath. "I'm not from around here. This is the only Network school that still runs the Competition. Not even the Boys School will do it now. Miss Amelia, however, com-peted and won. She went to school here years ago."

The deep chime of a grandfather clock announced midnight, and I yawned. Taking my cue, Miss Bernadette stood and pulled her white jacket over her slender shoulders.

"It's late, and you need sleep. Can I get you anything?"

"No. Thank you, Miss Bernadette, for staying with me."

"Then get some rest. Enjoy the chance to recover all day tomorrow."

She squeezed my hand, then slipped into the hallway.

I stared at the ceiling once she was gone to watch the candle light dance. When the movement of the shadows started to give me a headache, I extinguished the candle and stared at the darkness.

The next morning I ignored Camille's quiet knocks on my door and let them go to breakfast without me. My stomach still smarted and I had no desire to eat. Besides, I had someone I needed to talk to.

The sound of Miss Celia muttering to herself in the kitchen drifted up the back stairs and echoed down the empty second-year corridor. It felt odd being on this level. The decorations were a marked improvement. A gilded gold mirror reflected my pale face and gray eyes as I passed, trying to ignore how tired I looked. My feet didn't make a sound when I walked past an elaborate painting of a ship and an arrangement of nearly dead winterflowers a student had brought in the day before.

When I found the right door, I rapped with a single knuckle and held my breath.

"Who is it?"

"Bianca," I replied.

A long pause.

"Come in."

Elana looked up when I entered.

"I'm sorry if I'm bothering you," I said. "I didn't wake you up, did I?"

She sat on her bed with one shoe on. Her hair hung down her back in a neat braid. She motioned to her desk chair with a pale, drawn face.

"No, you're not bothering me. You just took me by surprise. Have a seat."

A dark velvet dress hung off her shoulders, falling in buttery waves to the floor, testament to her wealthy family background. The demarcation between students' backgrounds was never so apparent as on the weekend, the one day a week we could wear our own clothes. I wanted to touch the fabric, but kept my hands at my side. Her eyes flickered over my outfit, though she said nothing. I suppressed the urge to look over my plain black dress, with its elbow-length sleeves and high neckline.

"I wanted to make sure you were okay," I said, breaking the silence.

The door clicked shut behind me. A little larger than mine, her room had braids of dried yellow wildflowers and willow tree swatches ringing the window and headboard. A painting of two people that must have been her parents sat on the desk. Elana looked just like her mother, but had her father's dark hair. Like Elana, the neat room had a tidy, quiet appearance.

She studied me when I lowered myself to her wooden chair, as if searching for signs of insincerity. She turned away a few moments later, one hand pressed to her stomach. I knew how she felt.

"I'm better now, but it was a rough night."

Unsure of what to say next, I blurted out the first thing that came to mind.

"I tried to tell you. Honestly, I did. But I hadn't figured it out until–"

"It's all right," she stopped me. "I probably wouldn't have listened anyway. It's like I lost my head. I just started grabbing herbs as fast as I could, hoping for some relief."

We stared at each other, both recalling the bitter memory of the hot stabbing pains.

"Besides," she looked down at her hands in her lap, "I'm not sure I would have been good for the position. I began to question the idea after the first match, but this one confirmed it. I don't want to work for a woman who is willing to use Vibrio as a test for teenagers, no matter what my parents think."

Neither did I.

"I'm sure they'll understand," I said. A poor attempt at comfort, and I felt like curling into myself after the words came out.

Elana let out a bitter laugh. "I wish. Too bad I didn't just step away from the challenge at the beginning and spare myself the pain, huh?"

"Pain finds us all," I said, glancing at the circlus on my wrist. "Eventually."

When the silence stretched too long, I looked up to find her staring at me with a queer look on her face.

"You're kind of odd, Bianca."

I laughed. *And a raving lunatic, and a bit mad.*

"You're simple, aren't you?" She didn't wait for an answer, and I sensed she already had it. "Do you always go barefoot in the winter?"

I looked down to my chilly toes.

"If I can," I answered with a rare honesty I felt she deserved but didn't know why. "It feels better, like I'm not so restricted. It makes me feel like I can go anywhere."

"But you can't," she countered immediately. "You have to be responsible. You have to be here. You can't go and do whatever you want."

"Not yet," I said in a quiet voice. "But it reminds me that one day I will."

Elana took that in, with a subtle glint in her eyes that looked like tears. She turned away and blinked several times.

"I don't know why you're competing," she said, "and I don't really want to know. But now that we're not against each other, I can say that you'll be better against Priscilla than I would be. I hope you beat her."

The conviction in her words made it difficult to know what to say. "Thanks, Elana."

Elana motioned to the door with a soft jerk of her head. "You better get down for breakfast. Miss Celia hates it when people are late."

It was the kindest dismissal I could have expected. While I knew her disappointment over losing the Competition meant we wouldn't be friends, at least we weren't enemies.

She stopped me at the door. "Bianca?"

"Yes?"

"Good luck."

I tried to smile but couldn't muster the strength.

"Thanks."

Her hunched shoulders and exhausted eyes haunted me as I headed back to my room to put on a pair of shoes. Miss Mabel had used a forbidden potion on a group of teenagers who didn't know better. And, if she was anything like I imagined, she enjoyed seeing the results. The prospect of being her Assistant curled my lips like a tart candy.

A letter on the floor of my bedroom stopped me mid-stride. I stared at it with a mixture of anticipation and dread. Part of me wanted to win the Competition just to show Miss Mabel I wasn't afraid.

But I was.

Terror had me in her awful grip. I was nothing more than a big ball of nerves and fear. No amount of confidence or acting calm would take a curse away from a terrified sixteen-year-old in far over her head. I hid behind my own determination and confidence, pretending to be brave, pretending it would change reality, when fate wouldn't allow us to change anything. Would she?

I stared at the envelope.

You should never be afraid of anything, Papa said in the echoing chambers of my heart.

Yes. Of course. There must be a way. No more of this fear, this stress and worrying.

Confidence, I said, bolstering myself. Hiding my insecurities back in that little pocket in my mind, tucking the fear away to grow bigger and stronger until I dealt with it on a later day. *Confidence, Bianca.*

I picked up the letter. Three purple flowers, twine, and a thick envelope. The same handwriting on the front, the same quivering sensation in my body. Unlike Elana, I had no choice. And now it was down to me and Priscilla, the smartest, most talented girl in school.

This time the envelope didn't shake.

Dearest Bianca,

Congratulations on your advancement. If you win, I have great plans for you. I know your grandmother, Hazel, must be very proud, despite her recent illness.

In the past, I have enclosed start times and directions pertaining to the match. This time, I give you none. The third match may begin at any time, at any place. My only advice to you is to watch what you do, or say, wherever you are.

This is redundant but allow me to remind you again: Nothing is ever what it seems.

Always,
Miss Mabel

Inheritance Curse

"Girls! Come over here, please!"

Miss Bernadette called to the first-year students strung along the yard the next morning, two days after the second challenge. An angelic blue sky mocked our frozen fingers and noses, starting the day with a bitter cold.

"Is everyone paired off?" she asked. "I want you all in groups. No one should ever go into Letum Wood alone."

Especially not at night, with no light and no sense of direction.

Miss Bernadette's eyes met briefly with mine, thinking, no doubt, of my awful encounter with a creature of the woods.

The breakfast of hot cinnamon buns and warm milk sat as a sweet memory in our bellies, preparing us for the cold forage ahead. The risen sun shone bright, but the ground still glittered from the night's frost. I moved to the back of the crowd and found Leda a few feet away. We edged next to each other without a word.

Miss Bernadette stood on her toes and looked over the queue. Her lips moved as she counted in her mind.

"Good! We're all here. You have the list of cold weather herbs required for your book of samples. Please collect as many as you can find and come back when you're done. We'll begin classifying them by medicinal purpose tomorrow."

"Finally," I whispered, a cloud of white air billowing from my mouth, relieved to be out of the classroom for a change in scenery. A few girls grumbled about the cold, but Miss Bernadette bestowed her shining smile and the muttering faded.

"The sooner you finish," she said, "the sooner you'll have a mug of Miss Celia's vanilla bean hot chocolate in your hands to warm you up!"

Encouraged, the students immediately started into the forest in packs of two or three. Leda met my gaze.

"Ready?"

"I am," I said, gazing round. "But where's—"

"Hey girls! You ready?" Camille bounced up, ringlets flying, apple cheeks bright red in the cold. "Let's go. It's too chilly to stand still. I want to get my hands on some of that hot chocolate afterwards."

We followed Camille to an empty section of the woods. Camille immediately filled the quiet, as always.

"Did you hear the story?"

Leda rolled her eyes.

"No, and we don't want to. You know how I feel about gossip."

"I know, I know," Camille droned. "You couldn't care less." She looked at Leda askance, her voice nonchalant. "That's fine. I won't tell you about Priscilla's quibble with a first-year that got her in trouble."

Leda bit her bottom lip. I started a countdown in my head, waiting for the moment she would capitulate. There was nothing Leda enjoyed more than one of the third-year trifecta doing something wrong. If they got caught, that is.

Three . . . Two . . . One . . .

"Fine," Leda said, the bait too delicious to ignore. "But just this once!"

"Great!" Camille pounced toward her opportunity like a cat. "Last night, Ruby went into the hallway to go to the little girls room but didn't have a candle. It was urgent, so she went anyway. Naturally she didn't see Priscilla walking toward her, because Priscilla didn't have a candle either."

Leda made a poor attempt at hiding how much she wanted to know what happened by turning her face to the trees and letting out a sigh. But she edged a little closer, watching from the corner of her eye.

"What happened?" I asked, egging Camille on.

"Well," Camille said, drawing it out. "They smacked right into each other. Priscilla wore some kind of cream on her face so Ruby thought she was a ghost and screamed. Miss Celia came running down the corridor with a broom, yelling. And then Priscilla tripped on the hem of her nightgown and toppled head over heels, smearing the cream all over the place."

Leda and I stopped walking, both of us clutching our sides as we laughed. The sight of plump Miss Celia running with a broom over her head, and Priscilla going ankles up, was too much.

"Apparently her nose is swollen and she has a bruise on her chin where it hit a doorframe. Miss Celia made Priscilla stay up and clean the cream. Priscilla sent an emergency message to her father last night, asking him to get Ruby expelled and Miss Celia fired!"

Leda applauded, no longer ashamed to fully contribute to the conversation.

"Well done Ruby!"

"Let's send her flowers, shall we?" I asked.

"That's not the best part." Camille lowered her tone and glanced around, as if we weren't the only three people in sight. She bit her bottom lip in sordid excitement.

"Ruby told me in secret that she didn't recognize Priscilla. Her face was swollen and her nose larger than normal. She thinks that Priscilla performs a transformation spell on her face every day before class, and that's why she's so beautiful."

"I'll bet she was seething!" Leda cackled in delight, a hand pressed to her stomach.

"She's a horrid, wicked girl," I said. "No wonder she's so good at transformations. She does them every day."

"Yes, she is." Camille agreed, then sighed. "I'd just die for her hair, though."

Leda and I laughed again.

"Bianca!" Camille grabbed my arm, a sudden thought occurring to her. "Have you gotten the next letter yet?"

"Yes," I said. "Just last night."

"And?"

Camille's eyebrows rose as I recounted the letter.

"It didn't say anything about the match," she said in disappointment. "You don't even know when it will be?"

"No clue."

Camille shot Leda a look of question, but Leda firmly shook her head.

"No. I won't."

"Oh, fine," Camille muttered with a roll of her eyes. "Be fair."

I pointed out a few plants on our list, and Camille stepped forward to harvest them. Leda and I scrounged through the bushes nearby. When Camille slipped out of earshot to struggle with a particularly stubborn root, Leda stepped up to my side, fidgeting with the edge of her cloak.

"Bianca, can I, ah, ask you something?"

"Sure, I guess." I leaned back on my haunches.

She grimaced. "It's more of a confession." She paused to let me take that in, then blurted out, "I accidentally told Camille about your curse. I didn't mean to! It just came out."

I looked out to see Camille fall onto her backside, victorious, a wiggling root in her clutches.

"What do you mean it 'just came out'?"

"I don't know," she said, her face darkening. "She kept talking and talking. I couldn't get her to stop."

"That's a surprise," I said under my breath.

"I kept seeing glimpses of your future at the same time and got frustrated, which made the images come even faster. So I finally snapped at her to be quiet because I thought I saw something about your grandmother."

My eyes widened.

"What did you see?"

"Nothing," she said. "Nothing that makes sense. It all happens so fast, and sometime it's . . ." she trailed off. "Never mind!"

Not wanting to frustrate her further, I backed off on the interrogation.

"It's okay, Leda."

Leda slumped into the dirt next to me.

"Sorry," she mumbled. "Camille's harmless. Shocked that Miss Mabel would do something like that, but harmless. She won't tell anyone. She's kept my secret for years."

I let out a long sigh. It felt nice, actually. I hated secrets, even though they surrounded my life. "She would have found out eventually."

Relief flooded Leda's pale face. "I expected you to storm off and be angry."

"Just because I haven't yet doesn't mean I won't," I said, still a little tempted.

"Would you? I'd feel better."

"How about I make a scene in the dining room? I'll smear cream on your face and send you head over heels after dinner."

Leda managed a wry grimace I imagined she intended to be a smile.

"Thanks."

We started working through the plants in a comfortable silence until Leda broke it with a question. "Speaking of your curse, what kind is it?"

I hesitated and rested my weight on my fingers. They sank into the cold dirt, numbing the tips. If there was one thing I never wanted to talk about, the curse took first place. It only put me in a foul mood, like eating a bitter fruit. The horrible taste lingered, and once you knew what it tasted like, you couldn't forget for a long time.

"Does it matter?" I grumbled. "A curse is a curse."

Her forehead furrowed in confusion. "Maybe. Maybe not. Your future changes so much, more than most. It's . . . it's like there are really powerful influences outside your control that keep moving it. Most people are fairly in control of their future, and it usually shifts with their decisions. But you're different. I wondered if it was your curse controlling the outcomes."

Something in her tone made my blood run cold.

"It's an Inheritance curse," I said, after working the same spot of frozen ground for a plant with little success.

Leda abruptly stopped digging.

"An Inheritance curse?"

I nodded.

"Those are really rare," she said in a low tone. "Who received it?"

"My grandmother."

"The sick one?"

My heart squeezed. For me no other grandmother existed, but Leda couldn't know that. I'd never met Papa's family, and knew nothing about them.

"Yes."

"Your mother must have it then as well."

"That's how it works," I said with a clenched jaw, accidentally pulling a leaf too hard. The plant fell apart in my hands and I tossed it away.

"Is it affecting her?"

"Arthritis has already started to cripple her hands, if that's what you mean. Can we talk about something else?"

"Not yet, I just have a few more questions," she said, oblivious to, or not caring about, the sharp sting in my voice. She'd make a wonderful politician. "Is your grandmother going to die because of the curse?"

"Not if I can help it," I muttered. Leda tilted her head to the side.

"What do you mean?"

I set my jaw. "Nothing," I muttered. "Forget I said anything."

"Look what I found?" Camille said, breathless and rosy-cheeked as she rejoined us. "Some winter savory. Miss Bernadette said it's difficult to find! There's enough for all of us. Jackie'll be so jealous! Uh oh, is everything okay?"

She looked between Leda and I.

"Fine," both of us said at the same time. Camille dropped her pile of plants and fell to her knees by me.

"Did Leda tell you?" she asked, peering into my eyes. "It's my fault she told me your secret. I exasperated her. I do it often. I never mean to!"

"Yes."

"I think it's terrible," Camille declared. "I vow never to like Miss Mabel. And I won't tell anyone! I'm a good secret-keeper."

"Thanks," I said in a droll tone. "That means a lot."

Leda, never swayed from her original intent, broke into the conversation.

"You aren't thinking of trying to bargain with Miss Mabel are you?"

I glared at her.

"Let it go, Leda."

"Bianca, Miss Mabel isn't going to bargain with you for your grandmother's life. You know that, right?" she said.

"I don't know if it will work, but it's the only chance I have to save her," I snapped. "Satisfied? Are there any other happy things you want to talk about?" The echo of my acerbic tone bit like a razor as I picked at a few grass blades with vicious strikes, but I couldn't stop now. "The curse, my grandmother dying, the painful death my mother can't escape from? How about a few sick puppies or abandoned kittens for good measure?"

Leda reared back.

"Sorry."

She knelt in the grass and sat back on her feet, falling into silence while I attempted to piece my control back together with a few deep breaths. Contrition overcame me. None of this was her fault. Camille put a hand on my arm.

"It's okay, Bianca," she said in a soothing voice. "You've got a lot going on right now."

"I'm sorry." I looked up at Leda. "I shouldn't have said that."

"It's okay," she murmured. "I get it. Since I told Camille about your curse, consider us even."

But her curiosity hadn't waned; I could feel it in the air. I knew what she didn't dare to ask.

"Seventeen," I said, straightening up. "Miss Mabel cursed my grandmother at age seventeen."

Leda's eyes widened.

"Seventeen?" she repeated, casting a worried glance to Camille.

My stomach felt sick.

"No wonder you volunteered for the Competition," Leda said. "You're the third generation. If Miss Mabel doesn't remove it by your seventeenth birthday–"

I finished it for her.

"I'll die."

Camille gasped, her hands flying to her face. Leda opened her mouth several times to speak, but had nothing more to say.

"Oh, Bianca, no," Camille whispered. "No wonder you're Competing."

"I don't want to talk about it again," I said, making eye contact with both of them. "Winning the Competition is my only chance. I'll do whatever I need to in order to live. In the meantime, you tell no one. Okay?"

They both nodded a mute agreement. We quietly resumed our search for the right herbs, the silence speaking between us.

Hazel

Leda remained in her room that evening, holed up with a new stack of books on curses. No amount of pounding or pleading drew her out, so we left for dinner without her. Camille, Jackie and I descended the stairs, laughing when a statue of a forest nymph Miss Amelia had set out that evening startled Camille.

Miss Celia walked into the entryway from outside, bringing a blast of chilly air with her that cut through my dress and wrapped around my legs.

"Merry meet, Miss Celia," Camille called.

Miss Celia waved in an absent gesture. Her puffy face beamed bright red from the cold. Both sets of her sausage-like fingers worked at the strings on her cape with little success. Dark crept in from the outside with the icy wind that pushed against the school in thick gusts.

"Blessed be, but it's cold out there!" Miss Celia cried, finally succeeding with the thin strings. "I'm glad that delivery is over with. The good gods know I never want to venture out in the cold."

"What were you delivering?" I asked. Camille and Jackie continued to the dining room, leaving me standing on the stair alone.

Miss Celia's buxom chest swelled.

"An order of my cinnamon buns," she said with a little titter. "Ten dozen, with extra icing. It made me a nice sacran or two."

I slowed to a stop at the bottom of the steps. One or two of the golden, octagonal sacran coins seemed like a cheap price for so many cinnamon buns. Her pastries should net her at least three or four silver pentacles, but she looked so pleased I didn't say anything.

She shook a few stray leaves off the back of her cloak, and I couldn't help but notice the frayed hems and tattered edges. Miss Celia never looked poor, but her kitchen clothes typically bore speckled flour and tomato stains. Although everybody said that Miss Celia had been here for ages, I realized I didn't know much about her.

"Are you saving for something?" I asked.

She waved me off with a little cluck. "Just my retirement, like everyone else."

That should have been a few decades ago, I wanted to say but smiled instead.

She cast a wary eye toward the dining room and visibly shifted back into *Priestess of the Kitchen* mode. "I smell bread. Do Rebecca and Michelle have dinner ready? I hope they restocked the firewood and spiced the peaches."

I looked to the open dining room doors. Camille and Jackie stood inside, talking to Brianna, a second-year with full brown hair. She had a lovely nose, a warm smile, and reputation for being friendly to the first-years.

"They just rang the bell," I said.

Miss Celia's hands fluttered over her hair, soothing back the strands of gray and white. Instead of setting them right, she made them stand up on end, drifting in the drafty hallway.

"I guess I better get in there. I didn't mean to be so late. There was an emergency in Bickers Mill, and the apothecary had to leave in the middle of my order. Oh, well. So mote it be."

Emergency. Apothecary. Bickers Mill. My stomach clenched in fear. The sleepy village of Bickers Mill never had emergencies. I cleared my throat and tried to keep my tone even.

"What kind of emergency?"

"Oh, one of his elderly patients fell sick two nights ago. Poor thing," she crooned and hung her cape on an iron coat rack near the door. The pegs spiraled out like giant arms. It was a gargantuan piece of furniture that had startled me several times when I came down the stairs with only a candle. "It sounded like she wasn't going to make it."

"Did you hear a name?"

I realized I'd lost any claim to subtlety when Miss Celia gave me an odd look and her face dropped.

"Oh, Bianca. I forgot. Your family lives in Bickers Mill, don't they?"

"Yes. My grandmother is—"

"Hazel? Is her name Hazel?"

My heart stuttered and leapt into my throat.

"Yes," I whispered.

Miss Celia reached out and put a heavy hand on my shoulder.

"I'm sorry, Bianca. A woman who, now that I think about it, looked just like you, came running in, asking that he follow her. She mentioned a Hazel, and he left straight away."

I managed a weak smile, but inside I wanted to scream.

No! Not yet. Give me a chance to bargain with Miss Mabel. All I need is a few days!

"Y-yes. Thank you, Miss Celia."

"Come on," she said, motioning me to the dining room. "Let's get some warm food inside you, and you'll feel much better. That's a good girl."

"Actually," I said, digging in my heels. "I just realized I forgot something in my room. May I go get it?"

She hesitated, studied my face, and nodded.

"Take your time," she said, patting my shoulder again. "I'll set some dinner aside for you."

The sounds of the dining room faded behind me as I took the stairs two at a time. Three candles in my room blazed to life the moment I barged in. A feather flew into my hand, and a fresh sheet of messenger paper flapped onto the desk from my hidden cache below the mattress.

My hand trembled as I wrote:

Mama,

Miss Celia told me that Grandmother has fallen ill again. Please write with details as soon as you can. I may still have a chance to bargain with Miss Mabel, but I need as much time as you can give me.

All my love,
Bianca

I folded it, tossed open my window, and the paper flew out, disappearing over the haunting tree line of Letum Wood.

I Want To Be Great

Early the next morning a nightmare jarred me awake to the shadows of my bedroom.

I stared at the ceiling, panting, trying to erase the image of Grandmother lying in a casket, surrounded by a sea of black. Miss Mabel stood nearby. I couldn't see her; rather, I felt her. A raven flew overhead, circling and circling.

"She's not dead," I whispered, pushing the sticky hair out of my eyes. "She's not dead."

Yet.

I shoved the blankets off myself and slipped into the cold air of my bedroom to wake up. Dawn lingered on edge of the horizon, the lightening blue in the sky creating a jagged black outline of tree tops. My body shivered, staring into the cool morning. No letter had come during the night.

I clambered desperately for my clothes.

Too cold.

My candle gave a pathetic amount of light as I scrambled into the long white shirt and dark blue linen dress, still shaking. I never felt warm in a winter like this.

The low clang of Miss Celia moving around the kitchen greeted me on the stairs. She muttered to herself in bursts of agitation magnified by the clang of slamming pots. I padded down the stairs and hurried to the library undetected, wondering why she was working so early.

The candles in the library ignited into a low flame when I slipped inside, highlighting the dark shadows and aged oak of the bookshelves. The fire smoldered with coals and ash. I crouched down and added a few logs, stirring it into a blaze that heated the tip of my nose and loosened my stiff fingers.

I grabbed an empty bit of messenger parchment, a new feather, and a half-full ink pot, and settled onto a table near the fire.

Mama,

I wrote twice last night but haven't heard back. What's going on with Grandmother? Please write back soon.

Go well,
Bianca

The ink dried quickly. I folded the paper and stood up. Across the room sat a tall, skinny window. I grabbed the old handle and forced it open with a groan. My hair flew off my shoulders in a blast of cold wind, while the paper dropped into the night and disappeared from view.

The soft patter of footsteps caught my attention and I held my breath to hear more clearly. Someone approached. A student, probably by the light sound of her footsteps. She'd pass the library soon.

"Well, well. What have we here?"

Or not.

My blood turned cold, mimicking the icy draft that blew in from the window. I whirled around to see Priscilla standing in the doorway, her hair drifting about her shoulders.

"Hello Priscilla."

The wind slammed the window shut, sealing off the room.

"What are you doing down here?" she asked, stepping into the library.

"Getting warm by the fire."

Her eyes darted around, finally landing on the feather and leftover messenger paper on the table.

"Oh," she said, her mouth rounding out. "I heard about your grandmother. That's too bad."

The droop of her lips looked so sincere that I could only stare at her. Her unexpected twists and turns made me feel like I ran a race in a hedge, with walls so high I never knew where to go next.

"Thanks."

"How is she doing?" She took a few steps into the room and settled on a chair in the shadows near the fire, grasping a book. I barely caught the title before she covered it with her hand. *Advanced Beauty Transformation.*

Interesting.

"Fine," I lied and then started to the door, the best route of escape.

Second rule of every confrontation: map out your area. Know how to get away, and how others can get in.

"Oh, Bianca?" She motioned to the chair next to her with a pat. "Why don't you sit? We'll have a little chat."

"A little chat?"

"About school, of course," she said. "You're new, and I've been here for years. I can give you a few pointers."

"Yes, I'm sure the last two years have made you an expert," I said in a dry tone that she ignored.

"I wouldn't say expert, but I certainly know what I'm doing."

No doubt about that.

I lowered into the chair, keeping to the edge, trying to anticipate her trap. Priscilla set the book face down in her lap and folded her hands on top of it, turning to me with an inquiring gaze.

"How are things on the first-year floor? Is it still as shabby as I remember?"

"Yes," I drawled, eyeing her. She smoothed out a line in her skirt.

"I noticed that you hang around Leda and Camille a lot."

My eyes narrowed. I didn't trust this Priscilla. I preferred the snarky, deceptive third-year I met when I first arrived. This polite little bundle could be nothing but angles.

"Yes," I said, waiting. She studied me and, seeing something in my face, seemed to drop whatever plan she'd had before.

"Why are you doing this, Bianca?" she asked, trying to stare me down. "Are you trying to prove something as a first-year?"

The question struck a note of panic in me, but at least she wasn't playing a game anymore. I remembered Elana asking me the same question during the first match.

I'm doing this because it's my only chance to live. Whatever motivation you have, it's not stronger than mine.

"Why are you?" I asked.

Priscilla hesitated, her eyes calculating.

"Because I want to be the best."

An answer so blunt I couldn't doubt it.

"You think learning from Miss Mabel will do that for you?"

"Don't you?" she retorted immediately. "All of the greats of our time started in the Network school system and climbed their way to the top. Miss Mabel's has a reputation for turning out students that do very well."

No, I don't think that. Greatness doesn't develop because Miss Mabel runs the place.

"I think greatness depends more on you than on her," I replied instead, forcing myself to maintain eye contact. "It has nothing to do with outside influences."

Priscilla pondered my words for a moment, then changed the subject.

"We must have something in common, you and I," she said with a look that showed she was less than pleased about it. "I'm imagining it has something to do with our determination to win. But only one of us will."

"Indeed," I said.

"Leave the Competition, Bianca," she said. "At least spare yourself a little embarrassment. You're no match for my education level."

"Because I haven't been so far?"

Her hands balled into fists. Good. I unnerved her a little. Her aspirations to Assistant were in danger from a first-year. I understood her desperation but that didn't mean I felt any pity. If Priscilla really wanted greatness, she'd achieve it on her own. But that wasn't what she wanted. Priscilla wanted the fastest road to power.

And who didn't, really? Even I had felt the sweet tug of that desire before. Power to enact change. Power to keep my family and myself alive. Power was strength, and nothing compared to strength.

Perhaps we did have a few things in common.

"You've got more talent than I'd anticipated, I'll admit," she said slowly. "But I've been holding back, giving you a chance."

"I noticed that during the second match," I said, matching her cool tone. "When you headed for the herb table right behind Elana."

She leaned forward into the light of the fire, illuminating the freckles that smattered her nose, cheeks, forehead, and neck. Her anxiety was made apparent by the pitch of her voice.

"I'm serious Bianca. Get out now. I won't lose. Certainly not to a first-year. I've been planning for two years now."

Well I've been planning for eleven.

I opened my mouth to reply but stopped. Since when did Priscilla have so many freckles? I remembered her face as almost flawless, like porcelain, when I first met her. The firelight during the second match showed a few, but not nearly what I saw now. They gave her skin an entirely different color and tone.

"What?" she snapped, straightening. "What are you staring at?"

"Your freckles," I said. "I didn't know you had so many. I could have sworn your skin was—"

Her hands flew to her face with a gasp. The movement drew my attention to the sleeves of her shirt, which bulged. A subtle puffiness around her cheeks and jaw stood out to me next, then a tightness of her dress around the ribcage. Her stockings rolled halfway down her calves, too small for her legs.

Priscilla had gained weight.

"Are you okay?" I asked. Now that she was in the light she looked bloated. She moved back into the shadows so quickly that the chair scraped the floorboards with a loud groan.

"I'm fine!" she said with a sharp bark, standing up and turning her back to me. "Just remember: I'm going to win."

She escaped into the hallway with the slam of the library door behind her. I sank into a nearby chair and fell back, dissolving into laughter that, for the moment, made me forget the heavy burdens bearing on my chest.

Priscilla didn't make it to breakfast that morning.

Miss Celia's foul mood infiltrated the dining room. The entire school ate in silence, with Miss Scarlett looming in her usual spot near the fireplace, her arms folded across her chest and her eyes darting about, searching for rule-breakers like a hound after a hare. Her red bracelets jangled every now and then, a little reminder of her presence. Camille sent me a few miserable looks, but Leda stayed buried in a book. I had the distinct impression that she enjoyed the silence.

The gray spirit even affected Miss Bernadette, who set us to work copying vocabulary out of a book. Michelle brought us a tray of bread and cheese for lunch, saying that Miss Celia didn't want any girls in the dining room. By the time Miss Bernadette released us for dinner, students threw themselves out of the classroom, unable to get to their freedom fast enough.

"Finally!" Camille cried, bursting out of the room. "I hate those miserable walls. Classrooms," she shuddered, "they're like torture chambers."

I silently agreed. My head throbbed. Staying in the same room that long made me restless, and my legs itched in the heavy white stockings. I longed to peel them off.

"I thought it was a lovely day," Leda said in an offhand way, anchoring half a dozen scrolls against her chest with her arm. "We took enough notes to keep me busy studying all weekend."

"You're mad," I said, rubbing out the stiff muscles in my neck. "Really."

"I thought I was going to die when she started lecturing on the medicinal use of ginger root," Camille groaned. The day had been wretched. In between the vocabulary and lectures, Grandmother's ill health and mother's lack of communication pressed on me. Every other minute I checked the window, hoping for a message that never came. Soon enough I would succumb to the despondent cloud myself.

"What have you done?" A shrill voice cried as we walked by the closed dining room doors and toward the main stairs. "The pastry filling was supposed to be made with raspberries!"

Rebecca walked out of the kitchen, her face splotchy and her apron smeared with fruit preserves.

"Miss Celia's sitting on a devil's back today!" she muttered, stalking past us into the hall. "I've never seen the like before."

We backed against the wall to let her barrel past.

"What do you think is going on?" Camille asked. "The whole school has lost its mind."

Leda just shrugged, watching Rebecca charge out the back door.

"I don't know, but let's stay away from Miss Celia."

A group of third-years came up from behind, speaking in low voices. Leda signaled for us to slow down. Jade's high-pitched voice registered soon enough, and I caught a glimpse of her pug nose and blonde hair out of the corner of my eye.

"Are you serious?" one third-year asked in a low whisper.

"Priscilla won't come out of her room?"

"No!" Jade squealed in delight. "Not even for lunch, although she's been eating enough for all of us lately."

So much for friendship, I thought. Jade obviously bore ill will for losing the first match.

"She's always talking about her perfect hair," Jade continued. "Now it's falling out! Hey, move it," Jade snapped at us, like a dog herding cattle.

We dutifully moved away, allowing the three of them to push past. They moved into the third-year corridor from the stairs, laughing in loud whispers.

"What are they talking about?" Camille asked when they disappeared. "Priscilla's hair is falling out?"

I continued up the stairs, my thoughts churning.

"Maybe she's sick," I said, then told them about our encounter in the library that morning.

"Sounds like she's really stressed and has been eating too much," Camille said. "I do that too. I get hungry when I'm stressed. I raided the pantry once before an algebra test."

"Priscilla sick? Don't give me hope," Leda muttered. "Do you think that Ruby is right? She said Priscilla looked different when she ran into her the other night."

"I don't know," I murmured. "But something is going on. How else would she have gained so much weight?"

"All that beautiful hair," Camille sighed. "I hope it's not permanent."

The three of us peeled off to our separate rooms to get ready for dinner. I sat at my window until Camille knocked, staring out, waiting in vain.

The Winner

The first floor of the school had transformed.

I descended the stairs in mute awe, Leda at my side. Camille chattered with owl-eyed Isabelle a few steps behind until they both stopped with a gasp.

"What happened?" I whispered.

Lush green vines draped the walls of the entryway and twirled around the windows. Flowers hung from the chandelier in thick ropes, ending with a purple blossom. Brown branches wove through the bars along the staircase, making the entryway and staircase look like a jungle canopy.

"Are we expecting a visitor at the school?" Leda asked, plucking a flower off a wall of twisting green ivy. The petals disintegrated into a puff of smoke and the scent of honeysuckle floated by.

"Maybe Mr. Robert's School for Boys is coming!" Camille exclaimed.

She darted around, smelling all the blooms she could get her hands on. For every flower she touched, another appeared somewhere else. More students began to congregate, drawn in by the happy squawks of the girls already there.

"Well!" Miss Bernadette cried, walking down the stairs. A flower fell into her long, white fingers and didn't disappear in smoke. "This is a wonderful surprise. What's the occasion?"

No one could answer her because none of us knew.

"Look," Leda grabbed my arm. She pointed into the dining room. "It's in there as well."

We started down the stairs together, eager to arrive before the crowd. A verdant screen of leaves covered the dining room walls. Flowers the color of plums covered the ceiling and dropped throughout the room.

"It's beautiful," Camille whispered as we walked in. She spun around when a bloom fell and kissed her on the cheek. "Oh, it's so wonderful it hurts!"

"I feel like I'm going to drown in foliage," Leda said, dropping onto her usual spot on the bench and cracking open a book. But she didn't start reading right away, instead gazing around as she sat back.

The whole school milled through the room, surveying the mulberry blossoms and exclaiming over the subtle, sweet smell. The clang and clank of the kitchen had settled. I resisted the urge to creep over and peer in to see if Rebecca or Michelle had made it out alive.

"Bianca Monroe! Bianca?"

The sharp sound of Miss Scarlett calling my name broke through the excited chatter. I whirled around.

"Bianca! Where are you?"

She pushed through the crowd and into the dining room with all the grace of a bull, moving a few girls aside. I stepped forward.

"I'm here."

The room slowly quieted, girls craning around each other to find me. Miss Scarlett scanned the room, still searching.

"Bi–"

"Miss Scarlett, I'm here," I said from behind her.

She spun around to find me.

"There you are." Her breath came out in fast, erratic bursts. She turned and called into the entryway over her shoulder. "Marie, she's in here."

My heart plummeted into my stomach when a familiar pair of gray eyes hurried into the dining room.

"Mama?" I whispered.

She stopped in the doorway. Her reddened cheeks, bloodshot eyes, and tangled hair stole my breath. All the air left my body. I was weak and limp, unable to do anything but stand there.

"Bianca, there you are."

She sounded breathless and tired. Tears filled her eyes. It felt so good to see her, but it was so frightening at the same time that I didn't know what to do. The students parted to form a walkway, but I didn't have the strength to move. My knees felt like jelly.

Miss Bernadette stepped into the dining room near Miss Scarlett, who leaned in and whispered something in her ear. Miss Bernadette's flawless face went pale, and a hand flew to cover her mouth.

"Why are you here?" I managed to ask.

Mama swallowed, her voice faltering a little as she spoke.

"Your grandmother is very sick again. The apothecary says she won't survive the night."

A few girls gasped. I heard Camille give a startled cry. No one moved, including me. The dining room gelled into a nervous silence except for the low snap of the fire.

I stood there, not even sure I was breathing. The words ran through my mind again and again. It wasn't until I spoke that I realized how fast my heart pounded.

"She's going to die tonight?"

"We need to leave right away."

No amount of preparation for this day could have stopped this feeling; it was as if someone had scooped my heart out. I put a hand to my chest to quell the ache. Yes. We had to leave now. Take action. Do something.

"Y-yes," I said. "Of course."

"Do you need help packing?" Miss Scarlett asked, rigid as a board.

"No," I said, starting forward, my legs beneath me again. "I can pack."

Mama backed up, toward the dining room doors, carefully avoiding a few girls. "Please hurry, B. We must get back. She's all alone."

I stopped in the middle of the dining room. "B?" I whispered. Mother never called me anything but Bianca. Papa, and Papa alone, called me B. A creeping suspicion crawled up my spine.

"What's wrong?" she asked. "We need to go."

"Why did you leave Grandmother alone?"

She fumbled for a response, and my instincts bristled again. *Something's wrong here.*

"To come get you. Bianca, we don't have time!"

I looked up to Miss Scarlett.

"What about the final match?"

A few girls murmured in ripples of disbelief.

"Surely you can't be worried about the Competition at a time like this," Miss Scarlett said with bland apathy. "Your grandmother is dying."

"Can I compete when I return?"

"Does it matter?" she asked.

"Yes," I said with resolve. A flicker crossed her eyes. The amount of indifference laced in her tone impressed me.

"No, you may not."

The words infused me with panic. Without the position as Assistant, I had no chance. My life would end at seventeen. My mother would dwindle in death, alone, miserable, and in pain.

"You are worried about the Competition when your grandmother is dying?" Miss Scarlett asked, accenting each word. "You may never speak to her again. This is your last chance to see your grandmother."

"I know."

Several girls gasped. I heard the quiet murmur of words like *heartless* and *cruel* run through the crowd. Let them think what they wanted. For all I knew, they could be right.

"Bianca, I can't believe this," Mama whispered, stunned. A tear dropped down her beautiful cheek.

A warning ran through me again, like a shiver.

Something isn't right.

Mama wouldn't have left Grandmother to die alone. She would have sent a letter in response to mine. My heart raced. I hardly dared entertain the thought that kept coming to me.

Was this the third match?

"No," I said, breaking the silence. The risk of error was enormous, but so were the stakes. "I won't leave."

A couple of girls turned their backs to me. The rest of the dining room broke out in outraged whispers.

"Bianca!" Camille hissed. "Are you crazy?"

Leda silenced her by pinching her elbow.

"Very well," Miss Scarlett said. "We cannot force you to leave."

"Are you sure this is what you want?" Mama asked, her voice weak. "Miss Scarlett is right. You'll never be able to speak to your grandmother again."

"I know," I said. "But I have to compete."

More whispers. More stings. *Barbaric. Callous.*

"Compete," Mama whispered in disbelief, blinking. "You're choosing the Competition over your own grandmother." Her hands twisted in agitation. "I can't believe it."

Miss Mabel's words replayed in my mind.

Nothing is ever what it seems.

"I'm sorry," I said with greater confidence, straightening to meet Miss Scarlett's gaze. "I refuse to leave. I choose to stay and participate in the third match."

The room went pitch black.

Several girls shrieked. I stood my ground, waiting with clenched fists. I had a good idea of what would come next, and I wasn't looking forward to it.

The wine-colored flowers opened in the darkness. Their bioluminescent petals rolled apart, exposing white blossoms inside. My butterfly fluttered by.

One flower broke away from a vine and floated into the middle of the room. Another followed, and then another. The blossoms gathered in a pile on the floor. Like magnets, the others joined them. Where one left, another sprouted. Soon, a pillar of violet climbed to the ceiling and lit the room. Flowers flew through the air, sucked into the column.

The pillar shifted, spreading, morphing into the silhouette of a person. The top petals smoothed into lines of long blonde hair. Slender arms formed at the sides. The lights flowed to the ground in electric rivulets of lavender, illuminating a flowing skirt.

The light from the flowers vanished, drenching the room in blackness again. A few students cried out in surprise. When the candles flickered back to life, a stunning woman stood in place of the pillar. Her ebony dress spilled over her beautiful frame and pooled on the ground in an inky puddle of silk.

A pair of sapphire eyes met mine. Then a smile curved Miss Mabel's blood-red lips.

"Congratulations, Bianca. You are the winner."

All traces of my mother disappeared. My butterfly landed on my shoulder and evaporated in a poof of powder. I knew I'd never see it again.

I had a sinking feeling that the real challenge was just beginning.

Contracts and Requirements

Evil never looked so alluring.

Miss Mabel owned the room. Her elegant beauty captured every eye, and she knew it. They watched her move with a grace that belonged in a room far superior to a Network school.

"Darling students," Miss Mabel's voice called out, doting. "I'm so pleased to be here tonight. Your support of the Competition has been exemplary. To those who competed but did not win, remember this: if you have learned from the experience, the price was worth it."

She looked at Elana then, but Elana turned her gaze to the table.

"Tonight we will feast to celebrate! I know dear Miss Celia has worked very hard all day to bring you your very favorite goodies. Make sure to thank her for her hard work."

She circled around at the top of the room, looking out on the students, silhouetted against the fire. Her dress swirled around her legs and settled with a little sigh.

"Thank you for making Miss Mabel's School for Girls the most coveted school in the Central Network. Your hard work and dedication maintains our reputation. Continue to listen to your wonderful teachers and work hard to become the best witch you can."

Miss Mabel looked on all the students with an affectionate gaze, then turned to the teachers. "Miss Celia, you may begin the feast!"

Shock slid off the students like a discarded coat, and the room echoed with their excited cries. Camille turned to Leda and began to jabber at an incomprehensible speed. Leda stared at the floor, chewing on her bottom lip in frustration. I slowly backed away.

No one saw me slip into the hallway. Miss Bernadette startled me by grabbing my wrist as I started up the stairs.

"You aren't going to enjoy your own party?" she asked.

"No," I admitted. "I was going to collect my things."

Miss Bernadette smiled, but it didn't quite meet her eyes. "It's okay, I won't say anything to the students. Parties don't really seem like your kind of thing anyway. But I did want to congratulate you. This was a big accomplishment."

"Thank you, Miss Bernadette."

"You worked hard, and I'm proud of you. You stayed true to yourself," she hesitated, concern evident in her eyes. "I know you always will."

The implication of her words stayed with me long after she left, fading into the merry celebration that I had no part in. A flicker moved in the shadows, and Miss Mabel stepped into the light. Her wide blonde curls gleamed where they rested on her shoulders. Although pleasant, her voice sounded like a challenge.

"Are you ready, Bianca?"

I met her gaze.

"Yes, Miss Mabel."

Her smile appeared approving, but I wasn't willing to bet on it.

"Good. I believe you and I have a few things to discuss. Follow me, please. I'll talk to you in the attic. Your belongings are already there."

"The attic is mine," she said as we walked. "Miss Celia brings my meals and cleans it from time to time, but other than that no one is allowed. You may go into your room, my office when I give permission, and the classroom."

A sense of total isolation already wrapped around me, before I had even set foot on the attic floor, and I swallowed back the fear that rose with it.

Miss Mabel's fingertips trailed delicately along the elaborate iron railing of the spiral stairs. This staircase hid in the back corner of the school, unseen from the main hallway and illuminated by stained glass windows on each level. It twirled through all four stories, ending at the attic. Although the rails looked skinny, the metal black leaves and vines, images of plants native to Letum Wood, that ran through the bars made them sturdy and strong.

"Yes, Miss Mabel."

"Keep in mind that this stairwell is the only access."

And only escape, I thought, my stomach cramping from tying itself into knots.

Once we reached the top of the steps we faced a long hallway. Candles in iron sconces on the wall flickered, throwing light on the old wooden floor. To my right stood two open doors. The one across from the stairs looked into a nearly empty room about half the size of the classrooms downstairs.

"That's the classroom," she said, following my gaze. "Your bedroom is here on the left. Follow me. I'll show you my office."

My shoes echoed on the bare wooden floor as we walked.

For a witch of such power, her nondescript office surprised me. Blood red drapes and a window behind her large cherry wood desk drew my attention first. Bookshelves marched along one wall and half of another. An aged map of the Network filled the wall next to her desk. One exit, two windows. The sounds of the school weren't there anymore, even when I strained to hear them. It would be a very quiet world, existing almost completely apart from the rest of the girls.

She motioned for me to have a seat, but I resisted in a quiet voice.

"No, thank you."

Unbothered, she walked to the other side of her desk. Away from the adoration of the students, I thought she would be different, but I was wrong. She was as gracious and attractive in her own office as the dining room, inviting in the most dangerous way.

A few papers bearing my name, written in the same script as the letters I'd received, sat on her desk.

"I must say, Bianca, you surprised the entire school." Miss Mabel looked at me with a quick flash of her eyes. "Did you see the looks on their faces when you refused to leave? They hated you for being so selfish. It was lovely."

Lovely, or damning. They surely would hate me now. Their barbs attacked me anew. *Barbaric. Callous. Heartless.*

"I wasn't paying attention to them."

She gave me a blithe smile.

"I'm sure you weren't. I would have. I'm always aware of who's staring at me. Then again, most people always are. I'm dying to learn how you figured it out."

"I didn't know until the very end when you appeared."

She tapped her fingertips on the top of the desk. "The deception spell of your mother gave it away, didn't it?"

"Nothing gave it away, Miss Mabel." My lie came out with frightening fluidity. I wasn't absolutely certain until I'd seen Mama wringing her hands. The curse made her joints too sensitive for that kind of movement and pressure. "My response was sincere. I wanted to stay in the Competition."

A gleam came into her eyes.

"You erred on the side of loyalty to me, a very smart move. That was the main point. Your grandmother is fine, Bianca. She is not in any more danger of dying than usual. Didn't Miss Celia give an impressive performance the other night? She completed the task I asked of her, something I very much admire in someone who works for me. Although I will admit she felt terrible for lying to you about Hazel."

I took that in without a word, sensing that it would be important at some future date, but not knowing why.

"Do you want to know why I challenged you the way I did?" she asked.

I did, but I wouldn't admit how much. Understanding why she did things formed the pulse of my plans.

"Yes, Miss Mabel."

"Loyalty is a difficult thing to find these days. I can't afford an Assistant whose aspirations for other things are greater than their desire to work with me. Not even their family."

Or their life, I thought.

Seeing my unease, she straightened up with a smile that would have been reassuring if I hadn't known how diabolical she could be.

"Priscilla wasn't so lucky. She gains a few pounds, loses some skin integrity, and the girl comes unglued. Goodness. If anyone has the right to be vain around here, it's me. Now, we have only to go over the terms of your contract before we sign it and make this arrangement final."

Here it was. My only chance. I clenched my clammy fingers into my palms.

"I'd like to negotiate our contract, Miss Mabel."

A sly, enchanting smile crossed her face.

"Of course you would." Her voice had the slow drawl of someone enjoying a long-lost memory. "How delightful. It's about your grandmother Hazel, isn't it?"

My throat tightened like she had a grip on it. There was something unnerving about exposing the truth to her, even if she already knew it.

"Yes."

Miss Mabel spun around, giving me her back as she looked out the window behind her desk. I breathed easier, grateful to escape those sapphire eyes.

"She had an Inheritance curse if I remember correctly."

"She received the curse attending school here," I said, controlling my tone. The corners of Miss Mabel's lips twitched.

"That's right. It's all coming back to me now. Her family conspired against the High Priestess and she wouldn't even deny it. Oh, don't be upset. It wasn't my fault Bianca, truly. Hazel showed disloyalty to the High Priestess. This a Network school, so we had to expel and curse her. It was the punishment of choice at the time. That's outlawed now, of course. Unfortunately. Happy families make me about as sick as weddings."

My neck felt hot. Grandmother *had* conspired against the High Priestess at the time, Evelyn. A murderous leader, brutal and fiendish, reigning with fear, terror, and taxes. Our current High Priestess, Mildred, gathered a Resistance and overthrew Evelyn. My family had been part of the Resistance and staunch supporters of Mildred.

Unfortunately it earned my grandmother a curse. Not even Mildred could undo an Inheritance curse from before she took power, nor force the witch to reverse it.

Miss Mabel was just playing with me now. She remembered exactly what happened.

"If it wasn't your fault then take the curse away," I said through gritted teeth.

Miss Mabel laughed.

"Oh, Bianca. Don't you know the first rule of being an adult? Always keep a little leverage where you need it." She turned to me with a calculating gaze. "How old was Hazel when she received the curse?"

"Seventeen."

"Oh," she said with a soft croon. "An Inheritance curse passes on to the first-born daughter of every generation. That means the curse took affect with your mother at that age as well, yes?"

"Yes, Miss Mabel."

Her eyes sparkled. She lifted a perfect eyebrow.

"That means the curse will activate when *you* are seventeen."

"Yes," I whispered.

You heartless gargoyle.

"And you're the third generation."

Her implication hung in the air. I never broke eye contact.

The rule of three says you're going to die.

"Very interesting," she said in a low tone. "You have less than a year to try to get rid of the curse or your life is over. Poetic. Is this why you competed?"

My throat thickened. "Yes, Miss Mabel."

"Well, I like a girl who is willing to do what needs to be done. Tell me, what kind of negotiation are you wanting?"

I took a deep breath. It seemed as if I lived on the hinge of intense moments, each building on the next, that determined my life. But if any of them mattered, this one mattered most. This is where I stood or fell. This is what all my study, all my hours of training, all the sleepless moments of childhood, culminated in.

"Remove the curse from my family."

Miss Mabel stopped and took me in for several minutes. Her lazy smile returned, as if she'd just sized up a competitor.

"You want this very much, don't you? Yes, I see you do. Isadora mentioned something of your strength, but I never expected this." She paused to regard me. "You're just like Hazel, you know. You've got a real soft spot for family. Well, as a rule, I never give something without gaining something of equal value."

I didn't say anything, already prepared for that.

"So, what are you willing to give me?" she asked.

"Time."

Intrigued, she lifted an eyebrow and encouraged me to continue. I had planned out this conversation for years, and was terrified to find it going exactly as I'd thought it would.

"Five years of my life after I receive my marks."

"Well, that's quite an offer. What will I do with you during those five years?"

My throat constricted. Now things got dicey. I had to get her to agree to one purpose. If not, Miss Mabel could have me do anything she wanted. Surviving meant nothing if I had to live it at her beck and call.

"Teach for you for free. No pay, just room and board."

"Oh, Bianca. Girls like you aren't meant to be teachers." She scoffed. "I think we could find something far more useful for you."

The silence that followed pressed on my chest. I held my breath.

"Five years," she murmured, drumming her fingers along her arms. Her blue eyes glowed in the moonlight. "Quite an offer."

She spun around to face me.

"I'm not entirely opposed to a deal, but it will be on my terms, not yours. The Esbat should be coming up soon. Have you ever heard of an Esbat before, Bianca?"

The Esbat was a meeting of the Network's Council of Leaders. The ten oldest and most respected witches in the Network sat on the Council, and they met with individual coven leaders to discuss Network business. No one but those attending knew when it would be, and even they were only notified a day or two in advance.

"Yes, I've heard of it."

"I've been thinking about taking an Assistant with me to take notes for years now. I get so bored doing it myself, but I've never had a student I thought could complete the Esbat mark. It's so advanced and difficult. You've already shown a bit more spunk than the rest."

She paused, mulling it over.

"Yes, I think this will work. The Esbat meeting could pop up around then. If you can earn the Esbat mark, it may be worth your grandmother's freedom. Not yours or your mother's. Just Hazel's."

Her words echoed in my head. *Just Hazel's.* Both disappointment and hope whispered through me. It wasn't my life, but at least it could spare Grandmother some relief from her pain. The curse was more than just the slow destruction of bone and joints. It was a heavy weight that pressed down over time. My mother called it her invisible shackle, following her, waking with her, bearing down on her.

"Not that Hazel has much life left," Miss Mabel added as an afterthought. "Cheer up, Bianca. Everyone dies at some point, whether it's fair or not."

"Yes," I said with a steely voice. "But at least she wouldn't be in so much pain when she passed."

She acted as if I hadn't spoken.

"I need you to show me that you're worth something before I remove the curse from you completely. Prove yourself to me by finishing the Esbat mark in three weeks, then we'll ease Hazel's transition to death."

Stunned, I blinked several times, hoping it would clear my mind.

"Three weeks?" I repeated.

"Did I stutter?"

Her cool tone took on a sudden warning, her mood changing as fast as a blink.

"No, Miss Mabel," I said, truly disarmed for the first time.

The curriculum for the Esbat mark was the most difficult schoolwork the Network offered. The Network expired many marks, marks that faded away because times changed and so did needs. The Esbat mark lay dormant but not forgotten. Only a witch with a hope to work in the Network as a leader, or directly with the High Priestess, ever attempted the Esbat mark. It was all books, studying, and memorization. A veritable prison of classroom time and scrolls. For Leda, it would be heaven.

For me, hell.

A bolt of inspiration told me that she knew. Miss Mabel knew how much I hated bookwork, how difficult it would be to sit at a desk and memorize ancient languages, to concentrate for that long with no escape. My throat tightened just at the thought of it.

"Miss Mabel—"

"It's possible to pass it after only three weeks instead of the usual twelve week course, and has been done once before. At least, I think."

A quarter of the usual time. She'd found a weakness to exploit within minutes of when I met her. A weakness I'd never planned for.

You signed up for an interesting school year, Bianca, I silently chided myself. *One you'll be lucky to survive. You've already underestimated her.*

Isadora's warning came back to me with a flash.

"If I don't earn the mark?" I asked, using the last of my reserves to fake a confidence I didn't have.

"You'll still have the contract to work as my Assistant until you earn all three marks."

The words *and then you die* seemed to hang in the air.

Too simple.

"And?"

She smiled, "You're very wise, Bianca. Never get into an agreement you don't thoroughly understand. If you don't earn the mark, I'm not going to punish you. At least, not directly."

"Then what will you want?"

Miss Mabel walked to the other side of the room in a slow saunter. Her dress slipped over the floorboards with a whisper.

"If you do not complete the Esbat mark in three weeks' time, you will serve me for thirteen years from today. I'll extend the curse to cover the length of your servitude. You will not be allowed to see or speak to your family, no exceptions for death or sickness."

My heart stuttered. Thirteen years? I may never see my mother again. Grandmother would die without me. I'd be in bondage to Miss Mabel in dark magic hell and escape only through death at the end of it.

I floundered. It would be three sleepless weeks of learning new languages, creating impossible trust potions, and memorizing Network leadership structure. The idea made my head hurt. Miss Mabel waited with her hands folded behind her back.

Battles never go the way you plan, Papa always taught me. *The best talent any Guardian or Protector has is the ability to adapt his or her plan to the circumstances. Above all, have confidence in yourself.*

Of course I'd do it. I hadn't lived sixteen years waiting to die. I'd go out fighting, no matter what form the battlefield took, no matter how bleak the stakes looked. I squared my shoulders and met her steely gaze.

"I'll do it."

"Fantastic. I'll write up a contract tonight that you can sign in the morning. I love contracts. They prove what a good person I am."

She stopped, and took on a motherly tone. "Sweet Bianca. You do look tired. We have a lot to do tomorrow. Go to bed, darling. A good night's rest will help this all feel better."

In Vino Veritas

A thick book dropped on my desk with a thud and puff of dust the next morning, rattling the half-full inkwell. The quill, made of tiny emerald and gold feathers lay across the top of the desk, glistened with the wet ink I'd just used to sign the contract.

"Now that the contract is signed, we can move forward to your education. This is the textbook on the history of the Esbat."

Her long-sleeved, deep blue dress swished as she walked past me. From where I sat in the attic classroom, I could see out the back windows and into the gloom of the lifeless forest. One lonely desk stood in the middle of the floor. A fire crackled behind me. At the front, a blackboard ran from floor to ceiling and covered the whole wall, like Miss Bernadette's classroom. Cryptic swirls decorated the edges of the blackboard; it almost looked like an extension of Letum Wood.

The book smelled new, and the pages were undisturbed and fine, filled with symbols and script. I turned each page one at a time, perusing decades of information. The appendixes in the back contained three separate languages known only in the Central Network and allowed only in the Esbat.

"That is a special book. The High Priest is a very thorough man in his oversight of Network Education and has to approve every student who takes the Esbat curriculum. He put a special protective spell on this book that no one else knows, which makes it so only you and me can see the information. That prevents the secrets within from being gathered by unapproved eyes. The ink that you write your homework scrolls in is also special and will only be visible to you and I."

She held out her hand, palm up.

"Let me see your middle finger."

I hesitated, but she wiggled her fingers in an impatient gesture. I reached forward, holding my hand above hers, not wanting to touch her. She grabbed it, produced a small golden dagger in the center of her palm and pressed it to my fingertip before I could pull away. Her hands felt warm.

"Ouch!" I tried to jerk away, but she held me fast. A single red drop formed at the tip. She grabbed the inkwell and let the drop fall.

"There," she said, releasing my hand. "That will tie you to the ink."

Miss Mabel followed the same procedure, cutting a tip on the end of her middle finger. Once she squeezed a drop of blood out, the cut vanished.

"And that ties me. No one else will read your work. Once I'm done correcting the papers, I'll burn them as a precaution."

Tempted to heal my own cut, but not wanting her to see me perform the magic—she'd surely make me explain how I knew it—I sucked on the tip of the finger until the bleeding stopped. It tasted coppery, like putting a sacran coin in my mouth.

"The Esbat mark focuses on protecting the Network," Miss Mabel continued, positioning herself behind me to look over my shoulder. Her blonde hair swept my arm and sent chills across my skin. "Secrecy as well. There are several languages you'll need to learn, at least be passing conversant in, by the final test for the mark. They are used during the meeting and are typically the hardest part of the class."

I recognized a few words from old spells and history books Papa used to teach me. These languages had been around for centuries.

"To begin with," Miss Mabel said, "you need to read the entire book. I'll quiz you on it as soon as you're done. If you answer any question wrong, you'll read the book again before you go to bed. Any questions?"

"No."

"Miss Celia will bring your lunch up today in order to optimize your time. I'll be in my office. Do not bother me."

The sound of her shoes disappeared with the closing of a door. With a sigh, I glanced at the clock.

"You can do this," I said. "One day at a time."

I opened to the first page and began to read.

The day shifted away from me, chronicled in the crawl of the sunbeams across the floor as the hours passed. Miss Mabel gave no indication of life, not even a creak of the floorboard. The restless quiet made me uneasy, and I found myself staring out the window several times, lost in thought. Without meaning to, I spent most of my lunch hour just flipping through the pages to look at the painted pictures.

After the final event of the Competition, the solitude and silence were a welcomed reprieve, but I missed my friends. My thoughts often strayed to Camille and Leda, as well as Miss Bernadette's warm classroom.

Head throbbing, I turned the final page of the book later that afternoon and closed it in relief.

Take that, devil woman.

Miss Mabel swept into the classroom.

"When was the first Esbat held?"

Her words came in a fast, demanding clip. I straightened up, startled by her sudden entrance.

"O-over four hundred years ago."

"What is the most common ingredient among the four simple truth serums?"

My voice sat in my throat, paralyzed. I didn't remember reading about truth serums. She stopped and turned to look at me.

"Well?"

Grandmother sold ingredients for serums, potions, and simple baking spices at the shop in Bickers Mill. A wizened old man often came in, a worker at Chatham Castle. He bought spices for truth serums in high quantities from us all the time, so I took a wild guess.

"Gingko biloba?"

"Was that a question?"

"No," I said, more firmly this time, although my confidence wavered. "The answer is gingko biloba."

She narrowed her eyes, but continued. "Wrong. Tell me the names of the first High Priestess and Priest to use the language Dekkon."

I inwardly groaned. There had been too many names to keep track of who did what, but I did remember the pictures drawn and painted in the book. One in particular came to mind when I visualized the chapter. A painting at the beginning of the book with two people standing near a large throne. The High Priestess had black hair, reminding me of a woman named Viv. Although my guess could be wild, I threw it out anyway.

"Vivianne and Alexander."

Miss Mabel stood in front of my desk now, towering over me like a marble goddess. She launched into the lesson, drawing a breath of relief from me.

"The Esbat is a meeting of neighboring covens, Council Leaders, the High Priest, and the High Priestess. They meet to conduct business. How many Council Members?"

"Ten."

"Correct. Why is it so important to protect the Esbat meeting?"

This question was a summary of the entire textbook. "We discuss the needs of the Network at the meeting, which exposes our weaknesses."

Miss Mabel stared at me, then took a step away from the desk. It was easier to breathe when she wasn't looming over me.

"Yes, very good. It's unfortunate that we don't trust other Networks anymore. Once the mortals left centuries ago and we had no one to fight with, we naturally turned to hating each other. It hasn't been very many years since our own Network wasn't a very safe place to live. That was well before your time."

Evelyn reigned over the Dark Days, only part of the reason Miss Mabel cursed my grandmother. Anarchy was the leader; hysteria the rule.

"I've heard of them before," I said, realizing she expected me to say something.

Her smile seemed aggravated underneath her charm.

"Yes, I'm sure Hazel told you all about our darling High Priestess Mildred who swooped in and saved the Network from Evelyn. Let's not talk about her. Let's talk about potions."

Her abrupt twist in conversation surprised me, but I welcomed it. Potions meant action, not words.

"You can read all the books you want, but knowledge means nothing without action."

"Yes, Miss Mabel."

Then why did I sit here all day reading a book? I wanted to grumble, longing to feel the sun on my face.

"Tonight, I want to introduce you to a famous little gem that originated in the Western Network. They brought it over to our Network a few hundred years ago."

Her shoes clicked as she walked toward me, producing a glass of water in her hands. "It's important for you to know that simple truth potions are weak. Any attentive witch will know when they are influenced by one, and she can usually stop it through a few simple herbs. But not all truth potions are that easy."

My gut twisted as I sensed her direction. She sauntered to the corner of the room where a small shelf ran along the wall, filled with glass vials topped by corks. Humming as she looked over them, Miss Mabel picked a skinny little vial with an emerald liquid inside. Her hair swayed along her shoulders when she stepped away.

"This is Veritas. Have you seen it before?"

Papa told me wild stories of the confessions that witches made under the influence of Veritas, for good and ill. He'd warned me away from it with religious devotion.

"No, Miss Mabel," I cleared my throat. "I've never seen it before."

She tipped the vial upside down. The liquid clung to the walls of the glass, moving like clear green molasses.

"It's difficult to make," she said, studying it. "But easy to recognize. No other potion has this appealing shade of green. I'm quite fond of it. A single drop can extract superficial secrets from anyone. Two drops can reveal hidden information, and three will kill."

She pulled the cork, and it came off with a light pop. Placing the glass on my desk, she put a single drop of Veritas in the water.

This was not good.

She swirled the glass until the Veritas disappeared without a trace, then looked at me.

"Have you ever taken Veritas?"

I shook my head.

"I drank it once," she said, musing. "The Veritas dissolves clear, can survive in any liquid for an indefinite amount of time, tastes like mint, and burns going down. That's how most people know they've drunk it. But by then, it's too late. Most witches put it in wine, as it hides the aftertaste. I'm sure you've heard of *in vino veritas*? In wine there is truth."

She lifted the glass of water up to look through it, and I held my breath. If she demanded that I drink it, I would have no choice but to obey. Refusing to take it would only make her suspicious, but what if I said something about Papa under its influence? It could be disastrous.

"Some people will tell you to never take wine from a witch you don't know. I disagree. I never take wine from any witch. Ever."

She opened her hand, and the glass fell, shattering into a hundred crystal specks on the floor. The water evaporated in a fine mist, curling off the planks and into the air like an early morning fog.

"Veritas leaves no trace. If you suspect a liquid is tainted with it, let a single drop fall. If the liquid touches the ground, there is no Veritas."

As she headed for a bookshelf on the other side of the room, I breathed for what felt like the first time. The glass shards glittered and crunched on the floor as she strolled over them.

"As a leader, witches from different Networks may try and use Veritas against you to get our secrets. That's why we talk about it in the Esbat curriculum. Veritas is not allowed amongst the general public in our Network, thanks to our . . . annoyingly diligent High Priestess."

The ironic tone of her voice was no accident. Miss Mabel waved her hand, beckoning several books.

"You will make the Veritas serum. Once you have finished brewing it, you'll sample it in my presence so I can interrogate you. Everyone must sample Veritas once as part of the Esbat curriculum."

Any relief I felt at not drinking it tonight disappeared in a wall of anxiety. The books landed on the desk with a bang.

"These are some books to reference if you have questions."

"Yes, Miss Mabel."

Her sharp eyes narrowed in thought.

"You have three days to complete the potion, starting tomorrow morning. While it's brewing, work on these." She extended a thick roll of parchment. "Your homework questions are written in the Almorran language, so you'll need to translate them in order to answer correctly. For now, you may answer in our language."

She left me standing with a hollow feeling in my gut and the sound of Miss Celia walking up the stairs with our dinner.

Continuing On

Outside my new bedroom window, the woods gripped the darkness like a sponge, holding it in the naked trees.

This window was bigger than the last, with a ledge that jutted out and looked over the front of the school. I set a few little trinkets on it. A packet of lavender, a glass jar of my favorite peppermint salve, and a chipped mug from home. Mama's favorite cup for hot tea. The ceiling sloped, leaving only the window and a short wall just high enough for my headboard. But everything else in the room remained the same, right down to the scrawny mattress and undecorated walls.

I sat on the edge of the bed, a half-finished plate of brown bread and gravy sitting on my desk. If I started the first brew on the Veritas tonight, I could get it out of the way and study while it simmered. My lip curled in distaste at the thought of facing all those scrolls.

I perused the old books with increasing annoyance. A rust-colored book with a slip of yellowing paper wedged into the spine called to me first. I pulled the bit of parchment out of the spine.

"Veritas," I whispered the name of the potion. "Of course."

The herb pantry sat between the library and Miss Scarlett's classroom on the first floor, not far from the side entry. A sliver of light illuminated the bottom of Miss Mabel's door when I stepped into the hall, and I was glad to leave the attic behind for a while.

Camille's faint voice came through her thick door. Before I knocked, I heard Leda say something, and then it went quiet.

The door opened with a velocity I didn't think possible.

"Bianca!" Camille gasped, then threw herself into me with a hug that sent me backward. "Are you doing okay? Is Miss Mabel nice? Do you like your new room? Can we come see you?"

"Camille, calm down," Leda muttered, peeling her away. "Give her a second to breathe."

I disentangled myself from Camille's tight grip after she pulled me into her room. It felt like stepping into a messy bouquet of wildflowers. Clothing draped the back of the chair and headboard. Books cluttered the floor and built in shelves. The air smelled sweet. Too sweet.

A light blue quilt, decorated with a pink pillow and a stuffed teddy bear, stretched across her meager bed. A black and white drawing of two people sat on her window ledge. The shape of the man's face looked like Camille's. Her parents. They seemed very young in the picture.

"It's all right," I said while Camille shut the door behind me. "It's nice to know I've been missed."

"How are things?" Leda asked with her usual lack of preamble. "Miss Mabel seemed as horrifying as I expected."

"Yes," Camille agreed. "There's something a bit . . . creepy about her."

Creepy, or evil.

"But she's breathtaking. Those lips!" Camille squealed, falling back on her bed with a flop. "I'd die for lips like that."

"What happened?" Leda asked, astute as ever. "You're stressed."

I sat on the edge of the bed next to Leda and recounted everything, grateful to share the experience with them. Camille pushed up onto her elbows and listened, sprawled across the bed, her white stockings discarded into a corner of the room and toes wiggling free.

"She's a conniving witch," Leda muttered. "I knew it the moment I realized she cast the curse on your family. There's something not right about her."

Camille agreed with a low hum. "You better watch yourself, Bianca."

"Watch her is more like it," I muttered.

"It's very sad that she's so beautiful and so ugly at the same time," Camille said. "A little bit like Priscilla, isn't she?"

"A little bit too beautiful, I think," Leda said, her eyes landing on me. "Miss Mabel has been running the school for over forty years now. She must use some kind of transformative magic to look that way. She should be much older."

The thought made my skin crawl. I had the feeling that seeing the real Miss Mabel would be a horrifying experience and wondered what kind of festering soul hid under all that false perfection.

"Yes," I said feeling a little sheepish that I hadn't thought of it first. "She should."

"A lot of powerful witches do that to conceal their true age," Camille said, tugging on her hair and inspecting a wayward curl. "There was a witch in our village named Balinda that didn't look much over thirty, but she was well over ninety years old. I plan to do that. I want to die looking the way I do at twenty-five. Unless I look better at thirty, which is doubtful, considering how, uh, old my aunts seem."

"Balinda was also out of her mind," Leda said. "So how she managed to use transformative magic every day, I have no idea. The woman talked to her onions and thought her cat was a mule."

"Speaking of transformation," I drawled, a sudden thought coming to me. "How did Priscilla react when I won? Did she say anything?"

"Oh, she was pretty upset," Camille said in a prim tone, her lips pressed together in a poor attempt to hide a smile, "She, um, well–"

"First of all, she had been hiding in the kitchen the whole time. Then she threw a fit as soon as Miss Mabel left." Leda supplied the information with the droll tone that meant she enjoyed talking about it. "Miss Scarlett had to escort her into the hallway. I somehow found myself near the doors at the time and heard Miss Scarlett telling her to pull it together."

Camille laughed, falling backward onto the bed again, her arms thrown wide.

"She started to cry. It was wonderful, Bianca!"

The three of us dissolved into laughter, forcing away the dark cobwebs I'd already collected in the recesses of the attic.

"Jade and Stephany didn't come back to the dinner either," Camille said. "They sat up in Priscilla's room with her, pouting. Miss

Celia wouldn't let anyone take them food, even though they tried to get some first-years to knick them some. No one would do it. Miss Scarlett said that Priscilla, Jade, and Stephany were poor shows of sportsmanship and gave them six hours of kitchen duty."

Our mad fit of giggling continued as we discussed how Priscilla would look with flour in her red hair, Michelle ordering her around. Soon, the mirth subsided, leaving us clutching our stomachs.

I gazed down at the yellow parchment in my hand, a bleak reminder of my original intent. I let out a sigh.

"I better go," I said. "I have a potion to start and a huge scroll of homework to complete tonight, but I'll try to come down as often as I can."

"Uh oh," Leda said. "Did you say a huge scroll of homework?"

"Unfortunately," I grimaced.

Camille sent me a sulky glance. "Sounds like you won't be doing anything but studying."

"Yes," I agreed with the dismal tone of a martyr. "Sounds like it."

"Sounds like heaven," Leda muttered.

"Sounds like torture," Camille said at the same time.

"When will we see you next?" Leda asked, and then fell into a trance. She came out of this one quickly with a jerk of her head, a puzzled expression on her face.

"I should be there in the morning," I said.

"Okay," she murmured, lines of concern creasing her forehead. "See you then."

Camille threw her arms around me in another hug, and I slipped into the hall. The world still continued on down here without me, and for some reason, that gave me great comfort.

Liquid Curses

My bedroom didn't have a place for a fire, so I moved my supplies into the classroom and set up a work area by the hearth. Working with herbs came naturally after all the years at the shop, and the smell of sage calmed me. The first brewing began simply enough, allowing me time to start on the scroll of homework.

Translating the questions from ancient Almorran proved mind-numbing. My thoughts strayed, distracted by the upcoming Veritas interrogation. The corner where Miss Mabel had set the vial kept pulling my attention.

What if I tried the Veritas before she forced me to? I pictured myself accidentally stumbling onto Priscilla while under the power of Veritas. Or, even better, Miss Scarlett. Then she'd really know all the rules I broke.

No, taking it unsupervised could be the worst idea I'd ever had. Giving myself a drop of Veritas to see what it would do was a prodigious risk. Miss Mabel could walk in, and I'd be totally vulnerable.

But, a worried little voice in my mind reasoned, *not any less than when I take it in front of her.*

I shook my head, turned my back on the corner, and focused on the homework, scrawling out an easy answer to the question, *Who created the first trust potion?*

I stared at it for several minutes before I realized I'd written down *Veritas.*

Frustrated, I hastily blotted out the response.

Finally giving in, I swiveled back around and stared at the glass vials. If Miss Mabel interrogated me and I wasn't strong enough, she could get information about my father that I couldn't afford to betray. No amount of study and verb memorization could change that.

Annoyed, I threw the feather down and raked my hands through my hair. This wouldn't do. I had to find out.

Snatching the Veritas before I lost courage, I pulled the cork and let a single drop fall into the glass of water from dinner. I set the glass on the desk and stared at it for several minutes. All traces of Veritas fled.

With a shaking hand I grabbed the glass and chugged the whole thing.

The burning sensation in my stomach disappeared after a few seconds, but the effects were immediate and intense. The world started to spin.

Seconds later, I knew I'd made a grave mistake.

I struggled out of the classroom and started down the spiral stairs at a breakneck, frantic pace. The steps felt like they fell in uneven intervals, so I slipped and stumbled my way to the bottom with my eyes closed. When I opened them a slit to see where I was, the world spun.

Miss Celia's low hum drifted down the corridor from the kitchen, telling me I was in the main hallway on the first floor. An urge to speak overwhelmed me. My mouth opened on its own, but I slammed it shut so hard my teeth hurt.

I had to get out of there.

Lightheaded, I grabbed the wall and forced myself to walk away from the kitchen. My vision blurred when I opened my eyes, making the hall swim. A few third-year girls laughed from the library a few paces away. The desire to speak controlled me again. Somehow I struggled through it, groping for the side door that spilled into the yard.

The old handle on the side door rattled when I found it and pushed it open. It gave way with a groan just as the sound of the third-years swelled. I fell to my knees on the grass, kicked the door shut behind me, and crawled toward the tree line. The edges of my limited vision grew black.

"B-b-bad idea," I whispered, unable to stop myself. "I took Veritas, and it was a bad idea. R-r-really bad idea."

"Bianca! Over here."

My heart faltered as a dark silhouette approached my side. Leda's ash-blonde hair moved in front of me.

"Come on," she said, her lips pressed into a line.

She hooked an arm through mine and jerked me to my feet. Ignoring my cries of protest, we started into the trees. My balance plummeted. Every attempt to control my legs failed, and my stomach threatened to erupt.

"Walk, Bianca!"

"T-t-trying."

Leda groaned as I leaned my weight against her.

"Don't speak! Just . . . try to walk with me."

"I took Veritas. I-I took it out of the cupboard. It tasted like mint. I don't like it but I–"

Frantic, I tried to pull the words back, but realized I was making it worse.

"I-I need to control it. I need to know how–"

Leda cut me off. "Talk about something that doesn't matter until the Veritas works out of your system. It will help. What entries in the History of Witchcraft have you read in the past ten years?"

The answers poured out of me; I didn't even take a breath. The horrific lack of constraint terrified me. I recited things I didn't remember.

"Esbat. Rituals. History of Defensive Magic. Western Network. Northern Network. Sword making. Heartswords. Southern Network."

"Good," Leda said, panting. "Keep going."

"Persimmon. Hexes. Blighters. Eastern Network. Ruins."

Speaking restored tiny pieces of my balance. The undeniable relief felt like a flood of heat in the middle of winter. I couldn't gibber fast enough.

"Come on!" she muttered. "Walk!"

"Symbols. Chatham City. Letum Wood. Bellarmine jugs. Silent magic."

Leda jerked me into the tree line. Thorns ripped across my legs when she shoved me through a shadowy bramble bush. Several minutes of toil and struggle through the deadfall later, the words stopped without warning. There were no more.

"I-I can't stop it," I said. "Secrets. I-I'm supposed to say my secrets. M-my father taught me how to–"

"Books you've read," Leda panted, seeing the panic return to my face. "Tell me what books you've read."

After dragging me around a large oak tree, she let go with a grunt and collapsed on the ground.

It took fifteen minutes of recitation for my voice to slow and gain control. The potion's power faded, and my eyes focused on Leda's face.

"Are you all right?" she asked.

"No," I answered too fast. "I mean . . . yes, I'm fine."

I reached up and looked at my hand. It was clear. I could see again.

She let out a heavy breath. "That was close. I kept seeing Miss Celia leaving the kitchen to restock the firewood. It wasn't pretty after that, either."

"I didn't . . . I didn't know it would be so strong."

"Why would you take Veritas?" she asked with a condemning glare, making me feel like a fool. "Have you lost it? You're mad."

"I needed to know what it was like," I retorted with a snap, folding my arms across my middle, suddenly aware of how sensitive my head felt. Of all people, I felt the slap of censure from Leda hardest.

"You can't get that from a book?" she asked.

"Miss Mabel's going to make me take it," I said. "I needed to know what it was like. It seemed like the right thing at the time."

Leda considered this information, but it didn't seem to change her opinion.

"You're demented, Bianca. I knew you were pretty good with magic, but I didn't know you were out of your mind. If Miss Mabel found out–"

"I know!" I stopped her. "I know."

Knowing I'd end up hurting her feelings if we stayed on the topic of my poor choices, I asked her the first question that came to mind. Leda wasn't outside at night by chance.

"You saw me out here, didn't you?" I asked, the sound of my voice reverberating in an echo through my skull. "That's why you had a funny look on your face tonight when I went back to my room."

"Yes. And you're foolish for trying to best Veritas," she added for good measure, unwilling, as ever, to change the subject unless she wanted to. "Do you ever think before you act?"

"I get it," I growled. "I should have planned this differently." A headache thrummed through my sensitive skull. Every movement sent off a shot of pain. Despite her help, I wanted to get rid of Leda because I knew she was right. She'd saved me out here, but my pride wasn't ready to admit it. "You should go back before you get into trouble."

"I think I'm the one that's more qualified to determine what could happen. Give it a few more minutes." She peered through the forest. "Miss Celia is still restocking the wood pile."

A blessed silence followed. I closed my eyes and cradled my head in my hands. The twirling sensation changed into a hammer and anvil.

"It's okay. You're welcome," Leda said, just as I opened my mouth to thank her.

"Thanks," I said anyway, opening just one eye and managing to sound sincere. "I appreciate your help."

She bit her bottom lip.

"There's something I need to tell you, something I feel like you should know. I didn't want to tell you earlier because I worried it would concern Camille. She'll just stew on it all the time if she knows."

"What is it?"

"Something changed," she said. "I mean in your future. It's pressing on me more than ever. I see glimpses and flashes of it more often now, but it's—"

She broke off. I straightened up.

"It's what?"

"It's different. Instead of images I can't make sense of, occasionally all I see is darkness. Or gray." She pressed her hands to her eyes.

"I know that doesn't make sense, and I can't explain it very well. The future is always shifting and changing. It's like that for everyone. But yours is so pushy, so different."

Her revelation settled on me with all the weight of a boulder.

"Thanks for telling me," I said with a voice that didn't ease either of us.

Leda turned away with a huff of frustration, looking back at the school over her shoulder. She stayed in that position for a little while longer, then stood up.

"I think it's safe for me right now, but you need to be careful going back. Wait two minutes after I go inside."

Leda offered me a hand and helped me to my feet. White dots burst across my vision, and my entire skull pulsed in pain.

"Are you going to be okay?" she asked, avoiding my eyes. She'd be grateful to get back to her room, I could tell. I felt the same way.

"Yes, thanks again."

She started out of the trees and headed to the school, leaving me behind with a walloping headache. I leaned my head back with a groan and closed my eyes.

It would take more than one night to recover from this.

Experiencing Ignorance

"Your potion looks perfect for this stage," Miss Mabel said the next morning. "That color indicates you are on the second brew, which means you started last night. Didn't I tell you to begin this morning?"

She stepped away from my small cauldron, where a murky blue liquid bubbled, smelling like cheese. Her hands hid behind her back and the inscrutable expression on her face made my stomach clench in fear.

"No, Miss Mabel. You said the time began tomorrow morning. I decided to start early in case something went wrong."

"A very smart move."

Coiffed in a delicate bun at the nape of her neck, her hair glistened as she wandered through the early sunbeams. I let out a breath of relief as she moved past, her maroon dress waving.

"There's absolutely no reason to delay starting something that has to get done. You passed my test."

Miss Mabel smiled again, but it held a hint of promise that this wasn't the last test. Her praise gave me more paranoia than relief. Luckily, and despite my stress regarding her silent expectations, I saw no indication in her mannerisms that she knew I had taken Veritas.

"Did you finish the assignment?"

She approached my desk and rolled through the scroll sitting on top. My eyes burned from lack of sleep. I'd completely forgotten it after the Veritas and wouldn't have completed any of it if a nightmare hadn't woken me in the earliest hours of morning. My answers only filled the first part of the scroll.

"No, Miss Mabel," I swallowed a lump of fear in my throat.

She looked up in surprise.

"Why ever not?"

Because I spent the night trying to get ahead of you and still haven't recovered from a banging headache, thank you.

"I-it's a lot of information, Miss Mabel."

"That bodes well for the next three weeks," she muttered, shooting me a perturbed stare. "You can't even finish the first scroll on time."

"I'll finish it today, Miss Mabel."

She studied me.

"Yes, you will. Thirteen years of your life are hanging in the balance. I'm sure you're aware."

Yes. How could I forget the assurance of death and misery? It all came down to a couple of scrolls and a dash of bitter irony.

"Have you even started translating the Almorran language?"

"A little." *A very little.* "It's slow but doable."

Miserable and boring.

"At least you got that far. Well, I look forward to grading your assignments, which will be perfect."

A challenge. I heard it in her voice. *If you can't even finish the first scroll on time, then you'd better get them all right.*

"Yes, Miss Mabel."

"I have something new for you."

A small headache still nagged me from the Veritas, as if my brain was swollen inside my head, so the thought of learning had lost any appeal. Unable to do anything about it, I steeled myself for another miserable day.

Miss Mabel produced a jar of ink and a large peacock feather from her desk.

"Lovely," she sighed, staring at the feather, "isn't it? I just love peacocks. They are such attractive animals, very misunderstood. I don't believe vanity exists in the animal kingdom, so I don't know why they have such a bad reputation."

She stroked the fuzzy edge against her cheek and then turned her gaze to me. The vivid blue of the feather matched her eyes in a shocking way.

"What does a peacock symbolize, Bianca?"

"Beauty and power."

"Fantastic ideals, aren't they? Especially together." She twirled the feather between her fingertips as she approached my desk. "Now, smell this and tell me what it's made out of."

She extended the bottle of ink.

"I can't smell anything."

"Strange, don't you think? Most ink has a bitter scent. What you don't smell is ink made from the juice of unripened white mulberries."

She dipped the feather in the liquid and held it up. The tip didn't change. "It's a very special ink because it's the only white ink ever created."

Miss Mabel wrote across the top of the Veritas potion directions. Nothing showed up. She picked it up and motioned for me to take it to the hearth, where a low fire burned. "Go," she said. "Hold it up to the heat and see what it says."

Obeying her command, I crouched down near the flames. As if written that moment, Miss Mabel's words appeared.

Amusing, isn't it?

She came up behind me.

"Invisible ink?" I asked.

"Not exactly," she said, "but you're not far off. The combination of the peacock feather and that particular ink results in handwriting you can't see until it's exposed to heat from birch log fire. Most of the other Networks don't have access to birch trees, so this makes it easier for us to protect our documents. If you pass the Esbat mark and attend, you'll use this ink to take notes."

She turned around and walked back to her desk.

"I want you to do an analysis of the white mulberry ink and write a full report on its implications. It must be written in the Almorran language you are learning, in white ink that you make."

I was about to stand when another line of words appeared at the bottom of the page. Her voice faded into the background.

Experience overpowers ignorance.

My thoughts raced. What could this mean? It must have something to do with Veritas because it was written on the potion directions.

"Bianca?"

When I realized she had asked me a question, I whirled around. "Yes?"

She studied me, suspicious.

"I said that you need to finish this scroll of paperwork by tomorrow morning and complete a paper summarizing truth potions." Her eyebrow lifted in displeasure. "Is that a problem?"

"No, Miss Mabel."

She dropped the scroll on my desk.

"Best get to work now," she said. "The third brew will take more attention to detail than the first two did. And you have quite a few scrolls to catch up on."

"Yes, Miss Mabel."

She disappeared, leaving me with my unconnected thoughts and the beginnings of a plan.

After spending a day writing the paper and preparing the potion and two hours making white ink, I dissolved another drop of Veritas in some water and crept back out the side door, glass of water in hand. I still had scrolls stacking up, but couldn't stay inside any longer.

An icy wood embraced me when I slipped through the shadowed, naked trees. My breath billowed like a cloud. Not even my thick cloak provided enough protection from the heavy chill. When I couldn't see the light coming from the school, I downed the concoction in a single swallow and hoped for the best. The conversation with Leda haunted me.

Do you ever think before you act?

Unfortunately this time, I had thought about it. My decision remained the same.

My belly warmed with a flare of fire just before the blinding wall of vertigo. Expecting the dizziness didn't give me much of an edge, I still doubled over and wanted to die. This time, I covered myself with my cloak, locked myself into a ball, and didn't move.

Within minutes my throat ached from holding back the words. Even though no one would hear, I wouldn't allow myself to speak. I had to practice enduring it without talking.

Experience overpowers ignorance.

If my interpretation of this obscure phrase was correct, Veritas acted like a sickness. The more exposure, the faster the cure.

Bracing myself for more lightheaded agony, I burrowed my head into my arms and let the Veritas take control.

Without speaking, the rolling dizziness lasted almost three times as long. By the time it faded, my teeth ached and my head throbbed in pain. I crawled through the trees, my fingers and toes numb. By the time I made it back to the school, the dark hallways sat like tombs.

I collapsed onto my mattress and fell into a deep sleep.

The potion turned into a sludge not unlike loose tar by the end of the second brew the next morning. The acrid scent intensified my headache. Bleary-eyed, I read through the potion instructions again.

Miss Mabel walked into the room wearing a dress made of deep purple silk and white lace trim. Because of my second attempt with Veritas the night before, my sleep-deprived nerves left me with little patience. Attempting to hide my exhaustion was impossible, and I hoped she dismissed my bloodshot eyes as the result of trying to keep up with my homework.

"Starting the third brew?"

"Yes, Miss Mabel."

"Wonderful. We will test it in a couple days. Hand me your

scroll. You missed a couple on the homework you turned in at lunch yesterday."

My heart took a sudden dive. I couldn't pretend that her words surprised me. Instead, I awaited her judgment.

"Redo them today on top of the rest of the scrolls."

She handed them back.

"What did I miss?"

She smiled. "You'll have to figure that out, won't you?"

My nostrils flared. Not trusting myself to speak, I simply nodded once and accepted the scroll back. This would take a long time. I'd have to pay more attention to how I answered in the future.

"Miss Scarlett is teaching a lesson that fits in with the Esbat training on deception spells. She has an absolute talent for them, so you will sit in on her class today. You have one hour before it begins."

"Yes, Miss Mabel."

"When you return from the class," she spun around at the doorway, "you'll find several more scrolls of homework. Leave the first on my desk tomorrow morning and have the others ready when the Veritas is complete. I'm attending a meeting at Chatham Castle with the High Priestess and won't be back for two days, possibly three. While I'm gone, report to Miss Celia every morning. I have a list for you to complete by my return."

She strolled out and disappeared with the closing of her office door. I wondered what Priscilla would think of my supposed one-on-one learning time with Miss Mabel if she knew how little we interacted.

I turned back to the potion directions, knowing I preferred to learn from Miss Mabel from as far away as possible.

Deception Spells

Miss Scarlett didn't waver.

The third-year classroom was off-limits to first-and second-year students. As Assistant, I was the only exception. Most of the first-years didn't mind. We appreciated having a reason to not run into her. Her strict adherence to the simplest of rules quickly grew tiresome.

Not sure what to expect from her classroom, the bright silks and heady scent of cumin startled me. A warm, almost sultry breeze drifted through the air. Swatches of red and muted orange fabric hung from the rafters. Deep tones of burgundy and wine painted the walls, like stepping into a fire.

Miss Scarlett had a large desk in the back corner. A chalkboard filled most of the front wall, and several bookcases stood at the back. A massive brick fireplace in the middle of the farthest wall danced with flames. The calico cat sprawled on the stones of the hearth, asleep.

Sitting close to the fire and far from the others, I watched the students wander in. Most of them ignored me. Priscilla shot me a scathing glare and took her seat. Miss Scarlett's red bracelets announced her entrance at the very second the hour began.

"We shall begin now." She stood at the front of the room like a soldier at attention. The door slammed shut, the lock clicking. "Never be late."

I couldn't fathom why the third-year students seemed to have such a warm, kindred relationship with Miss Scarlett.

The class was smaller than I'd anticipated and involved only the few third-years working to get their Curses and Hexes mark. Priscilla and Jade sat in the front row, right next to Miss Scarlett's walkway. Unlike Miss Bernadette, who walked around the room to involve everyone and spoke in a quiet voice, Miss Scarlett remained rigidly in one spot.

"Deception spells are quite simple," she began. "They duplicate an object, deceiving you from the original."

Jade raised her hand, her blonde hair waving about her jaw, already prepared with questions.

"Can deception spells work on people?"

"Very astute question, Jade. A simple deception spell like we are learning today would not work on people. There are some that can create a replica of another person, but they are very advanced. You saw a perfect example during the third match."

Two students glanced in my direction, but I ignored them.

"Now, a deception spell has one major weakness. The person who cast the spell cannot tell the truth for its duration. It would run counter to the nature of the spell. No one, not even the High Priest or Priestess, can tell the truth while spinning a deception spell."

Miss Scarlett waved her hand. Several glowing embers leapt from the fire behind me and flew to the front of the room. They fell onto a spot on her desk but did not burn the wood.

"Observe these embers."

She put her sharp eye on all the students, ensuring she had their attention.

"Under the power of a deception spell, these embers would produce doubles that looked exactly the same. If you try to touch the identical object, it disappears. The spell would need to be recast."

She spoke the incantation aloud, and the embers multiplied into a new pile of glowing bark that could not be distinguished from its original. They popped with a *blip* when she touched them.

"Do you have any questions? No? Good. Split into partnerships. I'm going to have you practice on mushrooms."

The girls instantly slipped into pairs, leaving one person at the front alone. Michelle looked back, then stumbled through the desks with her awkward gait and long arms until she fell into the empty seat next to me.

"Hi," I said, surprised to see her in a class like this. What could baking have to do with the Curses and Hexes mark?

Her eyes flickered to mine through her thick bangs, then looked away.

"Hi."

We stayed quiet until Miss Scarlett approached.

"You're an Assistant now, Bianca. I expect Assistant-level results. If it's not perfect, I'm sending you back to the attic, and you can explain to Miss Mabel why you failed a third-year class."

Nice to see you too, Miss Scarlett, I wanted to say. *I'm already failing my own mark, thank you very much. I'm sure I don't need your help in showing Miss Mabel that I'm in over my head.*

Michelle averted her eyes to the floor as Miss Scarlett handed us two bulbous mushrooms and a paper with instructions.

"Michelle, you did a remarkable job on the Everyday Hexes test," Miss Scarlett said with a softened tone. "I have full faith that you will complete this well."

Once Miss Scarlett departed, Michelle peered at me from between clumps of hair.

"Does she scare you when she's that strict?" she asked.

I watched Miss Scarlett walk to the front of the class and sighed.

"No, because she's right. I should be able to do it. Does she scare you?"

"No. She's a really good teacher. I like her. She lets me study in her office sometimes because it's quiet."

She looked as if she wanted to say something else but stopped. I knew why she studied in there. Too many third-years gave her a hard time because of her gangly arms and large body. Seeking refuge with Miss Scarlett didn't help her reputation, but she didn't seem to mind.

Holding the paper so both of us could read it, I skimmed through the instructions. They were succinct, like Miss Scarlett, but easy to read. When I finished, I looked up to Michelle.

"Have you ever–"

Stopped by something that didn't look right, I glanced down to the table to find three identical mushrooms, in addition to mine. A hot blush crept across Michelle's face as she looked away.

"You already know how to do a deception spell?" I asked.

She popped the extra mushrooms.

"I learned awhile ago."

"Who taught you?"

"My older brothers."

"How many brothers do you have?"

"Five."

"Do you have any sisters?"

She shook her head, and her bangs swayed. Her family makeup explained her tomboyish characteristics.

"You did a perfect job." I studied the mushrooms. "Really."

Blushing again, she looked down.

"Thanks."

"Will you show me?"

Michelle demonstrated the right way to sound out specific syllables, and within my first two attempts, I made three duplicates of the mushroom. It felt so good to learn a magical skill again, to step away from the blasted scrolls choking me, that my awful mood began to be alleviated. Miss Scarlett popped them when she came to loom over us.

"Do it again," she commanded.

Michelle's nearly inaudible voice worked the spell. Another mushroom appeared onto the desk, and Miss Scarlett gave a nod.

"Good." Her approving tone shifted back to all business again as soon as she turned to me. "Now it's your turn."

I duplicated my mushroom with ease. Miss Scarlett left with only a nod of approval. We popped the mushrooms as she departed and sat in the quiet.

Michelle gazed up at me with her timid brown eyes.

"I'm glad you won the Competition," she said. "I knew I wouldn't have liked being Assistant. At first I felt stupid because I didn't make it past the first round. But when I saw Miss Mabel, I realized that I'm glad I didn't win. She's so beautiful and confident that she scares me."

"Then why would you compete?"

She shrugged, and her cheeks flushed. I wondered if her desire to win the Competition had something to do with wanting more friends.

"Why are you here at Miss Mabel's?" I asked to clear the air. Her face lit up.

"I want to be a baker at Chatham Castle."

"Really?"

"Yes." She looked away. "It sounds wonderful."

"You're taking the Culinary mark now, aren't you?"

"Yes. It's just Rebecca and me in the class, but I like it that way. I don't really like crowds, and Rebecca is nice. Miss Celia's been able to teach me a lot I didn't know already."

"Then why are you taking this class?"

"I still like doing other forms of magic. Then, if baking doesn't work out, I have a backup plan. It was my father's idea."

Miss Scarlett interrupted by calling our attention to the front.

"Thanks for working with me," I said and smiled at her. Struck with shyness again, Michelle mumbled a reply, grabbed her mushroom, and rushed back to her desk. She knocked over Priscilla's books and apologized profusely while she gathered them, her face a flaming red. Priscilla bestowed an exasperated look on her and rolled her eyes when Michelle walked away.

I tried to picture Michelle as the Assistant. When the image couldn't collect, I turned my attention back to the lesson with a sigh.

Sometimes I couldn't picture myself as the Assistant either.

Loyalty

I woke up the next day panting, sweaty, and disoriented.

Trying to figure out where I was only confused me further until I took in the familiar drapes on the window. The nightmare began to slip away, into the tendrils of night and my subconscious. I let the details go with it, not wanting to remember.

The wet pillow slapped my cheek when I dropped back, as I tried to work my way into reality for far too long. It did little to remove my fear of the upcoming interrogation.

Miss Mabel is gone. She is not questioning you. Miss Mabel is gone.

My desk stood against the door, barring the way out in case I tried to leave while under the influence of the Veritas. Taking it for the third time the previous night guaranteed a repeat of the same grueling experience, shortened not at all. Was I putting myself through this for nothing? I was no farther along than after the first exposure to Veritas.

Exhausted, but unable to relax enough to go back to sleep, I climbed out of bed and got dressed. Miss Celia would be up to get breakfast ready by now. I would go get my instructions for the day from her. Relief that I didn't have to face Miss Mabel propelled me down the stairs earlier than usual. I loved an early start to the day, even if I felt tired enough to fall asleep while walking down the stairs.

While she worked, Miss Celia hummed a quiet tune to herself that greeted me when I entered the kitchen. She jumped in surprise when she saw me.

"Bianca!" she cried, putting a hand on her chest. "You scared me! What are you doing, standing there like some kind of ghost?"

"I'm sorry, Miss Celia. I didn't mean to startle you."

She gave me a dirty look, but it softened when she regained her breath.

"What are you doing up so early?" she asked.

"I couldn't sleep. I thought I'd come report to you and get an early start on my lessons for the day."

She pulled a piece of paper from her apron pocket.

"That's very wise of you. Miss Mabel assigned you a heavy load."

Wish I could say that was a new occurrence.

"Thank you, Miss Celia."

Four new scrolls in a different language, two books to read, and a class with Miss Amelia on trust potions. I folded the instructions back into a small square and hesitated before turning to go.

Despite being so busy with homework that I studied while I ate, I felt a twinge of pity for Miss Celia, working all alone in the kitchen, day in and day out. I knew how that felt. It was no secret that she liked having people around, and I would do anything to avoid hitting the books again.

"Would you like some help, Miss Celia?"

She stopped drying a large bamboo bowl to stare at me.

"You want to help in the kitchen? You've got so much to do!"

"I don't mind."

Shocked speechless for several moments, she pointed to a pile of potatoes.

"Go ahead and peel them if you like. I certainly don't mind either."

The soothing, predictable routine of the warm kitchen helped relax my tense muscles. We worked in a companionable silence for a long stretch of time before Miss Celia broke it. Her tone was cordial in a way I'd never heard before.

"How do you like being the Assistant so far?" she asked.

"It's great." I had to choke the words out. "Miss Mabel has taught me so much already."

The lie wasn't entirely false, but I hoped it didn't sound as invented as it felt. Miss Celia continued kneading a lump of dough without seeming to notice.

"You look very tired," she remarked. "Are you staying up late to do homework?"

"Yes," I answered too quickly. Trying to ease my tone, I took a breath. "Miss Mabel has made the homework extra challenging."

Miss Celia smiled to herself.

"She loves to test her Assistants, but you can handle it. You would have never gotten the position if you couldn't. Mabel is the best teacher out there. Pressure and responsibility are driving forces, but only knowledge creates power."

Her small token of support had a surprising buoyant effect, giving me a little needed reassurance.

Confidence in all things, Bianca.

"Thank you, Miss Celia. How long have you worked here?"

"I started long ago, when Mabel, Miss Mabel's grandmother, ran the school. My husband and I lived at the northern edge of the Network. When he died, I wandered around for a while looking for a job, and ended up in Letum Wood. Mabel found me and took me in. I've been here ever since."

I stopped peeling the potatoes in surprise.

"Miss Mabel's grandmother was named Mabel?" I asked.

"Yes. She died several decades ago."

An unmistakable tension edged her voice.

"You are very loyal then," I said, changing the subject to bring the easy atmosphere back. Papa taught me that people give information better when they feel at ease. "To have stayed so long."

Affection bled back through her tone.

"Yes, well, I had a good hand in raising Miss Mabel myself after her mother left without any explanation. Mabel was only a baby at the time. How anyone could leave such a beautiful, calm child, I'll never understand! Anyway, I've said it before, and I'll say it again, I've lived here most of my life, and I'll die here. Mabel is my family, and that's all I need."

I didn't have an opportunity to ask her more. She quickly switched subjects, something in the speed of her change indicating she felt she'd said too much.

"Miss Mabel mentioned that you are working for the Esbat mark before the next meeting. That's very ambitious of you."

"I'm hoping to attend."

And dreading it, too.

"That mark will serve you well in the Network for the rest of your life. You should talk to Scarlett. She got the Esbat mark when she worked at Chatham Castle."

I almost dropped the slippery potato in my hands and scrambled with it for several seconds before regaining a firm grip. Miss Scarlett had the Esbat mark? Working hard to neutralize my tone, I asked, "Oh, she worked at Chatham, did she?"

"She's the best lie detector I've ever met, which makes for a great teacher. The woman could make Veritas with her eyes closed."

"That's very interesting," I murmured, and the silence collected again.

After putting the peeled potatoes in a pot, hanging up the towel, and wishing Miss Celia a good day, I took an apple, cut off a chunk of bread, and disappeared upstairs, Miss Scarlett on my mind.

I wasn't sure what I stood to gain by talking to Miss Scarlett, except for criticism about my responsibility to handle the Esbat mark on my own. The thought of losing control during the interrogation propelled me to her classroom against my better judgment.

The lull between lunch and the next set of classes, when the students gathered in their rooms to clean up after eating, seemed the best time to go. I took advantage of the opportunity. The deserted halls felt empty, the quiet sound of clanking glasses following me from the kitchen.

Sitting at her desk with a rigid, nearly inflexible back, Miss Scarlett didn't notice me standing in the doorway until I cleared my throat;

she had been focused on a letter. When she looked up, her eyes narrowed. A prim set of glasses sat on the edge of her nose.

"Yes?"

"I was wondering if you could answer a question."

Her sharp eyebrows lifted higher in expectation. Taking this as permission, I took a few steps into the room.

"It's about Veritas."

She turned back to the paper in her hands.

"If you have to ask me about it, I can't help you."

Undeterred, I took a few more steps toward her. The familiar blast of heat and spices hit me like a wave. Sandalwood. Her silky red drapes danced in a draft of cool winter wind from a slightly open window.

"Miss Celia mentioned that you had a particular talent for it."

"You're working for the Esbat mark, Bianca. You're an Assistant. You shouldn't have to ask for help."

"Miss Mabel isn't here, and I don't need help making Veritas. I just have a question about it."

Her steady gaze wasn't welcoming, but she hadn't thrown me out either. Hopeful, I held my breath and waited. She straightened even more, if it was possible, her bracelets dancing as she moved.

"Fine. What is it?"

"Is it possible to control Veritas? Well, to control yourself under its influence?"

She pulled her glasses off her face with a flick of her wrist.

"You must be facing the interrogation soon," she said. "When Miss Mabel gets back from Chatham?"

"Yes."

"A little worried?"

"I don't want to fail, Miss Scarlett."

"Or do you have secrets you don't want to divulge?"

My heart hammered so hard I worried she'd see it through my ribs.

"No ma'am. I just don't like the thought of not being in control of what I say."

She paused for an uncomfortable length of time, her jaw set. I felt as if she rifled through my mind, like Isadora, trying to figure out for herself what I was trying to hide.

"So you think I'll tell you how to overpower it so you can be in control?"

"Can it be overpowered?" I grabbed onto this hope as if it were my last. Perhaps it was.

"Assuming you could handle a potion as powerful as Veritas, you don't have the time to try. It takes at least forty or fifty exposures to make a difference."

My stomach plummeted. A waste, all of it. I was out of time and facing an interrogation that could reveal dangerous secrets about Papa and me. I still had scrolls to finish, scrolls I'd put off so I could build an immunity I didn't have time for. None of it meant anything. Tears rose in the back of my throat, but I forced them away.

"That's only part of it," she continued, reading my mind. "You can never be entirely immune to Veritas, or everyone would do it. You become immune to the side effects. That takes a long time. Years of constant exposure."

"I see."

"The purpose behind questioning you with Veritas is to give you a chance to know what it feels like, not to test your control of it. No sixteen-year-old stands a chance at controlling a potion that strong. You'll pass the interrogation as long as you're still breathing at the end."

She turned back to her letter and dismissed me with a wave.

"That's all the information I have for you. You may leave me to my work."

I stared after her for a minute, listening to only the cackle of the fire. When she made it clear she'd forgotten me, I circled around and left.

A Frightening Euphoria

The next day passed much the same. In between meals, I buried myself in scrolls. Leda came up after lunch to study together. Although it seemed odd to me, I knew she felt some kind of friendship was forming as we sat in the same room saying nothing. Camille, unable—or unwilling—to do homework on a weekend, worked on a puzzle with a mousy girl named Grace in the first-year common room.

After dinner, I came to a stop at the top of the spiral stairs. The smell of plumeria filled the hallway, and I looked in the open classroom door to see a familiar curvy figure. My heart dropped into my stomach.

"There you are, Bianca darling. I made it back a little early and thought we could get a start on things tonight. Is your homework complete?"

Her cool smile set my nerves on fire. This unexpected return was no accident.

"Not entirely, Miss Mabel," I motioned to her desk and willed my hands not to shake. "I'm still working on the scrolls from today."

She rolled her eyes, as if that had been expected.

"Are you ready for your interrogation?"

Yes, please take all my secrets and destroy my family again. I've so been looking forward to giving you more leverage.

"Yes, Miss Mabel. Whenever you are."

I wasn't ready. I would never be ready. It was happening too fast, too unexpectedly. I wondered if I could warn Papa somehow. No, of course not. Already prepared, Miss Mabel handed me the glass of water. When I took it, I avoided touching her hand.

"Here's to the Esbat," she said.

Expecting warmth in my stomach after I drank, I stared at the glass when I felt nothing. An aftertaste followed, like the sweet tang of sugared grapefruit, instead of the usual hit of mint. I braced myself for the worst, waiting for the dizzying spiral in my head.

It never came.

"How are you feeling, Bianca?" Miss Mabel circled around me in a saunter, speaking in a lazy tone. "Do you feel unusual?"

Unusual. That was the only word to describe how I felt. I floated, drifting on an invisible current. The stress of the past week lifted off my shoulders and unburdened me. It was euphoric, and terrifying.

"Do you feel free?"

I looked at Miss Mabel in a happy kind of surprise. How wonderful. She hadn't given me Veritas after all.

A blithe smile curled her lips.

"Yes, you figured it out. It wasn't Veritas. You spent all that time taking it on your own. Why would I test you on something you've already experienced? That may come at a later date. Or it may not."

The weightless feeling whirled through my body and brain. Such blue eyes. Miss Mabel had trustworthy blue eyes.

What? I thought, shaking my head. *What are you thinking?*

Miss Mabel strolled in front of me, her eyes as sharp as a hawk.

"You saved us some time, you know, trying it on your own. I'm so happy you did. In fact, I devised that little test to see if you would. Experience really is the best teacher, isn't it? I like to see if my Assistants have initiative. You certainly have that in gobs, don't you?"

While she spoke, I hovered between enjoyment and serenity. It was difficult to be concerned with what she said. She didn't appear angry with me for taking Veritas. How could someone so beautiful be angry?

"You went to Miss Amelia's lesson on the specific ingredients in a trust potion yesterday. Do you remember?"

My carefree mind skipped back.

"Yes," I answered, not aware that I spoke until it was too late. "Yes, I remember. I just ate dinner. The milk tasted funny."

Was this sublime experience from a trust potion? How do I combat an existence so delightful? It had something to do with . . . I couldn't remember. As soon as my worries appeared, they drowned in an ocean of disinterest. I didn't want to lose this enchanting feeling.

"Trust potions work on a very different level than Veritas. All that awful vertigo really takes a toll. This is much more pleasant and soothing. It's so easy to trust me right now, isn't it?"

"Yes," I agreed in a dreamy voice. The feeling relaxed me. I never wanted it to leave. It felt so good to talk to her that I wanted to say more. "I took the Veritas three times. I didn't want to. I told Leda I didn't want to. She helped me not get caught."

Talking lifted me up, carrying me high and free. I could talk forever. Miss Mabel walked over to look out the window, her hands folded behind her back. I watched her in adoring reverence.

"What do you know about the High Priestess, Bianca?"

"Not much," I sighed and closed my eyes. It felt like a cloud held me suspended in the air, letting me sleep on a moonbeam.

"Do you believe that sometimes the High Priestess makes the wrong decision?"

Something nagged inside me like a sharp pinprick. What did the High Priestess have to do with this? My brain became fuzzy, and I floundered in confusion.

"I-I don't know. I don't want to think about that right now."

"I know you don't," she said, soothing me back into serenity. "Let's talk about something else."

"Yes," I agreed with a dreamy sigh. Everything felt so good here. Miss Mabel was so pretty, so trustworthy. She'd never hurt or betray me. "Something else."

"Do you ever crave power, Bianca?"

Power.

Power over my curse. Power over Grandmother's daily pain, and Mama's sad eyes. Power over Papa's job, and the secrets, and the Veritas.

Power over my own life.

"Yes," I said. "I do."

"You have many reasons to need it, what with the curse that may soon take your life and your dear Grandmother's."

Grandmother. Curse. These words from her lips snagged my joy, like a dark cloud, threatening, but not overhead yet.

"If I offered you a chance to have power, would you take it?" Mabel asked.

The answer came to my lips without hesitation.

"Yes."

Of course I would take it. Wouldn't I? Something inside me didn't feel right. Through the haze of enjoyment rose a mild state of panic, and the two feelings clashed.

I fought my own thoughts with a visible frown.

"Bianca?"

She faced me now. The light from the sunset silhouetted her in dripping shades of yellow and orange. My internal conflict deafened me. I wanted to fall into the overwhelming safety of tranquility and trust. But the peace couldn't win. What stopped it? I'd do anything to live like this forever. No cares. No troubles.

Oh, yes. My secrets.

The secrets kept me here. I had to let go of them. Once I let go, I would be free.

Miss Mabel strolled forward a few steps.

"You are fighting it, Bianca. Just give in. I can see the struggle in your eyes."

The desire to speak overwhelmed me, but my jaw wouldn't move. No matter how good the sweetness of answering tasted, my lips wouldn't open. My body trembled. The longer I waited, the stronger the desire to talk, to tell her all my secrets, to tell her to give me power, became. The assault bounced back and forth until I felt as if I battled myself for my own soul.

"Silly Bianca," she laughed under her breath. "A little power never hurt anybody. Think of the things you could do! I could train you and your impressive mind for great things. Don't you want to be great?"

Papa's dark eyes flashed through my mind. Priscilla's voice said, *I want to be one of the great ones.* Mother's laugh. Grandmother's arthritic hands. A new feeling built up inside me, gaining pressure like a bottle of expanding bubbles. The tips of my fingers tingled.

"Tell me, Bianca. Don't you want me to make you great?"

I dropped to my knees and yelled.

"No!"

Everything exploded. The elation shattered, the confusion disappeared, the weightless feeling evaporated. Once the cloud in my mind faded, I found myself panting. The muscles in my face had cramped from holding my jaw closed.

Miss Mabel stood over me with a knowing smile on her face.

"Very interesting," she murmured. "You're much stronger than I expected, Bianca. That's very good to know."

I stared at her feet, too weak to meet her eyes.

"Go to bed. You can have the rest of the night off."

She disappeared into the hallway as I put my head on my arms, exhausted.

I Must Know

The grass felt cold at my back, but I lolled in it anyway, drunk from the effects of the sun, however small. Even the air felt almost warm, a playful breath of spring that winter would soon snatch away, leaving nothing but the mocking laughter of a bitter frost. My eyes stayed shut, but turned up, trying to soak in every winter ray.

Clusters of girls littered the schoolyard, speaking and laughing in quiet bursts, desperate to soak up the light. Camille lay next to me, propped on her elbows, picking absently at the brown spears of grass beneath us.

"Jackie told me today that she wants to go into divination. Her grandmother is a Diviner," Camille said with a sigh. I opened one eye to see her hands mowing the grass with fierce strokes. The afternoon Jackie pointed out the raven in my odious drawing flittered back through my mind. Diviner seemed to fit her. "I think I should like to be a Diviner."

Leda looked over the edge of her scroll. Her white skin looked almost translucent in the sunshine.

"I thought you wanted to be an apothecary?" she asked.

"I do," Camille replied. "But I think I should like getting a set of Diviners' cards. They are so lovely. I think I'd like helping people see the decisions they face, so they can make good choices, based on what the cards say."

Leda snorted, drawing a perturbed glare from Camille.

"There's more to it than that and you know it," Leda said, as self-righteous as ever. "Divining isn't just seeing the future."

"I know," Camille muttered under her breath. "I'm not stupid."

Camille resumed watching the other groups of girls, a restless, unsatisfied look on her face. I closed my eyes again, wanting to block it out. I didn't want to think about the future or our purpose here at the school. I just wanted to sit and not see a scroll or Miss Mabel's face anywhere near me. I wanted to not think about the Esbat, the close call with the trust potion, or what it meant that I almost told her everything. The pressure of the mark was beginning to take its toll on my weary mind. Even small talk felt like work, so I stayed out of it.

"What about gardening?" Camille asked again, after the silence stretched so long I'd started to drowse off into that in-between where everything seemed to make sense, no matter how absurd. It was a safe world to live in, one without commitment or fear. "I think I'd like working in a garden."

Michelle and Rebecca stood at the distant garden plot, pacing out spots, planning what they would grow come spring as part of their mark. I thought idly of my favorite herbs, the ones Grandmother taught me to care for with her aged hands. *Basil,* her voice said in my mind, *is my favorite herb. It goes with anything and is so easy to grow in the Central Network. But you can never go wrong with rosemary.* A flash of homesickness overcame me, and I drifted on it, replaying the sweet memories of home.

"You'd have to get your fingernails dirty," Leda said with obvious condescension. "You wouldn't even plant pumpkins in the summer, remember?"

Her retort shook me from my reverie. I opened my eyes to watch both of them. I wondered what made Leda so ornery today. She wasn't giving a single inch, and poor Camille looked frazzled.

"Yes," Camille said in a defeated tone. "There is that. How about fashion? Brianna is going to design clothing, hopefully for the High Priestess. She'll be so good at it. She always looks wonderful. I might like fashion."

Leda rolled her eyes and made a point of picking up a scroll and holding it in front of her face so she couldn't see either of us. Camille's hopeful look dropped into a disappointed frown. Giving up with a sigh, I raised myself to one elbow.

"Is something wrong, Camille?" I asked.

"Bianca, I need plans!" The exclamation burst out of her with all the force of a gale, visibly taking some of her pent-up energy with it. "Everyone at the school knows why they are attending Miss Mabel's, and I don't. Leda wants to be a Coven leader. Priscilla is going into transformation. Jackie wants to be a Diviner. Isabelle is going to be an artist. Michelle and Rebecca want to work at Chatham and cook for the High Priestess. What am I doing?"

She threw her hands in the air in agitation, her apple cheeks flaring to a deep red. I noticed she didn't pinpoint my future goals, and I wondered what exactly they were. Live, for one. The rest would come later.

Hopefully.

"Isadora would never have admitted you if you were weren't meant to go here," I said, hoping it would be comforting but not feeling conviction in my words. "Are you saying she was wrong?"

"No," she muttered. "I'm saying she's crazy. I'm not good at anything."

Leda joined the conversation.

"You are failing geometry still."

Tears welled up in Camille's eyes.

"Not as badly as you're failing at friendship," I shot back. "At least Camille makes an effort."

I sent Leda a scathing glare, accompanied by a mild hex that made her sneeze several times in succession. It took her a couple of minutes to compose herself, and when she did, she ignored me completely.

"Camille, you'll find your place here," I said. "All of us wonder where we belong, or what's ahead of us. Just because some of these girls think they know what they want doesn't mean you have to."

At least you have a life to plan, I wanted to say.

"No I won't." She ducked her face into her hands, drawing the attention of a few second-years nearby. I waved them off with a low growl, but they only moved away a few steps before turning back to watch from the corners of their eyes. "The only reason Isadora let me in is because . . . because . . ."

She trailed off, her face slowly crumpling. I reached over and put a hand on her shoulder. The floodgates broke.

"She felt sorry for me!"

Even Leda's face seemed sober when I looked at her in question. She forgot to be vexed at me and shrugged. Camille's wails turned into stuttering, hiccup-like sobs. Unsure of how to comfort her, I patted her shoulder until the crying subsided. The second-years moved away, motivated by the nasty look Leda shot them while they stared. She could silently threaten in a way that I couldn't. It was admirable, and I thought of asking her for lessons once she'd gotten over her irritation. There was no one in the yard but us now.

"Camille, surely Isadora wouldn't let you into Miss Mabel's just because she felt sorry for you," I said. Camille pulled a handkerchief from her pocket and patted the tears off her face. "It doesn't work like that."

"I certainly don't have the educational requirements," she said, stuttering through fast breaths as she attempted to recover from crying. "I-I-Isadora said it h-h-herself."

The look on Leda's face that suggested she agreed. I pinched her arm and gave her a threatening glare.

"Say something nice," I mouthed.

"Camille, you'll find your place here," she finally said. "Do you trust me?"

Camille quieted and looked at Leda in surprise.

"I will?"

"Yes," Leda said, conviction in her tone. If Camille hadn't been so upset, she would have heard the annoyance beneath it. "You will."

"Will you—"

"Absolutely not," Leda cut her off. "I won't tell you what it is, or when you'll figure it out. Discovering it is half the battle, Camille. I won't take that away from you."

It was an incredibly mature thing for Leda to say, especially in light of her preceding heartless remarks, and for a moment I felt like we were a bunch of children trying to pretend like we were adults. But we weren't, nor were we close to it, and I felt grateful. We really didn't know anything.

Camille looked away, embarrassed. "I'm sorry," she said. "I didn't mean to be so emotional."

The sun slipped beneath the spiny spires of Letum Wood, casting us in a cool blanket of winter air again and giving me an excuse to break the conversation up. Camille's fears had stirred up far too many of my own. I didn't even know if I had a future to be afraid of, and it made me sad.

What would I do if I lived?

Eat a dozen cinnamon buns, I decided, trying to cheer myself up. *And gobs of frosting.*

"Let's go inside," I suggested, uncomfortable with where my thoughts headed. *The Esbat,* I reminded myself. *There's no reason to plan a future if you can't even make it past the Esbat.*

The three of us stood and shook off our skirts. Camille finished composing herself while Leda headed for the door, scrolls in hand. She threw it open, leaking the sweet smell of apple spice cake into the cool evening. She fell into a book as soon as we reached the dining room, Camille dropped into a conversation with Jackie, and I sat staring at the fire, my thoughts back where they belonged, twirling around the Esbat and the mounds of homework awaiting me.

Confidence, Bianca. Confidence.

The Esbat

Leda sat across from me, thumping her body onto the chair.
"You look horrible, Bianca."

"Thanks," I muttered, pushing a few bits of egg around my plate. I felt sluggish, like my brain worked underwater. Studying nonstop for the Esbat the past weeks had taken its toll, and the dark funk I lived in settled in my bones.

Almost done, I told myself. *The three weeks are almost done.*

A nightly run through Letum Wood maintained my sanity, but only just. The jaunts were my only adventure, my only out. They were the fingernail grip that kept me holding on when my world felt buried in scrolls and parchment. Although dangerous, the balance the moments of freedom gave me was well worth the price. Besides, Isadora watched on, evidently keeping my secret, for Miss Mabel never mentioned them.

"I think you look lovely," Camille said, shooting Leda a reprimanding look. "A bit tired, and pale, and a little peaked," she clarified with pinched lips. "But lovely."

Leda had a newsscroll in hand. She held it like a club, her knuckles turning white. I recognized the title right away.

The Chatham Chatterer
Revealing the troubles of Antebellum one edition at a time.

"Oh no," Camille whispered under her breath, eyeing the scroll with impressive trepidation. "Here she goes. Leda's crazy over the news."

Leda's flaring nostrils and pressed lips were all I needed to see. Something had perturbed her. Good. She always provided some relief from my bad moods when she got worked up over something.

"Anything interesting?" I inquired, hoping to goad her into a reaction. "Good news, perhaps?"

Camille kicked me underneath the table, and I shot her a dirty glare as my shin smarted. Leda took a deep breath, her skinny shoulders settling down a few inches.

"No," she said with haughty disdain. "Is there ever good news with leaders that are such imbeciles?"

Camille shot me a look of warning, then shook her head once. "Don't ask anymore," she mouthed, but Leda was already scrolling through the newspaper, preparing her attack.

"I hope you're not talking about the Central Network leaders," I said in a low tone that was more teasing than earnestness. "I happen to like the High Priestess."

"Have you met her?" Leda shot me a pointed glance, already knowing the answer.

"No."

"Then you can't know if you like her."

"Have you met her?" I shot back.

"No," she said with a stiff neck, her eyes averted.

"Then you can't know if you don't like her."

She scowled at my triumphant expression, finally giving in with a low mutter.

"Stop encouraging her," Camille hissed under her breath.

"Have you read this?" Leda asked both of us, holding it up, already over my victory. "It's atrocious."

"Here, Leda. Eat something." Camille shoveled a few eggs onto her plate and tossed a golden biscuit at her. "It always makes you feel better."

And stops you from talking, I thought.

"No, I haven't read it," I said, attempting unsuccessfully to stab a swollen, round sausage. Finally giving up, I grabbed it off the plate and bit off the end, earning an annoyed look from Camille.

"Blessed be. Have some decent manners, Bianca," she muttered.

"Dane is a fool," Leda said.

Camille groaned, scooting a few inches closer to Isabelle, who sat on her other side.

"Not Dane again!"

Leda ignored her, grabbed her napkin, and shook it over her lap with a whip so violent it almost snapped my eye. I leaned back and gave her the same dirty glare Camille had given me.

"Sure, sure," I muttered, suddenly wary of the storm on Leda's face. Maybe goading her hadn't been the best idea after all. "They're all idiots. You're going to become a Council Member and teach them a thing or two. I know. I've heard it before."

"I'll be a Coven leader first," she corrected me. "The Coven leader of Chatham City. Then I'll convince the High Priestess to stand up to Dane and all of the Western Network, and then I'll save the world."

A snort almost escaped me, but I turned it into a cough at the last minute. Leda was from a tiny border village, and she wanted to lead the largest city in the Network? I couldn't help admiring her ambition, but I feared it as well. Leda looked so certain of herself that I couldn't help but give her a dose of reality.

"Dane is going to gather the whole Western Network and start a war with us before you even graduate Miss Mabel's," I said, drawing from information I'd read in the past, as well as stories Papa'd been telling me for months. "I think you'll have to settle on writing the High Priestess a convincing letter to see if she'll prepare for battle. Maybe they'll name the war after you. At the very least, I'm sure a few Guardians would sacrifice their life for your honor."

A dreamy look came to Camille's face. For a second, Leda looked as if she was considering my proposal. Sarcasm wasn't her strong suit. She blanked out long enough for Camille to be startled out of her daydream and cast me a forbidding scowl.

"No." Leda shook her head, unable to hide her disappointment when she came back. "That wouldn't work. There's no guarantee that the High Priestess would get the letter. I'll have to think of something else."

If the determined set of her jaw meant anything, Leda would do just that.

"Oh, let's not talk about this!" Camille said. "Let's talk about something pleasant, please? Aunt Bettina always talks about politics over breakfast, and I hate it. Don't make me go through it now that I'm away from that crazy old bat."

I ignored Camille. Papa spoke about Dane and his ambitions all the time, and whenever he did, it tied my stomach in knots. Any trouble from the Western Network meant that Papa would have to go and investigate in total secrecy. No news out of the Western Network was good news, especially news of their soon-to-be-leader Dane. A sudden worrisome urge to find out everything I could swooped over me like the fell shadow of a nasty black bird.

"What does the *Chatterer* say about Dane?" I asked, ignoring Camille's desperate pinch on my arm.

Leda waved the newsscroll toward me without a word, buried in a book titled, *Economic History of the Eastern Network*. Clearly she was ready to be rid of us, vexed into silence before eating breakfast. It was an accomplishment that made me feel as if the day meant something. The scroll landed against my chest with a heavy thud.

"Thanks," I muttered.

The *Chatham Chatterer* was made of a long, thin parchment of surprising resiliency. Most witches bought one newsscroll a year to keep until it wore out. Every time the *Chatterer* released a new edition, the words would shift on the scroll, so that its owner didn't have to buy a new paper. Keeping the same parchment for long periods of time reduced waste and cost; it was one of the many ways the current High Priestess devised to save money and spread news quickly, something that had been sorely lacking in the Dark Days.

I glanced at the edition in the top right corner first. Fresh this morning. The *Chatterer* wasn't consistent. Sometimes it could go a week without any new articles, sometimes it would release them twice a day. Checking a newsscroll was the only way to know.

Leda's scroll was ripped in a few places and the ink smudged in spots where water must have damaged it. Like the second-hand clothes I'd seen her wear on the weekends, it had seen better days.

"Where'd you get this?" I asked, carefully skipping past a torn section of the scroll. She flushed and mumbled something about finding it.

"Leda is the oldest of nine brothers and sisters," Camille said in a low whisper only I could hear. "They don't have any money so she nabs newsscrolls from the street or gets them second hand and uses them until they give out. Looks like this one is just about there."

I glanced up at Leda in surprise, but the book completely obscured her face. Having been an only child, I couldn't imagine what a house full of kids would be like. No wonder Leda didn't like people.

After muddling through a few headlines, I found the article in question and started to skim it.

A pair of Protectors following up on a lead found a group of West Guards lost in Letum Wood, near the border crossing of the Central and Northern Network. The West Guards were later reported to be on a trip to the Northern Network for a training mission.

I skipped past the drivel, searching for any sign of my father in the newsscroll's words. Nothing. Papa was always somewhere between the lines, although they never used his name.

"Notice how they claimed to be on a training mission," Leda said. "The West Guards don't need training. They were going to the North to try to make a secret alliance with the Northern Network, I just know it."

"Is that why you think Dane is an imbecile?" I asked.

"No," Leda snorted, as if I'd offended her. "He's an imbecile because he shouldn't look to the North for help. They won't come down from their mountains to save any of us."

The article trailed off into a ramble about the recent history of the Western Network's volatile relations with the other Networks and a discussion of the Central Network's plans to increase security along the Borderlands by sending more Guardians. I let the scroll slide shut and handed it back to Leda, disappointed and relieved. Camille just let out a sigh and looked away, humming under her breath while she searched for a safer conversation.

"Interesting," I said, handing it back. "Thanks for sharing."

"Ooh, look!" Camille cried, grabbing my arm. She waved to the other side of the room, where the beautiful second-year Brianna walked in with a new scarf around her neck. Brianna waved back with a sparkling smile dotted by perfect dimples and settled next to another second-year who stroked the fabric. Camille's shoulders slumped. "Her mother is always sending her nice things. Bettina would never buy that. Wouldn't it be lovely to have a cape and scarf set like hers?"

I thought I heard her mutter *or a mother* under her breath but couldn't be sure. Leda dropped the *Chatterer* into her ratty bag with a livid glare.

"You'll fawn over fashion but you don't even care about real problems," she said in disgust. "We could go to war over this incident."

"You're right," Camille admitted with no remorse. "I don't care about the Western Network. But I do want that scarf."

I silently applauded Camille's sudden backbone. Leda glowered at my presumptuous smirk. She finished the rest of the meal in her book and made a point of ignoring us, her wrinkled brow casting a dark shadow over her face. Camille, distracted by a new deck of Diviners' cards Jackie received that morning, turned her back on both of us, leaving me to myself.

My thoughts returned to the Esbat, depressing me. The unknown expectations hung around like a lurking black storm. I tried to ignore it, but that just seemed to make the rain fall harder, threatening to down me. Some nights I woke from dreams of scrolls and ravens flying around my head. They attacked me, forming little paper cuts all over my hands, arms, and face. When I woke up, I thought I could feel blood and feathers on my cheek.

"Bianca? Hello?"

I jerked out of my reverie to find Camille waving her hand in front of my face.

"Are you there?"

"Sorry, what?"

She motioned around us. The dining room had emptied. Only Camille, Leda, and I remained behind. I let out a long breath.

"It's almost time for class," she said.

I stood up, rubbing my face to stimulate some energy. I'd been awake for four hours already, studying with the window wide open so I wouldn't fall back to sleep. Miss Mabel conversed with me in three different languages during lectures now, sometimes switching in the middle of a sentence. She held me accountable for any information she gave, whether I understood it or not. Which, most of the time, I didn't.

"Are you almost done with this mark yet?" Camille asked, studying me with a worried gaze. "You're starting to look . . ."

"Like death warmed over," Leda said, pushing away from the table. I could tell her comment alleviated some of her annoyed gloom. Although I wanted to snap back, I didn't have the energy to think up a proper retort. I let it slide.

"I meant to say haggard," Camille said.

"Soon," I replied with little conviction. "At least, I hope. The Esbat may come at any moment."

A blessing and a curse. I needed all the time I could get to study, but hated waiting. I found myself yearning for it to come and put me out of my misery.

I walked with them as far as the first-year classroom, waved to Miss Bernadette, and then started up the spiral stairs to my own personal prison. A gloomy sky greeted me, echoing the sentiments in my chest.

"I have good news," Miss Mabel said, sailing into the classroom and taking me by surprise. "Tomorrow is the last day of your three weeks. It's a lucky twist of fate, as I just received word that we have an Esbat meeting tomorrow night. Should all go according to plan, you could come take notes for me. I do hate carting those scrolls around. So cumbersome."

She wore a simple beige dress. It was the least elegant thing I'd ever seen her in, but with her hair down around her face, she had never looked more charming. It made breakfast feel like lead in my stomach.

A letter with the Network seal flew onto my desk behind her. I pulled out a bit of parchment and unfolded it. A letter from the Education Committee, acknowledging my test and setting the rules. The High Priest's signature filled the bottom: *Briton Marx.*

"The written portion will start first thing in the morning," Miss Mabel said, walking past the window that showed the gloomy sky.

Raindrops plinked against the window pane and chased each other on their way down. "You'll have four hours to complete it."

"And the application portion?"

"That depends."

"On the written portion?"

"Partially," she said, and left it at that. Although I made it a point never to expect things to go as normal when working with Miss Mabel, part of me hoped for predictability, just this once. The letter didn't give any more details. Miss Mabel's lips turned down in dismay as she stared out at the weather.

"Too bad about the rain," she lamented. "I wanted to show you a few advanced camouflaging spells that are optional to the curriculum."

The last thing I needed was optional learning. I could barely keep my head above water. I sent out a silent, grateful call to the bleary weather. She circled around to face me.

"Have you completed your summary on the historical impact of the Esbat today?"

"Yes, Miss Mabel."

"Did you write a paper on non-verbal lie detectors in the ancient Dorcali language?"

"Yes."

"Have you studied the format in which I will require you to take notes should you pass the test?"

No, but that one would be easy to skim over tonight.

"Briefly, Miss Mabel."

"Good. Take the day off to clear your head. Get some sleep. You look ghastly. Cramming won't help you at this point. If you don't know it already, it's too late."

To my surprise, Miss Bernadette greeted me with her stunning smile the next morning at the Esbat final. Her close-cropped hair shone a reddish cocoa in the light. The calico cat sat on her lap, purring low in her chest as I neared.

"Hello, Bianca." Miss Bernadette smiled. "It's good to see you again."

"Thank you, Miss Bernadette," I said, blushing when I sounded too earnest. "I miss your class."

"I'm sure you're surprised that I'm filling in for Miss Mabel. The High Priest doesn't like the teacher who instructed the student to give the test for the Esbat in order to prevent partiality. He's particularly careful when testing students for the Esbat mark."

Partiality, how absurd. I bit back the desire to laugh. Miss Mabel would burn off her eyebrows before she'd help me pass a test, but I couldn't deny a measure of relief. Knowing Miss Mabel wouldn't be around felt like loosening a corset. I could breathe again. My toes wiggled in my leather shoes, a blatant breach against the uniform that I didn't bother to correct. Miss Scarlett would have noticed, but I doubt Miss Bernadette would mind. The need to feel a familiar comfort overruled my fear of censure.

"Please," she motioned to a solitary desk. "Have a seat."

A weighty scroll an inch thick landed on my desk with a thud. Miss Bernadette dropped a pencil next to it. I stared in disbelief. It looked like a textbook. *Whoever wrote this must be witless,* I thought. *Surely this will take all day.*

"You have four hours to complete the exam. You are not allowed to leave the room. As soon as I say time is up, you must put your pencil down. Do you understand?"

"Yes, Miss Bernadette," I said calmly, instead of screaming like a shrew and running from the room. "I understand."

"Then you may begin."

Because of the increasing difficulty Miss Mabel had imposed on my homework through the weeks, the test was not hard. It unsettled me to realize she'd done me a favor by her ruthless and demanding tactics. The facts didn't lie. Miss Mabel was an excellent teacher. She was also a heartless witch, but at least she knew what she was doing.

When Miss Bernadette called for me to put my pencil down, I still had a bundle of unanswered questions at the back. Terror threatened to overwhelm me. *No! It can't be time already!* Would Miss Bernadette suspect the truth if I dropped candle wax on it, then claimed it had been an accident and demanded a retest?

Of course she would. The pressure of the last three weeks had finally made me dotty, I realized. Like the crazy old woman that babbled to her onions Camille told me about. Miss Bernadette took my test with a smile but a firm resolve. If she read the fear in my eyes, she said nothing about it.

"Good luck, Bianca."

Not knowing what to do next, I climbed the spiral stairs, numb, sat down on the edge of my bed, and waited. Thirteen years. Thirteen years attached to Miss Mabel with only death as my reprieve. I'd just brought a different curse upon myself tonight by not finishing the written final, one far more dangerous to me, and others, than the Inheritance curse.

Miss Mabel's curvy frame filled my doorway an hour later. I hadn't moved. I looked to the doorway, startled by her sudden appearance.

"You passed," she said.

I straightened up in shock.

"What?" I asked. It came out more like an accusation than intended. "I mean, h-how is that–"

"You leave for the Esbat meeting in thirty minutes. I'd grab my cloak if I were you; it's chilly out there. Meet in the hallway downstairs."

I came to my feet as she turned to leave.

"Wait, Miss Mabel. What about the application portion of the test? I have to demonstrate the skills you taught me in order to attend the Esbat."

Her eyes sparkled with mischief.

"I know. What better place to demonstrate your knowledge than during the Esbat?" She turned around to leave but stopped. "Oh, and Bianca? Take care not to make a single mistake on the next portion. You won't have that luxury this time. One wrong move and, well, it'll be a fun thirteen years."

She didn't need to say it. The written test must have barely met the minimum standard, if that. Only my ability to do magic would save me now. I sank back to the bed with quivering knees.

She was going to test me for the Esbat *at* the Esbat.

Is this what drowning feels like? I thought, then banished the thought with a shake of my head. *No, don't think about it. Confidence.* But my hands still trembled as I sat there, waiting.

The Anteroom

The gloom from yesterday's storm hung in the air like an unwanted visitor. It never settled, always moving past the wet school in clouds of fog.

"Miss Mabel has gone ahead of you," Miss Bernadette explained as we walked outside together. "You'll ride to the Esbat alone. She said to tell you she would meet you there."

An old man drifted out of the vapor on spindly legs, walking around a black carriage with large wheels and golden trim. A single fuzzy horse stood in front of it. The man's white hair stuck out over his ears like banners, but the top of his head was bald. He nodded to Miss Bernadette, but kept his pale blue eyes averted.

"Bianca, this is Augustus."

"Merry meet," I said with a polite curtsy. He nodded but kept moving. She gave me a soft smile.

"He's not used to much formality. Good luck tonight, Bianca."

Somehow I smiled back, then climbed into the carriage. The door closed, and the horse started forward. I stared out for awhile, watching the stalks of bare trees and shadows where the fog did not move. But my mind strayed far from the haunted appearance of Letum Wood and into deep dungeons and castle walls that I did not know.

We passed through three very small villages, comprised of cottages, pale torchlight, and dirt roads. Letum Wood towered high over them, a weathered canopy of leaves and twigs that blocked the gray sky. A few girls my age stood on the side of the dirt road, waiting for us to pass. I watched them with envy, and to make myself feel better, slipped my shoes and stockings off. Then I unbound my hair from the restrictive bun at the nape of my neck and settled in with a sigh for the duration of the ride.

Chatham City, stationed within eyesight of the High Priestess's Chatham Castle, was the largest city in the Network. Evening drew close by the time we sped through it. A man walked down the cobblestone street lighting torches, and women hurried by with woven baskets on their hips. Others wore elegant dresses, with silk bustles and skirts. Neither Grandmother nor Mama ever went as far as Chatham City, but I'd heard stories about it. The sprawling expanse seemed to never end, with thick air and brick buildings stacked so close together only the narrowest alleys remained. The air smelled like soot and burnt sugar.

"Almost there," Augustus called as we turned onto a long cobblestone road. Chatham Castle twinkled in the distance, set against the late blue sky. I pressed a hand to my stomach to quell the flutter of fear and watched the distance between me and my possible doom close.

"Here we are."

I stepped out of the carriage when we rolled to a stop so Augustus wouldn't have to work his way down.

"It's okay," I called up to him. "You can stay up there."

The gatehouse to Chatham Castle was a dominating, intense presence. Turrets stabbed the night sky on either side of the ancient stone wall like giant spears. The double-door iron gate leading to the inner bailey housed several Guardians, the soldiers of the Central Network. Flames from wide, shallow bowls danced high, growing as tall as my body. The gray walls looked dull in their expansive light.

Four Guardians stood on either side of the gate. Young men, it appeared, with somber faces. All of them stared at me.

"Well," Augustus nodded toward it with a jaunty cry. "Have at 'er."

"Wait," I stopped him as he lifted the reins, scanning the area, and glimpsing the unfriendly stare of the Guardians. "Where's Miss Mabel?"

He gave me an odd look.

"She's inside."

"What do you mean inside?" I asked, forcing my voice to remain even.

"Don't you know how to get in? Miss Mabel told me to bring you right to the gatehouse. Said you'd know what to do from here."

"She's not coming for me?"

"Course not!" he laughed, but his face fell into a perplexed expression. "Why would she? Don't you know why you're here?"

"I guess I do," I replied, trying to convince myself. I'd learned enough to know how to get into Chatham but never thought I'd have to do it on my own. Newcomers had to be escorted to the Esbat, which meant Miss Mabel waited inside for me, out of the chill.

One would hope.

"Better go then," Augustus said, inclining his head toward the intimidating gate. "Those Guardians are eyeing you. They won't let you stick around here for very long. Makes them nervous." He clucked his tongue and started down the road, calling over his shoulder, "I'll be at the pub in the meantime."

I balled my hands into fists at my side to contain my fury at Miss Mabel. "Yes," I said under my breath, leaving a puff of fog in the air. The carriage pulled away, clattering on the cobblestones as it flew back down the drive. "Go while you can, before she ensnares you into one of her many traps and you never escape with your soul."

Miss Mabel had done this on purpose. Flaunting me before the Guardians meant they'd follow me into the trees when I pursued the hidden door that would let me into Chatham, catch me, and throw me in the dungeon for trespassing Her Highness's grounds. If I had known Miss Mabel wouldn't be waiting for me at the gatehouse, I would have left Augustus in Chatham City at his pub and trekked out on foot.

No coincidence, I was sure.

Augustus was too far away to call him back, and, at any rate, that wouldn't do me any good. I hesitated, standing at the edge of the light flickering across the stones, unsure of my next step. One Guardian took a step forward, his hands folded in front of him, his eyes narrowed, assessing. His look said it all.

Decide what you're going to do, or we will decide for you.

I swallowed, then spun on my heels and ran into Letum Wood like a frightened child. When I looked over my shoulder, two of the Guardians had disappeared. Soon enough they'd be hidden in the trees, waiting for the perfect opportunity to nab me. It wouldn't take them long. My time to act was on a dying chain, disappearing one link at a time.

There was only one way to avoid the dungeon right now, and I faced it with grim resolve. It involved magic that, technically, a first-year student shouldn't know.

Transportation.

Miss Mabel couldn't have known I was able to do it. The Network school system didn't even offer it as an option because of the advanced nature of the magic involved. And in the hands of someone not confident enough in their ability to do it, it was dangerous. Fortunately I had enough confidence but not much time.

If I transported, I may have to explain it to Miss Mabel. If I didn't, I wouldn't make it to the Esbat, and I'd owe thirteen years of my life to my mortal enemy. The sudden rustle of wind, as gentle as a breath, made every muscle in my back freeze. A slight crack to my right, close to the ground, made the decision for me.

The Guardians had found me.

I instantly dropped into a ball, flying through the incantation under my breath. I felt the tug of a hand close around my cloak, a guttural shout, and then I fell.

The wind rushed my eyes, pressure bore down on my chest, and I stumbled forward, almost running into a brick wall.

It worked. I stood on the far eastern side of Chatham Castle, where the trees and brush grew close and intimate, too thick and gnarled to make it through on foot by trespassers who thought they had the courage to try.

My hand pressed against the wall of the castle to steady me. I tilted my head back and gazed up. The flying wall never ended, sending my vision into a dizzy whirl. The lightheaded feeling didn't abate when I looked away.

The Guardians were still watching me, I could feel it. They would have followed the impression of my magic the second I disappeared.

Their talents for that were unmatched in all of Antebellum. Not even the Eastern Network trained their forces so well, and they were the richest of the Networks.

I hoped that now that I was standing at this particular spot, the Guardians would give me some space. Transporting here could only mean that I came for the Esbat.

All the same, I didn't feel like pressing my luck. I pushed the dark hair out of my eyes and began to walk along the wall. A pressing drape of nettles and thorny bushes allowed only enough space to walk sideways without snagging my hair, which I did twice.

The stones on the outer castle wall appeared to be perfect, especially when I stood this close, but they weren't. My fingertips pressed into them as I moved past. Once the texture changed, becoming slightly gritty, I stopped. The subtle sandy veneer lasted for three full bricks across and twelve high.

A skinny door.

Gathering my courage, I repeated the ancient words that I'd memorized two weeks earlier. I'd been reciting the secret spells to myself every day in each of the three languages, just in case. The textured stones drifted back a few feet without a sound. I slipped inside and they closed behind me.

I stood in a small room, barely wide enough to turn around in. Behind me the wall became a single smooth slab, with no evidence of a doorway. The chilly air hit my throat with a damp gust and I shivered. A pale green torch burned at the top of four stone steps, illuminating the only door. The emerald flame would never fade out unless the castle ceased to exist, an eternal companion to the sturdy walls.

This was the anteroom. If I did anything wrong, I'd be trapped here until someone else came through. Since Mabel ensured I arrived late to the meeting, that meant it would be another month.

I couldn't help but wonder if Miss Mabel would intervene or just let me die with a sigh of regret that yet another student failed her. Isadora was not here to see, to protect me. I imagined some great tragedy hitting the Central Network and delaying the Esbat for months. Years, even. Then they'd find my bones here in the anteroom, one arm stretched to the wooden door.

I shook off the shiver in my spine, annoyed for spooking myself. *Pull it together, Bianca.* Well, there was no better way to disappoint Miss Mabel than to arrive at the Esbat, ready to conquer.

Four metal hoops lay in a row on the heavy wooden door. Every hoop sat above a different triangle, one of each of the alchemy symbols. Air. Fire. Water. Earth. If I used the wrong hoop to knock, even once, I would not be admitted.

Without hesitation, I grabbed the second and third and slammed them down at the same time. Two different tones resonated into the castle. Fire and water together made the unity symbol, which was an upside down and right side up triangle pressed together.

To my relief, the door groaned open. A butler stood just behind it. His perfectly starched uniform smelled like powder. Light from the torch next to me glinted off his slick black hair. He didn't say anything, just stared at me with dull eyes.

"I need to speak with the High Priestess. I'm here on business," I said.

His forehead furrowed.

"What proof do you have?"

My heart jumped into my throat, and I fought back the urge to smack my forehead. Proof. Of course he wanted proof. Why wouldn't he? Certainly I didn't look suspicious at all, a lone sixteen-year-old entering an ancient castle by a secret door. There was no way to make this less awkward.

Unfortunately, I had no proof. No Esbat mark, no reason for him to allow me in. Uncertain whether my empty circlus would help or not, I exposed my right wrist. He glanced at it, hesitated, then pulled the door toward him just enough to allow me admittance. He wrinkled his upper lip, and I knew that he had no idea what to do with me.

The room I stepped into consisted of gray stones and a ceiling that curved into a peak at the top. A crimson carpet covered floor, infused with golden threaded designs. Banners hung along the walls in blood red and gold, a large C drawn in the middle, a hat-tip to the Central Network flag and colors. Statues stood at random intervals in shallow bays. Well-lit by torches and candles, the area had very little shadow. My eyes had to adjust to the light.

The butler motioned for me to stay where I stood. On his way to the door, he ran into a short, slender woman in a gray dress. They spoke in low tones, casting uneasy glances my way. When he left, the woman approached me. Her hair hung in limp blonde curls on her head, held in place by a large black pin. Rigid, and not very welcoming, she stopped a few feet away and looked me over with a haughty glance. Too late, I realized I'd left my hair down and my shoes in the carriage. No wonder the butler thought I looked odd. I pulled my toes under the skirt, silently berating myself.

"Who are you?" she asked.

Miss Mabel's lessons came back to assist me.

If you are outside the Council room or if the doors to the Council room are unsealed, you should never say your name or reason for being there. Spies could be anywhere and may take many forms.

The suspicious glint in the woman's eyes meant she had no idea what was going on either. My heart sunk a little deeper, if possible. Miss Mabel had not informed them of my arrival. She wanted me to get into the meeting alone, as a stranger, even though a current member always escorted newcomers to the Esbat. When it came to Network secrets, no one took any chances.

"I can't tell you that," I said, swallowing back the nervous fear that rose in my throat.

The unwelcoming glower turned dangerous. "Then why are you here?"

"On business. I need to speak to the High Priestess."

"How old are you? Twelve?"

"Sixteen," I said through clenched teeth. *Better than fifty-four,* I almost snapped but decided I couldn't afford to have her as an enemy.

"But I don't know you. Why should I let you into Chatham Castle?"

Telling her I knew Miss Mabel would also be a mistake. It didn't even matter to them that I'd come in by a secret entrance that a lay person couldn't have broached, speaking another witch's name in association with the Esbat equated with treason.

Spies could be anywhere.

"I'm supposed to be here," I stated with false confidence. Even I wasn't sure anymore. "I can prove it."

"Oh really? No one told me you were coming."

"It must have slipped her mind," I retorted quickly, surprised at my own condescension. "I'm sure she is very busy."

She muttered something under her breath and folded her arms across her chest. Her eyes glittered.

"If you're supposed to be here," she said with a nasty snark in her tone, "prove it."

The last words came out punctuated with disdain, and I couldn't say I blamed her. The muscles in my throat seemed to spasm. My false bravado caught up to me. I couldn't prove it. I didn't even have the Esbat mark yet. I hesitated. She tapped her foot on the floor. Her eyebrows, lifted halfway into her hairline, seemed to ask, *Where is your courage now, little girl?*

Good question.

If I could at least get into the Council room, I might be able to defend myself to, or get myself imprisoned by, the Council Members who were there. Even that would be better than making it this far just to flounder in the hallway with the housekeeper. Better to die in pride than wallow in regret.

I just had to get past her.

"I can only address my business to the people who actually understand what I am here to say," I finally concluded, turning my nose up in a queenly move that would have made Priscilla applaud. "I'm not sure a servant would know my purpose."

Her anger deepened to murderous intent in a flash.

"I see," she said, tightening with scorn. "Well then, let's see you prove yourself to the Council."

I fought the urge to run away and leave it all behind me. Instead I straightened my neck to a pristine tightness.

"Yes, that will suffice. Thank you."

My dread doubled into a sickening pit at the bottom of my stomach as I followed her. What had I just done? The meeting could have started and the doors sealed with a protective spell. If someone from the outside tried to listen or cast a spell to eavesdrop, they'd only hear the false drone of a very boring meeting in the background, one that wasn't real.

If the doors were already sealed on this meeting, they'd have to break the seal to admit me. My stomach committed to a terrifying nosedive. I wasn't sure what the ramifications of breaking the seal were, but I knew they wouldn't help my cause.

I trailed a few steps back, walking in her long shadow down hallways dotted by paintings of wrinkled faces and landscapes, statues, and grand tapestries until we came to a set of closed double doors. The woman flung the doors open and stepped aside. Her face lifted into a delighted sneer.

"I hope they understand all you have to say."

A crowd of nearly thirty adults sat around a sprawling table; they all turned to face me at the same moment. Although I didn't know what to expect, their stoic, eerie silence wasn't it.

The room looked similar to the rest of the sprawling estate. Cold slate walls, a glittering chandelier with tiny candles that reflected light off the crystals, an oak table, and maroon banners. Skinny windows with shiny panes of glass filled the far wall.

An older woman in an elegant black dress stood directly across from me. She had short silver hair and biting eyes the color of cinnamon. Her imposing bearing and the rigid lines of her face gave her a determined, straightforward look. Here was a Council Member I didn't want to mess with.

"Who are you?" she demanded.

"I-I'm here on business," I said, taking a step forward. The doors chugged to a close behind me.

"I didn't ask what you were here for. I asked your name."

"I know what you asked," I said, hoping the trembling in my hands didn't transmit to my voice. The doors weren't sealed by magic yet. I would not say my name.

"Oh," she lifted an eyebrow. "You're just going to ignore it then?"

Several witches stood near the fireplace, the rest sitting in plush red chairs. They all gave me the same harpooning glare from over their wine glasses.

"The butler allowed me in," I offered instead, trying to veer away from further questions. My voice sounded less certain now. The faces surrounding me were not familiar. Where was Miss Mabel? I didn't dare look too far away from the commanding woman at the center to find out.

"The only reason they let you enter is because you have a circlus on your wrist," she said. Her voice was deep and succinct, and her indifference chilling. The way her glare bore down, when taken with her gritty voice, terrified me. "Strangers are usually killed on the spot."

"I know."

"The only reason you're alive right now is because you're young."

"But I'm not a stranger," I said in a pitiful attempt to elevate my drowning chances. "I've been in this Network my whole life."

"You're a stranger in this room!" she thundered. "Obviously you don't understand how suspicious you are. The only conclusion I can draw is that someone sent you here to spy on our Esbat. Do you agree?"

Although the sharp look in her eyes raked through me like a hot set of talons, I felt a thrill all the same. *Spy on our Esbat, eh? How about you see how it feels to look like a fool.*

"No, I do not agree," I replied in a calm voice, looking at the un-sealed doors with a deliberate gaze. "I never mentioned an Esbat. I'm here for business."

A few shocked expressions passed from participant to participant, but they remained silent. Whether they reacted to my cheekiness or to her fault in mentioning the purpose of the meeting with un-sealed doors, I didn't know. Either way, I knew drowning when I felt it. When the woman's face took on a perturbed, assessing stare, my chance at the Esbat mark disintegrated. Survival or occasional visitation from my mother while in the dungeons was the best I could hope for now. I curled my toes in again, hoping they didn't peep out the edges of my dress.

The woman glared at me for several minutes with regal superiority.

"I know your face," she said. "I've seen it before."

"Perhaps out in the Network?" I suggested.

"No, that's not it." she said with a peevish snap, then shifted the conversation so suddenly it took me a moment to catch up. "I will ask you once more. What is your name?"

I shook my head. "No."

"No? You will stand before all of us and refuse a command from one of your superiors? Would you like to give your refusal to the High Priestess instead? We can arrange that."

What little ground I had left rapidly slipped away, leaving me on precarious footing. Defending myself would only damage my chances further. I already faced failure and a thirteen-year sentence with Miss Mabel. A movement across the room caught my eye, and I looked up to see my beloved teacher standing near a painting of a peacock. My heart sped up when I noticed her grin.

She enjoyed this. Today was no longer just a test for the Esbat mark. It was a battle for the next thirteen years of my life.

"Answer the question or we will send you to the High Priestess," the woman demanded. "She won't give you a chance to explain yourself."

I hesitated as the two of us locked eyes. Something didn't feel right.

"There's nothing to explain," I said, trying to buy a few moments to think this out.

"Don't waste our time," she barked. "Tell us your name or we'll have the Guardians come in, take you into the dungeon for a few uncomfortable nights, and you can discuss it with the High Priestess then."

A metallic bracelet on the woman's wrist caught my attention with a gleam of light. An ancient language covered the front that I could just decipher.

SAC ERO DOS SUM MUS

I caught my gasp before it came out. I'd seen those words in the Esbat book. I knew what they meant, what the bracelet meant.

Nothing is ever what it seems.

My next move was a wild guess that risked my life, and my grandmother's—a chance decision that Leda would not approve. If it failed, Miss Mabel would own me until my twenty-eighth birthday. Grandmother, and possibly my mother, would die without me.

Given how close I felt to the edge of sanity, my mind seemed surprisingly clear. Every eye focused on me. Miss Mabel chuckled to herself as she tipped her head back and downed the last of her wine.

"I already have discussed it with the High Priestess." I moved into a low curtsy. "Or should I say, Your Highness?"

Searing Pains

A familiar, searing pain grew in my right wrist.

"You are smart for one so young," the High Priestess declared in a dramatically altered tone of voice, although she was still far from kind. "When your teacher suggested this as a method of testing you for your mark, I reluctantly agreed. I didn't think it would work, but obviously you did well."

Our eyes met and silence fell. The burning faded from my wrist, and I glanced down to see the two triangles of the unity symbol tattooed within the circlus.

"Well?" she asked. "Don't you have anything to say?"

"No, Your Highness," I responded, realizing I might need to atone for my lack of respect. "Except to thank you for the honor of your participation in this test." Just for show, I added another curtsy. When a few of my toes peeked out, I quickly straightened.

Her eyes narrowed to thin slits.

"You're a little impudent, aren't you?" she murmured, and then paused. "Yes, you are. You've got a bit of vinegar beneath that calm expression, not a very attractive trait for a young girl. Especially with that hair of yours. Don't you wear it in buns anymore?"

I resisted the urge to reach for it, imagining barbs from the thorn bushes hanging down my back. Certainly not how a respectable young girl should meet the leader of her Network, but I couldn't change what had happened. Camille would shake me when she found out. Miss Scarlett's lips would press into that disappointed line.

You only get one chance to introduce yourself to the High Priestess.

And I botched mine very thoroughly, to no great surprise. I had the condolence of knowing both curtsies passed, however, and took strength in that. Perhaps Miss Scarlett wouldn't condemn me to an eternity of etiquette lessons.

"Yes, Your Highness," I said for lack of anything else, curling my toes ever further. I nearly stood on them, and my joints smarted with pain. "The bun gave me a headache on my way over, and I forgot to replace it."

A long, willowy man at her side interrupted with a whisper I couldn't hear. He had a drippy nose and red eyes. The High Priestess waved him off.

"Yes, Donald, please seal the doors."

A clicking, whirring sound came from behind me, then swept through the room with a broad, methodical stroke. A burst of air moved past and all fell silent again.

"Go sit with your teacher," she said to me with the same dismissive wave. "We will now begin."

Relieved to be out of the center of the room, I turned to the right and walked to the end of the table with small steps that kept my feet within my hem. A woman with graying auburn hair met my eyes and smiled with the corner of her lips. Her eyes flickered to the floor and back to mine.

Horrified, I looked away as if we'd never made eye contact in the first place.

Miss Mabel smiled as I sat in the chair next to hers. The empty wine glass sparkled at her fingertips.

"Welcome," she whispered, a gleam in her eyes. "You did marvelous, throwing that error back in her face. I would have given you the Esbat mark for that."

I didn't say anything. The wine refilled itself in her glass when I sat down and pulled a roll of parchment, a jar of white ink, and the peacock feather out of my bag. I wondered if the wine made Miss Mabel a little too bold. It was a risky thing to say with the High Priestess so near.

The High Priestess focused her gaze on someone to the right. I made the assumption that Donald was the High Priestess's Assistant, as he constantly fluttered through papers, muttering to himself and watching her every move.

"As I was saying before we were interrupted, the High Priest could not attend this Esbat. He is sick at home today. Please do an invocation and blessing for healing on his behalf. Melinda from the Eastern Coven will address us first. Have the problems arising from the flood last month been resolved?"

On the other side of the room, a middle-aged woman with faded red hair and a concerned expression stood.

"Yes, Your Highness. The support team of builders from the Network rebuilt the bridges and restored supplies to our farmers. Thank you for your assistance."

"I'm glad it was sufficient."

Melinda sat down.

"Mr. Crabtree from Tillan's Cove Coven," the High Priestess said without missing a beat

I started to outline the events as the people in the room spoke, trying to commit their faces to my memory. It didn't take long to realize that most of the people were Coven leaders, here to present their communities' issues to the Network. Their assistants sat off to the side, and I imagined Leda there one day, with her pale face and high opinions.

There were people who never spoke at all. They lingered in the shadowy background with no particular purpose. Most of them looked to be in their thirties, but a few were middle aged. It wasn't until I counted ten of them that I realized they made up the Council of Leaders. Like Miss Mabel, they hid their true ages. Papa had told me stories regarding several of the Council Members, many of whom were at least ninety. I wondered about the High Priestess. Why didn't she hide her true age? Or did she?

One by one, the Coven leaders stood and reported their business. Unemployment in one Coven. Disappearance of a farmer and his family in another. Notice of a runaway school boy. Parents dissatisfied with the education system. A deception spell gone awry. There were at least forty covens in the Network, but not all were represented tonight.

The High Priestess called on Miss Mabel. Instead of standing as the others did, she remained in her seat with a subtle gleam of defiance.

"The Eastern Letum Wood Coven has no issues to report," Miss Mabel stated in a business-like tone. "I met with the lower leaders prior to coming. They voiced no concerns."

The High Priestess's eyes narrowed almost imperceptibly, but she accepted it with a nod.

"Very well. Bickers Mill Coven . . ."

Darkness surrounded the school by the time I returned. The warm light of candles dancing in the windows illuminated the school, defying a black band of vapor that shielded Letum Wood.

"Thank you, Augustus," I said in a weary voice as I exited the carriage. "Have a good night."

He nodded and drove off, his eyes a bit bloodshot from his time at the pub if his jovial singing on the road home gave any indication. The carriage evaporated into the fog with the slow plod of the horse, leaving me alone. I stayed there, breathing in the night until the chill seeped through my clothes and forced me inside.

I slipped through the hall, absorbed with thoughts of my grandmother. An eagerness like I'd never known gripped me. I wanted the curse removed tonight, this moment. Yesterday, even. Better to spare her as much pain as I could.

Despite the thrill of exultant joy hovering under my skin, a heavy exhaustion weighed down my legs when I started up the spiral staircase. I slowed down. It was late. The grandfather clock gonged below, announcing eleven o'clock. A new black rug ran the length of the stairs, as did bunches of black ribbon wreaths the students must have made for a celebration. Samhain must be coming up soon.

Every floor I passed was quiet, the sounds of life reduced to subtle creaks and the quiet shuffles of last-minute bedtime rituals. I envied them and didn't know why. Maybe it was because I wished to be asleep, my fatigued eyes drooping and weary.

Not yet. Grandmother awaited.

A single light illuminated the space underneath Miss Mabel's door. I held my breath and stood on the landing, listening. The shuffle of two voices came from her private bedroom. A giggle, then a rakish growl.

The throaty tones of a man's voice.

I quickly cast a concealment spell, intrigued. It fell over me in an icy rush. My body blended in with the background, becoming nothing more than floorboards and stone. As long as I stayed motionless, no one would see me. If I moved, they'd see ripples in the air, like heat waves. Once the spell was complete, I crept forward, pressing my back against the wall. It wasn't long before Miss Mabel's dulcet words met my ears.

"Oh, how you make me laugh!"

The same low growl repeated, followed by a chiding reprimand.

"Stop that," she said. "I don't want you drawing attention up here. Bianca will return any minute now. We can't afford discovery, can we?"

Fabric rustled. My heart thudded in my chest, drumming out a frightened rhythm. Who was the man?

"Then tell me about the Esbat," the unknown voice said. "Did I miss anything important?"

I didn't know his voice. He must be a Coven leader if he had missed the Esbat.

"Nothing but the same old complaints. Mildred looked horrid in her dress. I don't know how you put up with her every day."

The puzzle pieces of this unknown mystery man began moving together like the slow movement of a clock.

Tick.

"I try not to see her every day," he said in a wry drawl. "Did your Assistant earn the mark?"

The eagerness in his voice sent a chill through my body.

"Of course," Miss Mabel's voice purred. "As if you ever doubted my judgment, Briton."

Tock.

The High Priest. Miss Mabel was having an affair with the High

Priest. My nails gripped the chinks in between stones in the wall, anchoring me, reminding me that I wasn't imagining things.

"Did she really pass?" he asked.

Miss Mabel moved slightly, and her voice became easier to hear. She let out a long sigh, as if she savored every molecule of air.

"Yes, and that's not the most exciting thing," she said.

"What is?"

"She transported."

My blood ran cold, like little spears of ice attacking from the inside, paralyzing every muscle in my body. She knew. I didn't know how she'd discovered it, but she knew.

"A sixteen-year-old?"

Miss Mabel made a noise low in her throat.

"I don't believe it," he said.

"Believe it. I watched her. It's how she avoided the Guardians at the very beginning, just as I thought. It was a last minute adjustment to my plan but a good one."

The sound of pacing footsteps jolted me. I slid to the floor, my knees too weak to hold my body upright. This was not good. Not good at all. This evening was changing from bad to nightmare on a course I couldn't stop. I'd never felt so helpless in my life.

Reckless. My desperation tonight made me reckless. Leda's words haunted me.

Do you ever think before you act?

No, clearly I didn't, and now I'd pay.

"That doesn't prove anything," he said.

"It proves she's got courage, like I thought. Talent, too. She thinks quick on her feet. Her homework is atrocious, but her magic is strong. That's what really counts."

A silence fell that twisted my insides to shreds.

"She's capable yes, but will she have enough power?" he asked.

"I think so. I think she has a great deal more power than she lets on," Miss Mabel said in a voice I had to strain to hear. "Or knows about yet."

"How do you know she's strong enough for the task?"

"We'll find out soon," she said.

"What are you planning?"

"Nothing too extraordinary. I'm just going to test her a little, see if she can handle it." An innocent tone, as if she spoke of summertime or flowers. My chest rose and fell in desperate gasps, making me light-headed. I bowed my head into my knees and screwed my eyes shut, forcing my breathing to slow.

"Wonderful," he said. I could tell he meant it. "How?"

"I'm going to see how much control she has over her power when she experiences intense emotions. Once we turn those on, the power doesn't turn off."

"Ah," he said. "Pain?"

"No," she scoffed. "Something infinitely stronger."

I could hear the smile in his voice. "You're going to make her angry."

"Yes," she giggled. "Very angry."

I pressed my fingertips to my lips to prevent them from emitting a horrified cry. The High Priest's heavier steps followed. When I heard their voices again they were hushed, as if they spoke from an embrace. I could hear the individual words no more.

The sound of footsteps came from the spiral stairs, startling me. I shot to my feet, stumbling toward my bedroom with an out-of-my-mind pulse of fear. I had to get out of there, away from the suffocating evil of their words, away from the risk of getting caught.

Somehow in my hurry my foot caught on the loop of my bag. I bobbled, bouncing back and forth, trying to recover, but it only wrapped my ankles tighter together. My arms flailed as I reached for the wall to no avail. I shot forward, landing with a leaden thud, the floorboards skimming my face and chin.

The sound rang out through the attic, freezing time. The air was completely still. I held my breath.

Miss Mabel's door creaked open, spilling a shaft of light onto my body.

Wasted

My lungs burned. Tears stung my eyes from the fall, threatening to drip onto the floor. I didn't risk looking at the rest of my body to make sure the spell held.

"Sorry to bother you this late, Mabel," Miss Scarlett said. "I finished the paperwork for the third-years' Network Mark applications. They want only your signature."

It took all my control not to move when Miss Scarlett entered the attic, announcing herself with her inflexible voice. Her quiet footsteps were almost silent, as if she hovered just above the ground and only made the motions of walking to make it look real. My already sinking luck took on more water.

In only a few steps Miss Scarlett would trip over me.

Miss Mabel took another step forward. I felt the floorboard beneath my right foot shift from her weight.

"Did you fall, Scarlett?"

Her slow words and low tone made my heart plummet. Why hadn't I just minded my own business and gone to bed? Instead, I was seconds away from discovery, sprawled on the floor like a rug.

"Yes," Miss Scarlett stopped moving toward me. Her feet were so close it made my eyes cross. "I tripped on the stairs on my way up."

I blinked. Had Miss Scarlett just lied?

There had been a noise that caught my attention before I fell, but the idea of Miss Scarlett tripping on a stair seemed ludicrous. I'd never seen her stiff, upright spine bend.

"I see," Miss Mabel murmured with another step into the hallway.

The floorboard groaned in protest as she stepped to the left of my foot. I didn't need to see her face to know her eyes flickered around the room. The air felt so unfriendly I could almost smell her unease. "Are you sure? It seemed much closer than that."

"Quite sure," she said in a clipped tone, readjusting her shoulders as if fixing her dress would rebuff her embarrassment at being human like the rest of us. "It's getting late. Here are the papers. I trust you'll send them once you're done. Please excuse me. There are a few first-years just below you that I heard giggling. I would like to remind them of the rules before they go to bed."

I wondered if adhering the rules lent comfort to her ruffled pride.

Several scrolls tied in a bundle floated from Miss Scarlett's hands. Another stretch of silence that seemed like an eternity. My heart would give me away, surely. Couldn't they hear it slam against the floor?

"Good night, Scarlett," Miss Mabel finally said.

Miss Scarlett was already on her way down the stairs but stopped to ask over her shoulder, "Did Bianca pass the Esbat mark?"

No, no, no! I wanted to scream. Any mention of me would make Miss Mabel suspicious over my delayed return.

"Yes," Miss Mabel drawled. She hadn't moved an inch. My lungs burned again. "She passed. She should have been home by now."

Miss Scarlett nodded once.

"Good night, Mabel."

She started down the stairs. Even after the last sign of her presence had faded, Miss Mabel remained, waiting. Finally, when I wasn't sure I could stand it any longer, she shuffled backward. The light from the doorway slowly gathered together, narrowing into a thin stream that evaporated into black.

Had I imagined it, or did Miss Scarlett's eyes meet mine when she walked down the stairs?

Exhausted, I pressed my cheek to the cold floor, let out a deep breath, and closed my eyes.

The night lasted several eternities, dragging every minute as if it were a heavy club. I willed morning to come. Maybe the light would shine, illuminating the blackest shadows, the midnight gargoyles that I could feel breathing down my neck in the darkness. When I slept, it was for moments, filled with dreams of the High Priest, Miss Mabel, and the High Priestess all standing over me, telling me my birthday came the next day.

I tossed and turned, wondering what the overheard conversation meant, replaying it all in my head, mixing it with my dreams. Miss Mabel's giggle, the low voice of the High Priest, Miss Scarlett's eyes on me as she left. Snatches of phrases haunted me like the wail of wraiths.

Powerful emotions.

Stronger than pain.

Very angry.

I hovered between consciousness and sleep, trapped in the realm of dreams that dragged me into the depths with the demons, the fear, the unknown. I knew I wasn't awake, just as I wasn't resting. I was stuck in the middle, unable to get out.

I jerked out of the clutch of the monsters with a gasp, tearing myself away.

Several seconds passed before I realized something had awoken me. Sweat coated my skin. My heart fluttered like the wings of a hummingbird; thin, thready, fast. The black lingered outside, but I knew it was closer to morning than midnight by the short chimes of the distant grandfather clock in the library.

A soft, almost imperceptible tap sounded on my door.

I sat up. "Who is it?" I whispered. It came again.

My heart stuttered when I scuttled out of bed, pulled open my door, and saw Leda and Camille huddled outside, casting nervous glances down the hall.

"What are you doing?"

Leda quieted me with a violent wave of her hand and motioned to Miss Mabel's room with a jerk of her head. She grabbed Camille and shoved her inside. The moment I shut the door, Camille threw her arms around me.

"Are you all right?" she whispered without bothering to pull away, her cheek pressed to mine. "We've been so worried all night."

Leda peeled her back.

"Give her some air, Camille. Why am I always pulling you off her? Camille is right, Bianca. It hasn't looked good for you tonight," she said, turning to me. "I thought we better come check on how the Esbat went."

"What did you see?" I asked, breathless. Leda shrugged.

"Gray."

I wasn't sure if it was relief or fear that I felt in my stomach.

"Are you okay?" Camille insisted again, grabbing my hand with a comforting squeeze. "I've been so nervous for you all night! I couldn't sleep. It's good to see you here safe! I wanted to bring you some warm tea, but Leda said Miss Celia would be up soon."

"Let's hear it," Leda said, her eyes on me.

"Better sit down," I whispered, grateful beyond words that they had come. "It might take a while to explain."

They listened without interruption. Camille sat down halfway through, her knees wobbly. By the time I finished, Leda stood at the window with her hands behind her back, her jaw tight.

"She's rotten," Camille whispered. "Wicked and rotten, and I can't believe it."

"I can," Leda muttered.

"What do you think Miss Mabel is going to do?"

A dark feeling crept over me just thinking about it, as if saying her name brought the fog from Letum Wood into my room.

"I don't know," I whispered. "It could be anything."

"She wants to make you angry," Camille whispered, her face scrunched in thought. "That means she'll do something bad, or try to take something away that means a lot to you."

"You're a big comfort," I muttered.

I didn't like the direction she took because I had already been there myself. Leda leaned back against the wall, her arms folded across her chest. Her white nightgown peeked out from beneath her ratty scarlet robe. The big toe of her left foot stuck out from a slipper that looked too small by several sizes.

"Do you think she'll stop you from going to the Samhain Festival?" Camille asked. "It's tomorrow. I'd be angry if she tried to stop me from going, especially with all the food that's going to be there. Miss Celia is making pumpkin frosting for her cinnamon buns."

Attending a feast that celebrated death didn't sound appealing to me in the first place, not when I fought against my own impending demise every day. I wondered if I could use Miss Mabel as an excuse not to attend.

"I don't think she'll try that," I said, my neck emitting a pop when I tilted back to stare at the sloping ceiling. "Think a bit . . . bigger."

"That's not the only thing to worry about," Leda said. "Miss Mabel obviously has plans for you. That would scare me more than getting a little angry. Whatever she's up to is not going to be good."

"Would she give you a bad grade for no reason?" Camille asked, looking hopeful. A loopy giggle threatened my composure. Miss Mabel worked on a scale ranging from ruthless to inhuman. Grades weren't her kind of vindictive delight. I wondered if Camille spoke of her biggest fear instead of mine.

"No," I said as Leda rolled her eyes. "It would be far worse than that."

"Whatever Miss Mabel ends up doing, you'll have to be careful," Leda said. "She's going to make it hurt."

Her words were haunting. I pulled my knees to my chest to ward off a sudden chill.

"I know," I whispered.

We all fell silent, caught up in the ghostly swirls of the unknown future.

I ventured into the classroom the next morning to find Miss Mabel perusing a book. She slammed it shut as I walked in and shot me a smile. Eight or nine stacks of publications sat on my desk and the floor around it, occluding the whole workspace. Seeing my eyes on them, Miss Mabel swept her arm over the piles.

"Your new curriculum," she said. "Since you did so well on your first mark, I thought we'd jump right into your next one. Don't worry. I know now that you're awful at homework, so I'm going to give you a month to read all these. We'll play off your greater strength of using magic more than books this time."

The spine of one book read, *Contrivance Curses and Their Uses Today.* Another book I'd never heard of was called, *The Complete Anthology of Dark Curses and Hexes.* Confused, I read the titles again to make sure they were correct. Contrivance curses were rooted in a rare kind of magic the Network didn't allow. Miss Mabel ran her finger down one stack of encyclopedias with a look of innocent detachment.

"I thought you'd like to get the Advanced Curses and Hexes mark." The tone of her voice suggested that, even if I wasn't interested, I didn't have a choice.

"Advanced Curses and Hexes?" I asked before I could stop my-self. Another rare mark, one that flirted with lines of appropriateness. Approval to teach it was difficult to gain. I hadn't known it was an option.

Then again, she had a special *in* with the High Priest. Her warm bed and base desires could probably get courses far darker than this approved.

"Of course. It's always good to know how to curse someone, Bianca. One never knows when one might need that skill."

Her eyes flashed with another little smile.

"I have Network approval?" I asked, just to be contrary. After what I heard last night, I'd snarl and snap my teeth at her if it wouldn't make her suspicious. It felt good, mixing fear with a bit of courage, making me feel like I stood up to her, when really I depended on her for my life.

"You let me deal with them." A glint of something in her voice made me feel cold. "You'll have bigger things to worry about. We'll start immediately."

Deal with. Right. That's why she had the High Priest over last night.

She walked her fingers along several books as she spoke, peering at me over the top of one stack. A book lined with purple leather shot out of a nearby column and fell into my arms. It hit with a thud, taking the wind out of me.

"I want you to read about hexes and complete these papers. When your overview is finished, we'll start practicing."

My eyes widened. No one put the Advanced Curses and Hexes mark into action. The normal class practiced a few little hexes but not the higher levels. The potent curses could maim, or not respond to a counter-curse if executed wrong. This situation was escalating into realms best not explored. Even Papa wouldn't have expected this from me, and he challenged me in everything.

"Practice?" I repeated.

"Yes, of course," she said. "This is the advanced class, isn't it? The Network needs witches who understand how and why these curses are used. That way they can track down the people who use them. If you don't know how they work, how can you be of any use?"

"They practice them in a controlled situation," I said. Miss Mabel rolled her eyes.

"Yes, well, this is a controlled situation, isn't it? Now, I suggest you stop questioning my decisions."

I pretended like I didn't hear the bite in her tone. Who would I curse? I could think of a few volunteers: Priscilla, Jade, and Stephany to name a few. But no, I wouldn't even do that to them. So how would I practice? Ignoring my unease, Miss Mabel handed me a scroll of parchment. I suppressed the urge to ask if she could be my test subject, imagining how lovely it would feel to hit her in the face with an eternal wart curse.

"Miss Mabel, can I talk to you about—"

"Memorize these hexes, answer the questions, and prepare to demonstrate them tomorrow morning."

"Yes, but my—"

"There's an assigned list of reading on the board. Start on them. Good luck."

"What about my grandmother?"

The words exploded from my mouth, forcing themselves on her, leaving me speechless in their wake. I waited, my breathing stalled, for her response, looking between her perfect sapphire eyes.

Puzzled, she tilted her head to one side.

"What are you talking about?"

I blinked several times.

"Our agreement said you would free my grandmother from her curse if I got the Esbat mark in three weeks."

Her expression of innocence was too perfect to be real. When her confused stare deepened, an uneasy feeling began to spread through me, like the slow creep of water.

"Whatever are you talking about?"

"My grandmother's curse," I replied, an edge of desperation in my tone. "The contract we signed—"

"Are you talking about your contract with me? Because that doesn't have anything to do with the Esbat."

"Yes, it does."

"Your contract is an agreement to work with me through the duration of your education here. If you want to take a look at my records, that is all I have in my file."

"We both signed the agreement to free my grandmother!" I cried. "Here, in the classroom, when we signed the Assistant contract. If you don't remove the curse, she'll die!"

I shut my mouth with a snap as realization dawned on me.

Something infinitely stronger than pain.

Her eyes narrowed into devious slits.

"Then bring your copy of this agreement forward, and I'll have a look at it."

My heart pounded as she extended her hand, waiting. I didn't have a copy of the agreement, and she knew it.

"Or you can bring forward a witness that saw both of us sign the contract," she offered. "We can do it either way."

The cloying tone of her voice made me sick, and I wanted to throw up. No witness. I had no witness.

Unable to bear it, I looked away and tried to get control of my breathing. No. Of all the things to do, this was the worst of all. I'd never even thought of getting my own copy.

All that work, all those sleepless nights, wasted.

Very angry.

"I guess even the prodigy Bianca can't anticipate every test. Poor darling, don't you know that everyone dies eventually?"

It seemed to press on me, the disappointment, horror, and regret. Despite my luck in the past, I managed to fail the most important test.

"Miss Mabel, I don't—"

"I've done you a favor, and one day you'll thank me. Just let this be a personal reminder you'll never forget. When you decide to bargain for your own life or others, you should always have a witness. When negotiating, never leave without a signed copy of your own to prove it."

She drifted to the hall, humming softly.

"Let's not make any more bargains until you're in a better position to do so, hmm? Prove yourself by earning the three marks I have planned. We'll talk about your own life then."

Panic filled my chest as she disappeared. The purple book fell to the ground, and I followed, landing on my knees, trying without success to calm myself enough to make sense of the situation. As soon as my mind settled, the truth hit with chilling force.

Grandmother's health would continue to deteriorate until the curse took her life. My failure to anticipate Miss Mabel's deceitful nature would contribute to my grandmother's death. Isadora's aged voice flickered through my mind.

Don't underestimate her.

Moving as if blind, I groped for my room and shut the door behind me. As soon as I was alone, I pressed my back against the door and slid to the ground.

I buried my face in my hands and let loose the dangerous pressure expanding in my chest. It flowed in a great current of sobs until my shoulders shook and my eyes hurt from pressing my arms into them to try to stop the tears. But it wouldn't work, so I fell into the solitude and would not be comforted.

Samhain

P,

I need to talk to you. Sometime. Sometime soon. It's very important.

B

The messenger paper flew out the window with a flutter and disappeared into the chilly sky. I stared after it. My words read bare and pathetic, but I didn't know how else to write. I'd racked my brain all day. *Miss Mabel is planning on using me in an evil, nefarious plot, but I don't know what it is yet* or *Miss Mabel went back on her word to remove the curse from Grandmother* didn't convey it well. Besides, there was no telling when he would get it or what he could do. Papa should only be a last resort.

Desperation is an ugly thing. I thought, scrutinizing the spot where the paper disappeared. *Sorry, Papa. I hope this doesn't distract you too much.*

A squeal from downstairs startled me out of my thoughts. I quickly shut the window and crept to the door, grateful for any distraction. The giggling of first-years wound up the spiral staircase. A draft under the door brought the scent of cinnamon and cloves into my room.

"Bianca! Get out here!"

Camille whispered my name seconds before she grabbed the knob and shoved the door open. It slammed into my nose, sending me backward with a cry.

"Ow!"

Leda quickly spilled into the room next to her and shut the door behind them. Camille dropped to her knees on the floor with me, where I held the end of my nose and tried to clear my watery eyes.

"I'm so sorry, Bianca! I didn't know you were right there," Camille said, but her fervor died down in confusion. "Why were you standing right there?"

I waved her flapping hands away and got to my feet. My nose ached, but the stinging had started to subside.

"I thought I heard noises."

"Sorry, Bianca, I saw it happen after it was too late or I would have stopped her," Leda said, dropping onto my bed and not appearing all that remorseful. "You really need to decorate. Even I think the bare walls are getting depressing."

"It's the Samhain festival," Camille said, motioning to the door. "We've got to go or we'll miss the judging."

"Judging?"

"Yes, Michelle helped me make an apple pie for one of her projects. Mine is up against Brianna's in the Samhain Best of the Feast competition, and I've got to win!"

Camille stamped her foot in determination.

"I thought you loved Brianna?" I asked.

"Yes," she said. "But not when goodies are on the line. I'm going to win! Let's go."

"You made a pie?" I asked, skeptical. There were days I wouldn't trust Camille's attention span to differentiate sugar and salt appropriately.

"Yes! Now let's go, or I won't give you any."

Which wouldn't be the worst thing, Leda's face seemed to say.

Samhain, the yearly feast for the dead. How had I forgotten? I'd seen the decorations every time I went to the dining room for days now. Hollowed out pumpkins littered the school, lighting the way up the stairs with candles sticking out of the middle, and cluttering the tables in the library. Miss Celia made a special wax candle that smelled like allspice when it burned, so the aroma of pumpkin pie permeated the school. Gold foil tablecloths decorated the dining room at breakfast, and the broad green leaves of pumpkin vines grew along every fireplace mantel, twining themselves around the staircases.

"Oh, that's right," I said. "I forgot about the feast."

Camille shot me a look that made it clear she didn't think that was possible. Who would forget a feast? Leda cast an eye on the piles of books that scattered across my desk, studying *Contrivance Curses and Their Use Today* with a dark look. She turned her gaze to the floor, fading into her future-searching haze.

"Small wonder you even remember where you are." Camille looked at the books on my desk. "You've got half the library in your closet up here. Now come on!" she tugged on my hand impatiently. "We've got to go. If I'm not present I forfeit the reward."

"What is the reward?"

"Immortal glory and prestige for the rest of my life!"

"A basket of baked goodies to satisfy Camille's insatiable love for food," Leda said, earning a proper scowl from Camille, who jerked her away from the pile of books and produced a black crepe hair ribbon as we made it to the bottom of the iron stairs.

"Here," Camille said, handing it to me. "This will be all you need. At least you'll be wearing black to welcome the spirits of the dead to our feast on their behalf. No one will care if you're still in your school clothes. Besides, no one expects you to dress up anyway."

"They'll just be happy if you wear shoes," Leda said with a wry grin. I acted as if I didn't hear her reference to the first match, grateful she didn't know about my slip-up at the Esbat.

Leda wore a black dress, similar to Camille's in style, but obviously different in execution. One sleeve hit the elbow, the other ran to her wrist. Gaudy black and gold sequins scattered across the front in random array. Camille's looked more organized, but not by much. The sequins had been traded for large gold beads; the skirt's layers of sheer material fluttered as she ran down the stairs and came up just a bit too short behind the knee, something Miss Scarlett's eyes would not miss. I had a feeling the mistake came from poor planning, and not a girlish intent to display her legs. Both dresses had to be Camille's work, as I doubted Leda cared about something like how to thread a needle when hunger still existed.

"Miss Celia's already put the crossed brooms above the main door to signal the start of the feast," Camille said. "We're late!"

Three second-years on the main stairwell ahead of us wore equally outlandish black dresses, regaled with complicated shawls they had knitted in their free time. One sported a golden tiara. The others wore gold earrings.

"You look great in gold, Leda," I said, motioning with a cheery grin to the uneven hem of gold ribbon around the edge of her skirt.

Leda glowered at me as only Leda could.

"She does, doesn't she?" Camille said with a look of pride. "I thought about adding some more, but she said she wouldn't wear it. I've been working on it for days now. It's part of the reason I'm still failing Geometry."

The sound of the celebration met us as we descended into the soaring entryway. A few third-years bustled by, slipping out the side door and into the yard in gauzy black dresses sent from home. They didn't have poor attempts at elegance attached to them, like most of the first-years. Instead, they opted for a more alluring, refined look with sleek skirts and shimmering necklaces, easily upstaging the younger girls. Hundreds of candles floated in the air, illuminating the undersides of the trees that the fading sun couldn't reach. It created an eerie, death-glow kind of feeling.

Michelle and Rebecca worked with Miss Celia at the tables, frantically setting out all the utensils and plates. Food flew from the kitchen and out to the yard, descending into their appropriate spots. Miss Celia directed them as if they rained from heaven.

"Wow," Camille whispered, her eyes growing wider. "This is amazing! Look, they brought in Miss Jasmine. She's the most talented Diviner in this part of Letum Wood. Maybe she'll tell me about my future husband!"

Her voice turned into a shrill squeal. She charged forward, running into the group of girls gathered around Miss Jasmine and disappearing into the sea of black and gold fabric.

I gazed around, trying to hide my sudden flood of nervous insecurity. My school uniform stuck out like a specter in this sea of ebony. With everyone's black dresses twirling and moving in the crowd, my only tie to the group was the fragile hair ribbon still in my hand.

This is what you get when you set yourself apart. My attempts at self-soothing had little effect. *You can't save yourself from Miss Mabel and be like the rest of the students.*

The curse took away something I'd never have the chance to be a part of again. This girlish phase of friendship when dress up, in whatever form, was just another part of life.

Leda, as if reading my mind, grabbed the ribbon and pulled at my hair.

"Don't worry about them. You need the break today, after Miss Mabel pulled a trick like that."

I'd been too distraught to explain the disappointment of Miss Mabel's betrayal, but somehow Leda had known. She'd stopped me before I explained with a shake of her head, and I never had to say a word. Despite the lingering depression of being nothing more than a puppet for one of the most evil witches in Antebellum, the jovial mood of the yard did have a buoyant effect.

Leda tugged my dark hair into a ponytail at my neck. Priscilla and Jade weren't far away, surrounded by most of the third-years. Priscilla wore a sparkling black dress that hung from her shoulders to the floor, unlike the first-year dresses that cut off around the knees. By comparison, she made everyone look like the schoolgirls they were. Most students couldn't take their eyes off her, though their expressions said that they hated her for making them look so young and insignificant.

"Let's just have a good time," Leda said, tightening my bow with a vicious yank that made me grimace. I wasn't sure which of the two of us she was trying to convince. "Eat some pumpkin spice almonds and apple slices with caramel, and then go where we can't hear Priscilla and Jade laughing so much. It's nauseating."

Once she finished, we went to the table to peruse the piles of goodies, where Miss Celia shouted directions to a new piece of silver.

"Drat that platter!" she cried. "I wish Mabel hadn't insisted on getting rid of the old ones. They always did just what I wanted. I'm not familiar enough with the new trays. That makes them unreliable. Oh, dear. Grab that end, Rebecca!"

The round silver platter, leaves etched into its sides, dropped to the table with a clatter, spilling steaming cider onto the white table-cloth and upsetting a ceramic tray of pumpkin swirl cake.

Michelle approached with another tray loaded down with sugar-roasted cranberries, and I gave her a friendly smile.

"Merry meet, Michelle."

"Merry meet," she whispered, averting her eyes at first, but then looking back with a smile. "I hope you're enjoying the fun."

I gazed at the melee.

"Yes," I said without conviction. "It seems great."

Miss Celia let out a bellow from across the yard, and Michelle started like a terrified deer.

"Michelle!"

"I have to go!" she said, and her burly form moved with surprising speed, arriving just in time to stop a heaping tray of Miss Celia's fresh cinnamon rolls from toppling over and rolling across the yard. Leda handed me a cup of cider.

"Michelle moves pretty fast."

We stood on the edges of the party, feeling as awkward as I knew we looked.

"Care to talk about that stack of books Miss Mabel has you studying?" Leda asked. The troubled storm returned to her eyes.

"Not really," I said, but it wouldn't matter. Leda had her mind set on figuring it out.

"What mark are you completing now?"

I looked at the two triangles on my wrist and felt a little shudder just saying the words aloud. Eventually, the Esbat symbol wouldn't be the only mark there.

"Advanced Curses and Hexes."

Leda sputtered, coughing out some of her warm cider. I pounded her on the back and waved Miss Celia off when she ran forward to check on her.

"What?" she whispered as soon as everyone faded into the background. "Is that mark offered anymore?"

"I guess it is."

Leda shifted, uneasy.

"That isn't good, Bianca. Not good at all."

"You're telling me."

"Be careful," she warned. "I don't like the feel of this. Miss Mabel isn't . . ." she trailed off with a breath of frustration. "She's not predictable but neither is she unorganized."

The thought made me uneasy. I'd spent most of my life plotting against Miss Mabel. I didn't like the thought of her doing the same.

"Have you ever thought about why Miss Mabel is still here?" Leda asked.

"What do you mean?"

"If Miss Mabel cursed your grandmother because she supported Mildred, then that meant Miss Mabel supported Evelyn. Mildred executed all of Evelyn's followers when she took power."

Leda let the implication hang in the air.

I blinked. "But not Miss Mabel."

"Exactly. It's worth finding out. In order to not be killed, Miss Mabel must have proven her loyalty to Mildred somehow, don't you think?"

I looked out at the yard and thought it over. Why hadn't I considered that before? Miss Mabel would have been in league with Evelyn, like her grandmother. But then why wouldn't she have removed my grandmother's curse when Mabel was executed, if she was on Mildred's side?

"You're right," I said.

"We should probably go check on Camille."

Leda motioned to the table of desserts where Camille stood, proudly pointing out her pie to anyone that would look at it. I could see the dark edges and bumpy crust from where we stood. Someone attempted one little slice, likely Miss Scarlett, who stood off to the side with a pinched look on her face, taking it upon herself to be fair and try all the desserts. Most of the other confections had disappeared into the greedy mouths of students who couldn't get enough sugar.

"She looks okay," I said. Miss Celia bustled to the table, the prize basket of goodies in her hand.

"Yes, she is now." Leda let out a heavy sigh and shook her head. "But she won't be when Miss Celia announces that Brianna has won. Camille doesn't love anyone when there's pastries on the line."

We quickly made our way to the table, arriving just as Miss Celia called out for everyone's attention. But my mind was far from the applause and the gentle, surprised smile on Brianna's face or the flash of red embarrassment that faded to disappointment on Camille's.

I forced a smile for Camille's sake when she wandered over, dejected, her shoulders slumped. Then I pushed the thoughts of my grandmother, of Miss Mabel, far from my mind. Instead, I took Camille by the hand, and we plunged into the festivities, laughing until the light faded and the feast began beneath the pumpkin-colored sky.

Hexes

Miss Mabel came in the next morning with a mangy white cat trailing behind her, inching along with a limp. Clumps of fur were missing, one ear bled, and the ribcage jutted out from beneath the hair.

Still burning in the aftermath of her betrayal of our contract, I entertained myself by wondering how she would look if I put a boil on her face. My wrath sat deep in my chest, near my heart, pinching with every beat, threatening to crowd it out. I pushed it away so I could focus on the lessons, but it throbbed in the recesses.

"Hexes are too simple to dwell on for very long in an advanced class," Miss Mabel began. "We'll review a few of the main hexes today, and I'll test you on them later. After that, we'll move the majority of our emphasis to curses."

She spoke with ease, as if she didn't notice the hungry feline behind her. The cat let out a feeble *mew* and settled near the fire. I stood and handed Miss Mabel the scroll from yesterday. She tossed the homework on her desk without another glance.

"How are hexes different from curses?"

"They are generally milder," I responded, my eyes on the cat. "Curses last over time, while hexes rarely last more than a few hours. Hexes cannot be inherited," I added as a bitter aside.

"Exactly," she said and waved toward the cat. "This revolting little creature wandered into the kitchen this morning. He must've been in a fight awhile ago. His back leg is infected. He's going to die, making him a fantastic model to practice a few hexes on."

Appalled, I met her eyes.

"Miss Mabel, I can't—"

"You have to," she interrupted firmly. "You can't receive the mark without the ability to perform these hexes."

"Is this required in every advanced class?"

"No, but it's required in mine. He's going to die," she scoffed in a patronizing tone. "It won't hurt him."

The poor creature looked miserable, licking a swollen, red leg. My mind raced to find another plan. Even if it was going to die, I didn't want to torture him through the last hours of his life.

"It's a cat, Bianca. Get over it. You're an Assistant now. Stop acting like a first-year. Let's get started. I want you to cast a simple hex. Something elementary, like the itching hex."

The itching hex was short-lived but easy, more of an annoyance than a serious hex, like the sensation of a blade of grass constantly running along the skin. It generally lasted fifteen minutes, but I didn't know how it would affect a cat holding onto life by only a few days. Maybe less.

Miss Mabel folded her arms across her chest and arched her eyebrow when I hesitated. Her short-lived patience had already expired. My mind raced for a way to get her out of the classroom for just a few moments.

"Go ahead," she said.

I hesitated, staring at the poor creature. I'd come up with the outline of a plan, but chances that it would work were slim.

"Miss Mabel," I protested, hoping she'd get mad at me again, "he's dying. I don't want to—"

"Yes, very good Bianca. He is dying," she spoke as if she were addressing a child. Her tone sharpened. "Maybe this will help him die faster and stop his misery. Do it. Now."

Taking advantage of the precious moments she gave me as she spoke, I cast a silent incantation. Then I stared at her, acting speechless. Miss Celia's voice floated up the stairs, interrupting the tense moment.

"Miss Mabel? There's a problem down here I need some help with."

It took all my concentration to continue the spell and stare at Miss Mabel without changing my expression. Every word I said in my head was mimicked as Miss Celia. I hadn't expected it to work but felt a new power inside me give it strength. Where that power came from, I didn't know. But releasing it felt good.

"Take care of it," Miss Mabel said. "I'm busy."

"It's urgent!"

Miss Mabel hesitated.

"What is it?" she called back.

"A question regarding the order the grocer sent."

"That's urgent?"

I hesitated, lost.

"I think the milk is poisoned!"

My panic brought out a shrill note in Miss Celia's voice, which seemed to motivate Miss Mabel.

"Oh fine," she muttered, perturbed. I fought the urge to let out a sigh of relief, my heart beating a sharp staccato beneath my ribs. "I'll be right down."

Miss Mabel shot me a dangerous look as she took a few steps back.

"It would be very wise of you to complete the hex before I return."

As soon as she disappeared, I headed for the cat. He gave a pathetic little mew when I approached, clearly afraid but too tired to do anything about it. I scooped the bony figure into my arms and started to my bedroom.

A warm ray of light rested on my blanket, and I set him inside it. He attempted another weak sound but nothing came out. I had no food in my room so I offered him some water from a glass on my desk. His puny attempts at drinking took a long while. By the time I had made him comfortable, Miss Mabel's voice filtered up the stairs.

"Yes, Miss Celia. Just two minutes ago. It's all right. I'll figure it out."

My plan to avoid hexing the real cat wasn't a good one. It put me in a poor position, especially considering Miss Mabel's obvious ill humor with me already. Now she'd be suspicious because Miss Celia hadn't called for her. The cat curled into a little ball and tucked his nose into his tail.

After straightening up, I cast a deception spell. A second pathetic cat appeared on my bed, identical to the first.

"Come on," I whispered. The second cat followed me, hobbling like the real one. Miss Mabel's steps echoed down the corridor below; she was heading for the spiral stairs by the time I closed my bedroom door. Although I wanted to reach out and move the cat along, I didn't touch it lest the deception spell break. Miss Mabel started up the spiral stairs as I got the cat back into the classroom. Then I hexed the deception-spell cat and prayed Miss Mabel wouldn't ask me any important questions. If she caught me lying, she'd know this wasn't the real cat.

The cat suddenly let out an annoyed sound, much louder than any it had managed before, and raised itself up on all four legs. Then it turned in circles, trying to reach something on its back.

Miss Mabel walked in and threw me a suspicious look. After taking in the annoyed cat's angry hissing, she lifted an eyebrow but let the moment slide.

"See?" she muttered, folding her arms across her chest. "That wasn't so hard."

My palms were sweaty, and my heart pounded in my ears, but I managed a shrug. Even though the deception-spell cat wasn't real, the awful feeling that I tortured something else wouldn't leave. She stared at the cat in disdain as it chased its own tail.

"Nasty little thing. Now remove the hex."

My first attempt yielded minimal results. The cat stopped his agitated chasing but wouldn't settle in one spot. It circled around, uncomfortable. Miss Mabel corrected my speech, and with the next repetition the cat settled, standing like a weak pillar in front of the fire. Miss Mabel scrutinized me from her perch near the doorway, far from the reach of the cat.

"Let's try something else, like the double vision hex. That's more complicated."

Still uneasy, I cast the hex. The cat immediately jumped, looking around in confusion. Miss Mabel tilted her head as she watched, appearing both disgusted and amused as the cat wobbled around like a drunk.

"All right, now take it off."

The cat stopped tripping over his own feet after my second attempt. It ran under my desk and cowered. My heart broke.

Miss Mabel regarded me through narrowed eyes.

"I think your problem is your concentration," she decided. "The reason it's more difficult to remove a hex is because the magic is already at work. Magic is not stagnant. You have to really focus to make it stop. It's almost like pulling the magic back together. Does that make sense?"

Trying to stay mute, I forced myself to nod.

"Do you have something on your mind that would take your concentration away from the counter-hex?"

Her question didn't seem purposeful, but my heart stuttered all the same.

"No," I lied, grateful that the deception spell worked in my favor.

"Then it's a matter of practice. Keep working on it tonight. We'll try it again tomorrow afternoon." Her eyes fell on the cat. "If that nasty feline is still alive, we'll use it."

I nodded to acknowledge her orders. After casting one last uncertain glance at me, she disappeared into her office. The cat hid underneath my chair, peering at me with yellow eyes. I waited for several minutes before reaching forward to touch it. The deception-spell cat dissolved into a mist as I stroked its tail, grateful that the lesson was over.

For now.

Poke Root

Sorting through the herb pantry for the right concoction of herbs for a healing paste proved to be more time consuming than I'd planned. Worse still was how long the poultice took to prepare. By the time I was ready to wrap it around the kitty's swollen leg, lunch had started. The cat stirred as I cleaned the open gash and applied the sticky mixture. But he was too weak to protest and didn't move after I was done. I sighed in worry. An infection poultice at this stage was like a feather trying to stop an open artery.

After wrapping the leg, leaving some water nearby, and covering him with my blanket, I slipped down the stairs and into the dining room with the hope that my friends would have some advice.

Leda looked at me in surprise when I sat down.

"You smell like jasmine," Camille said, sniffing.

"Thanks, I think."

"Why are you so late?"

"I'm not that late," I said, motioning to her untouched food. "You haven't even started."

"That's because I was on kitchen duty." Her dramatic sigh turned into a pout. "Stephany yelled at me because her biscuit was cold. She's as nasty as Priscilla. But look! I dished up a plate for you even though you weren't here and I didn't know if you were going to come." Camille gave me a pointed look. I smiled at her in appreciation.

"Thanks, Camille."

Satisfied, she turned to her own plate and dove into her mashed potatoes, exclaiming over how creamy they were.

"So," I said a few minutes later, attempting a light tone. "Have either of you ever used poke root before?"

Both of them stopped mid-bite to give me a skeptical look.

"You want my advice on herbs?" Camille asked. "Are you kidding? You're the Assistant."

"That doesn't mean I know everything."

"I don't know anything about poke root," she said, slathering raspberry preserves on a piece of bread. "This bread, however, needs some more flour. A bit soggy."

"Didn't you used to work with an apothecary?" I asked her, recalling a time when Camille talked about working with a grumpy potionmaker named Fitz.

"Yes, but I sorted herbs. I never put them to use. Well, maybe once–"

Her face twisted in thought as I waited, holding my breath.

"No, actually, wait!" she cried. "I think I did. No. No, I'm wrong. I didn't. I don't know anything about pole root."

"Poke root."

"Whatever."

Leda shot Camille a questioning look. "So becoming an apothecary is off the list of possibilities now?"

"Yes," Camille responded with a careless shake of her hair. "Too much memorizing. But I'm not hopeless in the job search yet. I'm only sixteen and still in pursuit of beauty."

"Poke root is poison," Leda said, turning to me. "Why do you need to know about it?"

"It can be," I agreed, "if used in the wrong dosages."

"Is it for you?" Camille asked.

"No."

"Then who is it for?"

"I found a stray cat. I want to try and nurse it back to health, but it's in pretty bad shape. It's so sick I think I may need to use poke root to kill the infection. My grandmother talked about it, but it's so strong she hardly ever used it."

Camille's face turned down in instant sorrow.

"Oh, poor kitty! What are you going to name it?"

"Name it?" I asked. "I don't know. I'll just be happy to keep it alive."

"There's a massive book on herbs in the herb pantry," Leda said. "It has listings based on use of the herb and function. I'd start there. A paste won't be as strong as a tincture though, so you would be safer with that."

"I've got a poultice on it now," I said. "I'll see what that does. I might be working against fate as it is."

Miss Bernadette interrupted our conversation by walking up to our table. Camille let out a squeak of happy surprise.

"Hi Miss Bernadette!"

Miss Bernadette gave her beautiful smile in response. Her short hair had grown out just enough to begin curling at the base of her neck, giving her an impish look.

"Bianca," she turned to me, "Miss Mabel said you are going to participate in our Geography class for the next month. She wanted you to get a deeper understanding regarding the layout of our Network, especially Letum Wood. You and I will have a separate class emphasizing Chatham City, the interior of Chatham Castle, and the borderlands by the Western Network."

"Yes, Miss Bernadette," I said, noticing Leda's ruffled forehead.

Camille silenced her yelp of excitement by stuffing a fist over her mouth.

"We'll meet outside at the large oak tree by the front gate. Bring a cloak. We'll start with Letum Wood. Reading up from the book *The Complete History of Letum Wood* would help."

"I'll go find the book today."

Miss Bernadette smiled at us and departed, leaving her flowery scent behind. Leda shot me a look with one eyebrow lifted.

"I wonder why Miss Mabel is having you study the Borderlands between the Western and Central Networks?"

I shrugged, wondering the same thing myself.

"Maybe she wants me to learn more about the desert."

"What are you going to do about Miss Mabel's conversation with the High Priest?" she asked next. "Have you heard back from your father?"

"No," I growled, annoyed at the reminder. "He hasn't written me back. Until he does, there's nothing I can do."

This wasn't something I wanted to think about, not until I knew more of what Miss Mabel's plan involved.

Leda picked up on the finality in my tone and spent the rest of the meal buried in her thoughts and visions. Camille prattled off about a letter she'd received from her aunt Bettina, informing her that one of her friends from home was sick, and I tried to smile and keep up with the conversation but like Leda found my thoughts slipping far away.

Miss Celia swept into the dining room a few minutes later, dismissing everyone to their classes five minutes early.

Communication Spells

Miss Mabel surprised me after breakfast the next morning by taking me into her office. The open window admitted waves of chilly winter air. Her blood-red drapes drifted into the room like restless flags, and a few papers rustled on her desk. The change in temperature from the warm classroom gave me goose bumps.

"I can't stand stale air." Miss Mabel said as I trailed behind her into the middle of the barren office. "Also, I can't tolerate dust. Actually, I won't tolerate dust. Since you're my Assistant, you have the privilege of dusting my shelves. I'm too nice, aren't I?"

Yes, I wanted to mutter. *That's what your problem is.*

"I wouldn't get lazy if I were you," she said. "I intend to do a thorough inspection when you finish, and you don't want me to find any dust. I have some meetings to attend, so I'll be back in the evening."

"Yes, Miss Mabel."

"Perfect the hexes and their removals today. I'll test you when I return. Get started on the textbook *History of Curses* as well. Write up a summary of every chapter. Is that infernal cat still alive?"

"Yes," I said, thinking back to his feeble attempts at drinking milk this morning. The swelling in his leg had gone down, but the redness remained. Poke root seemed inevitable.

"Ghastly creature," she muttered and pulled her satin sleeves to her wrist. The sapphire dress she wore matched her eyes. When she put on her ebony cloak, her eyes were brighter than I had ever seen. Her alluring smile grew when she caught me staring at her.

"I know. It's a breathtaking dress, isn't it? Have fun, Bianca.

Tomorrow, we'll have a real party. I'm going to teach you how to organize my scrolls."

She left the office in a swirl of skirt and cloak. Although I listened, I never heard her walk down the stairs. Only the silence told me she was gone.

Today, she wasn't the only one with a meeting.

I extended my hand in a collection spell. Seconds later, specks of dust flew from all parts of the room and fell into my palm. A whirling gray cloud formed around me for several moments, forcing me to hold my breath. I ran to the window as soon as the room cleared and dumped the dust in a windless moment.

Satisfied that nothing remained on the shelves, the floor, or her desk, I slipped back into my room and grabbed an old grimoire I'd found in the library. The hand-written pages of someone's old spell book whirred as I flipped through to the back, scouring each line for the right words.

Communication spell.

The conversation with Leda during Samhain had haunted me for several days. Why wasn't Miss Mabel killed with the rest of Evelyn's followers? It wasn't something history books could answer. Only one person could.

Today, I meant to talk to her.

I'd done communication spells with my father during the long breaks when he couldn't come see me. An advanced communication spell wouldn't leave a trace. Because Isadora watched the comings and goings of the school borders, she'd know right away if I transported out. I'd lose my place as Assistant for breaking the rules and couldn't risk it.

The cat rustled a little and opened his eyes to give a pathetic call when I slammed the book shut, verifying the correct words. Encouraged by any sign of life, I stroked his bony head. Then I fed him some milk, checked his wound, and reached for my cape.

Homework would have to wait.

The trees were silent as sentinels when I glided past, my cloak trailing out behind me. Gray and calm, it felt as if the forest held its breath. Did it know what I was about to do? Did the skinny branches tremble when I passed by because they were afraid of the risk I took? If Miss Mabel found out, she'd force me to give an explanation as to why I didn't just write a letter. What could be so pressing in a student's life? She still had not tested me with Veritas, and I knew she wouldn't hesitate to use it if she felt I kept a secret.

Well into the woods, I crouched down and picked up a handful of dead leaves. Dirt trailed through my fingers as I clenched my hand in a fist around their brittle bodies. Once I reduced them to pieces the size of confetti, I cast my eyes around. Alone. Not even the sound of a bird in the unearthly quiet of Letum Wood.

As soon as the final syllable of the communication spell ended, I flung the earthen pieces toward the trees. Airborne, the particles of leaf and dirt stopped and hovered in position, sprawling through the air in front of me. They didn't move for a long time.

Finally, after what felt like hours, they began to tremble. The pieces doubled, then tripled, moving around in a haphazard dance until they pulled together in similar colors, forming the figure of a woman sitting propped up.

Light spread through the specks to create the grooves of a wrinkled face. I could see the contours of her smile, the crow's feet near her eyes, and the rustle of her silvery hair. When she spoke, a light breeze moved past.

"Bianca?"

"Yes!" I cleared my thick throat. "It's me, Grandmother."

"What are you doing?" she cried, surprised and elated. "Is everything all right?"

"I'm fine."

The love in her voice was more overwhelming than Veritas and infinitely more powerful. I struggled to keep myself from crying. I wanted to bury my head in her lap and feel her stroke my hair, to breathe in the soft scent of her lavender soap.

"I heard about the Competition," she said with a smile. "Congratulations! Although I'm not a bit surprised. You are so talented.

All of Bickers Mill is talking about it. Your mother said the shop had record sales after you won! Apparently we sold all the fresh thyme."

I blushed under her praise, but a bitter taste rose in my mouth, reminding me of my lost bet with Miss Mabel. I wasn't sure I had the strength to admit to Grandmother that I'd failed her.

"Thank you," I said instead.

"How is everything else going?"

"It's wonderful," I lied with a smile. "I'm learning a lot."

Grandmother studied my face, and her forehead puckered.

"You're a terrible liar, Bianca. You're miserable, and I don't blame you. And you look skinnier. I didn't think that was possible. Are you eating?"

"Yes, I'm eating plenty."

"Have you made any friends?"

"Two, actually. Maybe three," I amended, thinking of Michelle.

Her face lit up. It was so good to see her. I studied everything about her as if I would never see it again.

"That's wonderful! It's time you went and had some fun. Go transform your textbooks into candy, or sneak out to Mr. Gerard's School for Boys and kiss one of them. Oh, I guess you can't do that from Letum Wood, can you? It's too far away. Well, later. Maybe when you come home for summer break."

She ended with a wink, and I laughed. "What would I tell the teacher after I ate the candy? I'm not sure Miss Mabel would believe that I'd eaten my textbook."

She laughed as well. "I guess I didn't think of that!"

I sobered quickly.

"May I ask you a question?"

"Yes, of course."

"It's about the curse."

Grandmother took a breath as if steeling herself. She winced, and I could see by the rigid line of her lips that she was trying to hide it. Any movement caused her pain.

"Go ahead."

"Miss Mabel said she cursed you because you supported Mildred. Why didn't Mildred get rid of Miss Mabel when she took power?"

Grandmother blinked several times and tilted her head to the side. "Mildred did get rid of Mabel."

It was my turn to stare in surprise. We regarded each other for a few moments.

"But—"

"The High Priestess got rid of the original Mabel. Your teacher is her granddaughter, Miss Mabel."

My eyes widened. The conversation I'd had in the kitchen with Miss Celia filtered through my mind, and I remembered that Miss Mabel's grandmother raised her when her mother ran off.

"So Miss Mabel didn't curse you?"

"No. It was her grandmother, Mabel. Did you not know that?"

I felt as if the breath fell out of the bottom of my lungs, leaving me weak.

"No. No, I didn't."

"Mildred executed Mabel with the rest of the traitors that supported Evelyn, but her granddaughter, Miss Mabel, pled before the Council that her grandmother had forced her to be loyal to Evelyn."

"But Miss Mabel hates Mildred!" I cried.

"Has she said that?"

I searched my memory with an uneasy squirm. "Not in those exact words, but she's implied it."

Grandmother continued. "Well, for as many instances for which people gave evidence that Miss Mabel supported Evelyn, she had one to prove her loyalty to Mildred. Miss Mabel was part of the Resistance, you know."

My jaw dropped.

"She couldn't have been!"

"She was. There were many members who spoke up for her at the hearing with the Council. They voted to keep her, although I suspect that Mildred didn't like it. Mildred has never trusted Miss Mabel, but with the Council voting for leniency, and so many people standing up on her behalf, she had no choice."

"Was Miss Mabel playing both sides?" I asked.

"It's very possible." Grandmother's tone held a note of warning. "Miss Mabel is one of the most vindictive witches the Central

Network has ever seen. I wouldn't be a bit surprised to learn she planned it."

A sudden thought made my heart stutter. "If Mabel is her grandmother, then Miss Mabel could still remove the Inheritance curse, right?"

"Yes, of course."

I relaxed a little.

"What was her grandmother, Mabel, like?" I found myself asking, remembering again how Miss Celia had seemed uncomfortable even speaking about her in the kitchen that morning.

"Not too different from her granddaughter, only she had black hair. She was very selfish and, if I remember correctly, obsessed with power and greed. I think Mabel was friends with Evelyn only to seek the position of High Priestess herself. Miss Mabel was a teacher at the school when I attended here, and her grandmother still ran it as High Witch."

"Did you see Mabel very much?" I asked.

"No. There was something very unnerving about her. When I did see her, I was always glad to leave."

Miss Mabel had never spoken of the original Mabel, and neither had Miss Scarlett. It seemed odd not to commemorate the founder of the school, and I wondered if it had something to do with the original Mabel's execution. Grandmother stifled a yawn, and I could see that her energy was almost gone. The particles began to flutter in warning. Our time was almost up.

"I miss you," I said, not wanting to end the conversation on a subject so bleak but realizing too late that I'd introduced one far more depressing.

She smiled and made an attempt to touch my face, but we were too far apart. Brown and gray bits of earth fell to the ground and faded into the wind.

"We miss you too. But we are very proud of you, no matter what you do. You know that, right?"

"Yes."

"I'm sorry you have to do this," she said with a sad grimace. "No girl should have to fight for her own right to live."

"It's not your fault, Nana," I whispered. Her tired eyes lit up briefly at my childhood nickname for her.

"You have more commitment than anyone I've ever met, Bianca. You're a very special girl, destined for great things. Just remember to not get in your own way. Promise me?"

A tear fell down my cheek and landed on the leaves at my feet.

"I promise."

The spell began to fall apart. She reached for me again, her hand shaking as she did. The leaves dropped to the ground.

Nana danced away, settling into the wind and flittering from sight.

Tricks and Hexes

By midnight, I could cast and remove every hex with little effort. I glanced at the clock, let out a deep breath, and started at the beginning of the list one last time. Burying myself in studying blocked out everything else, giving me time to adjust to Grandmother's revelations about Miss Mabel.

The deception-spell cat I practiced on had long since resigned himself to the hexes and curled in a ball on the floor. While I was never really comfortable putting hexes on the creature, knowing it was nothing more than a puff of air helped.

After I ran through every hex and removal, I broke the deception-spell cat. A noise came from the hall. I spun around to see the silhouette of Miss Mabel in the shadows. She stepped into the doorway where a beam of firelight illuminated her face. Her skin looked like alabaster.

My heart jumped into my throat.

"You're up late tonight, Bianca. It's well past midnight."

A shiver of apprehension ran through me when I realized she had seen me pop the deception-spell cat. She concealed any gleam of surprise in her eyes with a cool shadow of indifference. My heart seemed to stall in my chest.

"Yes, Miss Mabel. I was just practicing."

"I see that."

There was no trying to get out of it. Miss Mabel advanced into the room a few more steps with an unreadable poise that terrified me.

"You did remarkably well. I just watched your last run-through. Let's count this as your test, shall we?"

"Yes, Miss Mabel."

She glanced at where the cat had once been and back to me. Her eyes looked silvery and thoughtful.

"It isn't often a student is able to get a trick by me. Congratulations."

I knew, without asking, that she referred not only to the cat but to the mimicking spell of Miss Celia's voice. There was nothing about this moment to celebrate, but everything to fear. I held my breath, waiting for her to pass judgment, to decide my punishment or fate.

"Go to bed, Bianca."

Miss Mabel watched me gather my scrolls and slip past her to my bedroom. She didn't move but stayed like a pillar, staring at the fire in the doorway when I shut my bedroom door. I leaned against the wall and let out a breath. The real cat gave a pathetic call when he saw me, then turned around and settled back to sleep.

I sat on the side of the bed to calm my racing heart. I didn't understand what just happened, but knew I hadn't done myself any favors.

The air was almost warm at three the next afternoon when we congregated outside for the Letum Wood Geography class with Miss Bernadette. Our breath left small puffs of trailing air behind. The chill pinched at the cheeks of the girls until they were a ruddy color, but didn't feel vicious.

A small queue of first-years stood in a loose huddle near the old oak tree. When Miss Bernadette arrived, her cheeks were a lovely pink color that contrasted her brown, fur-lined cloak.

"Letum Wood extends throughout most of the eastern side of the Central Network," Miss Bernadette began. "It fills up the North, reaches to the Borderlands, and spills over into the Eastern Network. Follow me, and we'll look at a few things that grow here."

Camille, Leda, and I fell into step with each other.

"I gave the cat poke root this morning," I said, breaking into the conversation first. Camille bit her nails with an intensity that could only mean she had a test coming up, and Leda stood several paces away from us, brooding, her lips and face puckered into an annoyed scowl. Their minimal response disheartened my already frustrated mood. I wanted to tell them about my encounter with Grandmother but decided against it. For some reason, I didn't want to share her.

"Oh?" Camille said, distant. "That's nice."

"I also had to amputate his leg. The surgery caused only a few bloodstains on my sheets. Miss Mabel even helped. She removed my curse."

I monitored their responses, but neither of them said another word. They just continued to trudge forward in their own worlds. I let out a sigh and looked at the moving body of cloaked sheep in front of us, following Miss Bernadette with loyal devotion. When nothing changed for the next fifteen minutes, except for Miss Bernadette's quiet drawl on the types of oak trees spread throughout the wood, I poked Camille in the ribs with my elbow.

"What's going on? You've chewed half your fingers off."

"Oh, Bianca!" she wailed, as if she'd just been waiting for me to ask. "I have a test today in Algebra and Geometry, and I just know I'm going to fail!"

I held up a hand to quiet her and looked to the front of the group to make sure no one else had heard the outburst. Of all the teachers, Miss Bernadette was the one I didn't want to upset. If she caught us not paying attention, I'd feel horrible.

"I'm sure you'll be fine, Camille," I whispered, turning back to her.

"I hate math, Bianca. Really! I just can't do it."

"Have you asked Leda for help?"

"Yes, but she won't look into the future for me on this one. She'll normally look ahead and tell me if my chances are good or not so I don't get so much anxiety. It's the not knowing that stresses me out!" Camille folded her arms and shot Leda a scathing glance. "She's been concentrating on something all morning and won't tell me what, but it's put her in a foul mood."

I looked to Leda, but she was no help, caught up in her thoughts and staring at a tree trunk with a blank expression on her face. Once she seemed to come halfway out of it, I nudged her too.

"What's got you?"

She turned to me with an impatient growl, but quickly stopped. Her different-colored eyes were bloodshot.

"Nothing," she said, obviously still vexed. She hesitated, opened her mouth to say something, then turned away in a huff and fell into another daze.

"See?" Camille said with a self-righteous sniff that would have made the snooty third-years proud. "She gets like this sometimes, trying so hard to make sense of something. Then she gets frustrated if she can't, which makes the curse even harder to control."

I studied Leda's hunched shoulders and clenched fists.

"Sounds like an awful cycle," I muttered with little sympathy, their bad moods making mine worse.

"Right," Camille snorted. "But not as bad as failing Algebra and having to take it again."

She fell to studying a small piece of parchment hidden in her palm, her lips moving in silent recitation as she read. Miss Bernadette called us forward, and the whole group moved as one, deeper into the forest.

I watched Leda with a suddenly wary eye as she stumbled along. What was she seeing, and why was it so important? When Leda didn't look my way again, I turned my back on her, ignoring her vexed expressions. The three of us spread out for the rest of the lesson, and the class faded by without me any wiser for it.

Vertigo

Miss Mabel waited for me in the classroom when I returned from breakfast later that week, a warm bowl of oatmeal sitting in my stomach. She gazed out the windows on the backyard, her arms folded across her chest. She spoke without looking at me as I entered the room.

"Are you ready for class today, Bianca?"

"Yes, Miss Mabel."

"Good."

A feeling like a punch to my midsection slammed into me. I tumbled to my knees and gasped. My vision swam for a few seconds; my scalp began to tingle moments before I blacked out. When I came to, Miss Mabel stood over me, her long blonde hair dangling around her face.

"Goodness! You certainly fell harder than I thought you would. Does your head hurt?"

Disoriented, I blinked several times. My right shoulder throbbed and the world still spun. My head pulsed with dull thuds.

"What h-happened?"

Using my left elbow to prop myself up, I pushed off the floor. Dizziness overwhelmed me. My vision failed, my fingers prickled, and I passed out again.

The sound of Miss Mabel chuckling brought me back around.

"Oh, I wouldn't do that," she stopped me from trying to sit up by putting a foot on my shoulder. It took a moment for my vision to clear enough to bring the shiny black boot into focus. "It'll make it worse."

My head fell back to the floor, where it hit with a bang and echoed through my skull. I groaned and closed my eyes as Miss Mabel lifted her foot.

"What you have just been hit with is a vertigo curse. Eventually, with time, the fits of vertigo will decrease to once an hour. Then, after a few days, they will only come once every two hours, and so forth. You get the idea. Eventually, you'd live with blacking out every four to five hours. Not intolerable, I think."

Her footsteps reverberated through my ears as she walked around me.

"As you know, I don't think education is very valuable unless it's hands-on. Especially for the Advanced Curses and Hexes mark. Wouldn't you agree? No one should be able to cast a curse if she doesn't know how it feels. This is an education you can't get anywhere else in the Network, Bianca. Trust me. Lucky for you, isn't it? I'm also doing it like this because your papers and homework make me cringe."

Then, as quickly as it came, the pain and dizziness faded. I opened my eyes, and Miss Mabel smiled.

"You may sit up now."

She walked to her desk as I pulled myself together and stood up. My head didn't dive up and down in a dizzy spell. It felt normal and clear. Once removed, there were no residual effects.

Before I had gotten very far, the punch came again, only stronger this time. I held onto my desk to keep from falling and gasped for air. Nothing happened. I swallowed back a tickle in my throat as I waited. But the sensation didn't go away. It grew into a scratch. Uncomfortable, I cleared my throat. My mouth felt like sand. The need to drink seized me.

Suddenly I was so thirsty, I would die.

Barely aware of my actions, I grabbed a glass of water Miss Mabel had set out and began to drink. It tasted so sweet. The heat abated when the moisture slid past my throat. But as soon as I emptied the glass, my baked mouth returned. No, it had never left. The water didn't quench my thirst. I still craved more. Miss Mabel sat down in her chair and lounged back with a teasing smile.

"Thirsty, Bianca?"

Trying to hide my desperation was useless. I couldn't fight a curse, as I already knew. *What is it about cursing me that she likes?* Instead, I clung to the desk and forced myself not to move. If I got near water, I would drink until I vomited, and then begin again.

"That feeling you're experiencing precedes every curse. Sometimes it's the only way you know you've been hit. I've seen some curses so strong that the initial wave knocks the person over. Isn't that wild?"

I was barely able to concentrate. All I could think of was cool blue water. The refreshing taste sliding down my mouth, past my scorched tongue, into my stomach. Moments before I gave in and broke away from my desk to search for something to drink, the feeling stopped. Relieved, I put my head in my hands and collected my breath.

"There are some curses you can cast that are silent, without precursor, meaning that there is no way of knowing when they hit you. They are a bit more advanced and complicated. Of course, we won't bother with those. Not today, anyway."

She sat up and strolled into the middle of the room. As soon as her footsteps paused, I straightened up.

"Ready for some more?" she asked.

Her high eyebrow and tilted head challenged me. She wanted me to say no, to quit. Both of us knew this lesson would go on for hours. I wondered if this was her way of getting retribution for the deception-spell cat and tricking her with Miss Celia's voice.

Or if this was just a part of her evil plan that I couldn't decipher. Either way, I couldn't turn back. The awful arithmetic of saving my own life and shucking off the Inheritance curse meant I had to stay, and succeed, at all costs.

"Yes, Miss Mabel," I said, not without some trepidation, my fists clenched at my side. "I'm ready."

Three hours.
Three grueling hours.
It took that long for Miss Celia to ring the little tinkling bell for

lunch. Miss Mabel had just started explaining how to cast a swollen tongue curse when the bell interrupted and she looked up in surprise.

"Oh, is it already lunch?" she asked in feigned shock. "Fabulous. I'm exhausted."

Maybe she'll choke on her lunch and I won't have to see her again.

I wanted to cast my own curse. One that would make the floorboards disappear beneath her and swallow her into an unforgiving chasm of black snakes. Instead I rested my forehead on the desk and waited for the spasms in my arms and legs to stop. *Blasted seizure curse.* They slowly subsided, leaving me weary and still.

I hadn't known there were that many curses in our whole world, ranging from continuous sneezing to the inability to swallow. The most frightening had been a suffocation curse. While I knew she wouldn't let me die, not yet, the constant sensation that I couldn't breathe terrified me into wanting to.

The most unsettling part was Miss Mabel's amusement as she controlled me like a puppet.

"Don't bother going downstairs to eat," she said. "I'll have Miss Celia bring you something. You have a class with Miss Amelia tomorrow afternoon on counter-curses that should serve as a good introduction. You also have a paper due tonight. I want a one thousand word essay on the differences between counter-curses and removing curses. Then, I want you to read chapters ten through fifteen from the textbook *Curses*. I'll see you tomorrow. If you have any questions, I'll be in my office."

So much for tuning down the homework that I'm so horribly bad at.

The moment she disappeared, I folded my arms, lowered my head, and tried not to think about how much I hated her. I wouldn't remember those instructions and would have to ask her to repeat them later, but I didn't care. Miss Celia came up after a sweet twenty minutes in which I hovered on the bridge between wakefulness and sleep, startling me into reality again. She carried a plate loaded with food.

"Bianca?" she cried, aghast. "Blessed be, are you all right?"

"Yes, Miss Celia." My voice echoed in the small cave my arms made.

"What happened?"

"Nothing." I straightened up to put her at ease. "I'm just tired today."

"Tired!" she exclaimed. "You look nearly worn to death! Are you getting enough sleep?"

"I'm okay," I managed. "Nothing a little lunch won't help."

She eyed me in disbelief and set the plate down. Sliced apples rested in a petaled design around a sandwich. The bread smelled buttery and felt warm. My stomach grumbled, but I wasn't sure I'd have the energy to chew. My midsection felt sore from all the precursors.

"It's nothing fancy today, I'm afraid. Just a sandwich and some fruit."

"That sounds great. Thank you, Miss Celia."

She hesitated. She didn't seem to want to leave but had no reason to linger.

"Are you sure you're all right?"

"Yes, I'm well."

"Okay," she sighed. "Then I'll leave you alone. Just let me know if I can do anything, all right?"

I nodded. She turned away to leave, then circled back with a little exclamation.

"Oh! I just remembered something. Brianna's birthday party is coming up soon. Her parents have asked us to have a little celebration for her seventeenth. Do you think you'll be able to come?"

"Maybe."

Living through the day would be a requirement, and I didn't feel up to it right then.

"We'll have yellow cake with red frosting," she added, as if that would entice me into a commitment. The thought of getting as far away from Miss Mabel as possible appealed to me more than the promise of sweets.

"I'll try, Miss Celia."

She gave me an awkward little pat on my shoulder. Tears welled up in my eyes, and I wondered how long I'd be able to endure.

"Get some rest, poor dear."

Miss Celia mumbled something under her breath as she puttered to the spiral stairs and left me in the quiet classroom. After staring at the sandwich for a long time, I pushed it away, dropped my head back onto my arms, and fell asleep.

Purple Flowers

"Bianca, try this: instead of saying the spell, I want you to focus on what you want to happen. Focus really, really hard. Can you do that?"

His dark eyes smiled at me.

"Yes, Papa. But I can't—"

"Just try it, B. That's all I ask. Think really hard about what you want, not what spell to use. That's how silent magic is different."

"It's hard!"

"I know. But you can do hard things. If we learn it now, it will help you be strong when you're older."

Sunbeams strayed through the trees, warming my skin. The air smelled like fresh dirt and leaves. We were in a wild, unknown part of the forest where no one would see us. The high sun in the sky meant we still had a few hours before Papa had to leave.

The last thing I saw before I closed my eyes was the delicate curve of the yellow petals.

"Okay," I whispered, uncertain. Then I turned all my thoughts to the yellow flower, trying as hard as I could to imagine it purple instead. Time passed, but I kept my eyes closed until the sounds of Letum Wood faded and all I thought of was a purple flower. When I heard a cry of delight, I opened my eyes to see a violet blossom in hand. The only signs of the original flower remained in the few streaks of yellow down the center of each petal.

"Mama! Papa!" I shrieked, waving it in the air. "I did it! Look, it's purple!"

"You did it!" Mama cried.

Papa gathered me in his arms and spun around. "I knew you could!" he said, exultant with pride. "If anyone could do it, you can, sweet B." The world blurred into green and brown streaks as we twirled, laughing. He set me down and then settled onto a rock near Mama, who rubbed a hand across his back.

"You aren't going to leave yet, are you?" I asked him, fiddling with the flower stem, wondering if I could find some others and make a crown.

"No, of course not. We still have a few hours left. See, look up at the sun. It's not on the horizon yet, is it?"

"No."

"Then we still have time! What if we play your favorite game?"

"Why can't we go to your house?" I asked. "We never go to your house, Papa. We always meet here."

The two of them exchanged a look that meant I wasn't supposed to know something. So many secrets. He pulled me in closer to him, then propped me up on his lap.

"We meet here in the forest because I have a very busy job. Sometimes it's dangerous. I don't want you to get hurt."

His gentle tone did little to soothe my sadness. Mama ran a hand down my face and gave me the smile that meant everything would be okay. Papa took her other hand.

"Mama said no one can know you're my Papa."

"For now, she's right," he said. "Maybe one day, when you're older, we can tell people. But for now we're going to keep it a secret, okay?"

I still didn't understand, but I knew that understanding it wouldn't change anything.

"Who is going to protect you, Papa?"

He smiled and softly chucked my chin with his knuckles. "I can take care of myself, Bianca. That's part of the reason I'm teaching you all these difficult things. Then one day you can protect yourself."

"Because I'm cursed?"

"Yes. That's why I'm making you learn difficult things. Do you know why it's important to learn?"

"Because it gives me power?"

"Yes. The more you learn, the more power you'll get. Then we can try to stop the curse before you're seventeen."

"Should I be scared of the bad witch that cursed Nana?"

He stared at me for a long time, then brushed a long lock of black hair away from my face.

"No, Bianca. You should never be afraid of anything."

Startled out of the dream by a loud noise, I jerked myself awake.

A booming roll of thunder reverberated off the walls of my bedroom. Rain pounded the window and roof in a sharp staccato. I gazed around to make sure it was just a dream, a vague memory stirring from somewhere in the back of my mind. Alone in my room, I sat at my desk. I'd fallen asleep over a half-finished scroll.

Shaken, I pushed the hair off my sweaty face, curled myself in a ball under the covers, and knew no more.

Divinings

I sat in the library that morning, watching a few dust motes drift in the beams of sunlight. The old tomes shed an aged smell, like moldy paper and rotting leather, but it comforted me, reminding me of Grandmother. A yellowing book sat open on the table. I stared at the words but didn't see them. The flicker of the fire held me in a captivated trance, lulling me like a wicked siren.

Until two bodies sank into the chairs in front of me.

"Hi Bianca," Jackie said, expertly shuffling a stack of cards between her two hands. Her tiny black curls poked out of her head in all directions as usual, contrasting with her smooth caramel skin. I envied her exotic beauty. "I came to practice Divining on you."

I didn't notice a question, recalling our previous conversation in which she'd expressed interest in trying. Luckily, I was in the mood for a distraction, so I straightened up.

"But I don't have any decisions to make right now."

A lie, partially. Life was full of decisions. Jackie scoffed and shot me a look that suggested she had the same thought.

"We're always making decisions," she said with a confident little shake of her head. "I'm just going to show you two paths. It's up to you to decide which decision leads to which path. That's all I can do."

"She just did it for me," Camille said, her eyes glowing. "If a handsome young witch warrior comes along, the results of that decision could spring some beautiful children!"

"Okay," I agreed, secretly hoping this wouldn't turn into a warbling, romantic adventure about finding my soulmate and also fearing that Jackie would actually have some skill. What if one of her paths held only darkness, while the other ended? Perhaps all my choices lead to a bad end, and Jackie would see it. What then?

Camille bounced in excitement.

"I can't wait!"

I can, I wanted to say, beginning to wonder if this was a good idea.

Jackie held out both of her hands. I put my palms against hers, not surprised to find them warm and soft. For a first-year, Jackie had it together. She was everything she should be, and everything most girls wanted to be, but she didn't seem to notice. She closed her eyes and let out a long breath.

It didn't take long before her relaxed face slowly began to crumble, to fall into deep grooves and worry lines. It aged her too many years. I wanted to pull my hands away, to jump up and tell her to forget it, but I feared the meaning of her expression.

Seconds later, Jackie's eyes snapped open. She looked at me with a troubled gaze.

"Let's see what the cards say now that I have your essence," she whispered, reaching for the deck, her hand trembling just a little. Camille, oblivious to our silent exchange, clapped to herself, shuddering in excitement.

Jackie shifted the first card off the top of the deck and flipped it over. I stared at a Guardian on a horse, a burning red sword in his hand, an expression of rage on his face. My heart fluttered as Jackie set it off to the right.

"The Guardian," she said in a low tone. "You will battle your enemies on this line. The Guardian doesn't appear idly. It means you have the skills needed to fight but does not guarantee victory."

"He's quite handsome," Camille said, studying his face. "Angry, too." I didn't look at him, or at Jackie. I didn't look anywhere, instead pressed my palms together on my lap and waited. She reached for the next card.

"The red scales," she said, announcing the next card and placing it to the left. "It means you'll execute justice on this line."

I thought of my curse, of Miss Mabel. *Justice,* I thought, overwhelmed by a sudden desire to have that power. *What a sweet word.* A few candles flared high and sputtered out, drowning the library in a low blanket of light. Jackie shot me a sharp look, her eyes narrowed.

"What an odd rush of wind. What's next?" I asked, trying to distract her. A few girls on the other side of the room let out annoyed cries as they re-lit the burned out candles, restoring the light in the room. Jackie hesitated, her hand hovering over the deck, then grabbed the next card.

"The High Priest of Spears."

A man with dark, nearly black, skin wearing a fur-lined cloak and a heavy crown stared back at me. He balanced four spears in one hand. Not all of them were sharp. A lion with a full mane roared from next to him. I knew what this card meant.

"He only has one eye," Jackie pointed out. Camille recoiled in disgust. "That indicates determination, purpose. But the four spears represent the four directions of the earth. When these are brought together in one purpose under the High Priest of Spears, war always ensues."

He sat next to the Guardian, a dark omen, to be sure. Jackie didn't hesitate. She moved onto the next card, clearly ready to be done with me. I didn't blame her.

"The High Priestess."

She overturned a card with a beautiful, flowing woman in a white gown. Jackie's face, which had taken on momentary relief when she drew the beneficial card, fell back into concern. Camille exclaimed over the long folds of the dress, untouched by the darkness that seemed so apparent to Jackie and me.

"A woman of tenacity and strength but, when wearing the mourning robes of white, signifies passage, death, and grieving. Taken with the card of justice, it could mean that death satisfies the uneven scales."

It felt as if a light bird pecked at my heart, eating it one piece at a time. Death would bring no justice to my grandmother, my mother, or myself. I looked away from the beautiful face of the High Priestess with a knot in my stomach.

"The next?" I asked, my voice a croak.

"The raven," she announced. We exchanged a look, and my thoughts fell back to the idle drawing I'd made. A drawing that may not have been so idle. I made a mental note to look at it again later. "Ravens mean . . . death, doom. Betrayal by friends or enemies."

Teachers.

"The last one," she said, pulling the card out without needing encouragement, "is the fool."

All of us stared at it in surprise.

"The fool?" I asked, gazing up at her. Her forehead furrowed into deeper lines. She lifted her shoulders in a half shrug. "What does that mean?"

The painting on the card showed a young witch walking along a path riddled with snakes that had coiled up to bite his ankles. He looked up, oblivious to the danger at his feet, a mocking smile on his face.

"It could indicate a purposeful blindness to the dangers. Looking away because you don't want to see what's really there," Jackie said, fidgeting.

"Denial?"

"Yes," she said with an exhale, looking between the three cards. Her eyes lifted to mine, to the cards, and back to mine. "I have to admit, Bianca. This reading may be beyond me. I'm not really sure what to make of it. The line on the left is confusing." She motioned to the scales, the High Priestess, and the fool. "There's no one united purpose in these three cards. But over here," she motioned to the cards on the right. The Guardian, The High Priest of Spears, and the raven. "These all indicate war and fighting."

Her chocolate eyes peered into mine.

"Are you fighting with someone?" she asked.

Yes. Dear Miss Mabel holds my life in her hands.

I pasted on a sweet smile, hoping to dispel the gloom, wishing I could take all of this back.

"Just my homework."

"Whatever you end up deciding," Camille said, pointing to the pile on the right and meeting my eyes. "Don't choose this way! It looks dangerous. If you choose the other way, you'll just be confused. I'd much rather have that."

Camille's light-hearted tone was forced. I could tell by the distressed look in her eyes that she'd caught on but tried to put a positive spin on it. Jackie chuckled under her breath and swept the two piles together.

"Yes, Bianca. Confusion is much better than war!"

Is it? I wanted to ask, but held my tongue.

Jackie shuffled the cards back into the deck, obliterating any evidence that the two paths existed. I asked her a question about her grandmother and soon the dark reading was forgotten, lost in our laughter as she told us stories of growing up with a Diviner.

By the time the three of us went to dinner, I could pretend I'd forgotten what Jackie had said, tucking it into the back of my mind, safe, forgotten, and far away. We dove with relish into Miss Celia's chicken pot pie, lost in a discussion about whether or not Camille would make a good Diviner.

Brianna's Birthday

Miss Mabel's voice wafted into the classroom the next day. I looked up, startled out of a summary I was writing on silent curses, not even aware that Miss Mabel was in the attic. Nor had I realized how quiet it had become in the school. A couple of white messenger envelopes sat underneath my bedroom door. I recognized Camille's handwriting on one of them. They must have been trying to get ahold of me, but I'd been too absorbed in homework to notice.

Setting aside the papers and textbooks that cluttered my desk, I rose from the chair and headed to her office, grabbing the messages from my friends as I went. Miss Mabel stood at the window, looking down on the yard. Girlish shrieks and laughter from the students playing below filtered through the open window.

"They just started the birthday party for Brianna. She's turning eighteen today. Or was it seventeen? Oh, I don't really care."

I peered past her to the queue of girls playing games in the grass. The storm from the night before left a crisp blue sky in its wake. The sun was warm enough that the air would be tolerable for an hour or two, but most of the girls still wore their cloaks. They hovered in small congregations, talking and giggling like jabbering birds.

"Isn't she a lovely girl?" Miss Mabel continued. "Such dark brown hair. It's almost as long as yours. Look, her friends made her a crown of white flowers. They're learning about simple transformation spells this week and doing quite well."

A pang of resentment stabbed me. Anything would be better than sitting up here, cooped in the attic's four walls, answering questions I didn't care about. I couldn't enjoy the happy scene. The cloying tone in Miss Mabel's voice set me on edge. She was up to something.

Her gaze narrowed.

"Wouldn't it be a shame if someone cast a curse on the birthday girl? It would certainly ruin her day, wouldn't it?"

My heart stuttered.

"Yes," I said slowly. "It would."

"All that beautiful curly hair of hers. Wouldn't it be awful if it became a head full of snakes at her party?"

I paused in shock. She wouldn't.

Miss Mabel turned and met my gaze with an easy smile, as if she'd read my mind. Her eyes seemed to say, *Yes, I would. And I plan too. So you better get to work.*

Panicked, I scrambled forward and leaned out the window, searching for Brianna through the crowd. Camille, Jackie, and a few other first-years had formed a circle with a group of second-years. The third-years watched from a distance, stuck on their usual haughty perch like preening birds. Hadn't Brianna shown up to her own party? Where was she?

Augustus stood in the tree line in case he was needed, awkward in the midst of so many teenagers. Miss Celia, red-faced and frazzled, shouted directions to Michelle as she followed behind a giant cake in the shape of a blood red heart.

Leda stood alone, a book in hand and a look of intense concentration on her face. Then she turned to find me in the window and met my eyes in fear. My panic doubled.

Where was Brianna?

Her full hair gave her away when her friends worked to push her into the middle of the human ring. She finally assented with a shy blush, standing alone in the center. Nothing in her hair gave me any indication that Miss Mabel had set the curse, but I wasn't optimistic enough to think she hadn't.

My brain sped through every option. If it had to do with hair, it would be a vanity curse. Or would it be an adjustment curse? No, that was only for tailoring and sewing.

"Oh dear," Miss Mabel exclaimed, "do I see something moving?"

Brianna's hair shifted, rearranging itself into small ropes. The students started a low, harmonic chant, the beginning of a blessing circle meant for birthdays.

"Tick, tick," Miss Mabel whispered with a grin.

I whispered the counter-curse for a well-known retribution curse under my breath and watched in relief as Brianna's hair calmed back into its individual curls. Then I combed the crowd to find no one any wiser.

My time to feel relief fell short.

Leda caught my eye and motioned to Camille with a jerk of her head. Camille opened her mouth to speak but nothing came out. She shook her head and tried again, puzzled. She stepped away from the circle, seeking Leda, her eyes wide and her face blooming cherry red.

A wave of fury rushed over me. Miss Mabel had cast a curse on one of my best friends.

"What a fun little party," she murmured.

I watched Camille's every move for clues as Leda rushed to her side. There were so many possibilities, and I didn't know how to narrow them down from so far away.

Miss Mabel used a weakness or exploited a strength with everything she did, so I took a wild guess and whispered the tongue-tied counter-curse. As soon as I did, words poured out of Camille like a dam releasing floodwater. She prattled in relief, pressing her hands to her cheeks.

"Well done, Bianca," Miss Mabel crooned. "You have an uncanny talent for counter-curses. I'm most impressed. You countered the curse I warned you about and one I didn't. Congratulations."

She stepped away from the window. My heart raced as I stared at the carefree scene below. Brianna stood with her hands folded in front of her, a lovely, appropriately shy smile on her face as the students finished her blessing and Miss Celia produced the rouge cake.

"Go have fun at the party, Bianca," Miss Mabel said from the doorway. "It looks like a great time."

Her low chuckle echoed in the room as she departed, disappearing into her personal quarters and leaving me at the office window, staring down, trying to pull myself together. Oh, how I hated her. I had to remind myself that she still held ultimate power over the curse, over my life, and until the moment that changed I'd have to hate her in silence.

I backed away until I hit the wall and sank to the floor, not sure how many more tests I could endure.

It Won't Kill You

I rapped on Leda's door with my knuckles, reassured by the movement of a shadow under her door.

"Are you awake?" I asked. She called out for me to enter, and I slipped inside.

The smell of syrup and melted butter breezed into the room with me. Leda stood at her desk, an organized thoroughfare of parchment, scrolls, books, and feathers. A few childish drawings from her younger siblings filled her wall, perfectly aligned and centered over her bed.

"Looks just like you," I said, pointing to one such picture that depicted a girl with a tan dress and no hair.

"They never draw my hair," she said with a rueful sigh. "It's so light they just say the paper counts. They ran out of blue crayon, so they drew a tan dress."

I chuckled under my breath.

"Do you miss your family?" I asked.

To my surprise, she had to think about the question before she responded.

"Yes, and no. I don't miss hiding in the closet to get some privacy or watering down the soup to make sure everyone gets enough. I thought, when I came to school, that I'd love the quiet. But sometimes I hate it, like it's too much."

Her face flushed a little when she looked at me.

"Anyway," she quickly said, whirling away to stuff her bag with essentials for school that morning. She didn't like to be unprepared. "I guess I do miss them sometimes."

Sensing her hesitancy at discussing something so personal, I changed the subject. "Where's Camille?"

"Probably still asleep," she said with a roll of her eyes. A braided rug, lopsided and bulging, covered the chilly wooden floor. The tidy, efficient room seemed warm and cozy, something I never felt in the attic. I would decorate my room, but that would make it feel too permanent, like I meant to stay. "We'll grab her on the way down. Let's go."

Camille met us in the hall, her eyes still swollen and bleary.

"Hi," she mumbled, rubbing one eye and yawning, her usual headband drooping over one ear. The three of us headed down the stairs for breakfast, where platters of steaming scrambled eggs, crisp bacon, and high stacks of thin, rolled cakes met our eager eyes.

"The Yule celebration is coming up soon," Leda remarked, her eyes on a glass box on the fireplace mantel containing remnants from the Yule log burned the previous year. Miss Celia would burn them again this year and keep a few pieces of the new log for the next Yule celebration, to act as a protective charm over the school.

The three symbols of Yule filled the dining room. Sprigs of holly and Letum Ivy decorated the fireplace mantels, while winterflowers covered the walls in decorative wreaths, fanning out like skinny fingers with small white and red flowers.

"Miss Celia must have decorated last night," I said, looking at the evergreen rushes and boughs. The Yule holiday celebrated the quiet bounty of the winter season, like evergreen and winterflowers. The evening of Yule, the students would gather around the large dining room fireplace to light the Yule log and feast while it burned. A bouquet of red winterflowers accompanied every meal that day, bringing the blessings to each table.

Camille's half-open eyes looked around with detached interest as she struggled to stay awake. I piled a few pieces of bacon onto my plate while Leda grabbed for the rolled thin cakes, but a change in the air drew my attention. I stopped and gazed around. No one else seemed to notice, chattering over their plates like a cacophony of squirrels.

I looked out to the hallway to see Miss Celia headed for the vestibule. Someone had knocked on the door. She pulled it open to admit a Messenger. He wore a heavy overcoat and a tan scarf over his face, re-linquishing an envelope over to her with a quick nod. She took it, her forehead creased, and disappeared in the direction of Miss Scarlett's office.

Whoever had sent a Messenger meant business. Although the everyday messenger paper we used to send messages home was mostly reliable, there was no telling when, or in what state, your letter would arrive. Shaking off the sudden chill that swept in the room from the open door, I turned my mind back to breakfast.

The meal continued without a hitch. I left my friends and climbed the stairs, my mind lingering over the bitter memory of Miss Mabel cursing the students. What would she have me doing today?

Miss Mabel stood at the blackboard, staring at a word she'd just written with her head tilted to the side. I slipped into my desk and waited. She waved for an eraser. It popped up and rubbed out the only word on the sprawling board.

Bindings

"A binding is simple, really," she said, spinning around to face me. "It's an agreement that binds two people together. Some would call it an unbreakable promise. Whatever you call it, a binding is a binding. If a binding is not fulfilled, the witch that did not complete her part will die. Do you understand?"

"Yes, Miss Mabel."

"Do you have any questions?"

"No," I said, wondering how a binding applied to Advanced Curses and Hexes.

"Good." She tossed the chalk into the air and shook off her hands. It flew in a graceful arc to her desk and landed with a little *plop*. An amused smile crossed her face. It raised alarms in me immediately. She cast her eyes out on the hallway and said with a jovial tone, "Due to the lovely change in plans, we'll talk about it more when you return."

"When I return?" I asked, turning in my seat as she sauntered out of the room. At that moment, Miss Celia huffed her way to the top of the stairs. She waved for me.

"Bianca," she wheezed as she came to a stop. Her lips were turned down, and she waved with a fluttering hand. "Come with me. Hurry now. Miss Scarlett needs you. Immediately."

She put a hand on my back as we walked down the stairs, escorting me to the library. A grim feeling crept into my bones. Why would Miss Scarlett need me so early in the morning? I found both Miss Scarlett and Miss Bernadette waiting by the fireplace in the warm library. Miss Bernadette fidgeted with the end of her sleeves, while Miss Scarlett stood, her arms folded across her chest.

"Bianca, please have a seat," she said. "Miss Bernadette needs to talk to you."

Miss Bernadette motioned me into a chair near her, but I stayed close to the doorway for a quick escape. Something terrible had happened. I could see it in their eyes. When she saw I wasn't going to move, Miss Bernadette opened her mouth to say something, but no words formed. She turned to Miss Scarlett, as if seeking help. She couldn't do it herself.

Stepping forward, Miss Scarlett spoke with an even tone that sounded foreign, as if it had come from someone else.

"Bianca, we just received a message from your mother," she said. "She included a note for you."

The Messenger at breakfast had come from my mother.

Miss Scarlett handed me an envelope with my name written in a familiar, graceful handwriting. I broke the gray wax seal with trembling hands, tearing the thin parchment in my hurry.

Dearest Bianca,

I don't know what to say except to tell you that your dear Nana is finally free. After years of pain and ill health, she hurts no more. She passed away in her sleep last night and is finally at rest.

Do not mourn her, sweet girl. She would not want you to. She is happy, and her burdens are gone. She loved you very much and spoke of you every day. I'll see you soon. Your teachers have my directions and will send you home now for the funeral.

All my love,
Mama

In the end, Miss Scarlett's sturdy demeanor pulled me through the horror of those moments. Once I finished reading, when my knees went weak and my vision spotty, her sharp voice broke through the haze.

"The funeral is tomorrow," she said. "We've already told Augustus to get the carriage ready. You need to go upstairs and pack."

Dazed, I looked back at the letter. It felt like an out of body experience, staring at the words that confirmed I would never talk to Grandmother again. This was nothing like the Competition. This was real. I could feel it in my bones.

"Come," she insisted. "Let's go pack."

Underneath it all, I understood Miss Scarlett's motivation. I needed to focus, to think about something else. The pain would go away if I didn't think about it. My heart wouldn't fall apart. My lungs wouldn't feel this fire, this consuming pain. I needed to think about something else. Something mundane. Something that would tie me back to reality.

Packing, yes. What should I take with me? Clothes. Shoes. Agony. Guilt. Should I pick my heart up off the floor and bring it along, bruised and disappointed?

"Come," Miss Scarlett demanded. She grabbed my shoulder and steered me to the hall. "Let's go get your things."

All of a sudden, we were in my bedroom, but I didn't remember climbing the spiral stairs.

"Where is your shoulder bag?" she asked.

I got down on my knees and pulled it out from underneath my bed.

"Do you have a white dress?"

"No."

Miss Scarlett rummaged through my closet.

"Then let's go find one. We have a closet with extra clothes. Follow me. Come on, walk."

Miss Scarlett spent the next twenty minutes making me complete small tasks. I existed from one moment to the next, in between flashes of Grandmother's eyes and Miss Scarlett's inquiries. When I spaced out and shock threatened to envelop me, she would snap her fingers in front of my face, demanding attention.

When the carriage was ready, Miss Scarlett walked with me down the quiet corridor, past the full classrooms. I heard the drone of Miss Amelia's voice in the background and realized the school continued to function without me. It had no idea that my world had just paused.

A classroom door opened, and Leda spilled into the hallway, followed by Camille.

"Bianca!" Leda yelled. Miss Bernadette stepped out from behind them and grabbed their arms.

"Stay here," she quietly commanded.

"Let us talk to her!" Camille demanded in an uncharacteristically sharp voice, her face flushed and limbs flailing. The hysteria in her voice increased with every sentence. "Let us go! She needs us, Miss Bernadette. We are her only friends. She needs a friend right now! I know she does. I know she does!"

But Miss Scarlett steered me away. I looked over my shoulder to see Leda peering after me in concern. She was fighting Miss Bernadette too.

We passed through the side door near the kitchen and out into the cold. Augustus's hunched profile sat like a gargoyle on top of the carriage. He wouldn't look at me. Miss Scarlett held the carriage door open and set my bag inside.

"Grief won't kill you, Bianca," she said. Her firm voice felt like an order. "Don't wallow in it. There is still life to live. There are still things for you to do."

She meant more than she said, but I was too numb to read into it. The door closed, and the carriage started for home.

Not Your Fault

The wind blew strands of hair across my face as I stared at Grandmother's headstone.

Leaves drifted through the graveyard on the wind. A few stray flower petals tumbled away from the bouquet resting at the base of her headstone. Trees ringed the area like protective guards, casting a naked canopy over the soil that would fill with leaves in the spring. For now, the world reflected the gray shadows in my heart.

A white candle burned tall and bright above her headstone. The freshly churned dirt that covered her body smelled like her herb garden, and a new wave of pain washed over me. Thirteen plants formed a long line over the fresh soil. The protective plant rosemary, one of her favorites.

Mother stood at my side, a pillar of strength in her white dress. Like all her clothes, it was in a simple style, with sleeves and a cinched waist. My bare toes dug into the cold soil. The white cloak I wore flapped a little in the breeze, my hair tangled out over my shoulders, abandoned.

Mama reached over and took my hand. Grandmother lay next to Grandfather's grave. His headstone showed signs of wear. He had died almost eighteen years ago, before I was a whisper of existence, but his candle stood tall above him still. Not burning, but not gone either.

"She knew she was going to die," Mama said. In the background, I heard the slow, mournful chant of Grandmother's friend Helen, a sweet old woman with thin lips and a knowing smile. She stood just outside the cemetery, calling a blessing of remembrance. With no other sound in the forest, her voice rang through the trees with surprising strength from her shriveled and bent body.

As if we could forget her, I thought.

"Nana wanted me to tell you that she loved you and was very proud of you. No matter what happened." Mama's voice shifted into a soft laugh, and I envied her ability to work past the pain. "She also wanted me to tell you to stop studying and go have some fun."

I was too gutted to appreciate the humor. Guilt and rage made it difficult to know what to say.

"I tried," I whispered. "I tried to bargain with Miss–"

She forbade me from continuing. "This isn't your fault."

"I was so close!" I cried, tears filling my eyes. "I completed my end of the bargain with Miss Mabel, but she went back on her word. She refused!"

"Bianca, you don't know if removing the curse would have saved her. You can't know. You have to move on. All of us die sometime. We can't prevent it, no matter how powerful we are."

Mama grabbed my face, forcing me to look into her eyes.

"Tell me you understand that this is not your fault."

I hesitated.

"Tell me, Bianca."

I nodded once, and it was true. "I understand." This had nothing to do with me. But it had everything to do with Miss Mabel.

My hatred swelled until it bubbled, seething and simmering beneath my skin like a separate supply of blood. I didn't stop it, didn't try to deter it. I embraced it instead.

Grandmother may be dead, taken by the curse, but I was not. I could gain power from intense emotion. Strength from hatred. It didn't matter that this anger had been what Miss Mabel wanted, or that it felt like I was walking into the hands of the enemy. She'd asked me once if I wanted power. Yes I did. And now I had it.

I knew exactly how I wanted to use it, and that was all that mattered.

Mama took a calming breath, and I wondered if she could feel the shift in my rage. She had a special talent for tuning into the emotions of those around her. I pushed the raging grief back, into the recesses of my mind where all the rest of it bubbled. I didn't want Mama to know, didn't want to tell her that Miss Mabel had her own plans for me, that Papa hadn't responded, and that I was so livid I thought it would break me from the inside out.

"It's going to be okay, Bianca," she said, putting her warm hand on my shoulder and staring deep into my eyes. "Everything will work out."

I didn't believe her.

"Certainly," I whispered instead. My lie must have worked, because she relaxed. Locking the anger safe and tight in my heart meant Mama didn't sense it anymore and the worried lines around her eyes receded a little.

"You get your stubbornness from your father, you know," she whispered, brushing a lock of hair away from my face. "Just like your fast mind."

All of her movements were slow and deliberate. She hid her pain. The curse would take her life in a few years. It would strengthen with each day until life was nothing more than a cruel repetition of the day before, her bones worked into bitter ash.

"Bianca, I'm worried about you going back to—"

"It'll be all right." I stopped her this time.

"I can't lose you, too," she whispered in a small voice. I wondered how my mother survived these horrible years. The pressing weight of the curse, loving a man who couldn't stay, watching her daughter move closer to death with every birthday. I wanted to ask her if it was worth it. She'd say yes, but I didn't want to hear it, and I didn't know why.

"You won't," I promised. My resolve echoed into the numb soles of my feet. *Confidence, Bianca. She needs to hear your confidence.* "Miss Mabel's not going to win. Not now."

Mama took me into her arms and held me close. I took a great deal of solace from the love in her embrace. We stayed there for several long moments.

"Come on, Bianca," she whispered, pulling away. "Let's go."

Helen's voice changed, switching from the low keen to a sweet melody. An honor chant. The white candle standing over Nana's grave flickered, then went out.

We will never forget.

I turned to follow Mama, then stopped, grabbed a few skinny twigs, and knelt in front of Nana's grave. After whispering a spell, the twigs braided themselves together. A small handful of forget-me-nots bloomed from the dead stalks, unfurling their blue wings like a new dove. I draped the crown of flowers around the headstone so it rested across her name.

"So mote it be," I whispered, leaving her a kiss on the tip of my fingers. Then I took my mother's hand, and we left Grandmother to rest in the quiet graveyard.

Powerful Chances

I stood at the window in my childhood room, arms folded across my chest, listening to the last of the villagers as they spoke with Mama. Most of the time their words were a murmur in the background, but occasionally I caught a few snippets.

"So sorry, Marie."

"Can we do anything?"

"How's Bianca holding up? They were so close."

My head hurt, pulsing pain with every beat. Below me sat my rickety old desk, built from a tree my mother and I had chopped down, and a feather pen so old it looked like it had molted. Ink dripped off the end, forming a tiny puddle. I'd sent three more letters to Papa without a word in response. I feared more for him than myself anymore. He'd never gone this long without responding. I didn't dare bring it up to Mama, who would only worry.

I turned around, looking over my shoulder when a waft of lemon on the air caught my attention.

Fog filled the room, carrying a citrus scent. Had I been so wrapped up in my thoughts I hadn't noticed? An expanding mist with a specific smell only came from a powerful transportation spell. I backed up against the wall and sucked in a hopeful breath.

Papa. Who else could it be? Maybe I'd wished him here, brought him here on the power of my aching heart alone.

The cloud thickened, and the lemon scent intensified. The mist filled the room until I could only see a few inches beyond my face. Small drops of water condensed on the ends of my hair and fingertips.

Although I expected someone to arrive, the scratchy voice still startled me.

"Why are you standing against the wall?"

My eyes widened.

The High Priestess's lumpy frame came into view, appearing as a swatch of fog moved aside. She wore a sparkling yellow dress that made her look sallow and old. Diamond earrings dripped from her ears and matched the petite silver crown nestled in her gray hair.

"Waiting, Your Highness."

"Well, don't just stand there. I didn't stop by for tea. Are you coming or not?"

As if I could refuse the High Priestess.

"Yes, Your Highness."

She turned, and I stepped forward, following her into the fog. It swallowed us like a giant maw as we walked six or seven steps, leaving my quaint little room and emerging into an opulent office.

A massive mahogany desk, at least nine feet long, stretched across the middle of the room. A wall of windows faced the dying embers of the red and orange sunset. No books, just paintings of parts of the Central Network adorned every available space. Instead of seeming chaotic, the effect was warm.

The mist faded when we stepped into the room. She extended her hand to me.

"Take my arm."

Proof that she wasn't a deception spell. I gripped her forearm in my hand, and she held mine, completing the formal greeting amongst unknown witches. She dropped it almost immediately.

So much for curtsies, Miss Scarlett.

"I brought you here to talk about Miss Mabel."

The mention of her name made me turn hot, then cold. This couldn't be good.

"Miss Mabel, Your Highness?"

"Your education started out as a quest to save yourself from a curse set by a corrupt teacher, but it's about to become much more than that."

I watched her carefully, more concerned by the tone of her words than by her detailed knowledge about me. I wasn't sure what to say, so I remained quiet, waiting for her to continue.

"I believe Mabel has plans to overthrow me as High Priestess."

I blinked.

"Overthrow you?"

"Yes."

My mind spun. The late meeting with the High Priest, the snarky comments about the High Priestess, Miss Mabel's questions during the trust potion test. They all swarmed me, spinning around my head like flighty birds.

The only question I could muster of the thousands that reeled in me was the one I feared the answer to the most.

"Why are you telling me?"

"There is reason to believe that she will use you as a means to get to me."

My eyes narrowed.

"What do you mean?" I asked slowly. Her expression never wavered.

"It's my belief that she plans to have you kill me."

The blood left my face and hands, pooling in my stomach and making me want to vomit. It couldn't be. Impossible. There was no chance. Sixteen. I was only sixteen.

"I'm sorry," I whispered. "What did you say?"

"Miss Mabel is going to have you kill me."

"It's not possible," I breathed.

"It's very possible," she countered. Her small eyes were firm, steely, even, but not afraid. "If you kill me, her hands are clean. The High Priest can offer her name up as my replacement and the Council would agree wholeheartedly. They love Mabel."

I just stared at her, sorting through this information. The strange world I'd been living in since starting at Miss Mabel's began to take form, and it resembled the shadows of a hideous beast. The Esbat curriculum, the Advanced Curses and Hexes Mark, practicing curses on a cat. Preparation, all of it, for one violent act of treachery. The conversation I'd overheard with the High Priest began to make sense.

"That's what they were talking about," I said, coming out of my thoughts. "I overheard them."

The High Priestess lifted an inquiring eyebrow.

"Overheard who?"

She listened as I explained what had happened the night of the Esbat. When I finished, her already beady eyes tapered down and she rubbed her lips together.

"Yes, just as I thought."

She spun and started toward her desk.

"So you knew about this?" I asked, following behind her.

"I've known she was up to something for a very long time, but it wasn't until I saw you at the Esbat that my suspicions were confirmed."

"The Esbat?" I questioned.

She sat in an ornate chair several feet taller than she was and motioned me into a seat across from it, which I reluctantly lowered myself into. Sitting down cemented the reality of what she told me, and I didn't need more reality.

"There is no need for a sixteen-year-old girl to be at an Esbat, Bianca. Mabel has never taken notes during an Esbat. She doesn't need them. She's got a strong memory. It was a bold move. Bold, or stupid. The two are often difficult to distinguish. My suspicion is that she was testing you and probably getting you more familiar with Chatham."

It sent my stomach into spirals.

"She's not just training me to kill you," I said, thinking about my lessons in the attic and clenching my teeth. A puppet. That's all I've ever been. The fire flared in the hearth with a sudden pop, and the High Priestess sent me a sharp look. I forced myself to calm down by taking a long breath. "She's training me to work for her, isn't she?"

"It's possible," she said, still watching me with a wary eye.

"She's going to use my curse as leverage. She'll remove it only if I kill you."

"I believe so, yes."

The vehemence in my tone surprised me, almost bringing me out of the chair.

"I won't do it."

"Won't you? Not even for your own life?"

"No!"

The High Priestess leaned forward. "Or the life of your mother, your friends?"

My heart nosedived. She was right. I'd do anything for my family, and Miss Mabel knew it.

You're just like Hazel, you know. You've got a real soft spot for family.

"There's nothing I can do about your Inheritance curse, Bianca. I can't force a witch to do or undo any curse or spell that was cast before I took rule. But we can get through this together, if you'll do exactly as I ask."

I took a deep breath and straightened my shoulders.

"Yes," I said. It was good to have an adult take over now, to tell me what to do. "Of course."

She nodded.

"She's going to try to put you in a binding tomorrow morning, during your Advanced Curses and Hexes final."

My final? It wasn't supposed to be for another week.

"How do you know?" I asked.

Her irritated tone indicated she didn't appreciate the question.

"I'm the High Priestess, Bianca. You'd be surprised at how much I know."

The comment made me nervous. Her eyes seemed to pierce through mine. There were more secrets she knew about. Ones that no one else knew. Ones that possibly involved my father. My heart flip-flopped.

"She's going to try to bind me into killing you tomorrow?" I asked, hoping to divert the conversation back, though the topic was twice as grim. Grim, but safer.

"Yes. She'll want to take power before the Western High Priest, Almack, dies, I believe. That could be at any moment if our reports are correct."

"What does the Western Network have to do with it?" I asked, my confusion deepening.

"Everything," she said. So simple but so encompassing. A tangled web that I couldn't even comprehend.

Katie Cross

"Miss Mabel is working with Dane," I whispered. It wasn't even a question. I could see it in the High Priestess's eyes. Dane would take over the Western Network. Miss Mabel wanted to take over the Central Network and join forces with the West.

She wanted a war.

"I want you to agree to her deal," the High Priestess said, pulling me back out of the deepening recesses of my mind.

"What?" I hissed, gaping at her, all concerns for rank and respect aside. That was her big plan?

"Do you need your hearing checked? I told you to agree to whatever deal she makes you."

"Your Highness, I-I can't."

"Yes, you can."

"I can't kill you!" I cried, jumping to my feet. Her infuriating composure made this worse. "I'm not that strong. I don't have enough magical power to get into Chatham Castle with that intent. The Guardians would detect it right away. My father would—"

I stopped myself seconds too late.

"If you don't agree to it, Mabel will kill you. Do you understand that?" she asked, her voice hardening. It was the tone of a woman who had been in charge for many years. "I will not have a student, or several of them, die because of me. If you don't do it, she may try to find someone else, someone we can't track or anticipate."

My legs weakened until I fell back to the chair. I didn't like it. Not at all. There had to be a better way.

"It's crazy," I whispered, staring at the intricate swirls of light red and gold on the carpet beneath me.

"It was a crazy man that came up with it. Fortunately, most of his ideas have a way of working out. He seemed to have an uncanny belief in you."

She gave me a probing look then, one that kneaded right into my soul. I knew what man she spoke of, and so did she. Somewhere, somehow, the High Priestess had discovered that my father worked for her. A man who was not allowed to have a family by history's traditions but did anyway.

"You know," I said.

"Yes. I know that Derek is your father. Why do you think I recognized you at the Esbat? You've got his face. His serious expressions."

I swallowed.

"Is he—"

"No. He's not in any danger from me. But I'd advise you to continue keeping his secret, as I have. The Council is not aware he has a daughter."

"How long have you known?"

"He told me before I swore him in as the Head of Protectors. Your father is a man of honor. He came to me in private to refuse the position when I offered it to him, knowing the Council wouldn't approve of him in such a high Network position because of you and your mother. Not unless he broke all ties with you and promised to never see or speak to you again. He refused to abandon you, and I forbade him from doing so. Instead, I promised to keep his secret, and the Council isn't any the wiser sixteen years later."

Tears filled my eyes, but I blinked them away. Of course Papa had told the High Priestess. Why had I assumed for all these years that he would deceive her?

Suddenly I felt very, very tired. It sank into my chest, a horror collapsing in on me that was too much to bear. Miss Mabel planned to attempt a coup, and the High Priestess wanted me to be a part of it. My father made a proposal in which I agree to kill the High Priestess, and it all started tomorrow, the day after my grandmother's funeral.

Absurd.

"Can't you just make her tell you?" I asked hopefully, though I already knew the answer.

She shot me a disapproving glare. "Do you really think I'd be talking to you right now if it was that easy?"

No, I didn't. Miss Mabel was too powerful to beat with potions or truth spells. Her soul-deep conniving and treachery went too far. It wouldn't be practical to kill her. Not yet.

"It's imperative that she think we are ignorant of her plans. Do you understand?"

Her words gave me chills.

"Is this the only way?" I asked. The High Priestess paused, her chest rising and falling.

"No. But Derek believes it's the best chance we have."

I stood up and kept my hands at my side. She must have known that injecting Papa into it would give me strength, and she was right. Not much, but enough.

"Very well," I said with a great deal more bravado than I felt. My hands were icy fists, my heart as skittish as a rabbit. I wondered if the High Priestess would still recruit me if she knew the depth of my fear. "How shall I inform you once I've accepted the binding?"

She opened her mouth to say something but decided against it.

"If you need any help, let Scarlett know."

It didn't slip my notice that she hadn't answered my question, but I pushed that aside in my surprise. My eyebrows shot up. "Miss Scarlett?"

"Yes. She's been my eye. Scarlett has worked for me for many years. Most of my information comes from her."

The woman I thought was a lonely spinster obsessed with rules had actually been a secret spy for the High Priestess. Her actions the night of the Esbat, when I tripped outside Miss Mabel's door, now made sense. Miss Scarlett had probably been listening to Miss Mabel's conversation as well and had covered for me when I fell.

"Yes, Your Highness," I said in a weak voice.

She paused, staring at me. Then she nodded her head in the direction of the fog gathering in the back corner of her office.

"Go, Bianca, and be well."

Halfway across the room, I stopped and circled around.

"How did this happen?" I asked. "How did she get so strong?"

The High Priestess let out a deep sigh. Even in the gleaming light of the opulent office, she looked weary. It was the first time I had seen her display anything but regal haughtiness. She seemed human. Beneath the rough exterior, she probably wasn't that bad.

"We all have the same chance to be powerful within us, Bianca. What it comes down to is the choices that we make along the way."

It wasn't an explanation, but I sensed she didn't have one. I didn't

think anyone had the answer. After gazing back one last time, I turned around and disappeared into the fog.

Darkness had settled on the school grounds by the time I returned. Torches illuminated the road to the school in yellow light, and candles flickered in the kitchen window. Miss Celia moved as a dull shadow behind the white drapes. Augustus nodded to me when I climbed down from the carriage.

"Thank you," I said, and he disappeared into the night.

The hall held no noise or light when I ventured down the main corridor and up the spiral staircase. I tuned my ear to the sounds of the school as I trudged upward. A rustle of sheets. The low whisper of second-years in the common area. A crackling fire. A light cough from the first-year floor. The fragrant smell of plumeria. My heart started to pound.

Plumeria.

Miss Mabel.

At first a shadow, her dark hourglass figure on the attic landing took shape like a goddess waiting for her sacrificial offering. I kept climbing as if she wasn't there until I made it to the last step.

I met her with a flinty gaze.

She didn't say anything when I stopped. For a moment, I feared I couldn't control my hatred enough to hide it. All the manipulations, the secret plans, the puppeteering behind my back caught up with me. After talking to the High Priestess, my fear and anger collided into a far greater mass than I had anticipated. I didn't know how to control these emotions, and I stopped trying the moment I saw her. The candlelight flared, blazing with bright light.

Miss Mabel straightened up, her chest rising. The lustrous blue in her eyes gleamed in the growing candlelight from the wall sconce. Delight, mirth, happiness. I saw it all in her face. She'd gotten the response she wanted from me now. Her low drawl, as slow as her languid smile, told me she knew how angry I felt and how loose that made my power.

"Welcome back, Bianca."

Not For Anything

The perfect morning for a most horrific scenario started too early.

A low storm seemed to churn just above the school, threatening flecks of ice and snow. Bitter gusts of wind hit the building, nipping the tips of my fingers and nose in my cool room. I stayed buried beneath my blankets, staring at the wall, reviewing every memory and scrap of information I could recall my father teaching me. I couldn't help the feeling in my gut that told me today wasn't going to end in a peaceful binding to murder our leader.

No, I was in the mood for a fight.

I didn't sleep, kept company by the calico cat that had strolled into my room on my return to the attic. She hadn't been around in weeks, and purred near my head in sleep. Camille and Leda sent me several messages as soon as I returned, their envelopes flying underneath my door like darts. I left them on my desk, unopened.

Miss Mabel stirred before I crept out of bed. Once I heard her movements, I grabbed my clothes from where I'd tucked them beneath my pillow to keep them warm and dressed under the covers. Another trick Papa had taught me.

The white cat appeared from hunting, his fur cold. He followed me into the classroom and settled near the fireplace. Miss Mabel whirled around. A cream-colored dress made her sapphire eyes seem especially bright. Her hair fell onto her shoulders in gleaming waves.

I loathed her and her stunning beauty.

"Good morning, Bianca."

"Miss Mabel."

You horrid dragon.

"I have a surprise for you today. Instead of stressing you out with last minute studying and memorization, I decided we'd do the Advanced Curses and Hexes final this morning."

I tried to sound surprised, but it came out strangled.

"Oh?"

"Yes. Isn't that kind of me?"

"Yes, Miss Mabel."

She smiled. "Wonderful. I'd like to get started as soon as possible. In an effort to make the best use of my time, I'm going to teach you your first lesson on your next mark, Advanced Defensive Magic, while we take your final."

I took a mental step backward and looked up. Something wasn't right. The extra layer of malicious intent in her eyes gleamed like a wobbly crystal chandelier.

"You've heard of a Mactos, haven't you?" she asked.

"Yes."

Miss Mabel began her usual stroll around me. Her dress fluttered out behind her with the quiet sound of swishing silk. Diffusing through the windowpanes in white beams, the sunlight illuminated specks in the air that swirled up behind her.

"As you should know from your reading, a Mactos is a magical fight between two witches involving a shield and a versatile little weapon called a blighter."

A flash caught my eye and I spun to the right. Seconds later, a burning red fireball skimmed my back, just missing skin. The heat of it burned my dress, leaving a singed smell in the air.

A blighter.

We stared at each other, surprised.

Did she just send an actual blighter at me?

Red blighters burned. Blue froze. Orange caused bruising and swelling. There were many others, all categorized by color and effect.

"Well, well," she whispered. Her coy smile chilled my bones. "What a fast little mover. Have you ever conjured a blighter before, Bianca?"

My quick reflexes had betrayed me. She hadn't expected me to move fast enough away from the blighter. She *wanted* it to hit me.

Well, two could play this game.

"No, Miss Mabel," I lied. *Underestimate me,* I silently dared her. *I'm not afraid of you anymore.* "I've never worked with blighters before."

She studied me with a knowing look. My lie hadn't been effective. "Hmm . . . well, this could be rather fun," she said.

Three green blighters materialized from different corners of the room, headed straight for me. They would paralyze whatever they hit and were exceptionally sticky and difficult to remove.

I grabbed a heavy book off my desk. The first blighter came on my right. I whacked it into the path of the second and used the book as a shield against the third. The first two crashed into the vaulted ceiling, and the third clung to the book cover like a glowing snail.

She stopped walking to stare at me.

"You have done this before," she said.

"I don't know what you're talking about."

"No," she mused. "I'm sure you don't. Oh, Bianca, this is better than I could have hoped!"

She stepped to the right, and I followed suit. We circled each other with slow, measured steps.

The familiar punch in my gut told me she'd cast a curse. My mouth went as dry as the desert, the telltale symptom of the thirst curse. I countered it and sent one of my own, but it seemed to slide right through her. She must have some kind of protective incantation in place.

"Oh good. I love a student that will fight back," she cried. The tan braided rug underneath my feet slipped, but I jumped onto my desk chair and kept my balance.

"Very nimble move. What about this one?"

Another curse hit me. I stumbled back and landed on the ground with both feet. My body began to itch with a vengeance. It felt like red fire ants crawling under my skin. I could barely concentrate, finally countering it with the narrowest margin of time but not soon enough to recover before I saw the next blighter.

Icy blue and trailed by particles of snow, it headed for me with unmatched precision. Ice blighters were notoriously fast, constructed of razor sharp crystals that could tear through flesh.

Acting on instinct, I ducked and lifted my hand, conjuring up a jagged shield of crystals to match the ice blighter. The fist-sized ball of ice hit with a crack, shattering both into a thousand glittering shards and sending me onto my side.

I held my breath, waiting for Miss Mabel's reaction. Dodging the simplest blighters could be shrugged off as luck, but a protective shield strong enough to destroy an ice blighter was no accident. Without meaning to, I had just made a decision that would change everything.

Miss Mabel stood in the center of the room, regarding me through narrowed eyes.

"Don't lie to me anymore, Bianca. You know defensive magic."

I shook the remaining flecks of the shield off and straightened. There was no going back now. My shoulders and hair glittered with melting shards of ice.

"Yes. Since I was a little girl."

Miss Mabel smiled, slow and catlike. Her conversation with the High Priest rang in my ears.

It proves she's got courage, like I thought. Talent, too. She thinks quick on her feet.

"Your father taught you?"

"I don't know my father," I said automatically.

"Right," she chuckled. "And I don't know my mother. Derek's defensive magic skills are the stuff of legend, you know. I can't imagine he'd raise a little girl in secret and not teach her how to protect herself in the big bad world. He's kind of a bleeding heart for family, I hear. A familiar weakness amongst your kin."

The sound of my father's name on her lips knocked my heart against my ribs like stone. Of course she knew my secret. What didn't she know?

More leverage, more power.

Always keep a little leverage where you need it.

A couple of blighters popped up from nowhere, but I sent them back to her with a quick deflection spell. Now that she knew, there was no reason to hide what I could do. The blighters spun in a short cyclone around her waist and dissipated.

She was sizing me up. Assessing my skills. Wanting to see exactly what I could do.

Another curse slammed me in the stomach. I hit the ground and struggled to stay conscious. A fainting curse. Somehow, in between waves of awareness, I completed the counter-curse in my head. The blackness receded, and I jumped to my feet in one clean move.

"Very good, Bianca. If Derek taught you defensive magic, you don't need me to teach you all of this fluff and nonsense, do you?"

A shot of liquid dread spread through my body. Oh, no. This wouldn't be good.

She waved to the chalkboard and my desk. It shot toward me, intent to ram me over. I stopped it in the middle of the room.

"We should have a little talent showcase, don't you think? Let's see what you can do in a real Mactos. Because I have an idea that you know enough to pass the Advanced Defensive Magic mark right now."

A wooden shield materialized in the air, hanging several feet away from me. Bolts and strips of iron held it together. It looked solid but worn, with blackened spots from red blighters.

"Go ahead." She motioned with a jerk of her head. "Let's see what you've got."

Defensive magic without a shield was like trying to plant a tree with no seed. But this wasn't my shield, so it wouldn't listen to my commands. Strong magic ran on familiarity.

"No," I said.

"No?" she repeated. "Why ever not?"

"Because that's not my shield."

Her lips tapered into a circle.

"Is this your shield?"

A shimmer filled the air, and soon another shield appeared. Made of thick oak, the front gleamed in the firelight, lined with golden Letum Ivy vines and silver flowers. I held up my arm and it flew over, latching itself on with a speed that almost knocked me down. She'd conjured my shield.

This wasn't a final or a school lesson anymore. It was an official Mactos. A battle for my life.

Her wooden shield flew back, reaching her just in time to stop a yellow blighter I sent that would have caused her muscles to contract and spasm to the point of uselessness. She peeked over the top.

"A yellow one? Very impressive."

She sent a hailstorm of copper blighters I hadn't seen in a long time. Copper blighters dissolved into a powder that burned the skin and turned into an acid when it came into contact with water, so washing it off only made it worse. Not wanting it near me, I flung my arm, sending the shield skyward. It slammed the blighters into the ceiling. The gold vines and silver flowers grew red with heat on my silent command, burning the blighters into ash.

"Delightful," Miss Mabel sighed. "All this training already complete."

I ducked a white blighter. My shield slipped over my back as the speedy ball ricocheted back, threatening to break my spine. Responding to a deep instinct, I commanded my shield into different positions over my crouched body, blocking the blighter with every attempt to hit me. The speed of a white blighter alone would knock me out, or break a bone.

"A good idea, but it won't last forever," Miss Mabel said as she leaned back against the wall, her arms folded across her middle. "White blighters just get faster the longer they go, you know."

I tightened my jaw and steeled myself. She was right. The longer I waited, the more dangerous this blighter became. I thought about trapping it between the wall and my shield, but the wall wouldn't contain it. The only thing that stopped a white blighter was contact with the intended target. Allowing it to hit my leg would cripple me, and I wouldn't risk any place on my back.

No matter how I looked at it, this would hurt.

I held out my left hand, grabbed the handle on the inside of my shield with my right, and braced myself. Two seconds later I felt a cool burn in my palm and closed my hand around it. The bones in my left hand cracked, and I let out a cry, falling off my feet from the impact. The blighter disintegrated.

"Oh, very self-sacrificing, Bianca. Also very wise. A broken hand is a small injury to deal with when it comes to white blighters. I would have done the same thing."

Enraged, my hand throbbing, I stood up. The pain was so strong it made my head dizzy, and I fell back to my knees with a shout.

"You wouldn't know anything about self-sacrificing," I muttered. Miss Mabel threw her head back and laughed.

I silently commanded a black blighter. It hovered in front of me, the size of my fist.

"Ooh," she said, her eyebrows elevating. "I think your powers have grown since Hazel died. Since you finally let yourself become so angry. I've never seen a student conjure such a large blighter before. How wonderful. Although, if you want to talk impressive, the big ones are more like this."

She produced a black blighter of her own. At least two times as large as mine, it hung in the air like a monstrous piece of coal. I steeled myself. Black blighters didn't fly well. Their thick density made them better weapons on the ground. If Miss Mabel's blighter came near me, it would crush my kneecaps in seconds.

"Let's see how you feel about this one, hmm?"

It crashed to the floor, cracking a couple boards as it rolled toward me. Using only one hand, I slammed my shield into the floor so hard it stuck, the bottom angle buried deep in the wood. Then I commanded my blighter to the other side of the room, as far away as I could get it. Miss Mabel's blighter rammed into the shield just as mine swooped in from the corner, slamming into the monstrous black lump with a resounding crack. Both blighters broke into several pieces and fell apart.

"Very wise," she said, making a tsking sound with her teeth. "Not many know that the only way to destroy a black blighter is with another black blighter. A bit like diamonds."

This wasn't looking good. I'd been in a constant defensive position. My broken hand would make it difficult to take control.

If you want to win, you have to be the one moving forward, dictating the rules. You can't let your opponent be in control, Papa's reassuring voice whispered from deep in my past.

The misshapen angles of my hand and the magnificent pains soaring through my arm were too crippling to ignore. I hauled my shield out of the floor with my right arm too late. A pink blighter sitting just in front of me caught my eye. It was swollen and bubbling, sprouting large pink pockets of air that spread in halos around it.

"No," I breathed and dropped my shield, kicking it down to cover the blighter a second too late. The pink foam exploded in a thundering boom, throwing me backward.

My right shoulder slammed into the wall of the classroom, reverberating through my teeth and rocking my spine.

I fell to the floor with another yell. Despite the white-hot explosion of pain through my head, and the dull ache of my shoulder wrenching out of its socket, my shield stayed true, protecting my face and body from the burning embers that flew through the air with me.

Miss Mabel stood amidst the carnage, cool and untouched. A burned spot in the floor remained as the only testament that the blighter once existed.

"The true test of a witch in a Mactos is their control over their shield," she said, stepping out of the haze. "You obviously know how to fight, how to use blighters, and how to defend yourself. But your shield use is your most impressive skill, Bianca. It indicates a high level of magical control and power. Most impressive. Impressive enough to earn the Advanced Defensive Magic mark."

I leaned back against the classroom wall with a grimace, hoping the pain would dispel so I could think. My shield settled in front of me, blocking my body. I panted, blanching with every heartbeat that hammered blood through my hand and arm. Sweat dribbled down my back. I tried to stand up but fell back with a useless cry, my right arm immobile and smarting. I stayed there, bracing myself for the next move, trying to figure out a plan.

Clarity came all too soon. I'd never win a Mactos against Miss Mabel.

"Now that I have your full attention," Miss Mabel said. "Let's discuss a few things."

An old leather book drifted from the top of a bookshelf at the front of the room. Pages floated out of the loose, broken spine like lazy leaves in the fall.

"My *Book of Contracts*," she explained, plucking one of the loose papers out of the air. "It's a favorite of mine, you know."

My shoulder spasmed with pain. I looked down to see the extent of the damage and found the telltale dimple that meant a simple dislocation. This wasn't the first time. I bit my bottom lip, bracing myself for what would come next.

In a Mactos, you respond to any injury the moment you can, Papa advised. I held my teeth together. This would hurt.

My shield responded to my thoughts, moving back to me, angling between my useless arm and my body. It began pushing my arm to the side. I grunted through the pain, my eyes screwed shut. An audible *pop* filled the air, and instantaneous relief flooded my whole arm, making it weak.

I struggled to my knees, fighting off a wave of blackness that started at the edges of my vision. This talk about her *Book of Contracts* could be a ruse. Any minute now she'd send another blighter, but I wasn't sure how I'd fight them off. Any minute now.

Be ready for anything, I coached myself, desperate. *Be versatile.* My knees almost gave out, but I straightened up. *Confidence.*

The *Book of Contracts* slammed onto the table as it opened, sending the pages flapping in a sudden gust of wind. A large peacock feather and a jar of black ink materialized on the table next to the book. A blank page sat open, staring at me.

She snapped her fingers and the feather began to write.

"You surprised me today, Bianca. I knew you had some hidden magic abilities, but nothing this extensive. You've earned two marks in one day, completing your circlus."

My breath caught. Of course! Why hadn't I seen it before? She wanted me to have a completed circlus. That had been her plan all along. A completed circlus meant power. The scratch of the feather filled the spaces in her speech. Her voice switched from the cackle of battle to the syrupy sweet tone she used to bargain.

"I had plans for you before, but now that I know you're so well trained, I think we'll do something a bit different. I have an offer to make you, Bianca. Something that could help you be great. I want to take you as my official Assistant. Not just my pupil, but my equal. Work with me, and I'll teach you things to do with this newfound power you never would have known otherwise."

Equal? A trickle of warm blood oozed from the corner of my mouth. I had bitten the inside of my cheek and could taste the metallic tang.

"Like what? Cursing people?" I laughed bitterly. "Destroying lives?"

She acted as if I hadn't spoken, maintaining her illusion of control.

"You have one task left to complete to prove that you're ready for such a wonderful education." She motioned toward the *Book of Contracts*. "All I want is for you to agree to it by signing. Once the task is completed to my satisfaction, you and I can move forward with your education."

"What is the task?" I asked, my voice hoarse.

"Nothing too difficult, really. You'll find out after you sign."

"I see," I whispered. "You'll sign me to complete a task of your choosing and then kill me, or let me die, or back out of your portion of the deal as soon as I complete it. Sounds great."

"Good, you're skeptical. I like it. If you want me to convince you, I'll sign it in blood. Nothing would bind me to it more."

She pulled a tiny golden blade from her wrist with a flash, dragged it across her thumb, and pressed it to the cream page.

"Satisfied?"

The crimson mark shone in the lamplight, now brighter than ever.

"I won't enter into any deal with you," I said. "Not for anything."

Her eyes flashed.

"Not for anything? Because I imagine you wouldn't want something awful to happen to your dear mother, would you? Like a second curse or a horrific illness that she never dies from? Or there's always Derek, the hero of the Central Network. How would the people react if they knew their beloved Protector had been lying to them all along?"

I stared at her with burning rage. The heat from my broken hand grew, expanding up my arm and through my ribs until it electrified my toes. My breathing sped up. I didn't feel the pain anymore. In fact, I didn't feel anything but euphoric hatred and all the power it gave me. It ran through me like a buzz. A savage pop came from the fireplace, and the light in the room flared.

"Don't touch them."

Her eyes tightened into slits. "Then don't give me a reason."

I stepped toward her with a snarl.

"I'll never put myself in your debt."

"Here's the thing, Bianca." She grabbed my arm and pulled me close with surprising strength, gripping so hard I thought the bone would break. I forced back a cry of pain.

Her mouth hovered near my ear, whispering. "If you don't sign the contract, I won't remove the curse. You will die this summer, and your father will be exiled to the Northern Network for lying to the High Priestess and the Council. Your mother will dwindle in a slow death, alone. Because I have ultimate power over her curse, I wouldn't mind extending her miserable, pathetic life so that she always remembers what she lost. Death will be the reprieve that she can't have."

She shoved me away.

"Do you want that kind of guilt sitting on your chest? Knowing that you'll pass but your mother won't, forced to cling to a bitter, painful existence?"

The hairs on the back of my neck stood up when the High Priestess's words came back to me.

I want you to agree to her deal.

Agreement or not, I wasn't sure I could do it now that I stood in front of her. The High Priestess couldn't have known what she was asking. I hated Miss Mabel too much. The fire crackled and fizzed, shooting up the chimney in great flames, filling the room with sticky heat. A bead of sweat trickled down my neck and ran along my spine.

"I won't do it. I won't tie myself to you."

"I can see you'll need some convincing," she said. "I'm sure this will help."

The familiar *whoosh* that preceded a human transformation spell came from the hall. Mama appeared in the doorway, her black hair loose over her shoulders. It took her a second to take in the burned floors, the overturned desk, the scattered books. She shook her head, disoriented, her gray eyes matching the broiling winter storm outside.

"Bianca!" she cried, starting for me. My heart stilled in my chest. *Mama.* What was she doing here?

"No!" I screamed. "Stop!"

She skidded to a halt, her eyes in panic. Miss Mabel tipped her a cold, hard smile.

"Welcome, Marie. Bianca and I were just about to discuss what her future looks like."

"Go back!" I yelled as Mother started toward me again. "You have to leave!"

"Make a decision, Bianca!" Miss Mabel said, excitement in her wild sapphire eyes. "Or I'll make her life more miserable than you could ever imagine."

Mama stopped to stare at me. I glanced from her to Miss Mabel in indecision. No matter what I did someone would suffer. Why couldn't Miss Mabel leave her out of this?

"Don't do it, Bianca!" Mama cried. "It's not worth it. She doesn't frighten me."

Miss Mabel took a threatening step toward Mama with vindictive spite.

"Silence, Marie. You don't know what you're saying. Time is up, Bianca."

"Wait!" I yelled, throwing myself between them. "I'll do it."

Miss Mabel pointed to the book.

"Sign it."

I hesitated and looked back to my mother. She shook her head, her face pale, lips compressed. "Don't do it," she pleaded without sound. "Don't sign that paper."

"I have to," I whispered.

"Don't do this, Mabel. She's only a girl," Mother said in a low voice, turning away from me. "Let me sign it for her."

"This is what Bianca gets for trying to play in an adult world."

"It's okay," I said, begging Mama to trust me with my eyes. I wished I could explain it to her. Would knowing the High Priestess's plans comfort her? No, because they didn't even comfort me. "It's okay."

Whether I wanted to reassure her or myself, I couldn't tell.

My footsteps echoed on the floor as I walked to the *Book of Contracts*, like a slow march to death. The feather lifted into the air as I approached. Only a few sentences in the whole binding stuck out to me.

I will see the unknown deed unto completion or forfeit my own life. If I communicate this contract to another soul, may my life be surrendered.

My accomplishment of the task guarantees the removal of my family curse.

With one last breath, I grabbed the feather, turned away, and signed the bottom line. The ink glittered a familiar crimson, matching Miss Mabel's bloody thumbprint.

The book slammed shut as soon as I pulled away.

"Wonderful!" Miss Mabel cried, all fury forgotten. "I love a good binding."

The *Book of Contracts* flew to her side. She wrapped an arm around it and anchored it to her waist. The sound of a door slamming sounded below, and a gaggle of shouting voices followed. My heart perked up in hope.

Papa.

Miss Mabel stopped in the doorway, her back to us. Although the sound of running feet filled the air, she didn't seem to be in a hurry.

"One last thing," Miss Mabel said, looking back at me over her shoulder. "I'll need you to be powerful, so don't be afraid to give in to how you feel after this moment, Bianca. Hatred is a mighty catalyst. You're going to need it if you want to survive the hell that's about to descend on the Central Network."

My eyes narrowed in an attempt to understand her meaning. But then a blinding flash of light interrupted the air, slamming into my mother's chest with a spray of sparks.

I gasped, only able to stare in fear.

Mama turned to me, a stunned look on her face. Her gentle gray eyes locked with mine and stopped my heart. She stood there for a few moments, trying to breathe.

"Mama! No!"

Everything slowed down.

I ran forward and caught her as she fell. My knees gave out, taking us to the wooden floor. A few tendrils of ebony hair fell away from her face. Her lifeless eyes stared at the ceiling.

Someone began to scream from far away.

Voices yelled. Feet flooded the floor. Someone grabbed my arm. Another passed behind me. The edges of my vision went dark. A pair of hands felt her neck. People spoke over me.

"We're too late."

"She's dead."

"Careful! Look at Bianca's hand."

"Gone. Mabel's disappeared."

I held on tighter as the world around me blurred. The far-away screams turned to guttural cries of pain.

All I could feel was the breaking of my own heart.

Making Chaos

A few flower petals fluttered to the ground from my clenched
fist.

The coldness made it feel like winter would stay forever.
Gray carpets covered the sky, blocking the sun and sending a piercing
wind. The edges of my white dress drifted in the breeze as I stared at
my mother's grave. A fresh-churned dirt so rich it was almost black
made a perfect rectangle in the ground and smelled like earth. Instead
of a line of plants over her grave, we put a circle of chrysanthemums
with a tree in the middle. Letum Ivy already snaked along the ground
and started the slow twirl up the slender trunk, accepting Mama back
to the earth.

Everything else was so similar to Grandmother's funeral that I
wasn't sure if I was dreaming or not.

I wished I was. Oh, how I wished I was.

Two new marks filled the circle on my right wrist. I didn't remember getting them. A seven-pointed Advanced Defensive Magic star
and the three interlocking circles in a row for Advanced Hexes and
Curses. Although I hadn't done magic at all in the past two days, I
knew I was different with a completed circlus.

Different, or stronger. Filled with rage, or grieving. Whatever it
was, I felt it. It coursed through me in hot streaks, never letting me
forget.

Hatred is a mighty catalyst.

Indeed.

Guardians ringed the perimeter of the cemetery, spaced at even intervals and facing outward. Even their presence couldn't comfort me. Who were they against Miss Mabel's barbarous cruelty? It knew no boundary.

That's why my mother lay in the cold ground, never to smile again.

Helen stood outside the cemetery, but this time her chant faded away. She held her face in her hands, her shoulders shaking. I recognized the words of a familiar invocation as she called on the heavens to give me light and energy, to banish the bitter sting of death. But she couldn't finish it, and I didn't know if that was my fault or not. I watched her for a long time, and then I saw movement far behind her, in the depths of Letum Wood. Isadora's foggy eyes met mine. I saw a knowing sadness, a mourning there. Her warning at the beginning of the school year haunted me.

Don't underestimate her.

The crunch of leaves announced that someone walked toward me, and I braced myself for another well-meant expression of solace from someone I didn't know. The footsteps came to a stop at my side. Isadora disappeared.

The High Priestess's scratchy voice broke the air.

"Miss Mabel is gone, and the High Priest is dead. She killed him shortly after murdering your mother."

"I'm not surprised," I murmured. "She loves chaos of her own making."

I didn't have the energy to look the High Priestess in the eye, so the two of us just stared at the deadfall. How could I look at her knowing I would one day kill her? Especially when I couldn't tell her that I'd signed the binding. I had the creeping suspicion that the High Priestess had known all along that I wouldn't be able to warn her. Had I known, I wouldn't have agreed. She must have understood that about me.

It would be a bitter secret, gnawing at my heart.

"What happens now?" I asked.

"I don't know," she admitted. "You changed all her plans."

Yes, and she changed mine.

"Marie's death will not be posted in the Chatham Chatterer as it occurred," the High Priestess said with little preamble. "It was an unfortunate accident while visiting her daughter at school."

A well of bitterness grew in my chest.

"You're covering for a murderer."

"No. We're playing our cards right. Miss Mabel will think that we're trying to cover up a scandal with the Network schools to ensure we always have students. But we are trying to avoid drawing the spotlight onto her. There's nothing Mabel loves more than attention."

"Who will know the truth?"

"You and I, your father, and a handful of Council Members I trust. They put the classroom back together and repaired it before they left."

I suppose that meant she had Council Members she didn't trust. Just thinking about it left me with a headache.

"If a few Council Members know the truth, Miss Mabel has no hope of becoming High Priestess by popular vote," I said.

"As I said before: you changed her plans. I think it's safe to assume that she's going to attempt to do what I did with Evelyn."

"An overthrow?" I asked.

"Yes."

Or she can have me do it from within. A young traitor, bound to an unknown task.

"Do you think she will try?" I asked.

"I have no doubt."

We said no more. There was nothing more to say.

The High Priestess glanced over her shoulder to the small queue of people talking to my father by the cemetery gate. His wispy brown hair fanned out around his face and neck. Dark circles colored the skin under his eyes and a layer of stubble across his chin, but he held himself together with surprising strength.

"What's going to happen to him?" I asked, following her gaze. The wind brushed a few tendrils of hair off my face. Helen had picked the chant back up, and it coalesced into the background.

"He's going to continue in his job."

"What about the Council? They aren't likely to be as lenient with him."

"You let me worry about them."

That was a kind way of saying that it wasn't going to be that simple.

"He's not the first Head of Protectors to have a secret. He never let his family life interfere with his work, which is an argument in his favor." The High Priestess shifted and pulled her white shawl back over a shoulder. "Not until recently, anyway. He's been adamant about controlling your safety and being with you at all times for several weeks now. It's caused a few more issues amongst my Protectors than I would have liked."

Our eyes met for the first time. The rough edge I normally saw there had softened a little, making her look more like a grandmother than a ruler.

"What do you mean?"

"It's as simple as it sounds. You weren't aware of anything unusual except for the sudden appearance of a white cat."

My eyes widened. "What?"

"After Derek learned that Mabel had you at the Esbat, he became concerned. He received permission from me and came the next day. He wasn't there all the time but returned as often as he was able."

Tears rose to my eyes. Papa had been with me all along as my white cat. That's why he never answered my frantic letters.

Vague memories played back in my mind, making my heart thump. He hadn't been alone. The calico cat at every Competition event. Her sudden reappearance after Grandmother died. The way the two cats curled around each other. Their frequent company whenever I was alone.

My nearly inaudible voice came out in a mournful whisper.

"My mother was the calico cat, wasn't she?"

"Yes. Once Derek realized your Mactos with Miss Mabel wasn't just a test for the mark, he left to warn me. Marie stayed to monitor the situation in case you needed help. Mabel forced her transformation at the end."

"But how did she know?"

"Mabel has many abilities, Bianca. They cannot always be explained."

It was a bitter pill to swallow.

"How did he get hurt before he came? If I hadn't nursed him back to health then—"

"He got into a fight with a stray critter when he transformed in the forest to avoid any chance of being seen. Apparently fighting is a bit different when there are four legs to coordinate."

We fell into silence again. I just wanted it all to go away, but it wouldn't. Not ever. This grim reality was here to stay.

The High Priestess motioned off to the side with a tip of her head.

"It seems I'm not the only one waiting to talk to you. I won't take up any more of your time. I'm not sure they'd let me anyway. Camille has been inching closer every minute. Leda seems protective of you. She hasn't stopped glaring at me since I arrived. They will soon overtake us."

Camille and Leda stood a few feet into the tree line, staring at me in their white dresses and hair ribbons. My best friends.

"Take your time here, Bianca. We'll wait by the carriages. You're coming to stay at Chatham Castle, where we can keep you near your father."

And near you, so I can murder you in your sleep at Miss Mabel's behest.

I couldn't look at her. My response felt choked.

"Thank you, Your Highness."

She pulled a pair of gloves out of a pocket and started sliding them over her wrinkled hands.

"This is a lot bigger than just you and me, Bianca. It has been for a while. I only kept the obvious wolves at bay when I overthrew Evelyn. Now is the time to flush them all out. It will be a painful, dangerous process. Keep that in mind."

I thought I knew what she spoke of. Miss Mabel and Dane. The Central Network and the Western Network. Council Members she couldn't trust. Death and war. She was telling me that it didn't start or end with Mabel, or my mother, or me. Bigger forces were at play, forces I hadn't yet imagined.

Forces I didn't want to imagine.

The wind stirred up a flurry of leaves as she departed.

Camille gave an awkward curtsy to the High Priestess as she walked past, but Leda ignored her and started right for me. They reached me at the same time, pulling me into a hug that would have knocked me over if it hadn't also held me up. A sob filled my throat with suffocating thickness.

When they pulled back, tears swam in Camille's large hazel eyes. For the first time since I'd met her, she had nothing to say.

"Bianca, this is my fault," Leda said in a wavering voice. "I didn't see—"

"No." I grabbed her arm. "This is not your fault. I would never expect you to foresee everything. An accident—" I stumbled over the words. "Just an awful accident."

We stared at each other. She finally nodded once, blinked several times, and looked away. Leda didn't believe me, but she said nothing.

"I'm not going to ask if you're doing okay," Camille said, squeezing my arm above the elbow to avoid my bandaged hand and restoring a sense of grounding to my upside-down world. "Because I know that you're not. I remember how it felt when my parents died. Your father told us how it happened while you were speaking to the High Priestess. A terrible accident, falling that way."

Camille tightened her grip on my arm again, the wide-eyed look telling me in no uncertain terms that they knew the truth. They knew, and it was enough.

"Thanks," I whispered, attempting a short-lived smile. Tears pooled in my eyes. Camille looked around, her gaze lingering on the two fresh headstones that represented nearly everything important to me.

"What happens now?" she asked.

"I'm moving to the castle."

Camille's eyes popped open in shock.

"Chatham Castle?"

"No," Leda muttered. "The other one."

"You're going to live with the High Priestess?"

Yes, my beautiful nightmare. I wondered how they would react if they knew what I'd gotten myself into.

"For now, anyway," I said dismissively, not wanting to get into details.

"I guess that's where you'd live when your father is the Head of

Protectors," Leda said, glancing back at him. He stood apart from the small queue, intent in conversation with the High Priestess. "He's a really nice guy, Bianca."

"Thanks."

"Are you still going to keep your grandmother's shop open?" Camille asked. My thoughts turned back to the Tea and Spice Pantry with a twist in my stomach.

"No," I said. "Papa talked to the lady that's been helping my mother and gave it all to her."

It had been a simple conversation between Papa and me, but it had closed a door. I couldn't go back and see the deep barrels and the swatches of lavender or smell the cloves. My heart wasn't strong enough.

"What about your curse?" Leda asked.

The real question. Winter's cold grasp would fade into the fresh life of spring. It would give way to summer and the end of my life.

"I don't know." I sucked in a deep breath and looked out on Letum Wood. "Miss Mabel is still out there. I have until the middle of summer."

"Are they going to close the school?" Camille asked.

"No." A conversation I overheard between the High Priestess and my father ran through my head. Miss Scarlett would run the school as usual. If Miss Mabel stopped in, she'd let them know. No one would notice Miss Mabel's absence. "It was just an accident. No reason to alarm anyone."

Right, their looks seemed to say.

Camille lifted my right hand.

"Your circlus is complete," she said, glancing at me in surprise. Her voice was small, like a child's. "You're all done then. For real."

A call from the road caught our attention. Augustus pulled up with the same faded horse and creaky carriage I'd taken to the Esbat. He waved for Camille and Leda.

Camille whirled back around.

"Are we ever going to see you again?" she asked, clutching my hand even tighter.

"Of course," I said.

"She's going to invite us to the castle." Leda closed her eyes, then opened them. "Really soon."

I responded with a breathy laugh.

Camille's eyes grew watery. She threw herself against me with all her usual force and didn't let go for a long time.

"Thanks for being my friend, Bianca," she said into my shoulder, and I held her extra tight. "Merry part." She whirled around without another word and ran off, her hair bouncing, her white stockings flashing. Leda and I faced each other. Her eyes were exceptionally bright today, their divergent coloring highlighted by her white-blonde hair.

"Merry part, Bianca. Go well."

She put a kiss on the ends of her fingers and blew it to me. I smiled, and she walked away.

Once they had departed, I turned back around to face my mother's grave. I didn't know how long I'd been standing there when I looked up to the soft, warbling descent of white snowflakes. Papa stood at my side. He moved as silently as the snow. He wrapped a strong arm around my shoulder. I leaned into him, inhaling the musky scent of leaves and mint. For just a moment, I felt safe. I was a little girl in his arms blinking away the snowflakes on my eyelashes. There were no secrets. No fears. Just Papa.

"You ready to go home, B?"

No I wasn't ready. There was no home, not at Chatham. If Mama wasn't there, it would never be home. Just an intimidating, walled prison that guaranteed my proximity next to the High Priestess, when I was bound to murder her whenever Miss Mabel desired. But I couldn't tell him that.

"Yes, Papa."

I knelt down and picked up two twigs. They braided themselves together and blossomed into two creamy white lilies. I set them on the top of her headstone and straightened up.

It felt as if I stood on the brink of something grand and horrible, a great chasm yawning on all sides, waiting for me to take one wayward step or to stumble where I stood. No matter where I went, I faced the darkness alone. It wouldn't be long before I met up with Miss Mabel again. We were caught up in a sick symbiotic relationship that would only end in death.

All our lives were ticking away now. The High Priestess. My father. Myself. The Central Network.

"So mote it be," I whispered.

And then I walked away, my heart in the ground behind me.